MICHAEL CHABON is the Pulitzer Prize-winning author of *The Amazing Adventures of Kavalier & Clay*. His first novel, *The Mysteries of Pittsburgh*, was a national bestseller. Chabon's stories have appeared in *The New Yorker* and *GQ*, and in a collection published in 1999, *Werewolves in Their Youth*. He was nominated by *The New Yorker* as one of the 20 Writers for the 21st Century. His first book for children, *Summerland*, was published in 2002 and a novella, *The Final Solution*, in 2005. He lives in Berkeley, California, with his wife, novelist Ayelet Waldman, and their four children.

Visit www.AuthorTracker.co.uk for exclusive information on your favourite HarperCollins authors.

D1434276

By the same author

The Mysteries of Pittsburgh
Werewolves in Their Youth
The Amazing Adventures of Kavalier & Clay
Summerland
The Final Solution

MICHAEL CHABON

Wonder Boys

HARPER PERENNIAL
London, New York, Toronto and Sydney

Harper Perennial
An imprint of HarperCollins*Publishers*
77–85 Fulham Palace Road
Hammersmith
London W6 8JB

www.harperperennial.co.uk

This edition published by Harper Perennial 2006
1

First published in Great Britain in 1995 by Fourth Estate

A catalogue record for this book
is available from the British Library

ISBN-13 978-1-85702-405-0
ISBN-10 1-85702-405-2

Printed and bound in Great Britain by Clays Ltd, St Ives plc

To Ayelet

Let them think what they liked, but I didn't
mean to drown myself. I meant to swim till I sank –
but that's not the same thing.

                                    Joseph Conrad

The author would like to thank
Mary Evans and Douglas Stumpf
Tigris and Euphrates of this little empire.

WONDER
BOYS

THE first real writer I ever knew was a man who did all of his work under the name of August Van Zorn. He lived at the McClelland Hotel, which my grandmother owned, in the uppermost room of its turret, and taught English literature at Coxley, a small college on the other side of the minor Pennsylvania river that split our town in two. His real name was Albert Vetch, and his field, I believe, was Blake; I remember he kept a framed print of the Ancient of Days affixed to the faded flocked wallpaper of his room, above a stoop-shouldered wooden suit rack that once belonged to my father. Mr. Vetch's wife had been living in a sanitorium up near Erie since the deaths of their teenaged sons in a backyard explosion some years earlier, and it was always my impression that he wrote, in part, to earn the money to keep her there. He wrote horror stories, hundreds of them, many of which were eventually published, in such periodicals of the day as *Weird Tales, Strange Stories, Black Tower,* and the like. They were in the gothic mode, after the manner of Lovecraft, set in quiet little Pennsylvania towns that had the misfortune to have been built over the forgotten sites of visitations by bloodthirsty alien gods and of Iroquois torture cults—but written in a dry, ironic, at times almost whimsical idiom, an echo of which I was later to discover in the fiction of John Collier. He worked at night, using a fountain pen, in a bentwood rocking chair, with a Hudson Bay blanket draped across his lap and a bottle of bourbon on the table before him. When his work was going well, he could be heard in every corner of the sleeping hotel, rocking and madly rocking while he subjected his heroes to the gruesome rewards of their passions for unnameable things.

As the market for pulp horror dried up in the years after the Second World War, however, the flecked white envelopes with their fabulous New York addresses no longer appeared so regularly in the Belleek tea tray on my grandmother's piano; presently they ceased to arrive altogether. I know that August Van Zorn tried to make an adjustment. He changed the settings of his tales to the suburbs and laid a greater emphasis on humor, and he tried, without success, to sell these tame and jokey pieces to *Collier's* and the *Saturday Evening Post*. Then one Monday morning when I was fourteen years old, of an age to begin to appreciate the work of the anonymous, kindly, self-loathing man who'd been living under the same roof as my grandmother and me for the past twelve years, Honoria Vetch threw herself into the swift little river that flowed past the sanitorium, through our town, down to the yellow Allegheny. Her body was not recovered. On the following Sunday, when my grandmother and I came home from church, she sent me upstairs to take Mr. Vetch his lunch. Ordinarily she would have gone herself—she always said that neither Mr. Vetch nor I could be trusted not to waste the other one's time—but she was angry with him for having declined, among all the empty Sundays of his life, to go to church on this one. So she cut the crusts from a pair of chicken sandwiches and set them on a tray along with a salt-shaker, a white peach, and a King James Bible, and I climbed the stairs to his room, where I found him, with a tiny black-rimmed hole in his left temple, sitting, still slowly rocking, in his bentwood chair. In spite of his fondness for literary gore, and unlike my father, who, I gathered, had made a mess of things, Albert Vetch went out neatly and with a minimum of blood.

I say that Albert Vetch was the first real writer I knew not because he was, for a while, able to sell his work to magazines, but because he was the first one to have the midnight disease; to have the rocking chair and the faithful bottle of bourbon and the staring eye, lucid with insomnia even in the daytime. In any case he was, now that I consider it, the first writer of any sort to cross my path, real or otherwise, in a life that has on the whole been a little too crowded with representatives of that sour and squirrelly race. He set a kind of example that, as a writer, I've been living up to ever since. I only hope that I haven't invented him.

The story—and the stories—of August Van Zorn were in my thoughts that Friday when I drove out to the airport to meet Crabtree's plane. It was impossible for me to see Terry Crabtree without remembering those fey short stories, since our long friendship had been founded, you might say, on August Van Zorn's obscurity, on the very, abject failure that helped crumple the spirit of a man whom my grandmother used to compare to a broken umbrella. Our friendship had itself, after twenty years, come to resemble one of the towns in a Van Zorn story: a structure erected, all unknowingly, on a very thin membrane of reality, beneath which lay an enormous slumbering Thing with one yellow eye already half open and peering right up at us. Three months earlier, Crabtree had been announced as a staff member of this year's annual WordFest—I had wangled him the invitation—and in all the intervening time, although he left numerous messages for me, I'd spoken to him only once, for five minutes, one evening in February when I came home, kind of stoned, from a party at the Chancellor's, to put on a necktie and join my wife at another party which her boss was throwing that evening down in Shadyside. I was smoking a joint while I spoke to Crabtree, and holding on to the receiver as though it were a strap and I stood in the center of a vast long whistling tunnel of wind, my hair fluttering around my face, my tie streaming out behind me. Although I had the vague impression that my oldest friend was speaking to me in tones of anger and remonstrance, his words just blew by me, like curling scraps of excelsior and fish wrap, and I waved at them as they passed. That Friday marked one of the few times in the history of our friendship that I wasn't looking forward to seeing him again; I was dreading it.

I remember I'd let my senior workshop go home early that afternoon, telling them it was because of WordFest; but everyone looked over at poor James Leer as they filed out of the room. When I finished gathering all the marked-up dittoed copies and typed critiques of his latest odd short story, shuffling them into my briefcase, and putting on my coat, and then turned to leave the classroom, I saw that the boy was still sitting there, at the back of the classroom, in the empty circle of chairs. I knew I ought to say something to console him—the workshop had been awfully hard on him—and he seemed to want to hear the sound of my voice; but I was in a hurry to get to the airport and irritated with him for being such a goddamn spook all the time, and so I only said good-bye to him and started out the door. "Turn out the light, please," he'd said, in his choked little powder-soft voice. I knew that I shouldn't have, but I did it all the same; and there you have my epitaph, or one of them, because my grave is going to require a monument inscribed on all four sides with rueful mottoes, in small characters, set close together. I left James

Leer sitting there, alone in the dark, and arrived at the airport about half an hour before Crabtree's plane was due, which gave me the opportunity to sit in my car in the airport parking garage smoking a fatty and listening to Ahmad Jamal, and I won't pretend that I hadn't been envisioning this idyllic half hour from the moment I dismissed my class. Over the years I'd surrendered many vices, among them whiskey, cigarettes, and the various non-Newtonian drugs, but marijuana and I remained steadfast companions. I had one fragrant ounce of Humboldt County, California, in a Ziploc bag in the glove compartment of my car.

Crabtree walked off the plane carrying a small canvas grip, his garment bag draped over one arm, a tall, attractive person at his side. This person had long black curls, wore a smashing red topcoat over a black dress and five-inch black spikes, and was laughing in sheer delight at something that Crabtree was whispering out of the corner of his mouth. It didn't appear to me, however, that this person was a woman, although I wasn't entirely sure.

"Tripp," said Crabtree, approaching me with his free hand extended. He reached up with both arms to embrace me and I held on to him for an extra second or two, tightly, trying to determine from the soundness of his ribs whether he loved me still. "Good to see you. How are you?"

I let go of him and took a step backward. He wore the usual Crabtree expression of scorn, and his eyes were bright and hard, but he didn't look as though he were angry with me. He'd been letting his hair grow long as he got older, not, as is the case with some fashionable men in their forties, in compensation for any incipient baldness, but out of a vanity more pure and unchallengeable: he had beautiful hair, thick and chestnut-colored and falling in a flawless curtain to his shoulders. He was wearing a well-cut, olive-drab belted rain-coat over a handsome suit—an Italian number in a metallic silk that was green like the back of a dollar bill—a pair of woven leather loafers without socks, and round schoolboy spectacles I'd never seen before.

"You look great," I said.

"Grady Tripp, this is Miss Antonia, uh, Miss Antonia—"

"Sloviak," said the person, in an ordinary pretty woman's voice. "Nice to meet you."

"It turns out she lives around the corner from me, on Hudson."

"Hi," I said. "That's my favorite street in New York." I attempted to make an unobtrusive study of the architecture of Miss Sloviak's throat, but she'd tied a brightly patterned scarf around her neck. That in itself was a kind of clue, I supposed. "Any luggage?"

Crabtree held on to the blue canvas grip and handed me the garment bag. It was surprisingly light.

"Just this?"

"Just that," he said. "Any chance we can give Miss Sloviak here a lift?"

"I guess that would be all right," I said, with a faint twinge of apprehension, for I began to see already what kind of evening it was going to be. I knew the expression in Crabtree's eye all too well. He was looking at me as though I were a monster he'd created with his own brain and hands, and he were about to throw the switch that would send me reeling spasmodically across the countryside, laying waste to rude farmsteads and despoiling the rural maidenry. Further he had plenty more ideas where that one came from, and if the means of creating another disturbance fell into his hands he would exploit it without mercy on this night. If Miss Sloviak were not already a transvestite, Crabtree would certainly make her into one. "What hotel is it?"

"Oh, I *live* here," said Miss Sloviak, with a becoming blush. "That is, my parents do. In Bloomfield. But you can just drop me downtown and I'll get a cab from there."

"Well, we do have to stop downtown, Crabtree," I said, trying to demonstrate to all concerned that my traffic was with him and that I considered Miss Sloviak to be merely a temporary addition to our party. "To pick up Emily."

"Where's this dinner we're going to?"

"In Point Breeze."

"Is that far from Bloomfield?"

"Not too far."

"Great, then," said Crabtree, and with that, he took Miss Sloviak's elbow and started off toward Baggage Claim, working his skinny legs to keep up with her. "Come on, Tripp," he called over his shoulder.

The luggage from their flight was a long time in rolling out and Miss Sloviak took advantage of the delay to go to the bathroom—the ladies' room, naturally. Crabtree and I stood there, grinning at each other.

"Stoned again," he said.

"You bastard," I said. "How are you?"

"Unemployed," he said, looking no less delighted with himself.

I started to smile, but then something, a ripple in the muscle of his jaw, told me that he wasn't joking.

"You got *fired*?" I said.

"Not yet," he said. "But it looks like it's coming. I'll be all right. I spent most of the week calling around town. I had lunch with a couple of people." He continued to waggle his eyebrows and grin, as though his predicament only amused him—there was a thick streak of self-contempt in Terry Crabtree—and to a certain extent, no doubt, it did. "They weren't exactly lining up."

"But, Jesus, Terry, why? What happened?"

"Restructuring," he said.

Two months earlier my publisher, Bartizan, had been bought out by Blicero Verlag, a big German media conglomerate, and subsequent rumors of a ruthless housecleaning by the new owners had managed to penetrate as far into the outback as Pittsburgh.

"I guess I don't fit the new corporate profile."

"Which is?"

"Competence."

"Where will you go?"

He shook his head, and shrugged.

"So, how do you like her?" he said. "Miss Sloviak. She was in the seat beside me." An alarm clamored somewhere, to tell us that the carousel of suitcases was about to start up. I think that both of us jumped. "Do you know how many airplanes I've boarded with the hope in my heart that my ticket would get me a seat next to someone like her? Particularly while I'm on my way to *Pittsburgh*? Don't you think it says a lot for Pittsburgh that it could have produced a Miss Sloviak?"

"She's a transvestite."

"Oh, my God," he said, looking shocked.

"Isn't she?"

"I'll just *bet* that's hers," he said. He pointed to a large rectangular suitcase of spotted pony hide, zipped into what looked like the plastic covering for a sofa cushion, that was emerging through the rubber flaps on the carousel. "I guess she doesn't want to have it soiled."

"Terry, what's going to happen to you?" I said. I felt as

though the alarm bell were still reverberating within my chest. What's going to happen to me? I thought. What's going to happen to my book? "How many years have you been with Bartizan, now anyway? Ten?"

"It's only ten if you don't count the last five," he said, turning toward me. "Which I guess you weren't." He looked at me, his expression mild, his eyes alight with that combination of malice and affection expressed so neatly by his own last name. I knew before he opened his mouth exactly what he was going to ask me.

"How's the book?" he said.

I reached out to grab the pony-skin valise before it passed us by.

"It's fine," I said.

He was talking about my fourth novel, or what purported to be my fourth novel, *Wonder Boys,* which I had promised to Bartizan during the early stages of the previous presidential administration. My third novel, *The Land Downstairs,* had won a PEN award and, at twelve thousand copies, sold twice as well as both its predecessors combined, and in its aftermath Crabtree and his bosses at Bartizan had felt sanguine enough about my imminent attainment to the status of, at the least, cult favorite to advance me a ridiculous sum of money in exchange for nothing more than a fatuous smile from the thunderstruck author and a title invented out of air and brain-sparkle while pissing into the aluminum trough of a men's room at Three Rivers Stadium. Luckily for me an absolutely superb idea for a novel soon followed—three brothers in a haunted Pennsylvania small town are born, grow up, and die—and I'd started to work on it at once, and had been diligently hacking away at the thing ever since. Motivation, inspiration were not the problem; on the contrary I was always cheerful and workmanlike at the typewriter and had never suffered from what's called writer's block; I didn't believe in it.

The problem, if anything, was precisely the opposite. I had too much to write: too many fine and miserable buildings to construct and streets to name and clock towers to set chiming, too many characters to raise up from the dirt like flowers whose petals I peeled down to the intricate frail organs within, too many terrible genetic and fiduciary secrets to dig up and bury and dig up again, too many divorces to grant, heirs to disinherit, trysts to arrange, letters to misdirect into evil hands, innocent children to slay with rheumatic fever, women to leave unfulfilled and hopeless, men to drive to adultery and theft, fires to ignite at the hearts of ancient houses. It was about a single family and it stood, as of that morning, at two thousand six hundred and eleven pages, each of them revised and rewritten a half dozen times. And yet for all of those years, and all of those words expended in charting the eccentric paths of my characters through the violent blue heavens I had set them to cross, they had not even reached their zeniths. I was nowhere near the end.

"It's done," I said. "It's basically done. I'm just sort of, you know, tinkering with it now, buddy."

"Great. I was hoping I could get a look at it sometime this weekend. Oh, here's another one, I bet." He pointed to a neat little plaid-and-red-leather number, also zipped into a plastic sleeve, that came trundling toward us now along the belt. "Think that might be possible?"

I grabbed the second suitcase—it was more what you'd call a Gladstone bag, a squat little half moon hinged at the sides— and set it on the ground beside the first.

"I don't know," I said. "Look what happened to Joe Fahey."

"Yeah, he got famous," said Crabtree. "And on his fourth book."

John Jose Fahey, another real writer I'd known, had only *written* four books—*Sad Tidings, Kind of Blue, Fans and Fadeaways,* and *Eight Solid Light-years of Lead.* Joe and I became friends during the semester I spent in residence, almost a dozen years ago now, at the Tennessee college where he ran the writing program. Joe was a disciplined writer, when I met him, with an admirable gift for narrative digression he claimed to have inherited from his Mexican mother, and very few bad or unmanageable habits. He was a courtly fellow, even smooth, with hair that had turned white by the time he was thirty-two years old. After the moderate success of his third book, Joe's publishers had advanced him a hundred and twenty-five thousand dollars in order to encourage him to write them a fourth. His first attempt at it went awry almost instantly. He gamely started a second; this novel he pursued for over two years before giving it up as fucked. The next try his publisher rejected before Joe was even finished writing it, on the grounds that it was already too long, and at any rate not the kind of book they were interested in publishing.

After that John Jose Fahey disappeared into the fastness of an impregnable failure. He pulled off the difficult trick of losing his tenured job at the Tennessee college, when he started showing up drunk for work, spoke with unpardonable cruelty to the talentless element of his classes, and one day waved a loaded a pistol from the lectern and instructed his pupils to write about Fear. He sealed himself off from his wife, as well, and she left him, unwillingly, taking with her half of the proceeds from his fabulous contract. After a while he moved back to Nevada, where he'd been born, and lived in a succession of motels. A few years later, changing planes at the Reno airport, I ran into him. He wasn't going anywhere; he was just making the scene at McCarran. At first he affected not to recognize me. He'd lost his hearing in one ear and his manner was inattentive and cool. Over several margaritas in the airport bar, however, he eventually told me that at last, after seven tries, he'd sent his publisher what he believed to be an acceptable final manuscript of a novel. I asked him how he felt about it. "It's acceptable," he said coldly. Then I asked him if finishing the book hadn't make him feel very happy. I had to repeat myself twice.

"Happy as a fucking clam," he said.

After that I'd started hearing rumors. I heard that soon after our meeting, Joe tried to *withdraw* his seventh submission, an effort he abandoned only when his publisher, patience exhausted, had threatened him with legal action. I heard that entire sections had needed to be excised, due to aimlessness and illogic and an unseemly bitterness of tone. I heard all kinds of inauspicious things. In the end, however, *Lead* turned out to be a pretty good book, and with the added publicity value of Joe's untimely and absurdist death—he was hit, remember, on Virginia Street, by an armored car filled with casino takings—it did fairly well in the stores. His publishers recouped most of their advance, and everybody said that it was too bad Joe Fahey didn't live to see his success, but I was never quite sure that I agreed. Eight solid light-years of lead, if you haven't read the book, is the thickness of that metal in which you would need to encase yourself if you wanted to keep from being touched by neutrinos. I guess the little fuckers are everywhere.

"Okay, sure, Crabtree," I said. "I'll let you read, I don't know, a dozen pages or so."

"Any dozen pages I want?"

"Sure. You name 'em." I laughed, but I was afraid I knew which twelve pages he would choose: the last twelve. This was going to be a problem, because over the past month, knowing that Crabtree was coming to town, I had actually written five different "final chapters," subjecting my poor half-grown characters to a variety of biblical disasters and Shakespearean bloodbaths and happy little accidents of life, in a desperate attempt to bring in for a premature landing the immense careering zeppelin of which I was the mad commander. There were no "last twelve pages"; or rather, there were sixty of them, all absurdly sudden and random and violent, the literary equivalents of that windblown, flaming airfield in Lakehurst, New Jersey. I aimed a cheesy smile at Crabtree and held it, for just a minute too long. Crabtree took pity on me and looked away.

"Check this out," he said.

I looked. Wrapped, like the two suitcases, in heavy, clear sheeting that was held in place by strips of duct tape, a strange, black leather case was coming toward us, big as a trash can, molded according to a fanciful geometry, as though it had been designed to transport intact the heart, valves, and ventricles of an elephant.

"That would be a tuba," I said. I sucked my cheek in and looked at him through a half-closed eye. "Do you suppose—?"

"I think it has to be," said Crabtree. "It's wrapped in plastic."

I hoisted it from the carousel—it was even heavier than it looked—and set it beside the other two, and then we turned toward the ladies' room and waited for Miss Sloviak to rejoin us. When, after a few more minutes, Miss Sloviak didn't come back, we decided that I ought to rent a cart. I borrowed a dollar from Crabtree and after a brief struggle with the cart dispenser we managed to get the cart loaded, and wheeled it across the carpet to the bathroom.

"Miss Sloviak?" called Crabtree, knocking like a gentleman on the ladies' room door.

"I'll be right out," said Miss Sloviak.

"Probably putting the plastic wrapper back onto her johnson," I said.

"Tripp," said Crabtree. He looked straight at me now and held my eyes with his for as long as he could manage, given the agitated state of his pleasure receptors. "Is it really almost done?"

"Sure," I said. "Of course it is. Crabtree, are you still going to be my editor?"

"Sure," he said. He broke eye contact with me and turned back to watch the dwindling parade of suitcases drifting along the baggage carousel. "Everything's going to be fine."

Then Miss Sloviak emerged from the ladies' room, hair reestablished, cheeks rouged, eyelids freshly painted a soft viridian, smelling of what I recognized as Cristalle, the fragrance worn both by my wife, Emily, and also by my lover, Sara Gaskell. It smelled a little bitter to me, as you might imagine. Miss Sloviak looked down at the luggage on the cart, and then at Crabtree, and broke out into a broad, toothy, almost intolerably flirtatious lipsticked grin.

"Why, Mr. Crabtree," said Miss Sloviak, in a creditable Mae West, "is that a tuba on your luggage cart, or are you just glad to see me?"

When I looked at Crabtree I saw, to my amazement, that

he had turned bright red in the face. It had been a long time since I'd seen him do that.

CRABTREE and I met in college, a place in which I'd never intended to meet anyone. After graduating from high school I took great pains to avoid having to go to college at all, and in particular to Coxley, which had offered me the annual townie scholarship, along with a place as tight end on the starting eleven. I was and remain a big old bastard, six-three, fat now and I know it, and while at the time I had a certain cetacean delicacy of movement in the wide open sea of a hundred-yard field, I wore quadrangular black-rimmed eyeglasses and the patent-leather shoes, serge high-waters, and sober, V-necked sweater-vests my grandmother required of me, so it must have taken a kind of imaginative faith to see me as a football star with a four-year free ride; but in any case I had no desire to play for Coxley—or for anyone else—and one day in late June, 1968, I left my poor grandmother a rather smart-assed note and ran away from the somber hills, towns, and crooked spires of western Pennsylvania that had so haunted August Van Zorn. I didn't come back for twenty-five years.

I'll skip over a lot of what followed my cowardly departure from home. Let's just say that I'd read Kerouac the year before, and had conceived the usual picture of myself as an outlaw-poet-pathfinder, a kind of Zen-masterly John C. Frémont on amphetamines with a marbled dime-store pad of lined paper in the back pocket of my denim pants. I still see myself that way, I suppose, and I'm probably none the better for it. Dutifully I thumbed the rides, hopped the B & Os and the Great Northerns, balled the lithe small-town girls in the band shells of their hometown parks, held the jobs as field hand and day laborer and soda jerk, saw the crude spectacles of American landscape slide past me as I lay in an open boxcar and drank cheap red wine; and if I didn't, I might as well have. I worked for part of a summer in a hellish Texarkanan carnival as the contumelious clown you get to drop into a tank of water after he calls you pencil-dick. I was shot in the meat of my left hand in a bar outside La Crosse, Wisconsin. All of this rich material I made good use of in my first novel, *The Bottomlands,* 1976, which was well reviewed, and which sometimes, at desperate instants, I consider to be my truest work. After a few years of unhappy and often depraved existence, I landed, again in the classic manner, in California, where I fell in love with a philosophy major at Berkeley who persuaded me not to waste in wandering what she called, with an air of utter, soul-enveloping conviction that has since led to great misery and that I have never for one instant forgotten, my gift. I was pinned to the spot by this touching tribute to my genius, and stayed put long enough to get together an application to Cal. I was just about ready to blow town— alone—when the letter of acceptance arrived.

Terry Crabtree and I met at the start of our junior year, when we landed in the same short-story class, an introductory course I'd tried every semester to get into. Crabtree had signed up for it on an impulse, and gotten in on the strength of a story he'd written in the tenth grade, about an encounter, at a watering place, between the aging Sherlock Holmes and a youthful Adolf Hitler, who has come from Vienna to Carlsbad to rob invalid ladies of their jewelry. It was a remarkable trick for a fifteen-year-old to have performed, but it was unique; Crabtree had written nothing since then, not a line.

The story had weird sexual undertones, as, it must be said, did its author. He was then an awkward, frail young man, his face all forehead and teeth, and he kept to himself, at the back of the class, dressed in a tight, unfashionable suit and tie, a red cashmere scarf tucked like an ascot into his raised lapels when the weather turned cool. I sat in my own corner of the room, sporting a new beard and a pair of little round wire-rims, and took careful notes on everything the teacher had to say.

The teacher was a real writer, too, a lean, handsome cowboy writer from an old Central Valley ranching family, who revered Faulkner and who in his younger days had published a fat, controversial novel that was made into a movie with Robert Mitchum and Mercedes McCambridge. He was given to epigrams and I filled an entire notebook, since lost, with his gnomic utterances, all of which every night I committed to the care of my memory, since ruined. I swear but cannot independently confirm that one of them ran, "At the end of every short story the reader should feel as if a cloud has been lifted from the face of the moon." He wore a patrician manner and boots made of rattlesnake hide, and he drove an E-type Jaguar, but his teeth were bad, the fly of his trousers was always agape, and his family life was a semi-notorious farrago of legal proceedings, accidental injury, and institutionalization. He seemed, like Albert Vetch, simultaneously haunted and oblivious, the kind of person who in one moment could guess, with breathtaking coldness, at the innermost sorrow in your heart, and in the next moment turn and, with a cheery wave of farewell, march blithely through a plate-glass window, requiring twenty-two stitches in his cheek.

It was in this man's class that I first began to wonder if people who wrote fiction were not suffering from some kind of disorder—from what I've since come to think of, remembering the wild nocturnal rocking of Albert Vetch, as the midnight disease. The midnight disease is a kind of emotional insomnia; at every conscious moment its victim—even if he or she writes at dawn, or in the middle of the afternoon—feels like a person lying in a sweltering bedroom, with the window thrown open, looking up at a sky filled with stars and airplanes, listening to the narrative of a rattling blind, an ambulance, a fly trapped in a Coke bottle, while all around him the neighbors soundly sleep. This is in my opinion why writers—like insomniacs—are so accident-prone, so obsessed with the calculus of bad luck and missed opportunities, so liable to rumination and a concomitant inability to let go of a subject, even when urged repeatedly to do so.

But these are observations I made only later, over the course of many years' exposure to the workings of the midnight disease. At the time I was simply intimidated, by our teacher's fame, by his snakeskin boots, and by the secrets of the craft which I believed him to possess. The class covered two stories every session, and in the first go-around I held the last slot on the schedule, along with Crabtree, who, I noticed, made no effort whatever to write down the axioms that filled the smoky air of the classroom, nor ever had anything to contribute to the class beyond an occasional terse but unfailingly polite comment on the banality of the work under discussion that afternoon. Naturally his aloofness was taken for arrogance, and he was thought to be a snob, in particular when he wore his cashmere scarf; but I had noticed from the first how bitten were his nails, how soft and unimposing his voice, how he flinched whenever someone addressed him. He stayed in his corner, in his ill-fitting suit, looking forever pale and faintly queasy, as though our company disgusted him but he was too kind to let on.

He was suffering from the disease, I suspected—but was I?

Hitherto I'd always felt certain of my own ability, but as the weeks passed, and we were burdened with all the inescapable shibboleths and bugbears of the trade of writing—knowing what was "at stake" in a story, where the mystical fairy-fire of epiphany ought to be set dancing above a character's head, the importance of what our teacher liked to call "spiritual danger" to good characterization—the inevitable overshadowing of my own effort by cool Crabtree's made it impossible for me to finish anything. I stayed up all night long at the typewriter for the week before my story was due, drinking bourbon and trying to untangle the terrible symbolical mess I had made out of a simple story my grandmother once told me about a mean black rooster that had killed her dog when she was a little girl.

At six o'clock on the last morning I gave up, and decided to do an unconscionable thing. My mind had been wandering for the last hour through the rooms in which my grandmother had passed her life (a year before this I'd telephoned home from some booth in the middle of nowhere, Kansas, and learned that the woman who raised me had died of pneumonia that very morning), and all at once, with the burnt-sugar flavor of bourbon in my mouth, I found myself thinking about Albert Vetch and the hundreds of forgotten stories into which he had poured all the bitterness of his cosmic insomnia. There was one story I remembered fairly well—it was one of his best—called "Sister of Darkness." It was about an amateur archaeologist, naturally, who lived with his invalid spinster sister in a turreted old house, and who, in the course of poking around the ruins of a local Indian burial mound, stumbled upon a queer, non-Indian sarcophagus, empty, bearing the faded image of a woman with a sinister grin, which he carted home in the dead of night and with which he became obsessed. In the course of restoring the object he cut his hand on a razor blade, and at the splash of his blood upon it the sarcophagus at once grew warm and emitted an odd radiance; his hand was healed, and at the same time he felt himself suffused with a feeling of intense well-being. After a couple of tests on hapless household pets, which he injured and then restored, our man persuaded his crippled little sister to lie in the sarcophagus and thus heal her poliomyelitic legs, whereupon she was transformed, somewhat inexplicably as I recalled, into an incarnation of Yshtaxta, a succubus from a distant galaxy who forced the hero to lie with her—Van Zorn's genre permitted a certain raciness, as long as the treatment was grotesque and euphemistic—and then, having drained the life force from the unlucky hero, set out to take on the rest of the town, or so I had always imagined, half hoping that a luminous ten-foot woman with fangs and immortal cravings might appear sometime at my own window in the most lonely hour of the Pennsylvanian night.

I set to work reassembling the story as well as I could. I toned down the occult elements by turning the whole nameless-Thing-from-beyond-Time component into a weird psychosis on the part of my first-person narrator, played up the theme of incest, and added more sex. I wrote in a fever and it took about six hours to do. When I was finished I had to run all the way to class and I walked into the room five minutes late. The teacher was already reading Crabtree's story aloud, which was his favored way of having us "experience" a story, and it didn't take me long to recognize that I was hearing, not a garbled and badly Faulknerized rehash of an obscure gothic horror story by an unknown writer, but the original "Sister of Darkness," the clear, lean, unexcitable prose of August Van Zorn himself. The shock I felt at having been caught, beaten, and most of all preceded at my own game was equaled only by my surprise on learning that I wasn't the only person in the world who'd ever read the work of poor old Albert Vetch, and in the midst of my mortification, of the dread that stole over my heart as the professor slid each page of the manuscript under the last, I felt the first glow of the flickering love I continue to bear for Terry Crabtree.

I said nothing during the discussion that followed the reading of Van Zorn's story; nobody liked it very much—we were all far too serious-minded to enjoy such a piece of black foolery, and too young to catch the undertone of sorrow in its style—but nobody recognized it either. I was the one who was going to get busted. I handed my story to the professor, and he began to read, in his manner that was flat and dry as ranchland and as filled with empty space. I've never been able to decide if it was his tedious way of reading, or the turgid unpunctuated labyrinthine sentences of Mocknapatawpha prose with which he was forced to contend, or the total over-the-top incomprehensibility of my demysticized, hot-hot-sexy finale, composed in ten minutes after forty-six hours without sleep, but, in the end, nobody noticed that it was essentially the same story as Crabtree's. The professor finished, and looked at me with an expression at once sad and benedictory, as though he were envisioning the fine career I was to have as a wire-and-cable salesman. Those who had fallen asleep roused themselves, and a brief, dispirited discussion followed, during which the professor allowed that my writing showed "undeniable energy." Ten minutes later I was walking down Bancroft Way, headed for home, embarrassed, disappointed, but somehow undiscouraged; the story hadn't really been *mine,* after all. I felt oddly buzzed, almost happy, as I considered the undeniable energy of my writing, the torrent of world-altering stories that now poured into my mind demanding to be written, and the simple joyous fact that I had gotten away with my scam.

Or nearly so; as I stopped at the corner of Dwight, I felt a tap on my shoulder, and I turned to find Crabtree, his eyes bright, his red cashmere scarf fluttering out behind him.

"August Van Zorn," he said, holding out his hand.

"August Van Zorn," I said. We shook. "Unbelievable."

"I have no talent," he said. "What's your excuse?"

"Desperation. Have you read any of his others?"

"A lot of them. 'The Eaters of Men.' 'The Case of Edward Angell.' 'The House on Polfax Street.' He's great. I can't believe you've heard of him."

"Listen," I said, thinking that I had done far more than hear of Albert Vetch. "Do you want to get a beer?"

"I never drink," said Crabtree. "Buy me a cup of coffee."

I wanted a beer, but coffee was undeniably easier to be had in the purlieus of the University, so we went into a cafe, one that I'd been avoiding for the past couple of weeks, since it was a haunt of that tender and perceptive philosophy major who'd pleaded so sweetly with me not to fritter away my gift. A couple of years later I would marry her for a little while.

"There's a table under the stairs, at the back," said Crabtree. "I often sit there. I don't like to be seen."

"Why is that?"

"I prefer to remain a mystery to my peers."

"I see. So why are you talking to me?"

" 'The Sister of Darkness,' " he said. "It took me a few

pages to catch on, you know. It was the line about the angle of his widow's peak lying 'slightly out of true with the remainder of his face.' "

"I must have remembered that one wholesale," I said. "I was working from memory."

"You must have a sick memory, then."

"But at least I have talent."

"Maybe," he said, looking down cross-eyed at the flame of a match as he cupped his hand around the end of a filterless cigarette. He smoked Old Gold then. Now he's changed to something low-tar and aqua-colored; a faggy cigarette, I call it when I want to make him pretend to get mad.

"If you don't have talent, how'd you get in?" I asked him. "Didn't you have to submit a sample of work?"

"I had talent," he said, extinguishing the match with an insouciant shake. "One story's worth. But it's all right. I'm not planning to be a writer." He paused a moment after he said that, to let it sink in, and I got the feeling that he'd been waiting to have this conversation for a very long time. I imagined him at home, blowing sophisticated plumes of smoke at the reflection in his bedroom mirror, tying and retying his cashmere scarf. "I'm taking this class to learn about writers as much as writing." He sat back in his seat and coil by coil unwrapped the scarf from his neck. "I intend to be the Max Perkins of our generation."

His expression was grave and earnest but there was still a slight wrinkling of mockery at the corners of his eyes, as though he were daring me to admit that I didn't know who Maxwell Perkins was.

"Oh, yeah?" I said, determined to match his grandiosity and arrogance with my own. I had spent plenty of time impressing my own mirror with bons mots and intrepid writerly gazes. I had a Greek fisherman's sweater that I used to put on and flatter myself for having Hemingway's brow. "Well, then, I intend to be the Bill Faulkner."

He smiled. "You have a lot farther to go than I do," he said.

"Fuck you," I said, taking a cigarette from the pocket of his shirt.

As we drank our espressos I told him about myself and my wanderings over the past few years, embellishing my account with shameless references to wild if vague sexual encounters. I sensed a certain awkwardness on his part around the subject of girls and I asked if he was seeing anyone, but he grew monosyllabic and I quickly backed off. Instead I told him the story of Albert Vetch, and I could see, when I had finished, that it moved him.

"So," he said, looking solemn. He reached into the pocket of his overcoat and pulled out a slim hardback book in a buff-colored dust jacket. He passed it to me across the table, two-handed, as though it were an overflowing cup. "You must have seen this."

It was a collection, published by Arkham House, of twenty short stories by August Van Zorn.

"*The Abominations of Plunkettsburg and Other Tales,*" I said. "When did this come out?"

"A couple of years ago. They're a specialty house. You have to go looking for it."

I turned the deckled pages of the book Albert Vetch hadn't lived to hold. There was a laudatory text printed on the jacket flaps, and a startling photograph of the plain, high-browed, bespectacled man who had struggled for years, in his room in the turret of the McClelland Hotel, with unnameable regret, with the emptiness of his external life, with the ravages of the midnight disease. You certainly couldn't see any of that in the picture. He looked relaxed, even handsome, and his hair was just a bit unkempt, as befitting a scholar of Blake.

"Keep it," said Crabtree. "Seeing as how you knew him."

"Thanks, Crabtree," I said, flush once more with a sudden unreasonable affection for this small, skinny person with his scarf and his awkwardness and his studied displays of arrogance and scorn. Later they lost that quality of studiedness, of course, and hardened into automatic mannerisms not universally admired. "Maybe someday you'll be my editor, huh?"

"Maybe," he said. "You need one, that's for sure."

We smiled at each other and shook hands on it, and then the young woman I'd been avoiding came up from behind and poured a pitcher of ice water onto my head, drenching not only me but the book by August Van Zorn, ruining it beyond repair; or at least that's the way I remember it happening.

THE windshield wipers played their endless game of tag as we sat parked on Smithfield Street, smoking a little piece of Humboldt County and waiting for my third wife, Emily, to emerge from the lobby of the Baxter Building, where she worked as a copywriter for an advertising agency. Richards, Reed & Associates's major client was a locally popular brand of Polish sausage famous for its generous dimensions, which made writing ad copy a simple but delicate matter. I saw Emily's secretary come through the revolving door and shake open her umbrella, and then her friends Susan and Ben, and then a man whose name I had forgotten but whom I recognized as the Engorged Kielbasa from an office skit a couple of Christmases earlier. There were all kinds of other people spinning out into the soft gray evening, dentists and podiatrists, certified public accountants, the sad-looking Ethiopian man who sold half-dead flowers from a small kiosk in the lobby; looking skyward, covering their heads with outspread newspapers, laughing at the glittering, rain-slick prospect of a Friday night downtown; but after fifteen minutes Emily had still not appeared, even though she was always downstairs waiting for me on Fridays when I came to pick her up, and eventually I was forced to admit to myself what I had been fervently denying all day: that sometime early this morning, before I awoke, Emily had walked out on our marriage. There'd been a note taped to the coffee machine on the kitchen counter, and a modest void in all the drawers and closets that had been hers.

"Crabtree," I said. "She left me, man."

"She what?"

"She left me. This morning. There was a note. I don't know if she even *went* to work. I think she might have gone out to her parents' place. It's Passover. Tomorrow's the first night." I turned around and looked at Miss Sloviak. She was sitting in the backseat, with Crabtree, on the theory that Emily would have been getting into the front with me. They had the tuba back there with them as well, though I wasn't entirely sure how that had happened. I still didn't know if it really belonged to Miss Sloviak or not. "There are eight of them. Nights."

"Is he kidding?" said Miss Sloviak, all of whose makeup seemed in the course of the ride in from the airport to have been reapplied, very roughly, an inch to the left of her eyes and lips, so that her face had a blurred, double-exposed appearance.

"Why didn't you say anything, Tripp? I mean, why did you come down here?"

"I guess I just . . . I don't know." I turned back around to face the windshield and listened to the commentary of the rain on the roof of my car, a fly-green '66 Galaxie ragtop I'd been driving for a little less than a month. I'd had to accept it as repayment of a sizable loan I'd been fool enough to make Happy Blackmore, an old drinking buddy who wrote sports for the *Post-Gazette* and who was now somewhere in the Blue Ridge of Maryland at a rehabilitation center for the compulsively unlucky, playing out the last act of a spectacular emotional and financial collapse. It was a stylish old yacht, that Ford, with a balky transmission, bad wires, and a rear seat of almost infinite potential. I didn't really want to know what had just been going on back there.

"I was sort of thinking maybe I'd just imagined it all," I said. As a lifelong habitué of marijuana I was used to having even the most dreadful phenomena prove, on further inspection, to be only the figments of my paranoid fancy, and all day I had been trying to convince myself that this morning at about six o'clock, while I lay snoring with my legs scissorforked across the freshly uninhabited regions of the bed, my marriage had not come asunder. "Hoping I had, I mean."

"Do you feel all right?" said Miss Sloviak.

"I feel great," I said, trying to decide how I did feel. I felt sorry to have driven Emily to leave me, not because I thought that I could have done otherwise, but because she'd tried very hard for many years to avoid an outcome to which she was, in a way that would always remain beyond my understanding, morally opposed. Her own parents had married in 1939 and they were married still, in a manner that approximated happiness, and I knew she regarded divorce as the first refuge of the weak in character and the last of the hopelessly incompetent. I felt as you feel when you've forced an honest person to lie for you, or a thrifty person to blow his paycheck on one of your worthless tips. I also felt that I loved Emily, but in the fragmentary, half-narrative way you love people when you're stoned. I closed my eyes and I thought of the lash of her skirt snapping around her as she danced one evening in a bar on the South Side to a jukebox that was playing "Barefootin'," of the downy slope of her neck and the declivity in her nightgown as she bent to wash her face in the bathroom sink, of a tuna salad sandwich she'd handed me one windy afternoon as we sat on a picnic table in Lucia, California, and looked out for the passage of whales, and I felt that I loved Emily insofar as I loved all of these things—beyond reason, and with a longing that made me want to hang my head—but it was a love that felt an awful lot like nostalgia. I hung my head.

"Grady, what happened?" said Crabtree, leaning forward to rest his chin on the back of my seat. I could feel the ends of his long hair against my neck. He was giving off a faint whiff of Cristalle himself now, and the dual memory of Emily and Sara it stirred up inside me seemed particularly cruel. "What did you do?"

"I broke her heart," I said. "I think she found out about Sara and me."

"How?"

"I don't know," I said. She'd been looking a little lost ever since coming home a few days before from a lunch at Ali Baba with her sister, Deborah, who was working as a research assistant in fine arts at the University of Pittsburgh. Deborah must have picked something up on the academic grapevine and sisterly passed it along. "I don't suppose we've really been all that discreet."

"Sara?" said Miss Sloviak. "That's where the party's going to be?"

"That's right," I said. "That's where the party's going to be."

IT was above all a formal exercise in good behavior, the first staff party of the WordFest weekend, a preliminary shaking of hands before they rang the bell and the assembled guests all came out swinging. It was held early in the evening, for one thing, so that people had to keep dinner plates balanced in their laps; and then at around quarter to eight, just when supper was finished and strangers had grown acquainted and the booze began to flow, it would be time to go off to Thaw Hall for the Friday night lecture by one of the two most distinguished members of that year's staff. For eleven years now the college, under the direction of Sara Gaskell's husband, Walter, the chairman of the English Department, had been charging aspiring writers several hundred dollars for the privilege of meeting and receiving the counsel of a staff of more or less well-known writers, along with agents, editors, and assorted other New Yorkers with an astonishing capacity for alcohol and gossip. The conferees were housed in the college dormitories, left vacant over the spring holidays, and guided like passengers on a cruise ship through a tightly scheduled program of lit crit shuffleboard, self-improvement talks, and lessons in the New York publishing cha-cha-cha. The same kind of thing goes on all over the country, and I don't think there's anything wrong with it, any more than I find anything amiss in the practice of loading up an enormous floating replica of Las Vegas with a bunch of fearful Americans and whipping them past a dozen tourist-oriented ports of call at thirty knots. I usually had a friend or two among the invited guests, and once, several years ago now, I came across a young man from Moon Township with a short story so amazingly good that on the strength of it alone he was able to sign up an unwritten novel with my agent, a novel long since finished, published to acclaim, sold to the movies, and remaindered; at the time I was on page three hundred or so of my *Wonder Boys*.

Because WordFest had been conceived by Walter Gaskell, the first party was always held at the Gaskells', an eccentric, brick Tudor affair, a crooked witch's hat of a house set back from the street in a leafy pocket of Point Breeze that had been carved, Sara once told me, from the estate of H. J. Heinz. There were vestiges of a massive old wrought-iron fence along the sidewalk, and in the Gaskells' backyard, beyond Sara's greenhouse, lay a pair of rusted rails, buried in the grass, the remnants of a small-gauge railroad that had been the childish hobby of some long-dead Heinz heir. The house was much too large for the Gaskells, who, like Emily and me, never had children, and it was filled from crawl space to attic with the inventory of Walter Gaskell's collection of baseball memorabilia, so that even on those rare occasions when I went over to see Sara and we had the place to ourselves, we were never alone; the grand, dark spaces of the house were haunted by the presence of her husband and by the fainter ghosts of dead ballplayers and tycoons. I liked Walter Gaskell, and I could never lie in his bed without feeling that there was a coarse thread of shame running through the iridescent silk of my desire for his wife.

I'm not, however, going to say that it was never my intention to get involved with Sara Gaskell. I'm a man who falls in love so easily, and with such a reckless lack of consideration for the consequences of my actions, that from the very first instant of entering into a marriage I become, almost by definition, an adulterer. I've run through three marriages now, and each time the dissolution was my own fault, clearly and incontrovertibly. I intended to get involved with Sara Gaskell from the moment I saw her, to get involved with her articulate fingers, with the severe engineering of combs and barrettes that prevented her russet hair from falling to her hips, with her conversation that flowed in unnavigable oxbows between opposing shores of tenderness and ironical invective, with the smoke of her interminable cigarettes. We had an apartment we used, in East Oakland, that belonged to the college; Sara Gaskell was the Chancellor, and I met her on my very first day on the job. Our thing had been going on for almost five years now, according to no discernible progression other than the one leading from the crazed fumbling of two people's hands with a key in an unfamiliar lock to the installation in the Guest Apartment of cable television so that Sara and I could lie on the bed in our underwear and watch old movies on Wednesday afternoons. Neither of us wanted to leave our spouses, or do anything to disturb the tranquil pattern of what was already an old love.

"So is she *pretty*?" whispered Miss Sloviak as we came scraping up the flagstone steps to the Gaskells' front door. She gave my belly a poke, reproducing perfectly the condescending but essentially generous manner of a beautiful woman with a homely man. "*I* think she is," I was supposed to say.

"Not as pretty as you," I told her. Sara wasn't as pretty as Emily, either, and she had none of Emily's delicacy of skeleton or skittish grace. She was a big woman—tall and busty, with a large behind—and as with most redheaded women what beauty she possessed was protean and odd. Her cheeks and forehead were wild with freckles, and her nose, although cute and retroussé in profile, had a way of looking bulbous when viewed straight on. By the age of twelve she had already reached her present height and bodily dimensions, and I believe it was as a result of this trauma—and the demands of her professional position—that her everyday wardrobe consisted almost entirely of control-top panty hose, plain white cotton blouses, and shapeless tweed suits that spanned a brilliant spectrum from oatmeal to dirt. She imprisoned her glorious hair within its scaffolding of pins, painted a thin copper line across her lips for makeup, and aside from her wedding ring the only jewelry she generally wore was a pair of half-moon reading glasses tied around her neck with a length of athletic shoestring. Undressing her was an act of recklessness, a kind of vandalism, like releasing a zoo full of animals, or blowing up a dam.

"I'm so glad to see you," I told her, whispering into her ear as she stepped aside to let Crabtree and Miss Sloviak into the oaken foyer of her house. I had to whisper rather loudly because the dog, an Alaskan malamute named Doctor Dee, found amusement in greeting every one of my appearances in the Gaskells' house, regardless of the circumstances, with an astonishing display of savage barking. Doctor Dee had been blinded in puppyhood by a brain fever, and his weird blue eyes had an unnerving tendency to light on you when his head was pointed in some other direction and you thought, or in my case hoped, that he had forgotten all about you. Sara always blamed the hostile reception I got on his fever-addled brain—he was a loony dog to begin with, an obsessive burrower, a compulsive arranger of sticks—but he had also been Walter's dog before he was Sara's, and I supposed that had something to do with his feelings about me.

"Hush, now, Dee. Just ignore him, dear," she told Miss Sloviak, taking the newcomer's hand with the faintest glint of scientific curiosity in her eye. "And Terry, it's nice to see you again. You look very dashing."

Sara was good at the handshaking part of her job and she appeared delighted by our arrival, but her gaze was a little unfocused, there was a tense pleat in her voice, and I saw at once that something was bothering her. As she leaned to accept a kiss from Crabtree, she took a false step and lurched suddenly forward. I reached out and caught her by the elbow.

"Easy there," I said, setting her back on her feet. One of the chief pleasures of the opening party of WordFest, at least for me, was the opportunity it afforded to catch a glimpse of Sara Gaskell in high-heeled shoes and a dress.

"I'm so sorry," she said, blushing all the way down to the backs of her freckled arms. "It's these goddamned shoes. I don't know how anyone can walk on these things."

"Practice," said Miss Sloviak.

"I need to talk to you," I told Sara, under my breath. "Now."

"That's funny," said Sara, in her everyday, bantering tone. She didn't look at me, but instead aimed a sardonic smile at Crabtree, whom she knew to be in on our secret. "I need to talk to you, too."

"I think he needs to talk to you more," said Crabtree, handing her his coat and Miss Sloviak's.

"I doubt it," said Sara. The dress—a fairly amorphous

black rayon number with a boxy bodice and cap sleeves—
rode up a little behind and clung to the fabric of her panty
hose, and as she clattered around the foyer, arms and throat
bare, ankles wobbling, hair piled atop her head with the relative haphazardness she reserved for festive occasions, there
was an awkward grandeur to her movements, an unconscious
headlong career, that I found very appealing. Sara hadn't the
faintest idea of how she looked, or of what effect her deino-
therian body might have on a man. Balanced atop those modest two-inch spikes of hers she projected a certain air of
calculated daring, like one of those inverted skyscrapers you
see from time to time, sixty-three stories of glass and light set
down on a point of steel.

"Tripp, what did you *do* to this dog?" said Crabtree. "He
can't seem to take his eyes off your larynx."

"He's blind," I said. "He can't even see my larynx."

"I bet he knows how to find it, though."

"Oh, now, hush you, Doctor Dee," said Sara. "Honestly."

Miss Sloviak looked uneasily at the dog, who had assumed
his favorite stance, directly between me and Sara, teeth bared,
paws planted, barking operatically.

"Why doesn't he like you?" Miss Sloviak said.

I shrugged, and I felt myself blushing. There's nothing
more embarrassing than to have earned the disfavor of a perceptive animal.

"I owe him some money," I said.

"Grady, dear," said Sara, passing the overcoats along to me.
There was a patent note of stratagem in her voice. "Will you
go and toss these on the bed in the guest room?"

"I don't think I know how to find the guest room," I said,
although I had on several occasions tossed Sara herself down
onto that very bed.

"Well, then," said Sara, her voice alight now with panic. "I'd better show you."

"I guess you'd better," I said.

"We'll just make ourselves at home," said Crabtree. "How about that? Okay, now, old Doctor. Okay, old puppy dog." He knelt to pet Doctor Dee, pressing his forehead against the dog's tormented brow, murmuring secret editorial endearments. Doctor Dee stopped barking at once, and began to sniff at Crabtree's long hair.

"Could you find my husband, Terry, and ask him to lock Doctor Dee up in the laundry room for the rest of the party? Thanks, you can't miss him. He has eyes just like Doctor Dee's, and he's the handsomest man in the room." This was true. Walter Gaskell was a tall, silver-haired Manhattanite with a narrow waist and broad shoulders, and his blue eyes had the luminous, emptied-out look of a reformed alcoholic's. "That's a lovely dress, Miss Sloviak," she said as we started up the stairs.

"She's a man," I told Sara as I followed up after her, carrying an armful of topcoats.

IN the summer of 1958 it was reported in the Pittsburgh newspapers that Joseph Tedesco, a native of Naples and an assistant groundskeeper at Forbes Field, had been suspended from his job for keeping an illegal vegetable garden on a scrap of vacant land that lay just beyond the wall in center right. It was his third summer at the ballpark; in the years before this he had failed at several modest enterprises, among them a domestic gardening business, an apple orchard, and a nursery.

He was careful in his work but terrible with money, and he lost two of his businesses through disorderly bookkeeping. The rest of them he lost through drink. His well-tended but rather overexuberant patch of tomatoes, zucchini, and romano beans on tall poles, some four hundred and twenty feet from home plate, had caught the unfavorable notice of a real estate broker who was attempting to close the deal for the sale of the ballpark site to the University of Pittsburgh, and soon afterward Mr. Tedesco found himself sitting, in his vast undershorts, in his living room in Greenfield, while his former crewmates went on chalking foul lines and hosing down the infield dirt. Then his tale of injustice made the papers; there was a public outcry and a protest from the union; and a week after the scandal broke Mr. Tedesco was back on the job, having fulfilled his promise to dig up the offending plants and transplant them to his own postage-stamp backyard on Neeb Avenue. A few weeks later, just after the all-star break, at his youngest child's and only daughter's eighth birthday party, Mr. Tedesco had too much to drink, choked on a piece of meat while laughing at a joke, and died, surrounded by his wife and children, his two grandchildren, and his rows of Early Girls and lima beans. With an almost mysterious affection his daughter would afterward remember him as a big, fat, shiftless, and overexuberant minor craftsman, with bad habits, who committed a kind of suicide-by-appetite.

I'm not sure how much of that I've got right, but it shows the lengths to which I've had to go in order to account for why a woman as sensible and afraid of disorder as Sara Gaskell would ever waste an hour on a man like me. Her mother, whom I'd met on two occasions, was a sad, strong, undemonstrative Polish lady with a black wardrobe and a white mustache who worked in a laundry. In raising her half-orphaned daughter, she had brought to bear all of her considerable armaments in a largely successful effort to expunge Joseph Tedesco's evanescent legacy of failure and excess, and raise a woman who would always go for the sure thing, however modest. Thus Sara had submerged an early love of literature to the study of accounting, following this with a Ph.D. in administration. She'd refused the proposals of the first two great loves of her life in order to pursue her career, and then, having found herself Chancellor of our college at the age of thirty-five, allowed herself to marry.

She chose the head of the English Department: his affairs were in order, his career well-established, his habits husbandly, and he kept his seven thousand books not simply alphabetized but grouped by period and country of origin. As the eighth child of a poor Greenfield family she was attracted to Walter's genteel manners, to his Dartmouth education, his knowledge of sailboats, his parents' penthouse apartment on Central Park West. Her mother approved of him; Sara told herself that he was quite literally the best she could hope for. Nevertheless, in spite of all her mother's efforts, there remained a wild and sentimental Neapolitan streak in Sara, and this, along with some faint Electral residue she saw crackling in the air around me, may also help to explain her willingness to endanger her stable existence for the doubtful pleasure of my company.

The other explanation I used to make to myself was that my lover was an addict and I was a manufacturer of her particular drug of choice. Sara would read anything you handed her—Jean Rhys, Jean Shepherd, Jean Genet—at a steady rate of sixty-five pages an hour, grimly and unsparingly and without apparent pleasure. She read upon waking, sitting on the toilet, stretched out in the backseat of the car. When she went to the movies she took a book with her, to read before the show began, and it was not unusual to find her standing in front of the microwave, with a book in one hand and a fork in the other, heating a cup of noodle soup while she read, say, *At Lady Molly's* for the third time (she was a sucker for series and linked novels). If there was nothing else she would consume all the magazines and newspapers in the house—reading, to her, was a kind of pyromania—and when these ran out she would reach for insurance brochures, hotel prospectuses and product warranties, advertising circulars, sheets of coupons. Once I had come upon the spectacle of Sara, finished with a volume of C. P. Snow while only partway through one of the long baths she took for her bad back, desperately scanning the label on a bottle of Listerine. She'd even read my first book, long before she ever met me, and I liked to think that she was the best reader I had. Every writer has an ideal reader, I thought, and it was just my good luck that mine wanted to sleep with me.

"You can toss them in there," she said, in a stage voice, pointing me like a tour guide into a small, pale blue room with a parquet floor and a bay window, high-ceilinged like all the rooms in the house. I carried the coats in and Sara followed, closing the door behind us. On the left-hand wall, alongside an Empire armoire, hung two large sets of baseball cards in oblong frames. I'd examined them in the past and I knew they represented the championship New York Yankee teams of 1949 and 1950. The opposite wall was covered in framed photographs of Yankee Stadium, taken at various epochs in its history. Against this wall lay the headboard of a bed with newel posts and a frilly white dust ruffle. Its surface was white and smooth and bare of any wraps or other gar-

ments. I spread Sara out across it. Crabtree's and Miss Sloviak's coats slid to the floor. I climbed onto the bed beside
Sara and looked down at her anxious face.

"Hi," I said.

"Hi, big guy."

I lifted the skirt of her party dress and placed the palm of my
hand against the outcropping of her left hip, where the waistband of her panty hose cut into the skin. I slipped my hand
under the elastic and reached for the ten thousandth time for
the wool of her pussy, automatically, like a luckless man div-
ing for the rabbit's foot in his pocket. She put her lips against
my neck, beneath my earlobe. I felt her trying to relax her
body against mine, joint by joint. She worked at the topmost
button of my shirt, got a hand inside, and cupped my left
breast.

"This one's mine," she said.

"That's right," I said. "All yours."

We didn't say anything for a minute. The guest room was
right over the living room and I could hear a flashing ribbon
of Oscar Peterson fluttering below us.

"So?" I said at last.

"You go first," she said.

"All right." I took off my eyeglasses, stared at the spots on
their lenses, put them back on. "This morning—"

"I'm pregnant."

"What? Are you sure?"

"My period is nine days late."

"Still, nine days, that doesn't—"

"I'm sure," she said. "I know I must be pregnant, Grady,
because although I gave up all hope of ever having a child a
year ago, when I turned forty-five, I really only reconciled

myself to the notion a couple of weeks ago. Or, I mean, I realized that I'd reconciled myself to it. You remember we even talked about it."

"I remember."

"So, naturally."

"How do you like that."

"How do *you* like it?"

I thought about that for a moment.

"It sort of makes for an interesting complement to my news," I said. "Which is that Emily left me this morning." I felt her grow still beside me, as if she were listening for footsteps in the hall. I stopped talking and listened for a moment until I realized that she was only waiting for me to continue. "It's for real, I think. She went out to Kinship for the weekend, but I don't think she really plans on coming home."

"Huh," she said, matter-of-factly, trying to sound as if I had just imparted some moderately interesting fact about the manufacture of grout. "So then, I guess what we do is divorce our spouses, marry each other, and have this baby. Is that it?"

"Simple," I said. I lay there for a few minutes, with my head thrown back, looking at the wistful, sunstruck faces of ballplayers on the wall behind us. I was so conscious of Sara's strained and irregular breathing that I was unable to breathe normally myself. My left arm was pinned underneath her and I could feel the first pricklings of trapped blood in my fingertips. I looked into the sad and competent eyes of Johnny Mize. He appeared to me to be the sort of man who would not hesitate to counsel his mistress to abort the first and only child she might ever conceive.

"Is your friend Terry's friend really a man?" said Sara.

"I believe so," I said. "Knowing Crabtree as I do."

"So what did he say to you?"

"He wants to see the book."

"Are you going to show it to him?"

"I don't know," I said. My hand had gone numb now, and my left shoulder was starting to tingle and shut down. "I don't know what I'm going to do."

"Neither do I," said Sara. A tear pooled at the corner of her eye and then spilled out across the bridge of her nose. She bit her lip and shut her eyes. I was close enough to her to study the cartography of veins printed on her eyelids.

"Sara, honey," I said, "I'm stuck." I gave my arm a gentle tug, trying to free it. "You're lying on my arm."

She didn't move; she only opened her eyes, dry once again, and gave me a very hard stare.

"I guess you're going to have to chew it off, then," she said.

I drank for years, and then I stopped drinking and discovered the sad truth about parties. A sober man at a party is lonely as a journalist, implacable as a coroner, bitter as an angel looking down from heaven. There's something purely foolish about attending any large gathering of men and women without benefit of some kind of philter or magic dust to blind you and weaken your critical faculties. I don't mean to make a big deal out of sobriety, by the way. Of all the modes of human consciousness available to the modern consumer I consider it to be the most overrated. I stopped drinking not because I had a drinking problem, although I suppose I may have, but because alcohol had mysteriously become so poisonous to my body that one night half a bottle of George Dickel stopped my heart for almost twenty seconds (it turned out I was allergic to the stuff). But when, after counting off five discreet minutes, I followed Sara and the sparkling pearl of protein lodged in the innermost pleats of her belly back down to the First Party of the Weekend, I found the prospect of navigating the room sober to be more than I could face, and for the first time in months I was tempted to pour myself a drink. I was reintroduced to a shy, elfin man whose prose style is among the most admired in this country, whose company I had enjoyed in the past, and this time found him a leering, self-important old windbag who flirted with young girls to stave off the fear of death; I met a woman whose short stories have broken my heart over and over again for the last fifteen years and saw only the withered neck and hollow stare of a woman who had wasted her life. I shook hands with talented students, eager young staff members, colleagues in the department whom I had good reasons to admire and like, and heard their false laughter, and felt their discomfort with their bodies and their status and their clothes, and smelled the stink of sweet beer and whiskey on their breath. I avoided Crabtree, to whom I felt I had become nothing more than a colossal debit on the balance sheet of his life; and as for Miss Sloviak, that man in his dress and high heels—that was too sad even to think of. I was in no kind of shape to talk to anyone. So I sneaked through the kitchen and slipped out onto the back porch to blow a jay.

Although it wasn't raining anymore the air was still heavy with water, and rain gutters were ringing all over Point Breeze. A fine mist of light hung in a cloud around the Gaskells' illuminated house. I could see the panes of Sara's greenhouse glinting black in the distance like wet iron. She had been obsessed for several years now with forcing her for-sythias and pinching her hothouse chrysanthemums, but I supposed things might get a little wild in there if she decided to grow herself a baby. This didn't seem likely, given that the chancellor of a college was among the last people in America required to build a career out of such outmoded materials as probity and temperance and good repute. Through a deter-mined program of sheer dumb luck and liberal applications of THC I had managed never to impregnate a woman before, but I knew that she and Walter had not made love in several years, and that the child had to be mine. I felt astonished and a little afraid suddenly to find myself lost, after so long, in the elephant-white hills of abortionland. *An awfully simple opera-tion* went the line. *They just let the air in.* I felt pity for Sara and remorse toward Walter, but more than anything I felt a sharp disappointment in myself. I'd spent my whole life waiting to awake on an ordinary morning in the town that was destined to be my home, in the arms of the woman I was destined to love, knowing the people and doing the work that would make up the changing but essentially invariable landscape of my particular destiny. Instead here I was, forty-one years old, having left behind dozens of houses, spent a lot of money on vanished possessions and momentary entertainments, fallen desperately in and abruptly out of love with at least seventeen women, lost my mother in infancy and my father to suicide, and everything was about to change once more, with unfore-seeable result. And yet for all that I still had never gotten used to the breathtaking impermanence of things. The only part of my world that carried on, inalterable and permanent, was *Wonder Boys*. I had the depressing thought, certainly not for the first time, that my novel might well survive me unfinished. Then I reached into the pocket of my shirt and took out the last inch of the joint Crabtree and I had smoked in the car as we waited for Emily to show up.

I had just lit the ragged end of it, and was staring down at one of Doctor Dee's cryptic stick arrangements, when I heard the squeak of rubber soles on wet grass. I looked up to see someone step out from the shadows around the back porch and start across the yard, toward the greenhouse, into the light. It was a man, tall and wearing a long coat, his hands thrust into his pockets. He skirted the corner of the greenhouse and kept walking until he came to the pair of long dull shining bands that cut across the Gaskells' yard from east to west and that once had borne the young empire builder across the breadth of his miniature domain. I started when I saw the man in the Gaskells' yard, and for an instant I was afraid—Sara and Walter had been robbed a couple of months before—but then I recognized the long coat, and the stooped shoulders, and the slicked-back hair, black and shining like a pane of the greenhouse. It was my student James Leer, standing between the rails, with his face raised to the sky, as though waiting for a hurtling phantom engine to come and cut him down.

I was surprised to see him. The students invited to this First Party at the Chancellor's house were usually conference interns, the typists and telephone clerks, the program staplers and ad hoc chauffeurs. For a talented young writer you could always bend the rules a little, to give him or her the chance to hobnob with real writers, in their natural habitat, and James Leer was indeed talented, but he was not the kind of young man who inspired people to bend rules for him, and I tried to remember if I could possibly have invited him to come myself. He stood for a moment like that, gazing up at the starless sky, then pulled his right hand out of his pocket. There was a gleam of silver glass or metal, the flash of a mirror, at the end of his crooked arm.

"James?" I said. "Is that you? What are you doing?" I stepped down from the porch, still holding on to the fatty, and started across the grass toward him.

"It's a fake," said James Leer, holding out his hand to me, palm upward. Upon it lay a tiny silver pistol, a "ladies' model" with a pearl handle, no bigger than a deck of cards. "Hello, Professor Tripp."

"Hello, James," I said. "I didn't know what you were doing out here."

"It's my mother's," he said. "She won it in a penny arcade in Baltimore, in one of those machines with the claw. When she was in Catholic school. It used to shoot these little paper caps, but you can't find the right kind anymore."

"Why do you carry it around?" I said, reaching for it.

"I don't know." His fingers closed around the little gun and he slipped it back into the pocket of his overcoat. "I found it in a drawer at home and I just started carrying it around. For good luck, I guess."

The overcoat was a trademark of his. It was an impermeable thrift-shop special with a plaid flannel lining and wide lapels, and it looked as though it had been trying for many years to keep the rain off the stooped shoulders of a long series of hard cases, drifters, and ordinary bums. It emitted an odor of bus station so desolate that just standing next to him you could feel your luck changing for the worse.

"I'm not supposed to be here, in case you were wondering," he said. He shifted his shoulders under the weight of the knapsack he carried, and looked me in the eye for the first time. James Leer was a handsome kid; he had eyes that were large and dark and always seemed to shine with tears, a straight nose, a clear complexion, red lips; but there was something blurry and indeterminate about his features, as though he were still in the process of deciding what kind of a face he wanted to have. In the soft light radiating from the Gaskells' house he looked painfully young. "I crashed. I came with Hannah Green."

"That's all right," I said. Hannah Green was the most brilliant writer in the department. She was twenty years old, very pretty, and had already published two stories in *The Paris Review*. Her style was plain and poetic as rain on a daisy—she was particularly gifted at the description of empty land and horses. She lived in the basement of my house for a hundred dollars a month, and I was desperately in love with her. "You can say I invited you. I ought to have, anyway."

"What are you doing out here?"

"I was about to smoke a joint, as a matter of fact. Would you care to join me?"

"No, thank you," he said, looking uncomfortable. He unbuttoned his overcoat, and I saw that he was still wearing the tight black suit and skinny tie he had seen fit to wear to the discussion of his story that afternoon, over a faded glen plaid shirt. "I don't like to lose control of my emotions."

I thought that he had just diagnosed his entire problem in life, but I let it pass and took a long drag on the joint. It was nice standing out in the darkness, in the damp grass, with spring coming on and a feeling in my heart of imminent disaster. I didn't think James was all that comfortable standing next to me this way, but at the same time I knew he would have felt much worse inside, on a sofa, with a canapé in his hand. He was a furtive, lurking soul, James Leer. He didn't belong anywhere, but things went much better for him in places where nobody belonged.

"Are you and Hannah seeing each other?" I said after a moment. Lately, I knew, they had been palling around together, going to movies at the Playhouse and Filmmakers'. "Dating?"

"No!" he said immediately. It was too dim to see if he blushed, but he looked down at his feet. "We just came from *Son of Fury* at the Playhouse." He looked up again and his face grew more animated, as it generally did when he got himself onto his favorite subject. "With Tyrone Power and Frances Farmer."

"I haven't seen it."

"I think Hannah looks like Frances Farmer. That's why I wanted her to see it."

"She went crazy, Frances Farmer."

"So did Gene Tierney. She's in it, too."

"Sounds like a good one."

"It's not bad." He smiled. He had a big-toothed, crooked smile that made him look even younger. "I kind of needed a little cheering up, I guess."

"I'll bet," I said. "They were hard on you today."

He shrugged, and looked away again. That afternoon, as we had gone around the room, there was only one member of the workshop with anything good to say about James's story: Hannah Green, and even her critique had been chiefly constructed out of equal parts equivocation and tact. Insofar as the outlines of its plot could be made out amid the sentence fragments and tics of punctuation that characterized James Leer's writing, the story concerned a boy who had been molested by a priest and then, when he began to show signs of emotional distress through odd and destructive behavior, was taken by his mother to this same priest to confess his sins. The story ended with the boy watching through the grate of the confessional as his mother walked out of the church into the sunshine, and with the words "Shaft. Of light." It was called, for no apparent reason, "Blood and Sand." Like all of his stories, its title was borrowed from Hollywood; he had written stories called "Swing Time," "Flame of New Orleans," "Greed," "Million Dollar Legs." All of them were opaque and fractured and centered on grave flaws in the relations between children and adults. None of the titles ever seemed to connect to the stories. There was a persistent theme of Catholicism gone badly wrong. My students had a hard time knowing what to think about James Leer's writing. They could see that he knew what he was doing and that he had been born with the talent to do it; but the results were so puzzling and unfriendly to the reader that they tended to inspire the anger that had flared up in workshop that afternoon.

"They really hated it," he said. "I think they hated it more than any of the other ones."

"I know it," I said. "I'm sorry I let things get a little out of control."

"That's all right," he said, shrugging his shoulders to regain a purchase on the straps of his knapsack. "I guess you didn't really like it either."

"Well, James, no, I—"

"It doesn't matter," he said. "It only took me an hour to write it."

"An hour? That's remarkable." For all its terrible problems, it had been a dense and vivid piece of writing. "That's hard to believe."

"I think them all out beforehand. I have trouble sleeping, so that's what I do while I lie there." He sighed. "Well," he said. "I guess you probably have to go back in. It must be almost time to go to that lecture."

I held up my wristwatch to catch the light. It was nearly twenty-five minutes to eight.

"You're right," I said. "Let's go."

"Uh, well," he said. "I—I think I'm just going to go home. I think I can catch the 74."

"Nonsense," I said. "Come on inside and have a drink before we go to the lecture. You don't want to miss that lecture. And have you seen the Chancellor's house? It's a beautiful house, James. Come on, I'll introduce you around." I mentioned the two writers who were this year's guests of honor.

"I met them," he said coldly. "What's with all the baseball cards, anyway?"

"Dr. Gaskell collects them. He has a lot of memora——— oh." The air before my eyes was suddenly filled with spangles, and I felt my knees knock against each other. Reaching out to steady myself, I took hold of James's arm. It felt weightless and slender as a cardboard tube.

"Professor? Are you all right?"

"I'm fine, James. I'm just a little stoned."

"You didn't look so well in class today. Hannah didn't think so, either."

"I haven't been sleeping well, myself," I said. As a matter of fact I had, during the last month, been experiencing spells of dizziness and bewilderment that came over me suddenly, at odd moments of the day, and filled my skull with a glittering afflatus. "I'll be fine. I'd better get my old fat body inside."

"Okay, then," he said, freeing his arm from my grasp. "I'll see you on Monday."

"Aren't you coming to any of the conference seminars or anything?"

He shook his head. "I don't think so. I—I have a lot of

homework." He bit his lip and then turned and started back across the lawn, toward the house, hands jammed once more into his pockets, the fingers of his right hand, I imagined, curled around the smooth pearly handle of his imitation gun. The knapsack pounded against his back and the soles of his shoes squeaked as he left me, and I don't know why, but I was sorry to see him go. I felt as though he were the only person whose company I could possibly have enjoyed at that moment, awkward and isolate and hopeless as he was, disquieted and bewildered by the proliferating symptoms of the midnight disease. Oh, he had it, all right. Just before James started around the corner he looked up, at the back windows of the house, and stopped dead, his face raised to catch the light spilling out from the party. He was looking at Hannah Green, who stood by the dining-room window with her back toward us. Her yellow hair was mussed and scattered in all directions. She was telling a story with her hands. All the people standing in front of her had bared their teeth to laugh.

After a moment James Leer looked away and started off. His head was absorbed into the sharp black shadow that fell from the side of the house.

"Wait a minute, James," I said. "Don't leave yet."

He turned, and his face reemerged from the shadow, and I walked over to him, flicking the burnt end of the joint into the air.

"Come on inside the house for a minute," I said, lowering my voice to a whisper that came out sounding so sinister and friendless that I suddenly felt ashamed. "There's something upstairs I think you ought to see."

WHEN we walked back into the kitchen, the party was breaking up; Walter Gaskell had already led a large contingent of staff members off to Thaw Hall, among them the shy little elf in the turtleneck sweater who was to address us that evening on the subject of "The Writer as Doppelgänger." Sara and a young woman in a gray service uniform were busy scraping out bowls into the kitchen trash, stretching plastic wrap across plates of cookies, shoving corks back into half-empty bottles of wine. They had the water running into the sink and didn't hear us as we slipped past into the living room, where a crew of students was gathering up streaked paper plates and ashtrays filled with cigarette butts. I felt very stoned, now that I was inside, light and insubstantial as a ghost, and far less certain than a few minutes earlier of my motives in sneaking James Leer up to the Gaskells' bedroom to show him what was hanging from a silver hanger in Walter Gaskell's closet.

"Grady," said one of the students, a young woman named Carrie McWhirty. She had been among James Leer's most cruel detractors that afternoon, and she was herself a truly terrible writer, but I nevertheless held her in a certain tender and pitying regard, because she had been working on a novel, called *Liza and the Cat People,* since she was nine years old; almost half her life, longer even than I'd been working on *Wonder Boys.* "Hannah was looking for you. Hi, James."

"Hello," said James, glumly.

"Hannah?" I said. At the thought that she had been looking for me my heart was seized with panic or delight. "Where'd she go?"

"I'm out here, Grady," called Hannah, from the foyer. She stuck her head into the living room. "I was wondering what happened to you guys."

"Uh, we were outside," I said. "We had a few things to discuss."

"I don't doubt it," said Hannah, reading the pink calligraphy inked across the whites of my eyes. She had on a man's plaid flannel shirt, tucked imperfectly into a baggy pair of Levi's, and the cracked red cowboy boots I'd never once seen her go without, not even when she prowled the house in a terry-cloth bathrobe, or a pair of sweatpants, or running shorts. In idle moments I liked to summon up an image of her naked feet, long and intelligent, aglitter with down, toenails painted red as the leather of her boots. Beyond the mess of her dirty blond hair, however, and a certain heaviness of jaw— she was originally from Provo, Utah, and she had the wide, stubborn face of a Western girl—it was difficult to see much of a resemblance to Frances Farmer; but Hannah Green was very beautiful, and she knew it all too well, and she tried with all her might, I thought, not to let it fuck her up; maybe it was in this doomed struggle that James Leer saw a sad resemblance. "No, but really," she said. "James, do you need a ride? I'm leaving right now. I was planning to give your friends a ride, too, Grady. Terry and his friend. Who is she, anyw—— hey. Grady, what's the matter? You look kind of wiped."

She reached out to put a hand on my arm—she was a person who liked to touch you—and I took a step away from her. I was always backing off from Hannah Green, pressing myself against the wall when we passed each other in a wide and empty hallway, hiding behind my newspaper when we found ourselves in the kitchen alone, with an admirable and highly unlikely steadfastness that I had a hard time explaining to myself. I suppose that I derived some kind of comfort from the fact that my relationship with young Hannah Green remained a disaster waiting to happen and not, as would normally have been the case by this time, the usual disaster.

"I'm just fine," I said. "I think I'm coming down with something. Where are those two?"

"Upstairs. They went to get their coats."

"Great." I started to call up to them, but then I remembered James Leer, and the piece of Walter's collection I had promised I would show him. He was leaning against the front door of the house, looking out at nothing at all through the mist on the sidelights, right hand jiggling in his overcoat pocket. "Hey, uh, Hannah, could you take them for me, and I'll drive James? We're not, uh, we're not quite through here."

"Sure," said Hannah. "Only your friends went up there to get their coats, like, ten minutes ago."

"Here we are," said Crabtree, holding Miss Sloviak's upraised fingers in one hand as he followed her down the stairs. She chose her steps with care, and the escort Crabtree was giving her seemed to be not entirely an act of gentlemanliness. Her ankles were wobbling in her tall black pumps, and I saw that it could not be an easy thing to be a drunken transvestite. Crabtree's metallic green suit showed not a wrinkle, and he was wearing the smug, blank expression he assumed whenever he thought he might be causing a scandal, but as soon as he saw James Leer his eyes got very wide, and he let go of Miss Sloviak's hand. She took the last three steps all at once, unintentionally, and fell against me, enveloping me in her long smooth arms and a disturbing odor of Cristalle and something else that was rank and spicy.

"I'm so sorry," she said with a tragic smile.

"Hello there," said Crabtree, giving James Leer his hand.

"James," I said, "this is my oldest and best friend, Terry Crabtree, and his friend, Miss Sloviak. My editor, too. Terry, I've told you about James, I'm sure."

"Have you?" said Crabtree. He had yet to let go of James Leer's hand. "I'm sure I would remember."

"Oh, listen, Terry," said Hannah Green, tugging at Crabtree's elbow as if she had known him all her life. "This is the guy I was telling you about. James Leer. Ask him about George Sanders. James will know."

"Ask me what?" said James, freeing his pale hand at last from Crabtree's grip. His voice shook a little and I wondered if he was seeing what I saw in Crabtree's eyes, the mad conquistador glint, looking at James Leer with a wild surmise. "He was in *Son of Fury*."

"Terry was saying how George Sanders killed himself, James, but he didn't remember how. I told him you'd know."

"Pills," said James Leer. "In 1972."

"Very good! The date, too!" Crabtree handed Miss Sloviak her coat. "Here," he said.

"Oh, James is amazing," said Hannah. "Aren't you, James? No, really, watch this, watch this." She turned to James Leer, looking up at him as though she were his adoring little sister and thought him capable of limitless acts of magic. You could see the desire to please her freezing up all the muscles of his face. "James, who else committed suicide? What other movie actors, I mean?"

"All of them? There are way too many."

"Well, then, just a few of the big ones, let's say."

He didn't even roll back his eyes in his head, or scratch reminiscently at his chin. He just opened his mouth and started counting them off on his fingers.

"Pier Angeli, 1971 or '72, also pills. Charles Boyer, 1978, pills again. Charles Butterworth, 1946, I think. In a car. Supposedly it was an accident, but, you know." He cocked his head sadly to one side. "He was distraught." There was a trace of irony in his voice but I had the sense it was there for our benefit. It was clear he took his Hollywood suicides—and Hannah Green's requests—very seriously. "Dorothy Dandridge, she took pills in, like, 1965. Albert Dekker, 1968, he hung himself. He wrote his suicide note in lipstick on his stomach. I know, weird. Alan Ladd, '64, more pills, Carole Landis, pills again, I forget when. George Reeves, Superman on TV, shot himself. Jean Seberg, pills of course, 1979. Everett Sloane—he was good—pills. Margaret Sullavan, pills, Lupe Velez, a lot of pills. Gig Young. He shot himself and his wife in 1978. There are more but I don't know if you would have heard of them. Ross Alexander? Clara Blandick? Maggie McNamara? Gia Scala?"

"I haven't heard of *half* of those," said Hannah.

"You did them alphabetically," said Crabtree.

James shrugged. "That's just kind of how my brain works," he said.

"I don't think so," said Hannah. "I think your brain works a lot more weirdly than that. Come on. We have to go."

On his way out the door, Crabtree shook hands with James yet again. It was not hard to see that Miss Sloviak's feelings were hurt. Evidently she was not too drunk to remember whatever it was she and Crabtree had been doing upstairs in the guest room, or to feel that this entitled her to dwell within the radius of his attention for at least the remainder of the evening. She refused to let Crabtree take her arm and instead made a point of taking hold of Hannah Green, who said, "What's that you're wearing? It smells so familiar."

"Why don't you come out with us after the lecture?" said Crabtree to James Leer. "There's this place on the Hill I always get Tripp to take me."

James's ears turned red. "Oh, I don't— I wasn't—"

Crabtree gave me a pleading look. "Maybe your teacher can convince you."

I shrugged, and Terry Crabtree went out. A few moments later, Miss Sloviak reappeared in the doorway, her cerise lipstick neatly applied, her long black hair glossy and blue as a gun, and reproached James Leer with her eyes.

"Didn't you forget someone, wonder boy?" she said.

WHEN Marilyn Monroe married Joe DiMaggio, on January 14, 1954—a week after I turned three years old—she was wearing, over a plain brown suit, a short black satin jacket, trimmed with an ermine collar. After her death this jacket became just another item in the riotous inventory of cocktail dresses and fox stoles and pearly black stockings she left behind. It was assigned by the executors to an old friend of Marilyn's, who failed to recognize it from photographs of that happy afternoon in San Francisco years before, and who wore it frequently to the marathon alcoholic luncheons she took every Wednesday at Musso & Frank. In the early seventies, when the old friend—a B-movie actress whose name had long since been forgotten by everyone but James Leer and his kind—herself expired, the ermine-collared jacket, shiny at the elbows now, and missing one of its glass buttons, was sold off, along with rest of the dead starlet's meager estate, at a public auction in East Hollywood, where it was purchased, and presently identified, by an acute Marilyn Monroe fan. Thus it passed into the kingdom of Memorabilia. It made a circuitous pilgrimage through the reliquaries of several Monroe cultists before it jumped sectarian lines and fell into the hands of a man in Riverside, New York, who owned—for example—nineteen bats once swung by Joe DiMaggio, and seven of the Yankee Clipper's diamond tie bars, and who then, after suffering some financial reverses, sold the errant jacket to Walter Gaskell, who hung it in a special low-humidity section of his bedroom closet, with a foot of space on either side of it, on a special corrosion-free hanger.

"Is that really it?" said James Leer, with all the shy reverence in his voice I'd anticipated on first promising to show him the silly thing. He was standing beside me, in the Gaskells' silent bedroom, on a fan-shaped patch of carpet that had been flattened by the constant passage across it of the heavy, fireproof closet door, in the course of Walter's periodic visits to his treasures, which he made dressed in Yankee pinstripes, tears streaming down his lean and chiseled cheeks, mourning his Sutton Place childhood. In five years I'd never yet arrived at the foundation of the grudge that Sara Gaskell bore her husband but it was manifold and profound and no secret of his was safe from me. He kept the closet locked, but I knew the combination.

"That's really it," I said. "Go ahead and touch it, James, if you want to."

He glanced at me, doubtfully, then turned back to the cork-lined closet. On either side of the satin jacket, on special hangers of their own, hung five pin-striped jerseys, all bearing the number 3 on their backs, ragged and stained at the arm-pits.

"Are you sure it's all right? Are you sure it's okay for us to be up here?"

"Sure it is," I said, looking back over my shoulder at the doorway for the fifth time since we'd come into the room. I had switched on the overhead light and left the bedroom door wide open to suggest that there was no need for skulkery and I had every right to be here with him, but each creaking of the house or last-minute clatter from downstairs made my heart leap in my chest. "Just keep your voice down, all right?"

He reached out with two tentative fingers and touched them to the yellowed collar, barely, as though afraid that it might crumble to dust.

"Soft," he said, his eyes gone all dreamy, his lips parted. He was standing so close that I could smell the old-fashioned brilliantine he used to slick back his hair, a heavy lilac perfume that, combined with the Greyhound-station smell of his over-coat and the waves of camphor emanating from the closet, led me to wonder if throwing up might not feel kind of nice right about now. "How much did he pay for it?"

"I don't know," I said, though I'd heard an outlandish fig-ure quoted. The DiMaggio-Monroe union was a significant obsession of Walter's, and the subject of his own magnum opus, his *Wonder Boys,* an impenetrable seven-hundred-page critical "reading," as yet unpublished, of the marriage of Marilyn and Joe and its "function" in what Walter, in his lighter moods, liked to call "American mythopoetics." In that brief unhappy tale of jealousy, affection, self-deception, and bad luck he claimed to find, as far as I understood it, a typically American narrative of hyperbole and disappointment, "the wedding as spectacular antievent"; an allegory of the Husband as Slugger; and conclusive proof of what he called, in one memorable passage, "the American tendency to view every marriage as a cross between tabooed exogamy and corporate merger." "He never tells Sara the truth about how much he pays for these things."

That interested him. I wished immediately that I hadn't said it.

"You're really good friends with the Chancellor, aren't you?"

"Pretty good," I said. "I'm friends with Dr. Gaskell, too."

"I guess you must be, if you know the combination to his closet, and he doesn't mind your being, you know, here in their bedroom like this."

"Right," I said, watching him closely for signs that he was fucking with me. A door slammed, somewhere downstairs, and both of us started, then grinned at each other. I wondered if the smile on my face looked as false and uneasy as his.

"It feels so flimsy," he said, turning back to the closet, lifting the left sleeve of the satin jacket with three fingers, letting it fall. "It doesn't feel real. More like a costume."

"Maybe everything a movie star wears feels like a costume."

"Hey, that's really deep," said James, teasing me for the first time that I could remember. At least I thought he was teasing me. "You ought to get stoned more often, Professor Tripp."

"If you're going to fuck with me, Mr. Leer, I think that you ought to start calling me Grady," I said. "Or Tripp."

I'd intended just to return the teasing a little but he took me very seriously. He blushed and looked down at the ghostly fan imprinted in the fibers of the carpet.

"Thank you," he said. After that he seemed to feel a need to get away from me, and from the closet, and he took a step into the bedroom. I was glad to have a little distance between me and his hair. He looked around at the Gaskells' bedroom, at the high, molded ceiling, the buttery old Biedermeier dresser, the tall oak armoire with its mirrored door that had lost the better part of its silvering, the thick pillows and linen duvet on the trim bed, looking white and smooth and cold as if it had been buried in snow. "This is a nice house. They must be pretty well off, to have all these things."

Walter Gaskell's grandfather had at one time owned most of Manatee County, Florida, as well as ten newspapers and a winner of the Preakness, but I didn't tell that to James.

"They do all right," I said. "Is your family well off?"

"Mine?" he said, poking himself in the sternum. "No way. My dad used to work in a mannequin factory. I'm serious. Seitz Plastics. They made mannequins for department stores, and display heads for hats, and those flattened-out sexy legs that they use to sell panty hose. He's retired now, though. He's old, my dad. Now he's trying to raise trout in our backyard. No, we're really poor. My mom was a fry cook before she died. Sometimes she worked in a gift shop."

"Where was this?" I said, surprised, because despite his overcoat that stank of failure and the shabby thrift-shop suits he wore, he had the face and mannerisms of a rich boy, and sometimes he showed up for class wearing a gold Hamilton wristwatch with an alligator band. "I don't think I ever knew where you're from."

He shook his head. "No place," he said. "Near Scranton. You haven't heard of it. It's called Carvel."

"I haven't heard of it," I said, though I thought it sounded vaguely familiar.

"It's a hellhole," he said. "It's an armpit. Everybody hates me there."

"But that's good," I said, wondering at how young he sounded, regretting that vanished time when I too had believed that I united in my fugitive soul all the greatest fears and petty hatreds of my neighbors in that little river town. How sweet it had felt, in those days, to be the bête noire of other people, and not only of myself! "Now you've got good reason to write about them."

"Actually," he said, "I already have." He hefted the stained canvas knapsack on his shoulder and inclined his head toward it. It was one of those surplus Israeli paratrooper numbers that had caught on among my students about five years before, with the winged red insignia on the flap. "I just finished a novel that's kind of about all that."

"A novel," I said. "God damn it, James, you're amazing. You've already written five short stories this term! How long did *that* take you, a week?"

"Four months," he said. "I started it at home, over Christmas break. It's called *The Love Parade*. In the book I call the town Sylvania. Like in the movie."

"What movie is that?"

"*The Love Parade*," he said.

"I should have known. You ought to let me read it."

He shook his head. "No. You'll hate it. It really isn't any good. It sucks, Prof— Grady. Tripp. I'd be too ashamed."

"All right, then," I said. As a matter of fact, the prospect of crawling across hundreds of pages of James Leer's shards-of-glass style was less than appealing, and I was glad that he had let me off the hook of my automatic offer to read his book. "I'll take your word for it. It sucks." I smiled at him, but as I said it I saw something swim into his eyes, and I stopped smiling. "Hey, James, hey. I didn't mean it. Buddy, I was just kidding."

But James Leer had started to cry. He sat down on the Gaskells' bed and let his knapsack slide to the floor. He cried silently, covering his face. A tear fell onto his old acetate necktie and spread in a slow ragged circle. I went over to stand beside him. It was now seven fifty-three, according to the clock on the night table, and downstairs I could hear the click of Sara's heels as she rushed around, switching off lights, gathering up her purse, taking a last look at herself in the pier glass hanging in the foyer. After a moment the front door squealed on its hinges, then slammed, and the bolt turned in the lock. James and I were alone in the Gaskells' house. I sat down on the bed beside him.

"I'd really like to take a look at your novel," I said. "Really, James."

"It isn't that, Professor Tripp," he said, his voice little more than a whisper. He wiped at his eyes with the back of his hand. There was a pearl of snot in one of his nostrils and he inhaled it. "I'm sorry."

"What's the matter, buddy? Hey, I know the workshop was awfully hard on you, it's my fault, I—"

"No," he said. "It isn't that."

"Well, what is it?"

"I don't know," he said, with a sigh. "Maybe I'm just depressed." He looked up and turned his red eyes toward the closet. "Maybe it's seeing that jacket that belonged to her. I guess I think it looks, I don't know, really sad, just hanging there like that."

"It does look sad," I said. From outside I heard the engine of Sara's car bubble to life. It was one of the few successful stylish gestures that she had managed to make—a currant red convertible Citroën DS23, in which she liked to tool around campus with a red and white polka-dot scarf on her head.

"I have an extra hard time with stuff like that," he said. "Things that used to belong to people. Hanging in a closet."

"I know what you mean." I pictured a row of empty dresses, hanging in an upstairs closet in a soot-faced redbrick house in Carvel, Pennsylvania.

We sat there for a minute, side by side on that cool white snowbank of a bed, looking over at the scrap of black satin hanging in Walter Gaskell's closet, listening to the whisper of Sara's tires in the gravel drive as she pulled away from the house. In another second she would turn out into the street and wonder why Happy Blackmore's Galaxie was still sitting dark and deserted along the curb.

"My wife left me today," I said, as much to myself as to James Leer.

"I know," said James Leer. "Hannah told me."

"Hannah knows?" Now it was my turn to cover my face with my hands. "I guess she must have seen the note."

"I guess so," said James. "It seemed like she was kind of happy about it, to tell you the truth."

"She what?"

"Not—I mean, Hannah said a couple of things that, well. I never got the impression, you know, that she and your wife actually *liked* each other. Very much. I mean, actually it sounded to me like your wife kind of *hated* Hannah."

"I guess she did," I said, remembering the creaking silence

that had reached like the arm of a glacier across my marriage, in the days after I'd invited Hannah to rent our basement. "I guess I don't really know a whole lot about what's going on in my own house."

"That could be," said James, a certain wryness entering his tone. "Did you know that Hannah Green has a crush on you?"

"I didn't know that," I said, falling backward on the bed. It felt so good to lie back and close my eyes that I was afraid to stay that way. I sat up, too quickly, so that a starry cloud of diamonds condensed around my head. I didn't know what to say next. I'm glad? So much the worse for her?

"I think so, anyway," said James. "Hey, you know who else I forgot? Peg Entwistle. Although she certainly was never a big star. She only made one movie, *Thirteen Women*, 1932, and she just had a bit part in that. It was the only part she ever got."

"And?"

"And she jumped off the 'Hollywoodland' sign. That's what it used to say, you know. Off of the second letter *d*, I think."

"That's a good one." The cloud of stars had parted, but now I was unable to clear my head of a thick blue smog that had begun to form inside it, and the lilac smell of James's hair oil was just too much. I felt that if I didn't stand up at once and get moving I was going to pass out, or vomit, or both. I felt weak in my arms and legs, and tried to remember the last time I'd had something to eat. I'd been forgetting to take my meals lately, which is a dangerous sign in a man of my girth and capacity. "We'd better skedaddle, James," I said, in a mild panic, taking hold of James's scarecrow arm. "Let's get out of here."

Forgetting that I had left wide open the door of Walter Gaskell's closet, I got up and hurried out of the room. I switched off the bedroom light behind me, leaving James Leer sitting alone in the dark for the second time that day. As I stepped out into the hallway I heard a low rumbling sound that raised all the hairs on the back of my neck. It was Doctor Dee. Sara had freed him from the prison of the laundry room and he crouched in the hall, belly to the ground, paws outspread, his black lip peeled back from his yellow old teeth. His wild eyes were staring fixedly at the empty air beside me, at some distant arctic peak.

"James?" I said. "Guess who's here? Hello, Doctor Dee. Hello, you old bastard."

I flattened myself against the right-hand wall of the hallway and tried to brush past him, but he came at me. I panicked and lost my balance, stumbling over Doctor Dee, accidentally giving him a sharp kick in the ribs. The next instant I felt a stab of pain in my foot, somewhere in the vicinity of my ankle, and then I fell to the floor, hard. Doctor Dee scrambled to his feet and stood over me, his throat filled with a single long rolling syllable.

"Get away from me," I said. I was afraid, but not too afraid for it to occur to me that dying torn to pieces by blind, mad dogs had a certain mythic quality that might work well in the section of *Wonder Boys* in which I planned to have Curtis Wonder, the oldest of the three brothers who were the central characters of my book, meet the fate that his colossal pride and his lurid misdeeds had earned for him. I raised my fist, as Curtis might, and tried actually to punch Doctor Dee, as you would slug a man, but he caught the blow in his teeth, as it were, and worked his jaw around the meat of my hand.

There was a sudden sharp crack! as of a rock against the

windshield of a car. Doctor Dee yelped. His tail jerked straight up into the air like an exclamation point and ratcheted around a few times on its hinge. Then he toppled over onto my legs. I looked up, my ears ringing, and saw James Leer, standing half in the shadow of the doorway, the pretty little pearl-handled pistol in his hand. I yanked my legs out from under Doctor Dee and the dog landed with a soft thud against the floor. I rolled down my sock. There were four bright red holes in my foot, on either side of my Achilles tendon.

"I thought you said that was a cap gun," I said.

"Is he dead? Did he bite you bad?"

"Not so bad." I pulled my sock up and scrambled up onto my knees. Carefully I passed my hand around Doctor Dee's head and cupped the moist tip of his snout in my fingers. There was no trace of his breath against them. "He's dead," I said, climbing slowly to my feet. I could feel the first delicate tickle of pain in my ankle. "Shit, James. You killed the Chancellor's dog."

"I had to," he said miserably. "Didn't I?"

"Couldn't you have just pulled him off me?"

"No! He was biting you! I didn't—I thought he—"

"Easy," I said, laying a hand on his shoulder. "Okay. Don't freak out on me."

"What are we going to do?"

"We're going to go find Sara and tell her, I guess," I said, feeling the desire for a sweet poisonous glass of bourbon steal over me like a fog. "But first I'm going to get cleaned up. No. First you're going to give me that cap gun of yours."

I held out my hand, palm up, and he obediently set the pistol on it. It was warm, and heavier than it looked.

"Thanks," I said. I slipped it into the hip pocket of my

blazer, and then he helped me into the bathroom, where I washed out the puncture holes with foaming hydrogen peroxide and found a pair of Band-Aids to cover them up. Then I rolled up my sock again and tugged down the leg of my trousers, and we went back out into the hall, where the handsome old dog lay dead.

"I don't think we should leave him lying there," I said.

James said nothing. He was so lost in working out the ramifications of what he had done that I don't think he was capable of speech at that moment.

"Don't sweat it," I said. "I'm going to tell her that I did it. That it was self-defense. Come on."

I knelt down beside Doctor Dee and wrapped my arms around his heavy head. A dark red smear was turning to purple in the fur around the base of the right earflap, and there was a smell of burnt hair. James knelt and took hold of the dog's hindquarters, a dazed, almost sweet expression on his smooth face.

"A little curl of smoke came out of the bullet hole," said James.

"Wow," I said. "I wish I could have seen that."

Then we carried Doctor Dee down the stairs and along the endless driveway to the street, where we laid him out in the back of my car, on the seat, beside the tuba.

By the time we arrived for the lecture, both of the school's main lots were full, and we ended up parking in one of the quiet residential streets at the other end of campus from Thaw Hall, under an old stand of beech trees, at the foot of some happy professor's driveway. I cut the engine and we sat for a moment, listening to the rain drop like beechnuts from the trees and scatter across the canvas top of the car.

"That sounds nice," said James Leer. "It's like being in a tent."

"I don't want to do this," I said, filled with a sudden longing to be lying on my back in a little tent, peering up through the silk mesh window at Orion.

"You don't have to. It's dumb for you to tell her you did it, Professor Tripp. I mean, it's a lie." He picked at the threads fraying along the hem of his long black coat. "I don't care what she does to me, to tell you the truth. She probably *should* kick me out."

"James," I said, shaking my head. "It was my fault. I shouldn't have sneaked you up there in the first place."

"But," said James, looking confused, "you knew the combination."

"True," I said. "Think about that one for a minute or two." I looked at my watch. "Only you can't, 'cause we're late." I grabbed hold of the handle and leaned against the door. "Come on, help me get him into the trunk."

"The trunk?"

"Yeah, well, I'm probably going to have to drive a bunch of people over to the Hi-Hat after the lecture, buddy. There isn't going to be a whole lot of room for *people* with a tuba and a dead dog in the backseat."

I climbed out of the car and tilted my seat forward. My fingers were cold and I could feel a very faint envelope of heat around the body of Doctor Dee as I passed my arms beneath it. I lifted without crouching first to gain leverage, and felt a sharp twinge in the small of my back. There was a vinegar tang of blood in my nose. James had gotten out of the car by now, and he came around to help me pitch the stiffening old pup into the trunk, alongside Miss Sloviak's bags. We slid the body as far back as we could, under the rear dash, until there was a sound like a pencil snapping in two, and we jerked our hands away.

"Yuck," said James, wiping his hands against the flaps of his overcoat. That garment bore the stains of all manner of hell, bad weather, and misfortune, but I wondered if it had ever before been used to wipe away the invisible effluvium of a dead dog. Quite possibly so, I imagined.

"Now the tuba," I said.

"That's a big trunk," James said, as we jammed in the leathery old case that looked so much like the black heart of some leviathan. "It fits a tuba, three suitcases, a dead dog, and a garment bag almost perfectly."

"That's just what they used to say in the ads," I said, reaching for Crabtree's garment bag. I palpated its pockets for a moment, then zipped open the largest of them. To my surprise I found that it was empty. I felt around in the next largest pocket, and then in a third, and found that they were empty, too. Laying the bag open across the other luggage, I unzipped its main compartment. Inside there were a pair of white dress shirts, a couple of paisley neckties, and two suits, glinting faintly in the streetlight.

"They're the same," said James, lifting the uppermost suit and peering underneath.

"What's that?"

"His suits. They look just like the one he has on now."

He was right: the suits were both double-breasted, with peaked lapels, cut from the same kind of sleek metallic silk. Although it was difficult to tell their color, you could see that they matched each other and the suit he was wearing. I thought of Superman's closet at the North Pole, a row of shining suits hanging on vibranium hooks.

"I find that odd," I said, finding it somehow pathetic. I'd always thought there was something a little pathetic about Superman, too, way up there in his Fortress of Solitude.

"I guess he doesn't like to have to worry about what he's going to wear," James said.

"I guess he doesn't like having to *remember* to worry." I zipped the garment bag closed and stuffed it back into the trunk. "Come on, Crabtree," I said, "I know you're holding." I pulled on the handles of the canvas grip, and it weighed so little that when it came free it nearly flew out of my hand.

"Whose tuba *is* that, anyway?" said James.

"Miss Sloviak's," I said, plunging my hand into the grip, hoping, with an odd foretaste of horror, that it did not contain nothing at all. To my relief I discovered three pairs of boxer shorts, bundled into little balls, rolling around like marbles inside the bag. Wrapped up in one of these bundles I felt something hard, and my fingers curled around it. "Actually, no, it isn't. I don't know who it belongs to."

"Can I ask you something about her?" said James.

"She's a transvestite," I said, pulling out what proved to be an airline bottle of Jack Daniel's. "Hey. How do you like that?"

"I don't like whiskey," said James. "Oh. So. Is—is your friend Crabtree—is he—gay?"

"I don't like whiskey, either," I said, handing him the bottle. "Open that. Most of the time he is, James. Bear with me now. I'm going to make another dive down to the wreck." I stuck my hand back into the grip and fished out another rolled-up pair of boxers. "Some of the time he isn't. Oh, my goodness. What have we here?"

Inside the second roll of underwear there was a small prescription vial of pills.

"No label," I said, examining the outside of the vial.

"What do you think they are?"

"Looks like my old friend Mr. Codeine. That'll be good for my ankle," I said, shaking out a pair of thick white pills into my palm, each of them marked with a tiny numeral 3. "Have one."

"No thanks," he said. "I'm fine without them."

"Oh, right," I said. "That's why you were standing out there in the Gaskells' backyard trying to decide whether or not to kill yourself. Right, buddy?"

He didn't say anything. A gust of wind blew a handful of rain from the trees and it splashed against our faces. The bell over in the Mellon Campanile rang out the quarter hour, and I thought of Emily, whose father, Irving Warshaw, had been a young metallurgist assigned to the casting of the steel bell back in the late forties. An experimental and later discredited method had been employed in the bell's manufacture, leaving it to toll in a voice that was off-key and faintly mournful and that usually reminded me of old Irv, to whom I had been a constant source of disappointment.

"I'm sorry I said what I said, James." I took the bottle from him and unscrewed the lid. I tossed one of the codeine pills into my mouth like an M & M, and downed it with a swallow of Dickel. The whiskey tasted like bear steaks and river mud and the flesh of an oak tree. I had another swallow because it tasted so good. "I haven't had any of this stuff in four years," I said.

"Give me," said James, biting his lip in anger and trepidation and a childish desire to force himself into being a man. I handed him the pill and the dark little bottle. I knew it was irresponsible of me but that was as far as my thinking on the subject went. I told myself that he could hardly feel worse than he already did, and I suppose that I told myself that I didn't really care. He took a long, careless pull from the bottle, and half a second later spat out the whole mouthful.

"Take it easy," I said. I peeled the soggy pill from the lapel of my jacket and returned it to him. "Here. Why don't you try that again?"

This time he was more successful. He frowned.

"It tastes like cordovan shoe polish," he said, reaching for the bottle again. "Another sip."

"There isn't any more," I said, giving the bottle a demonstrative shake. "These things don't hold a whole lot."

"Look inside the other ball of underpants."

"Good thinking." In the remaining pair of boxers was another little bottle of bourbon. "Hello," I said. "We're going to have to confiscate this, too, I'm afraid."

James smiled. "I'm afraid so," he said.

We ran splashing through puddles all the way to Thaw Hall, passing the little bottle back and forth between us, avoiding a group of young ladies who glared at us, and when we got to the hall and came laughing into the high, gilt lobby, James Leer looked thrilled. His cheeks were flushed, and his eyes were full of water from the bite of the wind on his face. As I stood, doubled over, at the closed doors to the auditorium, trying to catch my breath, I felt him place a steadying hand on my back.

"Was I running funny?" I said.

"A little. Does your ankle hurt bad?"

I nodded. "It'll be all right in a few minutes, though. How are you feeling?"

"All right," he said. He wiped his nose with the back of his hand, and I saw that he was trying to keep himself from smiling. "I guess I'm feeling sort of glad I didn't kill myself tonight."

I stood up and put my hand on his shoulder, and reached out with my other hand to open the door.

"What more could you ask for?" I said.

THAW Hall had served as a preliminary exercise for the architects who later went on to build the old Syria Mosque. The exterior was trimmed with sphinxes and cartouches and scarabs, and the lobby and auditorium were all pointed arches, slender pillars, a tangled vegetation of arabesques. The seats and the loges were arranged around the stage in a kind of lazy oval, just as in that late, lamented concert hall, only there were far fewer of them—seats, I mean—and the stage itself was smaller than that of the Mosque. The place held about five hundred in the orchestra and another fifty up above, and by the time we got in there every one of the blood red velvet seats was taken, and at the creaking of the door hinges every one of those five hundred heads turned around. Some folding chairs had been set up at the back, in the standing aisle, and James Leer and I took a couple and sat down.

We hadn't missed much; the elfin old novelist, I later discovered, had commenced his lecture by reading a lengthy extract from *The Secret Sharer,* and it didn't take long for me to pick up the thread of his argument, which was that over the course of his life as a writer he—you know the man I mean, but let's just call him Q.—had become his own doppelgänger, a malignant shadow who lived in the mirrors and under the floorboards and behind the drapes of his own existence, haunting all of Q.'s personal relationships and all of his commerce with the world; a being unmoved by tragedy, unconcerned with the feelings of others, disinclined to any human business but surveillance and recollection. Only every once in a while, Q. said, did his secret sharer act—overpowering his unwilling captor, so to speak, assuming his double's place long enough to say or do something unwise or reprehensible, and thus to ensure that human misfortune, the constant object of the Other Q.'s surveillance and the theme of all his recollections, continued unabated in Q.'s life. Otherwise, of course, there would be nothing to write about. "I blame it all on him," the dapper little man declared, to the apparent delight of his audience, "the terrible mess I have made of my life."

It seemed to me that Q. was talking about the nature of the midnight disease, which started as a simple feeling of disconnection from other people, an inability to "fit in" by no means unique to writers, a sense of envy and of unbridgeable distance like that felt by someone tossing on a restless pillow in a world full of sleepers. Very quickly, though, what happened with the midnight disease was that you began actually to crave this feeling of apartness, to cultivate and even flourish within it. You pushed yourself farther and farther and farther apart until one black day you woke to discover that you yourself had become the chief object of your own hostile gaze.

There was a lot I could agree with in Q.'s argument—but I soon found myself having a tough time concentrating on his words. The mark of Doctor Dee's teeth on my ankle had dulled with the codeine to a faint pulse of pain, but things had also gone smeary at their edges. I could feel the machinery of my heart laboring in my chest, and there was a jagged codeine cramp in my belly. I was drunk on five swallows of Jack Daniel's and a heavy dose of oxygen from our run across the campus, and all the radiant things around me, the stage lights, the gilt wall sconces, the back of Hannah Green's golden head seven rows away from me, the massive crystal chandelier suspended above the audience by the thinnest of chains, seemed to be wrapped, like streetlights in a mist, in pale, wavering halos. As soon as I managed to focus my eyes on them, however, the halos would vanish. I smelled something dank and somehow nostalgic in the air of Thaw Hall, dust and silk and the work of some devouring organism—rotten ball gowns, ancient baby clothes, the faded flag with forty-eight stars that my grandmother kept in a steamer trunk under the back stairs and flew from the porch of the McClelland Hotel on the Fourth of July. I sat back in my chair and folded my hands across my stomach. The warm ache of codeine there felt sad and appropriate. I wasn't worrying about the tiny zygote rolling like a satellite through the starry dome of Sara's womb, or about the marriage that was falling apart around me, or about the derailment of Crabtree's career, or about the dead animal turning hard in the trunk of my car; and most of all I was not thinking about *Wonder Boys*. I watched Hannah Green nod her head, tuck a strand of hair behind her right ear, and, in a gesture I knew well, raise her knee to her forehead and slip her hands down into her boot to give a sharp upward tug on her sock. I passed ten blissful minutes without a thought in my head.

Then James Leer laughed, out loud, at some private witticism that had bubbled up from the bottom of his brain. People turned around to glare at him. He covered his mouth, ducked his head, and looked up at me, his face as red as Hannah Green's boots. I shrugged. All the people who had turned to look at James now returned their gazes to the podium; all except one. Terry Crabtree was sitting three seats away from Hannah, with Miss Sloviak and Walter Gaskell between them, and he kept his eyes on James Leer for just a second or two longer. Then he looked toward me, winked once, and arranged his studious little face into a playful expression that was supposed to mean something like What are you two up to back there? and without really meaning to I gave him back an irritable frown that meant something like Leave us alone. Crabtree looked startled, and quickly turned away.

The milkweed tufts of a codeine high are easily dispersed; all at once, in the aftermath of Leer's mad guffaw, I found myself going over a particular troublesome scene in the novel, for the one thousand and seventy-third time, in the manner of a lunatic ape in a cage at the zoo, running his fingers back and forth along the iron bars of his home. It was a scene that took place immediately before the five ill-fated endings I'd tried out over the last month, in which Johnny Wonder, the youngest of my three doomed and glorious brothers, buys a 1955 Rambler American from a minor character named Bubby Zrzavy, a veteran of U.S. Army LSD experiments. I'd been trying for weeks to imbue this purchase with the organ rumble of finality and a sense of resolution but it was an irremediably pivotal moment in the book: it was to be in this car, rebuilt from the chassis out by mad Bubby Z., over the course of ten years, according to the cryptic auto mechanics of his addled neurons, that Johnny Wonder would set out on the cross-country trip from which he would return with Valerie Sweet, the girl from Palos Verdes, who would lead the

Wonder family to its ruin. That I had written so much already, without even having gotten to Valerie Sweet, was one of the things that had been making it so difficult for me to force the book to any kind of conclusion. I was dying for Valerie Sweet. I felt as though I had been writing my entire life just to arrive at the page on which her cheap pink sunglasses made their first appearance. At the thought of forgoing her, as my zoo-monkey brain returned yet again to the insoluble question of how I could get myself out of the seven-year mess I had gotten myself into, it was as if the power flowing into Thaw Hall had suddenly ebbed. Then a dazzling burst of static passed like rain across my eyes, and I caught a bloody whiff of the inside of my nose, and a bitter shaft of acid rose from my belly.

"I have to get out of here," I whispered to James Leer. "I'm going to be sick."

I got up and pushed through the doors to the lobby. It was deserted, except for a couple of kids—one of whom I recognized vaguely—slouched against the main doors, propping them open with their bodies, smoking and blowing their bored smoke out into the evening. I nodded to them and then hurried toward the men's room, moving as quickly as I could without looking like a man who had to heave and was trying not to do it on the rug. The whiff of static, the burst of red blood in my nose, the nausea, none of these symptoms was new to me. They had gripped me at odd moments for the past month or so, along with an attendant sense of weird elation, a feeling of weightlessness, of making my way across the shimmering mesh of sunshine in a swimming pool. I looked back at the kids by the door and recognized by his goatee a former student of mine, a stunned-looking, moderately talented young writer of H. S. Thompsonesque paranoid drug jazz who had dropped by my office one afternoon last year to inform me, with the true callousness of an innocent heart, that he felt the college was cheating him by taking his money to put him through writing classes with a pseudo-Faulknerian nobody like me. Then the corridor to the bathrooms turned sideways on me, and I felt so feverish that I had to lay my cheek against the cool, cool wall.

When I came to, I was lying on my back, with my head propped up, and Sara Gaskell kneeling over me, one light hand on my brow. The cushion she had fashioned for my head felt soft on the outside, but at its center there was something hard as a brick.

"Grady?" she said, in a careless voice, as though she were trying only to attract my attention to an interesting item in the newspaper. "Are you still with us?"

"Hello," I said. "I think so."

"What happened, big guy?" Her eyes darted from one corner of my face to another, and she licked her lips, and I saw that despite her tone of unconcern I had given her a fright. "Not another one of these dizzy-spell things?"

"Kind of. I don't know." Your dog is dead. "I think I'll be all right."

"Do you think I ought to run you over to the E.R.?"

"Not necessary," I said. "Is the thing over?"

"Not yet. I saw you walk out, and I—I thought—" She wrung her hands a little, as if they were cold. "Grady—"

Before she could say whatever difficult thing she intended to say to me, I sat up and kissed her. Her lips were cracked and slick with lipstick. Our teeth touched. The play of her fingers along the back of my neck was cold as rain. After a moment we parted, and I looked at her face, freckled and pale and alive with the look of disappointment that often haunts the difficult faces of redheaded women. Presently we kissed again, and I shivered as her fingertips ran like raindrops down my neck. I slipped my hands down into the back of her dress.

"Grady—" She let go of me, and drew back, and shook herself. She took a deep breath. I could feel her physically readopting some resolve she had made, some promise not to let me kiss away her doubts. "I know tonight is a terrible night to try to deal with the kind of things we need to deal with, here, sweetie, but I—"

"I have something to tell you," I said. "Something hard."

"Stand up," she said, in her most Chancelloresque voice, reacting immediately to the note of fear that had crept into my voice. "I'm too old for all this rolling around on the floor." She rose a little unsteadily on her heels, tugged down the hem of her black dress, and held out a hand to me. I let her pull me to my feet. Her wedding ring was like a cold spark against my palm.

Sara let go of my hand and looked over her shoulder, down the corridor. There was no one coming. She turned back to me, trying to make her face expressionless, as though I were the college comptroller come to deliver some bad financial news. "What is it? No, wait a minute." She pulled a pack of Merit cigarettes from the purse she sometimes carried on formal occasions. It was a flashy silver beaded thing no bigger than twenty cigarettes and a lipstick, a gift from her father to her mother fifty years before, and utterly unsuited to either woman's character. Sara's regular handbag was a sort of leather toolbox, with a brass padlock, filled with spreadsheets and textbooks and a crowded key ring as spiked and heavy as a mace. "I know what you're going to say."

"No, you don't," I said. Just before she lit her cigarette I thought I caught a faint whiff of burning bud in the air. Those kids standing out in the lobby, I thought. It smelled awfully good. "Sara—"

"You love Emily," she said, looking down at the steady flame of the match. "I know that. You need to stay with her."

"I don't think I really have any choice there," I said. "Emily *left* me."

"She'll come back." She allowed the flame to burn all the way down to the skin of her fingers. "Ow. That's why I'm going to—not have this baby."

"Not have it," I said, watching her maintain her cool administrator's gaze, waiting to feel the sense of relief I knew I ought to be feeling.

"I can't. There's no way." She passed her fingers through her hair and there was the momentary flash of her ring, as if her russet hair itself were flashing. "Don't you think there's just no way?"

"I don't see any way," I said. I reached out to give her hand a squeeze. "I know how hard it is—for you to—lose this chance."

"No, you don't." She jerked her hand away. "And fuck you for saying you do. And fuck you, too, for saying . . ."

"What, my girl?" I said, when she did not continue. "Fuck me too for saying what?"

"For saying that there's just no way I could have this baby." She glanced away from me, then back. "Because there is, Grady. Or there could be." From out in the lobby came a loud squeal of hinges and a burst of human murmuring. "He must be finished," she said, looking at her watch. She blew a cloud of smoke to hide her face, and reached up to brush away the tear that hung from an eyelash of her left eye. "We should go." She sniffled, once. "Don't forget your jacket."

Sara knelt down to retrieve my old corduroy blazer, which she had stripped from my body and folded into a pillow for my head. As she peeled it away from the carpet, something tumbled out of one of the pockets and clattered to the floor, where it lay shining like the hood ornament of a madman's Rambler.

"Whose gun is that?" said Sara.

"It isn't real," I said, stooping to get to it before she did. I was tempted to stuff it into my pocket, but I didn't want her to think that it was anything important enough to hide. I held it in the palm of my hand for a moment, giving her a good look at it. "It's a souvenir of Baltimore."

She reached for it, and I tried to close my hand around it, but I was too slow.

"Pretty." She ran the tip of her index finger across the mother-of-pearl handle. She palmed the little pistol and slipped her finger through the trigger guard. She lifted the muzzle up to her nose. "Hmm," she said, sniffing. "It really smells like gunpowder."

"Caps," I said, reaching to take it away from her.

Then she pointed it at my chest. I didn't know how many bullets it held, but there was no reason to think there might not be one more.

"Pow," said Sara.

"You got me," I said, and then I fell on her and caught her up in a bouncer's embrace.

"I love you, Grady," she said, after a moment.

"I love you, too, my monkey," I said, as with a twist of her thin wrist I disarmed her.

"Oh!" said a voice behind us. "I'm sorry. I was just—"

It was Miss Sloviak, standing at the head of the corridor,

balanced atop her heels, hand on her hip. Her face was red, but her cheeks were streaked with mascara, and I could see that it was not the flush of embarrassment.

"It's all right," said Sara. "What's the matter, dear?"

"It's your friend, Terry Crabtree," said Miss Sloviak, looking at me harshly. She took a deep breath and passed her fingertips through her black curls, several times, quickly, in a way that somehow struck me as very masculine. "I'd like for you to take me home, if you don't mind."

"I'd be happy to," I said, starting toward her. "I'll meet you all later, Sara, over at the Hat."

"I'll walk you out to the car," said Sara.

"Well, it's kind of a hike," I said. "I'm parked all the way over on Clive."

"I could use the air."

We walked out into the lobby. It was completely deserted now, except for a sweet remnant of marijuana smoke in the air.

"I'm going to need one of my bags," said Miss Sloviak, as we headed out of Thaw Hall. "From the trunk."

"Are you?" I said, looking levelly at Sara. "All right."

A pair of doors slam-slammed behind us, and I heard a low, nervous chuckle, like that of someone trying to remain calm on a roller coaster in the last instant before free fall. James Leer emerged from the auditorium with his arms outspread and draped across the shoulders of Crabtree, on his right, and on his left across those of the young man with the goatee who'd dropped by during office hours to let me know that I was a fraud. They each had a grip on one of James's armpits, as if he might at any point collapse, and they were whispering all the usual platitudes of encouragement and reassurance. Although he looked a little queasy he seemed to be walking steadily enough, and I wondered if he weren't just enjoying the ride.

"The doors made *so* much noise!" he cried. He watched in evident amazement as his feet in their black brogues followed each other across the carpet. "Whoa!"

As the two men steered their charge toward the men's room, Crabtree happened to look my way. He raised his eyebrows and winked at me. Although it was only nine o'clock he had already gone once around the pharmacological wheel to which he'd strapped himself for the evening, stolen a tuba, and offended a transvestite; and now his companions were beginning, with delight and aplomb, to barf. It was definitely a Crabtree kind of night.

"This is so *embarrassing*! You guys had to carry me out!"

"Is he all right?" I said, as they maneuvered James past us.

"He's fine," said Crabtree, rolling his eyes. "He's *narrating.*"

"We're going to the men's room," said James. "Only we might not make it in time."

"Poor James," I said, watching as they turned into the hallway.

"I don't know what you guys have been giving him," said Miss Sloviak. "But I don't think he needs any more of it."

Sara shook her head. "Terry Crabtree and James Leer," she said, punching me on the shoulder, hard. "Leave it to you to make *that* mistake. Wait here."

She went after them, and I stood awkwardly beside Miss Sloviak for half a minute, watching her take irritable puffs on a black Nat Sherman and blow them out in long blue jets.

"I'm sorry about all this."

"Are you?"

"It's just pretty much your standard WordFest behavior."

"No wonder I've never heard of it before."

A minor squall of applause gathered and blew through the auditorium. Then the doors burst open again, and five hundred people poured into the lobby. They were all talking about Q. and his rascally double, the latter of whom had apparently ended the lecture with an unflattering remark about the cumulative literary achievement of Pittsburgh, comparing it with Luxembourg's and Chad's. I waved to a couple of my offended colleagues and nodded carefully to Franconia Epps, a well-to-do Fox Chapel woman of a certain age who had been attending WordFest for the last six years in the hope of finding a publisher for a novel called *Black Flowers,* which every year she raveled and unraveled, Penelope-like, according to the contradictory whims and indications of a dozen half-interested editors, but which in each incarnation managed to retain its surprising although not, unfortunately, redeeming number of scenes involving well-to-do Fox Chapel women of a certain age and a variety of leather appliances, artificial male genitalia, and tractable polo ponies with names like Goliath and Big Jacques. A gang of literary young men surrounded Miss Sloviak and me, all talking at once, batting one another with rolled programs, taking out their cigarettes. A few of them were students of mine, and they were about to draw us into their conversation—they had their eyes on Miss Sloviak—when suddenly, as if touched with an electric prod, they drew apart and opened a path for Sara Gaskell.

"Hello, Chancellor."

"Hello, Dr. Gaskell."

"Gentlemen," she said, nodding coolly, and then leveling toward me the same administrative and vaguely condescending green eyes. She had slipped off her wobbly high heels, and the silver beaded purse was nowhere to be seen.

"He was sick, but I think he'll be fine," she said, looking both generally and specifically disgusted. "No thanks to you and your idiot friend."

"I'm glad to hear that."

"Go on, take Antonia home. I'll look after Mr. Leer."

"All right." I leaned against the door, letting in a blast of cool April air. "Sara," I said, lowering my voice, almost mouthing the words. "I didn't get to tell you—"

"Later," she said, lightly pushing me out the door with the bare toes of her right foot. "You'll tell me later."

"I'm going to have to," I said to Miss Sloviak, as we hurried through the rain back to the leafy end of campus where I had left my car. The air was warm and fragrant with lilac and as we ran it was hard not to hear the clatter of Miss Sloviak's heels as the very signature of romantic haste. When we got back to the car she stood beside me at the trunk, and her eyes grew very large when I lifted the lid.

"I had a little accident," I said. "I know this looks pretty bad."

"Listen," said Miss Sloviak, yanking her pony-skin suitcase out from under the stiff brush of Doctor Dee's tail, "all I—yhew!—all I want to do is get home and never see any of you authors ever again, okay?"

"I know how you feel," I said, looking down sadly at what remained of Doctor Dee.

"Poor thing," said Miss Sloviak, after a moment. She set her bag on the lip of the trunk, pulled it free from its plastic sleeve, and unzipped it. "He kind of gave me the creeps, though, with those eyes."

"Sara doesn't know yet," I said. "I couldn't tell her."

"Well, don't worry about me," said Miss Sloviak, as she

detached her long black curls and laid them in the valise with a look of affectionate regret, like a violinist retiring her instrument for the night. "I'm not going to say anything."

THE story goes that I sucked too avidly at my mother's breast, and caused an abscess to bloom in the tender flesh of her left nipple. My grandmother, less kind in those days than afterward, disapproved strongly when at seventeen my mother had married, and managed to instill her daughter with a powerful sense of ill-equipment for the task of mothering me; the failure of her breast to bear up to the ardor of my infant lips filled my mother with shame. She didn't go to the doctor as quickly as she ought to have. By the time my father found her, collapsed across the keys of the hotel's piano, and got her into the county hospital, a staph infection had already taken hold of her blood. She died on February 18, 1951, five weeks after giving birth, and thus, naturally, I've no memory of her. I can, however, manage to recall a few things about my father, George Tripp, called Little George to distinguish him from my paternal grandfather, his namesake, from whom I'm supposed to have inherited my Big George body and appetites.

Little George gained a regrettable measure of fame in our part of the state when he killed the young man who, among other prospective achievements, was to have become the first Jewish graduate of Coxley College in its eighty-year history. My father was a policeman. In killing this bright young man, whose father owned Glucksbringer's department store on Pickman Street, across and two doors down from the McClelland Hotel, he believed, without much justification as it turned out, that he was defending himself from an armed assailant. He'd returned from Korea missing the lower third of his right leg, along with a few crucial extremities, I believe, of his spiritual frame, and in the aftermath of his murderous error of judgment and subsequent suicide there was much specula-tion as to whether he ought to have been made a policeman at all. He had gone into the army with a reputation for flakiness and come home amid rumors of psychiatric collapse. But like all small towns, ours necessarily possessed a nearly infinite ca-pacity to forgive its citizens their personal failings, and since Big George had been chief of police for forty years until he suffered a fatal aneurysm at the poker table in the back room of the Alibi Tavern, my father was permitted to carry a .38 and wander the streets at midnight, his peripheral vision tor-mented by whispering shadows.

I was not quite four years old when he killed himself, and most of my memories of him are no more than shards and chance survivals. I remember the reddish blond hairs of his veiny wrist, caught in the links of his expanding watchband; a crumpled package of his Pall Malls, lying red as a ranunculus on the windowsill of his bedroom; the chime of a golf ball rattling into a Belleek teacup as he lined up putts across the broad front parlor of the hotel. And I can remember one time when I heard him come home from work. As I said, he had the night shift, eight to four, and got in at the darkest hour of the morning. Every day my father vanished behind the door to his bedroom as I was waking and reappeared just as I was going to bed; his invisible arrivals and departures were as mys-terious to me as snowfall or the sight of my blood. One night, however, I was awake to hear the laughter of the silver bell on the hotel's front door, the deliberate creaking of the back stairs, my father's angry cough, and then the next thing I remember I was standing in the doorway of his bedroom, watching Little George as he undressed. I used to pretend to myself, and tell my lovers, that in remembering all this I was recalling the night on which my father did himself in. But the truth is that he'd been suspended—with pay—for two weeks when he soul-kissed the blue barrel of his service revolver. So I don't know which night this must have been, or why its memory should have outlasted any other. Maybe it was the night my father shot David Glucksbringer. Maybe you just never forget the sight of your father taking off all his clothes.

I see myself peering through the half-open door of his bedroom, cheek pressed into a corner of cold oak molding, watching as the great blue man who lived in our hotel, with his high-crowned hat, his broad epaulets, his heavy golden badge, with bullets on his belt and a fat black gun, transformed himself into somebody else. He removed the hat and set it upside down on the dresser. A few strands of thin, sweaty hair stuck to the leather band inside and then remained standing atop his head, wavering like undersea plants. Carelessly he splashed whiskey into a shot glass, and then knocked it back with one hand as he unbuttoned and yanked off his uniform shirt with the other. He sat down on the bed to unlace his coffin black shoes, and kicked them into a corner of the room. When he stood up again, he looked smaller, more frail, and very tired. He stepped out of his trousers, exposing the pale orange prosthesis with its suggestion of discrete toes and its complicated harness work of leather. After that he went to the bedroom window, I think, and stood for a moment, looking at the desert topography of frost on the glass, the empty street, the mannequins posed in their little spring dresses in the luminous windows of Glucksbringer's. He pulled his sleeveless undershirt up over his belly and head, tugged his boxer shorts down to his ankles, and sat down on the bed again to unbuckle the strange contraption he owned instead of a foot. Then there was nothing left of him to remove. I was at once fascinated and horrified by the act of diminishment he had just performed; it was as though I were being permitted to see the crippled, balding, adipose gnome who dwelt within the brazen simulacrum, the lumbering golem I had learned to call my father.

I was thinking of this as I drove Miss Sloviak home to Bloomfield, as we headed east along Baum Boulevard and she turned herself into a man. She took a jar of cold cream and a bottle of nail polish remover from a black zipper bag in the suitcase on the seat between us, and set them on the lowered door of the glove compartment. With a succession of cotton balls she wiped the makeup from her face and stripped her nails of their pale pink armor. She reached up into her dress for the waistband of her panty hose and dragged them down along her smooth legs to her feet. Then she extracted a pair of pressed Levi's from the suitcase, unfolded them, and, with some difficulty, slid them up under the skirt of her black dress, which she then tugged up over her head and off. Her brassiere was black Lycra, padded, with a pearled ribbon at the junction of the cups and a neat pair of small protuberances meant to simulate erect female nipples; the chest beneath it was small but muscular, and free from hair. She put on a striped pullover, white socks emblazoned with a polo pony, and a pair of white Stan Smiths. The cold cream and acetone went back into the zipper bag, and the black dress, black pumps, and the airy tangle of panty hose were folded and tucked into the pony-skin valise. I was sorry I had to concentrate on the road, because her performance was impressive. She had assembled her male self with the precision and speed of an assassin in the movies snapping together the parts of his rifle.

"My name is Tony," said the former Miss Sloviak as we turned onto Liberty Avenue. "Now that I'm home."

"How do you do," I said.

"You don't seem all that surprised."

"I've been having some trouble with my surprise reflex lately," I said.

"Did you know I was drag queen?"

I thought about the right answer to that one for a minute. I considered the nature of the response that I hoped for in the wake of the deceptions I practiced on the world.

"No," I said. "I thought you were a beautiful woman. Tony."

Tony smiled. "I'm getting there," he said. "It's this next street. Mathilda. Left here. And then another left onto Juniper."

We pulled up in front of a small, brick two-story house, set close to but not quite touching its neighbors, with a light on in the upstairs dormer and a statue of the Blessed Virgin standing in the front lawn. Our Lady was sheltered under a kind of arching white band shell, painted on the inside with all the stars in the dome of heaven.

"I wish I had one of those in my front yard," I said. "All we have is a Japanese beetle trap."

"That's an old bathtub she's standing under," said Tony. "The other half of it's buried in the ground."

"Neat," I said. The engine dropped down into idle. A shadow drew aside the curtain in the dormer window and pressed itself against the glass. "Well."

"Well."

"Okay, then, Tony."

"Okay, Grady." He held out his hand to me, and we shook. "Good-bye. Thanks for the ride."

"Sure," I said. "Hey, uh, Tony, I'm sorry if it—if things didn't—turn out so well. Tonight."

"No biggie," he said. "I just really should have known better. Your friend, Crabtree, he's just looking for, I don't know, novelty, or whatever. He's into collec, like, collecting, you know, weird tricks. Mind?" He angled the rearview mirror toward himself and checked his bare face for makeup, for lingering traces of Miss Antonia Sloviak. Like many transvestites he was far more beautiful as a woman—as a man his nose was hawkish and his eyes were set too close together—and he gazed a moment wonderingly at the plainness of his face. He ran his fingers through his jarhead-short hair. He couldn't have been older than twenty-one. "That's kind of a problem I run into a lot."

"He's writing his name in water," I said.

"What's that?"

It was the half-regretful term—borrowed from the headstone of John Keats—that Crabtree used to describe his own and others' failure to express a literary gift through any actual writing on paper. Some of them, he said, just told lies; others wove plots out of the gnarls and elf knots of their lives and then followed them through to resolution. That had always been Crabtree's chosen genre—thinking his way into an attractive disaster and then attempting to talk his way out, leaving no record and nothing to show for his efforts but a reckless reputation and a small dossier in the files of the Berkeley and New York City police departments.

"It's what he's always done, you know," I said. "But now . . ." I put my hands on the steering wheel and rocked it from side to side. "I get the feeling he's going through the motions a little bit."

"Because his career's ruined, you mean?"

"Jesus," I said. I squeezed the wheel tightly, as if we were about to fishtail on an icy road, and pressed my foot against the brake pedal, although we weren't going anywhere. "Is that what he told you?"

"He said he hasn't had a success in ten years and everyone in New York thinks he's kind of a loser," Tony said. He angled the mirror back toward me, and as he fiddled with it I caught a flash of my own swollen, sleepless face. "After that it was hard not to feel sorry for him."

"But I guess he helped you there, didn't he?"

"He did his best." Tony lay a hand on the sleeve of my jacket. His fingernails, though bare, were still extravagant and nasty. "I'm sure your book is so good that he'll be able to keep his job."

I didn't say anything.

"Isn't it?"

"Sure," I said. "It's a gem."

"Sure it is," he said. "I have to go, all right?" I nodded. "Are you going to be okay?"

There was the rattle and slam of a screen door, and we turned toward the house. The porch light had come on, yellow and haloed in the rain, and I saw a small, white-haired man watching us from the top step, a hand raised to his forehead.

"My pop," said Tony. "Hey!"

Something darted down the steps, past the statue of the Virgin, and then there was a scrabbling sound at the passenger door, and a sharp, white grin at the window.

"Shadow!" He opened the door to admit a fat, charcoal

blue poodle who appeared delighted to see Tony Sloviak again. "Hi, girl!" The dog scrambled to get her forepaws, then her hind legs, up onto Tony's lap, and proceeded to work over his face with her slow pink tongue. Tony turned his head this way, that way, laughing and pushing her down. "My dog," he said.

"I gathered that."

"Oh," he said, "who's my baby? Yes. You. You. Oh, who's my—hey! Shadow!"

The dog dropped down from his lap, back out of the car, and cut suddenly away to the right. The next instant we heard her, at the back of the car, whistling a low sad canine tune.

"She found Doctor Dee," I said.

"Grady," said Tony, putting his hand to his mouth. "My other bags. I'm going to need to get in there."

"That's fine," I said. I cut the engine. "Just as long as you get back out."

We went around to the rear of the car, watched carefully by Shadow and the slender old man on the porch. I popped open the lid of the trunk.

"Stay down, Shadow," said Tony, lowering his hand like a harness around the poodle's shoulders so that she was unable to execute her apparent intention of leaping into the trunk and paying her last respects to Doctor Dee. "Hey, Grady, what, uh, what did happen to that poor husky dog?"

"James Leer shot him," I said, pulling out the plaid Gladstone bag and setting it on the ground. "It was kind of a misunderstanding."

"That kid's fucked up," said Tony. "And when your friend Crabtree gets through with him, he's going to be even more fucked up."

Michael Chabon

I fished out Crabtree's empty garment bag and then slammed shut the lid of the trunk.

"I'm not sure that's possible," I said, but I wasn't being honest. In my heart I believed that James Leer could still be saved, though not by Terry Crabtree; and if he could be saved, then he could always be made more fucked up.

"So, what, he packs a gun, that kid?"

"Sort of," I said. I switched the garment bag to my left hand and reached into the hip pocket of my jacket for the stainless little pistol. "He was carrying this. Actually, at one point tonight, to tell you the truth, I caught him pointing it at himself."

" 'me see?" Tony held out his hand. "My brothers all have, like, fucking gun collections, if you can believe it." I handed it over to him. Shadow watched it pass between us with mild interest, holding, as a dog will, to the imperishable belief that anything might possibly be something edible. "Pearl-handled. A twenty-two. This kind only holds one shot, I think."

I glanced up to the porch, but the old man appeared to have given up on his inconstant son and gone back inside, turning out the porch light behind him. All the other lights in the house seemed also to have gone out. I thought I could see now why Miss Sloviak had been less than eager all evening to come home. Tony looked up from the pistol in his fingers and shook his head.

"Figures," he said.

"What do you mean?"

"Well, because this is the kind of a gun that, you know, like, Bette Davis would carry? In her beaded purse?" He grinned. "I bet that kid would be much happier if he could be

Bette Davis shooting herself, instead of some big-lipped little boy in a stinky old overcoat."

Tony closed his fingers around the gun, and his lids with their long eyelashes fluttered twice and then closed. He brought the pistol delicately to his lips. Though I knew the gun was empty now, I was frightened at the sight of that. For the first time it registered in my weedy old brain that James Leer, my student, had intended to kill himself that evening.

"I'd better go," I said. "I think I need to rescue James Leer."

Tony lowered the pistol and started to give it back to me. I pushed his hand away.

"Keep it. I think it suits you."

"Thanks." He looked up at the dark, shuttered face of the house and frowned. "I just might need it myself."

"Ha," I said, fumbling in my jacket pocket for my car keys. I knew I'd been holding them a second or two before.

"Hey, you know, uh, Grady, maybe I'd just go on home if I were you," said Tony, as I got back into my car. "You look to me like you need to rescue yourself."

"That's not a bad idea." I closed my eyes. I saw myself pulling into the driveway of our ivy-clad house on Denniston Street, hanging my coat on the newel post of our stairs, falling down backward into the fragrant riot of coverlets and bed-clothes on our never-made bed. Then I remembered that there was nothing, no one, waiting for me at home. Without really wanting to, I opened my eyes and nodded once to Tony. I started to roll up my window, then stopped. "Oh, shit, buddy," I said. "What about that fucking tuba?"

"Keep it," said Tony. He reached out and slapped me

three times softly on the cheek, as you might pat the tremulous cheek of a baby. "It suits you."

"Thanks a lot," I said, and rolled up the window. As I pulled away from the curb, heading back up Juniper Street, I watched in the rearview mirror as Tony Sloviak, carrying his bags, climbed the long stairway up to his father's house, past the benedictory embrace of Our Lady, his little black dog nipping at his heels with every step he took.

CRABTREE and I had discovered the Hi-Hat together, in the course of one of his first visits to Pittsburgh, during the period between my second and third marriages—the last great era of our friendship, of our pirate days, before stars were lost from certain constellations, when the woods and railroad wastes and dark street corners of the world still concealed Indians and poetical madmen and razor-sharp women with the eyes of tarot-card queens. I was still a monstrous thing then, a Yeti, a Swamp Thing, the chest-thumping Sasquatch of American fiction. I wore my hair long and tipped the scales at an ungraceful but dirigible two hundred and thirty-five pounds. I exercised my appetites freely, with a young man's wild discipline. I moved my big frame across the floors of barrooms like a Cuban dancer with a knife in his boot and a hibiscus in the band of his Panama hat.

We found Carl Franklin's Hi-Hat, or the Hat, as it was known to regulars, on the Hill, stranded in a forlorn block of Centre Avenue between the boarded-up storefront of a Jewish fish wholesaler and a medical supply company whose grimy display windows featured, and had gone on featuring ever since, a miniature family of headless and limbless human torsos dressed up in exact, tiny replicas of hernia trusses. On the avenue side there were only a fire door and a rusted sign that said FRANKLIN'S in looping script; you got in through the alley around back, where you found a small parking lot and a large man named Clement, who was there to look you over, assess your character, and pat you down if he thought you might be packing. He didn't come off as a very nice person the first time you met him, and he never got any friendlier. The owner, Carl Franklin, was a local boy—he'd grown up on Conkling Street, a few blocks away—who'd worked as a drummer in big bands and small combos during the fifties and sixties, including a stint in one of the late Ellington configurations, and then come home to open the Hi-Hat as a jazz supper club, aiming to attract a class clientele. There was a beautiful old Steinway grand, a luminous bar of glass brick, and the walls were still hung with photographs of Billy Eckstine, Ben Webster, Erroll Garner, Sarah Vaughan; but the place had long since devolved into a loud R & B joint, lit with pink floodlights, smelling of hair spray, spilt beer, and barbecue sauce, catering to a shadowy, not particularly sociable crowd of middle-aged black men and their ethnically varied but uniformly irritable dates.

I remember that I had been dangling unhappily from the rope of my new life as an English professor in Pittsburgh for about three months, friendless, bored, and living alone in a cramped flat over a Ukrainian coffee shop on the South Side, when Crabtree showed up, dressed in a knee-length leather policeman's coat, with a sheet of Mickey Mouse acid and sixty-five hundred dollars in severance pay from a men's fashion magazine that had just decided to fire its literary editor and get out of the unprofitable fiction business once and for

all. I was so glad to see him. We set out immediately to recon-
noiter the bars of my new hometown—Danny's, Jimmy
Post's, the Wheel, all of them gone now—landing in the Hat,
on a Saturday night, when the Blue Roosters, the house band
at that time, were joined onstage by a visiting Rufus Thomas.
We were not only drunk but tripping our brains out, and thus
our initial judgment of the welcome the Hat afforded us and
of the level of the entertainment was not entirely accurate—
we were under the impression that everybody there loved us,
and as I recall we also believed that Rufus was singing the
French lyrics of "My Way" to the tune of "Walkin' the
Dog." At a certain point in the evening, furthermore, one of
the patrons was badly beaten, out in the alley, and came stumbling back into the Hat with his ear hanging loose; Crabtree
and I, having consumed four orders of barbecued ribs, then
spent a fiery half hour unconsuming them, taking turns over
the toilet in the men's room. We'd been going back ever
since, every time Crabtree came to town.

It was about ten-thirty when I walked into the Hat and
submitted myself to the X-ray gaze of Clement. I was glad
that I'd thought to give Tony Sloviak the little gun; it was said
that if you tried to enter the Hat with a weapon concealed
even in the innermost recess of your body, Clement would
still do what was necessary to relieve you of it. The house
band was between sets, and the jukebox was playing Jimmie
Rodgers. I stood a moment on the apron of baby-aspirin-
orange carpeting that ran all the way around the lounge, trying to get my bearings. It had been a couple of years since my
last visit and things seemed to have deteriorated. The ply-
wood subfloor showed through the carpet, which was
pocked with cigarette burns and stained everywhere by substances whose nature I didn't care to speculate on. The wall of

mirrored tile was gapped like a bad smile with empty spaces. Behind the bandstand someone had defaced the big mural, which showed the proprietor wailing away behind an enormous fortress of a drum kit. His sticks were each equipped now with a pair of hairy testicles and he sported a Dalí mustache. The dance floor was dimpled with heel marks. I looked around, expecting to see a couple of tables surrounded by writers and WordFesters and a cloud of pink smoke, but there was only the usual crowd of Hat regulars, looking at me with expressions of derision or mild annoyance. I have no doubt that my face held a stupid aspect.

Out on the floor there were a handful of couples doing the buckethead and the barracuda and the cold Samoan, to the weary and inexorable groove of "Baby What You Want Me to Do," and near the center of the crowd of dancers were Hannah Green and Q., the man who haunted his own life. Hannah was an ungraceful but energetic dancer, capable of admirable feats of pelvic abandon, but the best you could say for old Q. was that he was making no effort to cling to some outmoded notion of dignity. It sounds uncharitable of me to say so, I know, but his attention seemed to be occupied less by his own movements than by the slow vertical mambo of Hannah Green's breasts. I waved to Hannah, who smiled at me, and when I looked around and gave my shoulders an exaggerated shrug, she pointed to a table in a far corner, away from the dancers, the bandstand, and all the other customers. At this table sat Crabtree and James Leer, behind a long, crazy skyline of Iron City bottles. James was slouched down in his chair, his head tilted against the wall, his eyes closed. He looked almost as if he might be asleep. As for Crabtree, he was staring off at, or past, the people dancing, with an expression of happy concentration. His arm was extended down and away from his body, at a delicate angle, as though he were about to choose a bonbon from a tray. His hand, however, wasn't in evidence; it had disappeared under the table, in the general vicinity of James Leer's lap. I shot what must've been a fairly panicked look at Hannah, who bared her teeth and screwed up her eyes, the way you do when an ambulance goes screaming by.

I stopped a waitress on my way over to the table and asked her to bring me a shot of George Dickel. By the time I got there, Crabtree's hands were both visible, and James was sitting more or less upright, his cheeks flushed. The high, flawless forehead that had led me to believe him a rich boy looked feverish, and his eyes were lustrous with something that might have been either euphoria or fear.

"How are you feeling, James?" I said.

"I'm drunk," he said, sounding very sincere. "I'm sorry, Professor Tripp."

I sat down beside Crabtree, glad to be off my feet. The pain in my ankle was getting worse.

"You're all right, James," I said, feeding him the same smile of reassurance I'd already fed him twice that day; the first time as his story was hung up for slaughter in workshop, and the second as I led him into the Gaskells' bedroom, telling him that everything was fine. "Everything's fine."

"Sure it is," said Crabtree. He handed me his bottle of beer, half full, and I tipped it back and took a long warm swallow. "Thought we'd lost you, Tripp."

"Where is everyone?" I said, setting the empty bottle before him with a flourish, as though I'd just performed some alcoholic parlor trick. "Did it work out to be just the four of you?"

"Nobody else showed up," said Crabtree. "Sara and what's

his name, Walter, they said they were going to go home first and then meet us here. But I guess they just decided to stay home. Curl up on the sofa with the dog."

I glanced at James, expecting a little guilt to show in his face, but he was too far gone for that. I doubted if he even remembered what he had done. He'd started to wink out again, his head drifting back against the wall.

"Is that just beer?" I said, jerking my head in his direction.

"Primarily," said Crabtree. "Although I gather you two staged a little raid on the Crabtree pharmacopoeia."

"That was a while ago," I said, reaching down to press my fingers against the bandage on my ankle. "He shouldn't be feeling any of that anymore."

"Well, you two missed a few bottles the first time," he said. He tapped the hip pocket of his dollar green jacket. "And James here was curious." He turned to watch the young man as his lips parted and a tiny flag of saliva flew from one corner of his mouth.

"He's out," I said.

We sat for a moment, watching the regular rise and fall of James Leer's chest within his glen plaid shirt. The skinny little tie had come halfway unknotted and drooped at his throat like a blown flower. Crabtree dabbed at the ribbon of spit with the corner of a cocktail napkin, tenderly, as though wiping a baby's mouth.

"He has a book," said Crabtree. "I hear he has a novel."

"I know it. Something about a parade. Love parade."

"Why didn't you tell me?"

"I just found out myself tonight. He's carrying it around in that knapsack of his."

"Is he any good?"

"No," I said. "Not yet he isn't."

"I want to read it," said Crabtree. An oily lock of hair had fallen down across James Leer's forehead, and he reached out to brush it back.

"Come on, Crabtree." I lowered my voice. "Don't do this."

"Don't do what?"

"He's a kid," I said. "He's my student, man. I'm not even sure if he's—"

"He is," said Crabtree. "Take my word for it."

"I don't believe that he is," I said. "I think it's more complicated than that. I want you to leave him alone."

"Is that so?"

"He's really fucked up right now, Crabtree." I lowered my voice all the way to a whisper. "I think he was planning to off himself tonight. Maybe. I don't know. Anyway, he's a mess. He's a disaster. I don't think he needs sexual confusion thrown into the mix right this minute."

"On the contrary," said Crabtree, "it could be just the ticket. Hey, what's the matter, Grady?"

"I'm fine," I said. "What do you mean?"

"Looked like you just, I don't know, winced."

"Oh," I said. "It's my foot. My foot's killing me."

"Your foot? What's wrong with it?"

"Nothing," I said. "I just—I fell."

"Yeah, you know, you look kind of shaken up," he said. His eyes had lost their fevered Cortés luster, and I thought I saw real tenderness in them for the first time all night. Our chairs were pushed close together and he leaned his shoulder against mine. I could still smell Tony's perfume on his cheek. The waitress arrived with my shot of Dickel and I sipped at it, feeling the slow poison work its way into my heart.

"I like the way she dances," said Crabtree, looking out

across the floor toward Hannah Green and Q. The selection now playing was "Ride Your Pony," by Lee Dorsey. One of the many features that marked the Hat as a survivor of the great lost era of Pittsburgh dives was its telephone jukebox. There was no actual box, only a coin-operated telephone, black and heavy as an old steam iron, mounted on a pillar at one end of the dance floor. Attached to this phone by an oft-repaired length of wire was a dog-eared, barbecue-stained playlist, typed a million years ago by some manic alphabetist, that featured over five thousand selections, grouped by genre. You picked your songs, dropped your quarters, and had a drunken, shouted conversation with an old Slovenian lady hidden away somewhere in Pittsburgh inside an underground bunker of black vinyl. A few minutes later you would hear your songs. At one time, according to Sara, many bars in town had been so equipped, but now the Hat was one of the last. "She shows a heavy Pharaonic influence, I'd say, in the elbow movements. With perhaps just a soupçon of Snoopy in the feet."

"How long have she and Q. been going at it?" I said.

"Too long for Q., I think," said Crabtree, shaking his head. "Look at him."

"I know it," I said. "Poor bastard."

I attempted to ignore the ivy fingers of desire for Hannah Green that climbed along my spine as I watched her dance.

"Hey," said Crabtree, "look at that guy."

He pointed to a table just at the edge of the dance floor.

"Who? Oh my." I smiled. "The one with the hair sculpture."

He was a small man, with delicate cheekbones and an amazing, radiant, processed pompadour, a cresting black tidal wave of hair atop his head. Many of the great hairdos of bygone ages, I'd found, survived to this day in isolated pockets of Pittsburgh. The guy was also wearing an elaborate velour warm-up suit, piped and embroidered with gold and crimson ribbon, and he was puffing on a long, thin cigar. His hands were too large for the rest of him, and you could see bright pink traces of some ancient injury puckered around the right side of his face.

"He's a boxer," I said. "A flyweight."

"He's a jockey," said Crabtree. "His name's, um, Curtis. Hardapple."

"Not Curtis," I said.

"Vernon, then. Vernon Hardapple. The scars are from a—from a horse's hooves. He fell during a race and got trampled."

"He's addicted to painkillers."

"He has a plate in his head."

"He lost a toe to sugar diabetes."

"He can't piss standing up anymore."

"He lives with his mother."

"Right. He had a younger brother who was a—trainer."

"A groom."

"Named Claudell. Who was retarded. And his mother blames Vernon for his death."

"Because, because, because Vernon let him—groom some mean stallion—and he got his head stove in. Or—"

"He was killed," said a sleepy voice, "when a gangster named Freddie Nostrils tried to shoot his favorite horse. He took the bullet himself."

We both turned to look at James Leer, who opened one bloodshot eye to regard us.

"Vernon, over there, was in on the hit."

"That's very good," said Crabtree, after a surprised moment. We watched as the eye closed once more.

"He heard what we were saying," I said.

Working on his sixth or seventh bottle of Iron, Crabtree did not look overly concerned by this. I took another few sips of poison from my shot glass. After a few minutes the silence between us seemed to have taken on an insufferable weight.

"Poor old Vernon Hardapple," Crabtree said, sorrowfully shaking his head. He smiled. "They always come out sounding so unlucky."

"Every story is the story of somebody's hard luck," I said, quoting the silver-haired cowboy writer in whose class we had met twenty years before.

"Hey, teach," said Hannah Green, bounding toward us in her sharp red boots. "I want you to come and dance with me."

We danced, to "Shake a Tail Feather," and "Sex Machine," and some scratchy Joe Tex number whose title I couldn't recall. I danced with Hannah until the band came off break, and as they climbed up onto the platform and got behind their various instruments I went back over to the table and hit up Crabtree for another codeine and a couple of whatever else he was selling. I needed something for my ankle, and something else for my sense of shame—don't think I didn't feel ridiculous, thrashing around out there like one of Picasso's wounded minotaurs, lumbering blindly after an angelic young girl. Crabtree had managed to revive James Leer, for the moment, and they were engaged with old Q. in an apparently intricate consideration of the function or meaning of the cockatoo in *Citizen Kane*. Crabtree was by no means a film buff but he had an excellent memory for narratives and his gothic imagination found much to appreciate in the work of my girth brother Orson Welles. Or at least that was the impression he wanted to give James Leer. Under the cold and inescapable gaze of Q. or his doppelgänger, Crabtree held out to me a palmful of blue grapeshot, pink moons, gray goldfish, little white pentagons shaped like tiny home plates.

"Christ, your hand looks like a bowl of Lucky Charms," I said. "Let me try one of those white ones."

I washed it down with something roiling around in a shot glass on the table in front of Crabtree that stank of ketones and aldehydes and that I thought might have been bad tequila. Then I went back out onto the floor and danced for another hour to what grizzled old Carl Franklin called the R & B stylings of Pittsburgh's very own Double Down, until I could no longer feel my ankle and had lost the better part of my shame. Hannah rolled up her sleeves, and unbuttoned the top two buttons of her flannel shirt, revealing the threadbare neckline of a white ribbed undershirt and a filigreed locket on a thin silver chain.

While she danced she kept her eyes closed and described solitary, interlocking circles across the floor, so that there were moments when I felt that she wasn't really dancing with me at all, but simply employing me as a kind of fulcrum, a hub on which to hang the whirling spokes of her own private revolutions. And no wonder, I thought; if I were her I certainly wouldn't have wanted anyone to think that I could possibly have chosen such an elephantine piece of machinery as myself, all vacuum tubes and gear work with a plain old analog dial of a face, such a dented, gas-guzzling old Galaxie 500 of a man, for a dance partner. But then she would open her eyes, favor me with her spacious Utah smile, and give me her hands, so that I could spin her for a second or two. Whenever our faces drew within each other's orbit I felt compelled to speak, generally to express my doubts about the wisdom of my dancing, with her, at all, and when Double Down broke their set again I was relieved, and I started for the table. But she took hold of my wrist, dragged me over to the magic black telephone, and dialed up three songs.

" 'Just My Imagination,' " she told the operator, without consulting the tattered playlist. " 'When a Man Loves a Woman.' That's right. And 'Get It While You Can.' "

"Uh oh," I said. "I'm in trouble."

"Hush now," said Hannah, as she reached up and put her arms around my neck.

"I'm going to regret this tomorrow," I said.

"That's nice," she said. "Everybody ought to have a hobby."

A few other couples joined us on the dance floor and we lost ourselves among them. I'd never been able to figure out exactly what was involved in slow dancing, so I contented myself, as I had since high school, with gripping my partner to me, letting out awkward breaths against her ear, and tipping from foot to foot like someone waiting for a bus. I could feel the sweat cooling on her forearms and smell a trace of apples in her hair. Somewhere in the middle of Percy Sledge's testimony the combination of substances I'd introduced into my bloodstream in the course of the evening reached a kind of equilibrium, and I forgot, for a moment, all the bad things that had already happened to me that day as a result of my foolishness and bad behavior, and all the good reasons I had

for leaving poor Hannah Green alone. I was happy. I kissed
Hannah's apple yellow hair. I could feel them unlimbering
the old siege engine down inside my boxers. I think that I
must have sighed, then, and for all the fizz and ichor flowing
at that moment through the ventricles of my heart, it must
have come out sounding unutterably sad.

"I've been rereading *Arsonist*," she told me, to cheer me
up, I supposed. "It's so great." She was referring to my second
novel, *The Arsonist's Girl,* an unpleasant little story of love and
madness I'd written during the Final Days, down inside the
doomed bunker of my second marriage to a San Francisco
weatherwoman whom I'll just call Eva B. It was a slender
book, whose composition had cost me a lot of misery, and I
had a pretty low opinion of it, myself, although it did contain
a nice description of a fire at a petting zoo, and a pretty good
two-page sex scene in which my reader was given a taste of
the heroine's rectum. "It's so fucking tragic, and beautiful,
Grady. I love the way you write. It's so natural. It's so plain. I
was thinking it's like all your sentences seem as if they've
always existed, waiting around up there, in Style Heaven, or
wherever, for you to fetch them down."

"I thank you," I said.

"And I love what you wrote in your inscription, Grady."

"I'm glad."

"Only I'm not quite the downy innocent you think I am."

"I hope that isn't true," I said, and at that moment I happened to catch a glimpse, in the smoky mirrored wall of the
Hi-Hat, of an overweight, hobbled, bespectacled, aging,
lank-haired, stoop-shouldered Sasquatch, his furry eye sockets dim, his gait unsteady, his arms enfolded so tightly around
the bones of a helpless young angel that it was impossible to
say if she was holding him up or if, on the contrary, he was

dragging her down. I stopped dancing and let go of Hannah Green, and then Janis Joplin ceased urging us not to turn our backs on love, and the last of Hannah's requests came to an end. In its aftermath we stood there, suddenly abandoned by the other couples, looking at each other, and all at once, as the pills and the whiskey fell out of balance in my bloodstream, I felt irremediably fucked up.

"So what are you going to do?" said Hannah, giving my belly a friendly slap.

My reply was something softheaded and mumbled about dancing with her all night.

"About Emily, I mean," she said, a little impatiently. "I—I guess she isn't going to be there when you get home."

"I guess not," I said. "Try not to look quite so pleased."

She blushed. "Sorry."

"I guess that I really don't know. What I'm going to do."

"I have an idea," she said. She fished around in the pocket of her jeans for a moment, and then pressed three warm quarters into my palm.

I steered myself over to the telephone, dropped in the quarters, and unhooked the receiver.

"You've got to help me," I said.

"Who is this?" said the voice of the thousand-year-old lavender-haired Ruthenian woman in cat-eye glasses and an angora sweater who dwelt within the secret heart of Pittsburgh, taking the requests of an ever-dwindling population of drunken and heartbroken lovers. "I can't understand what you're saying."

"I said I need to hear something that's going to save my life," I told her, reeling on the end of the telephone cord.

"This is a jukebox, hon," said the woman, sounding calm and a little distracted, as though wherever she was the televi-

sion was playing low or she had a copy of *Cosmo* spread open
on her ancient lap. "This isn't a real telephone you're talking
on."

"I know that," I said, unconvincingly. "I just don't know
what to ask you for."

I looked over at Hannah and tried to flash her the smile of
a competent and reasonable smiler, of someone who wasn't at
all worried that he was going to be sick, and going to fall
down, and going to hurt yet another young woman in the
course of a lifelong career of callous disregard. Judging from
the look of dismay that came over her face, I thought I must
have failed miserably, but then I saw that Q. had left the table
and was making his way across the crowded room toward
Hannah, his face grim and determined and haunted, as far as I
could see, only by alcohol, the writer's true secret sharer, the
ghost that lived in the dusty, bare corners of Albert Vetch's
and so many other midnight lives. As he approached, however, to ask her for the next dance, Hannah turned on him,
simply, and headed straight toward me, head lowered, blushing from her forehead to the nape of her neck at the thought
of her own rudeness.

"Just a minute," I told the Jukebox Crone, wrapping my
hand around the mouthpiece of the receiver. "Dance with
him, Hannah." I tried out another of my implausible smiles.
"He's a famous writer." I raised the telephone to my mouth
again. "Are you still there?" I said.

"Where would I go?" said the woman. "I told you, hon,
I'm not a real person. This is my job."

"But I don't want to dance with him, Grady." Hannah put
her arm through mine and looked up at me through her scattered bangs, searching my face, her eyes so wide and desperate
that I was alarmed. I'd never seen Hannah acting anything

other than the calm, optimistic Mormon girl she was, eternally polite, capable of stolid acceptance of locusts, misfortunes, and outlandish news about the universe. "I want to keep dancing with you."

"Please." I watched as Q. turned and walked with drunken precision back to the table in the far corner of the room, arriving just as the heads of James Leer and Crabtree surfaced into the pink beam of a floodlight from the bottom of a very deep kiss. James's eyes had gone all blind and his mouth was an empty O.

"I'm sorry," I said into the telephone, "but I have to hang up now."

"All right, all right," said the woman. She gave a curt little sigh and tapped her seven-inch tropical pink fingernails against her headset. "How about 'Sukiyaki'?"

"Perfect," I said. "And why don't you pick another two that you like?"

I hung up the phone, gave Hannah a sloppy and inarticulate hug, and apologized to her about forty-seven times, until neither of us knew what I was talking about and she said that it was all right. Then I hurried over to the table in the corner, where I laid my cold fingers against James Leer's feverish neck.

"In ten seconds," I told them, as I helped James to his feet, "this dance floor is going to be packed."

HANNAH said that she had never been there but she believed James Leer rented a room from his Aunt Rachel, in the attic of her house in Mt. Lebanon. Since neither of us felt like driving all way the out to the South Hills at two o'clock in the morning, I folded James into Hannah's beat-to-shit Le Car and sent them on home to my house. Crabtree and Q. would be riding with me. I figured it would be safer that way for all of us.

As I was about to close the door on him, James stirred and wrinkled up his face.

"He's having a bad dream," I said.

We watched him for a moment.

"I'll bet James's bad dreams are *really* bad," said Hannah. "The way bad movies are."

"Xylophones on the soundtrack," I said. "Lots of Mexican policemen."

James lifted a hand to the general vicinity of his right shoulder and patted it a few times, without opening his eyes, then pawed in the same way at his left shoulder, as if he thought he were home in bed and had lost track of his pillow.

"My knacksap," he said, as his eyes flew open.

"His bag," said Hannah. "You know that ratty green thing of his?"

James sent his pale hand spidering across his lap, his seat, the space around his long legs, then made a sudden grab for the door handle.

"You stay right here, little James," I said, squeezing him back into the car. I waved to Crabtree, busy just then propping Q.'s string-puppet body against the side of my car, and called out that I was going to run in and look for James's knapsack. Crabtree didn't bother to look up. Before I could register the fact that he was ignoring me, however, I'd already tossed him my keys. They rang out against his left shoulder and then splashed into a puddle at his feet. He fired a nasty look at me across the parking lot before he knelt down to retrieve them, one restraining hand on Q.'s waist.

"Sorry," I said.

As I limped back into the Hat and headed for our corner, the man we had fictionalized as Vernon Hardapple tried, without much success, to interpose his body between me and our table. His breath blew sour and warm at my face. His tall tsunami of hair had disintegrated into a kind of shivering pom-pom that stuck out all around his head. He was ready to mix it up with me.

"What were you looking at?" he asked me. His voice was raspy and his speech slow. Standing close to him I could see that his facial scars were the mark of some jagged and not very sharp object. "Something funny about me?"

"I wasn't looking at you," I said, smiling.

"Whose car you driving?"

"What's that?"

"That 1966 emerald green Ford Galaxie 500, out there, with the license plate that say YAW 332. That your car?"

I said that it was.

"Bullshit," he said, pushing lightly at my chest. "That's mine, motherfucker."

"I've had it for years."

"Bull*shit*." He brought his scarred face an inch closer to mine.

"It was my mother's," I said. Ordinarily I'm never too busy to get myself into a stupid argument with an angry and potentially dangerous person in an unsavory place. I was in a hurry to get James home and safely put to bed, however, and so I just brushed past him. "Excuse me."

He lurched in front of me.

"What were you fuckers *looking* at?"

"We were admiring your hair," I said.

He reached out for my chest as if to give me a shove. I took an involuntary step backward, and he stumbled against me. As he tried to regain his feet he tipped himself over sideways, and sprawled across the black Naugahyde seat of an empty booth behind him, which after a moment he found comfortable and appeared unwilling to leave.

"Sorry about your brother, Vernon," I said.

Our table hadn't been cleared yet. As I came closer I saw, underneath it, not James's knapsack but what I believed for a heart-stopping instant to be the mangled body of a bird, lying dead on the orange carpet. It turned out to be my wallet. My charge plates and several of the engraved business cards Sara had ordered for me on my last birthday were scattered across the floor around the the table. I gathered them up and slipped them back into the wallet, a fat black kidskin number Emily's parents had brought back for me from their trip to Italy, cut wide to hold continental bills. I returned it to the breast pocket of my jacket, not even bothering to check if all the cash was still there, as if I'd left my elegant Florentine wallet lying on the floor on purpose, where I knew it would be perfectly safe. In any case I couldn't have said how much cash there ought to have been. I started for the door, feeling perversely pleased, congratulating myself, as I always did at such moments, on not having been born an unlucky drunk. I tapped the comforting bulk of the wallet at my breast.

"See, now," I told Vernon, passing by the booth in which he'd taken up residence. "You just have to learn to be lucky like me."

Then I rolled on out of the Hat. My car and Hannah's were idling side by side at the center of the nearly empty parking lot, trailing long plumes of exhaust, their windows misted over. There were two dark shapes sitting in the front seat of my car, the smaller one, on the passenger's side, pitched a little to the right. For some reason it irritated me that Crabtree had gotten behind the wheel of Happy Blackmore's Galaxie. I walked over to Hannah's car and knocked on her window, and then the air around me was filled, an inch at a time, with the radiance of her face and with the wheezing of a tragic accordion. Hannah Green was big on tango music.

"No knacksap," I said. "He must have left it back at Thaw."

"Are you sure?" she said. "Maybe someone took it."

"No. Nobody took it."

"How do you know?"

I shrugged, and bent down to have a look at James. He'd slumped over against Hannah, now, and his head rested on her shoulder with an enviable snugness.

"Is he all right?" I said.

"I think so." She gave the hair over his ear a few unconscious strokes. "I'm just going to get him home and onto the sofa." She ducked her head and looked at me pleadingly. "The one in your office, all right?"

"In my office?"

"Yeah, you know it's the best one for naps, Grady." Over the course of the previous winter, as I read student writing or caught up on correspondence at my desk, Hannah had dozed off many times while studying on my old Sears Honor Bilt, her bootheels kicked up on the creaking armrest, her face sheltered under the tent of a sociology text.

"I don't think it's really going to make all that much difference to him right now, Hannah," I said. "We could probably stand him up out in the garage with the snow shovels."

"Grady."

"All right. In my office." I hung a couple of fingers over the edge of her window, and she reached up and took them in her own.

"See you at home," I said.

I walked around to the front of the Galaxie and waited for Crabtree to get out. The door swung open. Crabtree looked up at me, his face utterly blank.

"You shouldn't drive," he said.

"You should?" I said. "Get in back."

He continued to favor me with the polar expanse of his gaze for another moment, then shrugged, got out of the car, and climbed into the back. I slid in beside Q. and put the engine in gear. As I followed Hannah down the bumpy alley I was aware of a flickering shadow at the limit of my peripheral vision. The next moment there was something caught in my headlights, flagging us down with its wild dark arms. I braked. The arms cutting across the beams of light threw thirty-foot shadows against the screen of rainy air behind them.

"Jesus Christ," said Q., in a strangled whisper. *"It's him."*

"What's he want?" said Crabtree. It was only Vernon Hardapple again, but Q. seemed to be seeing someone else.

"Nothing," I said. "I had a little problem with the guy when I went back inside the Hat."

"Go around him, Grady."

"All right," I said.

"Oh my God," said Q., squeezing his head between his hands, as though to shore it up against collapse.

"Grady, go around him!"

"All right!" I tried to tiptoe the car around him, but the

alleyway was too narrow. One sidestep and he was standing in front of the car again. "Shit, man, there's no room."

"Look at those pink scars on his cheek," said Q., remembering himself. "It looks like he has another set of *lips*."

"Back up, then, idiot!" said Crabtree.

"All right!" I said, throwing the car into reverse. I rolled us back into the Hi-Hat's parking lot, then wrenched the wheel around to the left and, ignoring a one-way sign, started off down the alley in the other direction. Vernon was there, a funny, almost happy little smile on his face. I stepped on the brake again.

"Shit," I said, just before he rocked back onto his heels, swung his arms forward, backward, forward again. You could see him moving his mouth as he one, two, threw himself onto the hood of my car. He landed on his ass, with a surprisingly gentle report, and then quickly slid down the hood of my car to the grille, legs extended, like a child sliding down a banister. He managed to alight on his feet, turned around, took a deep bow from which he almost didn't recover, and aimed another blind smile through the windshield, directly at me. Then he disappeared.

"Who *was* that?" said Q., grinning with some odd but not unfamiliar combination of terror and delight. "What happened?"

"I had my car jumped on," I said, as though this were a service the Hat provided to its very best customers.

"Is it all right?"

I hoisted myself up on the steering wheel and tried to see how the hood looked. The light in the alleyway was bad and I couldn't see much of anything.

"I think it's okay," I said. "They made these things pretty heavy back then."

"Let's get out of here," said Crabtree. "Before he comes back with some friends."

I took off down the alley, out onto the empty avenue, then headed down Baum Boulevard, feeling once again that I'd made a narrow but foreordained escape from danger.

"After we drop Q., here, Crabtree," I said, "we have to make a stop at Thaw."

"Uh huh," said Crabtree. Now that the crisis was over, he settled back down into his sulk.

"I think James might've left his knapsack in the auditorium."

"Great."

"Do you remember seeing it when you, uh, escorted him out tonight?" I looked at him in the rearview mirror, and I didn't like what I saw. Crabtree was sitting back, arms folded behind his head, watching dark storefronts and deserted filling stations slide past him, an expression on his face of dumb amusement, as though he were the happiest man in the world, and all that he saw around him only increased the value and hue of his contentment. It was the closest that he ever came to screaming. "Crabtree?"

"Tripp?"

"Yes, Crabtree?"

"Please go fuck yourself."

"I'll do that," I said.

"Isn't this the way back to the college?" said Q. as we passed the Electric Banana.

"That's right," I said, impressed that he could recognize the route in the dark, drunk, after having seen it only once before.

"Well, I don't know if—that is, I'm not staying at the college, Grady."

"No?"

"No, I'm staying with the Gaskells."

"Is that so?" For an instant the sole of my foot slipped free from the gas pedal, and the car drifted for a few hundred feet on momentum, slowing almost to a stop. "Well, it's the way to their house, too," I said, after I could breathe again. I replaced my foot on the accelerator and drove us out to Point Breeze.

"I wonder what happened to them, anyway?" Q. said when I headed down the street that led to the Gaskells' driveway. The nearer we came to Sara's house the less inclined I felt to go forward. We crept along the fence of fearsome iron spikes. "They just never showed up."

In the end there was nothing more I could do to prevent it, and we turned into the Gaskells' gravel drive. Sara and Walter garaged their cars at night, and the driveway looked desolate, the house abandoned. A pair of floods set amid the bushes on either side of the narrow front porch searched the face of the house, throwing their light across its bays and shutters and dormers, riddling it with odd shadows. The harsh floodlights seemed to be there not to illuminate so much as to identify, to mark the Gaskells' house to passersby as one that had an infamous history, or was slated for imminent destruction. The wet wind blew through the branches of the pair of ancient apple trees in the front yard and filled the air with flowing scarves and snowdrifts of white petals. After a moment, I noticed that in an upstairs window a light was still dimly burning, and as I looked up something passed across the window blind. It was the window of Sara and Walter's bedroom; they were still awake. I could go in with Q., right now, and tell them about the burden I was carrying around in the trunk of my car.

"See you tomorrow," said Q., as he negotiated his way out of his safety belt. He worked the handle, and then pushed open the door with the toe of his Wallabee shoe. Wisely and with an air of long experience he took a moment to locate the ground before he tried to stand on it.

"Take it easy, now." Crabtree slid across the backseat and climbed out of the car before Q. could slam the door on him. He shook Q.'s hand, steadying him a little as he did so, then got in beside me.

"I'm looking forward to your talk tomorrow, Terry." Q. searched his pockets for a moment, a determined look on his face. His shirt was untucked, and the long thin strands of hair that he combed over his bald scalp were all standing on end, and I saw that in the course of the evening he had somehow managed to lose one of the temple pieces of his eyeglasses. When at last he found the key Sara must have given him, he looked so happy—so pleased with himself—that I had to turn away. I didn't look back at the house until he was already inside it.

"His old doppelgänger must be feeling pretty good about things right now," I said as we drove away. Crabtree said nothing. "What?" I asked him. "Come on, buddy. Don't do this. Talk. What's the matter?"

"Don't you know?"

"You're pissed off at me because I wouldn't let you mess with poor James Leer."

"Like it was any of your business."

"You're getting greedy, man," I told him. "Wasn't Miss Sloviak enough for one night?"

Crabtree repeated his earlier, anatomically impossible request of me. He had nothing further to add.

"Okay, look, I'm sorry," I said, to no effect. I made a few more halfhearted attempts to apologize, then let it drop, and we drove on in silence. I started thinking all kinds of maudlin thoughts, about things like Doctor Dee's empty food dish, and his rubber pork chop, and the length of leash chain hanging, forever slack now, from a bent nail in the pantry. Without knowing exactly how, I found myself, ten minutes later, in the service driveway alongside Thaw Hall, putting the car in park.

"Wait here," I said. "I'll be right back."

"Where would I go?" said Crabtree.

Yes, it was my lucky night. As I came around the side of the building to the front doors, I saw that the janitor was still at work, getting Thaw Hall ready for tomorrow's busy schedule of exciting WordFest events. He was a tall, stooped, shaggy-haired white kid, dressed in a blue jumpsuit, dragging a vacuum cleaner back and forth behind him across the carpet of the lobby, with a kind of dazed industriousness, like a paperboy towing a wagon full of newsprint. When I rapped on the glass he seemed to recognize me, and I wondered if he could possibly have been a student of mine.

"Traxler," he said, as he let me into the hall. "Sam. I had you in my freshman year. Then I dropped out."

"I hope it wasn't my fault," I said.

"It wasn't," said Sam Traxler. I hadn't expected him to take me seriously. I wished I could remember who he was. "Anyway, I'm in this band now. We're starting to play out a little. We're starting to make a little cash."

"Sam," I said, jerking a thumb toward the doors of the auditorium. "Did you already clean up in there?"

"Yep. Hey, did you lose a knapsack, Professor Tripp?"

He had it in the service closet, on the floor, between a zinc mop bucket and a black leather guitar case plastered over with stickers and decals.

"I thought that looked like a manuscript in there," he said.

"It is. Thanks a lot." I took the knapsack from him and started for the door.

"No problem," he said, accompanying me. I'd obviously provided him with a welcome distraction from his work. "Hey, is all that true about Errol Flynn and how he used to put coke on his dick? To make himself, like, last longer?"

"Christ, Traxler," I said. "How the fuck should I know?"

"Well, jeez," he said, pointing to the knapsack. He looked a little taken aback. "You're reading his biography, aren't you? It was all wrapped up in your sweater or whatever."

"Oh, yeah," I said. "Right. Yeah, that's true. He used to rub all kinds of things on it. Paprika. Iron filings. Ground lamb."

"Sick," said Sam, opening the door and holding it open for me. "Well, take care, Professor."

"See you, Sam," I said. "Hey, what's your band's name, anyway? I'll, uh, I'll look for you guys."

"We don't have a name," he said. "We came up with so many names that we just had to give up, you know? Meat Nickels. Bitter Dregs. The Ulnas. We couldn't agree. People just call us, I don't know, 'Sam and those dudes,' or 'Greg's band,' or whatever."

"Clever," I said, standing half in and half out of the door. As I listened to him I'd been fiddling with the strap on James's knapsack, and now it came loose. I held on tight to the flap as the knapsack's weighted-down bottom gaped against my thigh. Inside, tied with binder's twine to a neatly cut rectangle of shirt cardboard, lay James Leer's manuscript, two inches thick.

"That the new one?" said Sam.

I nodded. There was no title page, no hint of authorship: simply the words THE LOVE PARADE at the top of the first sheet of paper, followed by the numeral 1, and then, to start the thing off,

> On Friday afternoon his daddy handed him a hundred wrinkled one dollar bills and told him to buy himself a sport-jacket for the Homecoming Dance.

Two characters, an occasion, in the wad of tired money a whisper of some long history of poverty and thrift, and, above all, a quirky human voice to hang a story on. It was hard to do more in a good first sentence. I could have wished the kid would just break down and employ a comma, but at least the thing wasn't the usual scattering of fragments and chips. One of his short stories actually began with the lines "Ruined. The dinner was. Utterly," but in his novel he seemed to have left all that behind. Its second sentence read:

> He rode the Greyhound over to Wilkes-Barre and spent the money on a pretty chrome gun.

"Is it good?" said Sam.

"I don't know," I said. "It might be."

I stuffed the manuscript back into the knapsack, next to a kind of crude package—the biography of Errol Flynn, I supposed—wrapped hastily in a piece of soft black cloth. There was something familiar about the sheen of this fabric. I peeled back a corner of it, and saw a flash of yellowed ermine, and smelled a faint smoky flavor of cork. All at once the world seemed to draw a sharp breath; it started to rain, streaking the ink of James Leer's manuscript, spattering the satin jacket Marilyn Monroe wore as she and her sad-faced husband set off in their De Soto to meet their fate as married people.

"This isn't my jacket," I told Sam Traxler.

"I kind of figured that," said Sam.

Walking out of Thaw Hall, I felt myself arrive at the end of my luck. When I got back to the service road, the car and Crabtree were gone.

It was a mile and seven tenths from the campus to my house on Denniston. The intervening streets were broad and straight, lined with maples, chestnuts, and oaks that had been planted just after the First World War. All the houses I passed were dark, with cars arranged in their driveways as neatly as duck decoys on a mantelpiece. I limped right down the middle of certain streets, and stood for an entire minute in the center of a desolate intersection as the lights changed around me and the traffic signals swung from their cables in the wind. I walked for a hundred and sixty-two hours through an uncharitable sobering rain. The pain in my ankle grew worse the longer I walked and the soberer I got. I wished to the point of religious feeling that I had my little bag of Humboldt County with me. There was no marijuana in James Leer's knapsack; I confirmed this unsurprising fact several times. There were only, in addition to the three objects I already

knew about, an otherwise anonymous gold Cross pen inscribed FROM YOUR LOVING PARENTS, half a roll of breath
mints, twelve cents, and an autographed postcard of Frances
Farmer. I recognized the looping script as the hand of Hannah
Green. When I crested the last hill before my block I caught
the echo of some sad vibration, like the lowing of a passing
train. It was the bell in the Mellon Campanile, tolling three
o'clock.

My car wasn't in the driveway. It seemed to me that I had
never seen the driveway looking so empty before. I lived in a
nice, big, brick-and-ivy house, built in 1915 in the Prairie
style, quadrangular and spacious as a bank. Squat pillars held
up its three porches, and it had leaded windows, built-in window seats, cabinets, and bookcases, an office nook under the
stairs, a parlor, and enough bedrooms for a family of five. The
pantry was larger than apartments I had lived in and certainly
better provisioned. The wainscoting and the walls had been
repainted in careful tones of candle wax and eggshell. The
flower beds along the front walk were dark and animate with
primrose, crocus, narcissus. I dragged myself up the five steps
to the front door and let myself in. There was a smell of Froot
Loops cereal from the vase of freesias on the hatstand. I turned
on the hall light and was confronted by the faces of vanished
furriers, dry-goods merchants, printers, and chiropodists, in
wooden frames, hanging on the wall under the stairs, along
with their wives, children and grandchildren, two lavishly
bearded brother uncles, a long-dead cocker spaniel named
Shlumper, and nine members of a Zionist social club. When I
opened the hall closet to hang up my wet jacket, I was en-
veloped in a cloud of Cristalle. I stood there for a moment,
smelling Emily's coats. The refrigerator hummed to itself in
the faraway kitchen. I smelled her mackinaw, and her pea

coat, and the cracked black shearling which she had worn all through the winter of our courtship eight years before. She was living in her place on Beacon Street, then, near the park, and I remembered walking her home one night along the Panther Hollow bridge; halfway across we had stopped, and I had backed her up against the frozen rail to kiss her. I remembered the give of shearling between my fingers, soft and rough as the skin of her throat, and the way when I worked open its wooden buttons the coat had emitted a dizzying blast of her bodily perfumes, as if I were lowering myself into the deep black pocket of her bed.

For the first time I understood that I had driven Emily Warshaw from my life.

This was something I'd been trying to do for a long time—not intentionally, I swear, nor with any feeling of satisfaction, but in the automatic, methodical manner of a boy working on a loose tooth. Without reference to doppelgängers and the symptoms of the midnight disease it's hard to say why, exactly; but certainly a native genius for externalizing self-hatred may have had something to do with it. Not only would I never want to belong to any club that would have me for a member—if elected I would wear street shoes onto the squash court and set fire to the ballroom curtains.

It hadn't been love at first sight for Emily and me, it was true. We'd met through a friend of hers whose husband taught the nineteenth-century British novel in my department and presided over a weekly professorial poker game that I sometimes frequented during my lonely early days in Pittsburgh. At first sight I found her cold and aloof, if beautiful, and she thought that I was boastful, hyperbolic, alcoholic, and loud. We were right, of course. We saw each other casually a few times, with no result apart from a few awkward conversations. Then I heard that she had lost her job—photographing ingots and smelters for an ad shop with a lot of steel-industry accounts—and, through my friend the Dickensian, I put her in touch with an acquaintance of mine, a senior copywriter at Richards, Reed. This fellow liked her work and took her on, and Emily asked me to dinner, to thank me. Then she invited me home. A year later we were married. In those days I was tired and suspicious of love at first sight. In each of my first two marriages the come-out roll had turned up seven, and now it seemed reasonable to lay my money on the Don't Pass line.

I believe that I was inspired to marry Emily Warshaw by the artificial hopefulness of sex and by an orphan's trite desire for a home. The odd agglomeration of Warshaws, the product of a long and determined program of overseas adoptions, with its combination of Jews and Koreans, intellectuals, space cadets, and sharpies, no two of them related by blood, seemed to offer me the best chance yet to wire my wandering meteor to the armillary sphere of a family. This was a sincere if not entirely commendable motive for marriage, but I've since found that in the efforts of a husband and wife to stay together, a fugitive *chaleur* and a longing for home are no better guarantees of success than the ozone-blue flash of the Thunderbolt. For me the act of marriage has proven, like most of the other disastrous acts of my life, little more than a hedge against any future lack of good material.

I went into my office and found James Leer asleep, on the long green sofa, an unzipped sleeping bag pulled up to his chin. It was an old-fashioned bag that had belonged to Emily's dad, patterned with mallards and huntsmen and hounds. I could see it was, because the lamp on my desk was still on. I supposed that Hannah had left it burning for James in case he awakened in the middle of the night and didn't know where he was. His head lay at the end of the sofa nearest my desk, but she had angled the lamp's neck so that its light wouldn't shine directly in his eyes. I wondered if she was waiting for me in the basement, in her narrow bed, under a Stieglitz portrait of Georgia O'Keeffe, propped up on one elbow, hearing portents in the creaking of the ceiling overhead. For a second I allowed myself to imagine going down. Then I looked over at my desk. She'd turned the lamp, I saw, so that it cast its light squarely on the thick white slab of twenty-pound bond, on the towering pile, on the keep and insurmountable battlements of *Wonder Boys*. All at once I felt very tired. I set James's knapsack down on the floor beside the sofa and switched off the lamp. In a last, ill-advised spree of hopefulness I made myself walk all the way down the hall to the guest bedroom to look for Terry Crabtree. Then I forced my body up the stairs, and into the next empty room.

WHEN I woke on Saturday morning in our big sleigh bed there were black sky and stars at the window. It wasn't quite six o'clock. The pain in my ankle was still there, duller and more feverish than before. My hasty bandage work had come unraveled in the night, and I made out a Japan of dried blood on the sheets. I lay for a moment, riding the swell and roll of my hangover, clinging to the mattress and to the wreckage of my last dream. I'd already lost most of the details, but I could still recall its backdrop or central theme, which was the shadowy kingdom of mystery and spice hidden in the parting of Hannah Green's thighs. I groaned aloud, gritted my teeth, and took deep yogic breaths. After a few desperate minutes I gave up and went naked and half blind into the bathroom to throw up.

It had been several years since my last alcohol hangover and I found I'd lost the knack: instead of cool submission I fought against it, and after I was done being sick I lay crumpled like a chastened teenager on the floor beside the toilet, for a long time, feeling worthless and alone. Then I got up. I put on my eyeglasses, stepped into my moccasins, and tied on my lucky bathrobe, which made me feel somewhat better. Like most beloved items of clothing, this robe had once belonged to somebody else. I'd come upon it years ago, hanging in the upstairs closet of a beach house in Gearhart, Oregon, that Eva B. and I rented for a summer from a Portland family named Knopflmacher. It was an enormous white chenille number, threadbare at the elbows, with pink and red arrangements of embroidered geraniums on the pockets, and I didn't have too much doubt that it had been Mrs. Knopflmacher's. It had since become impossible for me to write wearing anything else. In one of its pockets I now found, to my delight, the charred half of a roach and a book of El Producto matches. I stood at the bedroom window, looking east, smoking the roach down to the last particle of ash and watching the sky for a hint of daylight.

After a few minutes I felt much better indeed, and I went downstairs to the front door for the paper. As I stepped out onto the porch, I saw the noble fins of Happy's Galaxie, poking out from behind the hedge that screened the driveway from the rest of the house. So Crabtree had found his way home, and he was all right: I could hear him snoring now, from all the way back in the guest room. Crabtree had a deviated septum that he was afraid to have a surgeon put right;

he was well known for the resonance of his leonine snore. Crabtree's snoring was loud enough to rattle the glass of water on the nightstand, to ruin his love affairs, to cause violent confrontations with neighbors in cheap motels. It was loud enough to kill bacteria and loosen centuries of dirt from the face of a cathedral. When I came back into the house—the newspaper hadn't arrived yet—I followed the snoring down the hall to Crabtree's room and stood for a while with my ear to his door, listening to the operation of his lungs. Then I went to the kitchen and started coffee.

While the coffee was brewing I drank a tall glass of orange juice, to which I added two tablespoons of honey, on the theory that an increase in my blood sugar, along with a massive dose of caffeine, would eliminate the last traces of my hangover. Pot for the nausea and the heaviness of heart, vitamin C for the cell structure, sugar for the depleted blood, caffeine to burn off the moral fog; it was starting to come back to me now—the whole praxis of alcoholism and reckless living. When the coffee was ready, I poured it into a thermos pitcher and carried it out to my office at the back of the house, where James Leer lay on the sofa, his head pillowed on his praying hands, like someone pantomiming sleep. The sleeping bag had slid partway to the floor and I saw now that he'd gone to bed naked. His suit, shirt, and tie were draped across the footrest of my old Eames chair, white BVDs folded neatly on top of the pile. I wondered if Hannah had undressed him, or if he'd managed it himself. He had the shrunken look of a tall person asleep, curled up into himself, his knees and elbows and wrists too large, his skin pale and freckled. His body had almost no hair and his naked little circumcised johnson was nearly as pale as the rest of him, white as a boy's—perhaps over time one's genitals emerge from the pots and bubbling vats of love permanently stained, like the hands of a wool dyer. I felt sorry for James Leer when I saw his penis. Carefully I redistributed the sleeping bag over his form.

"Thank you," he said, without waking.

I said, "You're welcome," and then carried the pot of coffee over to my desk. It was six-fifteen. I went to work. I had to slap an ending on *Wonder Boys* by tomorrow evening if I was going to let Crabtree see it. I took a sip of coffee and gave my left cheek an exhortatory smack. For the one thousandth time I resorted to the nine-page plot outline, single-spaced, tattered and coffee-stained, that I'd fired off on a vainglorious April morning five years before. As of this fine morning I was halfway through its fourth page, more or less, with another five pages to go. An accidental poisoning, a car crash, a house on fire; the births of three children and a miraculous trotter named Faithless; a theft, an arrest, a trial, an electrocution; a wedding, two funerals, a cross-country trip; two dances, a seduction in a fallout shelter, and a deer hunt; all these scenes and a dozen others I had yet to write, according to the neat headings of my stupid fucking outline: nine central characters' and a lifetime's worth of destiny that I had, for the last month, been attempting to compress into fifty-odd pages of terse and lambent prose. I reread with scorn the confident, pompous annotations I'd made on that distant day: Take your time with this, and This has to be very very big, and, worst of all, This scene should read as a single vast Interstate of Language, three thousand miles long. How I hated the asshole who had written that note!

Once again and with the usual pleasure I entertained the notion of tossing the whole thing out. With this swollen monster out of the way I'd be at liberty to undertake *The Snake Handler,* or the story of the washed-up astronaut who marooned himself in Disney World, or the story of the two doomed baseball teams, blue and gray, playing nine on the eve of Chancellorsville, or *The King of Freestyle,* or any of the dozen other imaginary novels that had fluttered past like admirals and lyrebirds while I labored with my shovel in the ostrich pen of *Wonder Boys.* Then I indulged the equally usual, not quite as pleasurable fantasy of taking Crabtree into my confidence, telling him that I was still years away from finishing *Wonder Boys,* and throwing myself on his mercy. Then I thought of Joe Fahey and, as always, rolled a blank sheet of paper into the machine.

I worked for four hours, typing steadily, lowering myself on a very thin cord into the dank and worm-ridden hole of an ending I'd already tried three times before. This one would oblige me to go back through the previous two-thousand-odd pages to flatten out and marginalize one of the present main characters and to eliminate another entirely, but I thought that of the five false conclusions to the novel I'd come up with in the last month, it was probably my best shot. While I worked I told myself lies. Writers, unlike most people, tell their best lies when they are alone. Ending the book this way, I told myself, would work out for the best; this was in fact the very ending my book had been straining toward all along. Crabtree's visit, viewed properly, was a kind of creative accident, a gift from God, a hammer blow to loosen all the windows my imagination had long since painted shut. I would finish it sometime tomorrow, hand it over to Crabtree, and thus save both our careers.

Every so often I would look up from my humming Selectric with its smell of hot dust and burnt wire—I'd tried to work on a computer but hated the way it turned writing into a kind of cartoon you sat back and watched—to see James

Leer twisting on the spit of his unimaginable dreams. The sound of my typing didn't wake him, or did not, at least, disturb him enough to make him want to get off the couch and move into a quieter part of the house.

Then, as I strapped my family of Wonders into the twin-engine Piper that, on its way to Lowell Wonder's rock-and-roll funeral in New York City, would slam into the impassive face of Weathertop Mountain—such was the ostrich shit I had obliged myself to shovel—I heard a whisper in my ears, like the crackling of soap suds, and a spray of bright static passed across my eyes.

"James!" I said. I clutched at the manuscript of *Wonder Boys* as if grabbing for a baluster, about to tumble headlong down an infinite flight of stairs. When I awakened, no more than a few seconds later, I was lying on the floor, with James Leer frowning over me, wrapped up in his sleeping bag like a B-movie Indian in a buffalo robe.

"I'm fine," I said. "I just lost my balance."

"I put you on the floor," he said. "I was afraid you might, I don't know, swallow your tongue, or something. Are you still drunk?"

I sat up on one elbow and watched as a last yellow meteor streaked across the dome of my skull.

"Of course not," I said.

James Leer nodded, shivered once, and tugged the sleeping bag more snugly around his shoulders. He took a step backward that turned abruptly into a kind of clumsy plié, then steadied himself against the back of my chair.

"I am," he said. The telephone rang, out in the living room. It was a new phone with all the modern functions—caller fragmentation and speed garbling and so on—and it didn't so much ring as sound an alarum, like a Porsche being broken into in the middle of the night. "Want me to get that?"

"Sure," I said, dropping my head back softly to the floor. I was sure that it must be Sara, calling to say not only that her dog was missing but that Walter had been robbed of a twenty-five-thousand-dollar black satin jacket. I closed my eyes, still faintly asparkle with optic fireworks, and wondered if I didn't have something evil inhabiting my brain, a malignant spider opening out its long black legs like the ribs of an umbrella. I asked myself what I would do if my doctor pronounced some fatal diagnosis over me then sent me back out into the wea-selly old world. Would I throw aside my work and concentrate instead on writing my name in water—picking up transvestites on airplanes, seducing sexually ambivalent virgins, driving around Pittsburgh in a borrowed convertible at four o'clock in the morning, looking for trouble? It pleased me for a moment to believe that I would; but in the very next instant I knew that with death in my body my only desire would be to curl up on the Honor Bilt with half a kilo of Afghan Butthair, roll numbers, and watch reruns of *The Rockford Files* until the girl in the black kimono came to take me away.

"Someone named Irv?" said James Leer, padding back into my office, a crooked smirk on his face. I guessed that he was still drunk enough for his hangover to be making him feel all grown up and dissolute. "I told him you might be a minute."

"Thanks," I said. I held out my hand to him, and he helped me to my feet. "Why don't you get yourself some breakfast? There's coffee in the fridge."

He nodded, a little absently, like a boy ignoring his mother's advice, and sat down on the sofa.

"Maybe in a minute," he said. He jerked his head toward

the bookshelf in the corner, on which sat a small television with a built-in VCR. "That thing work?"

"Uh, yeah," I said. I was always a little embarrassed about having a television in my office, even though I would never have watched it when I was supposed to be working. "I use it to look at ball games, sometimes, if Emily's trying to work, or sleep."

"What movies do you have?"

"Movies? Not too many. I don't really collect movies, James." I pointed to the scanty assortment of videocassettes stacked beside the TV set. "I think I still have *9½ Weeks* over there. Taped it off the cable."

James made a face. "*9½ Weeks*," he said. "Please."

"Sorry," I said. I started for the phone, gathering the flaps of my lucky bathrobe around me.

"Nice robe, Professor Tripp," said James.

"It's Irv, Grady," said Emily's father.

"Hello, Irv," I said. "How are you?"

"I could always be better," said Irv. "I'm having a little trouble with my *right* knee, now."

"What's the matter with it?" He'd had the left one replaced the year before, with a stainless steel joint of which he was inordinately proud, as though it were a spontaneous physical improvement produced through the cleverness of his own cells.

"I'm not sure," he said. "But it won't bend until ten o'clock in the morning."

"That could be a problem."

"Terrible," he agreed. "As a matter of fact it just started bending. . . ." There was a pause while he consulted his watch. Irv wore one of those fancy chronometer-style jobs the size of an Oreo cookie, capable not only of telling time, temperature, altitude, and barometric pressure but also of analyzing atmospheric composition and indicating the presence of alien life-forms. He had assembled it himself, out of a kit purchased from the back pages of *Popular Science*. "Twenty-two minutes ago. So, how are you?"

"I'm all right," I said. "I could always be better." I sat down on the pale yellow chintz love seat, patterned with a trellis of climbing red roses, that had forced the old green Honor Bilt into exile in my office. "How's Emily?"

"She's fine. I'd let you speak to her but she isn't here. She's in town with her mother. Doing a little last-minute shopping. Listen, Grady, you know what today is."

"Saturday?"

"Today is *erev pesach*. First night of Passover."

"That's right," I said. "Happy Passover."

"Grady, we're making the Seder tonight."

"I know you are."

"Deborah's here, she got here last night. Phil and Marie are driving up from Aberdeen."

"Uh huh."

"We'll be starting at sundown, of course, which today falls at—just a second." Another pause while, I supposed, he checked his trusty Chronotron 5000. "Six-eighteen."

"Yeah, well," I said, "Irv, listen. I—I have this WordFest thing, you know?" I'd spent a thousand hours in conversation with Irving Warshaw, on subjects that ranged from Mose Allison to dog racing to the tectonic plates underlying the state of Israel, but I'd never said a single word to him about the secret geologic forces that deformed the state of my marriage to his daughter. Irv saw no point in the discussion of human feelings: he was sad at funerals, proud of Israel, disappointed in his children, happy on the Fourth of July. He had no idea how crazy I was about him. "We do it every year."

"I know what it is," he said.

"Right, so anyway I have, you know, a lot of seminars to attend, and lectures, and all that." I was on the point of telling him that I had a lecture to deliver, but I stopped myself. Although I certainly didn't always tell him the truth, I'd never lied to Emily's father about anything, either. "I just don't think I'm going to be able to get away."

"No," he said. "That makes sense."

His voice sounded a little hollow.

"You okay, Irv?"

"I'm fine," he said. "You know. Pesach. It always falls on the day after the—the anniversary—of Sam. Of his death."

I had forgotten this unfortunate coincidence of lunar dates, though of course it recurred every year in spite of the fact that Sam had drowned sometime at the very end of April.

"Aw," I said. I clucked my tongue. "His *yahrzeit*. Isn't that it?"

"That's it," said Irv. "We lit the candle last night."

"I'm sorry, Irv," I said.

In response Irv made a kind of interrogative half grunt that sounded like the equivalent of an irritated shrug, as if to say, What are you sorry for?

"So," he said, after a moment, letting out the word like a sigh. "All right."

"All right, Irv," I said. Suddenly I felt that I might never speak to him again.

"Grady, my friend," said Irv. I caught the tiny fissure of grief that had opened in his voice.

"Buddy," I said, "did Emily know that you were going to be calling me?"

"Yes. She didn't want me to."

"Well, I'm glad that you did."

"Yes, I—well. I really hoped to see you at our table this evening."

"I'd love to be there," I said. "I wish that I could. I just don't think that it would be right."

"You have your conference."

"That's right."

"I understand."

"Love to everyone," I said.

When I went back into my office, I found James Leer sitting on the sofa, his legs drawn up into the tent of his sleeping bag, watching something black-and-white on TV; the sound was turned all the way down. When I walked in, he looked at me for a moment without seeming to know who I was. The blood had drained from his cheeks, his jaw hung slack, and his eyes were bleary with something that looked almost like sorrow. He was feeling his hangover now.

"You have *9½ Weeks* and *Year of the Dragon*," he said, as if these were not movies but scabies and mange. "And that's it."

"I like that Mickey Rourke," I said. "So what's this you're watching?"

"*Lured,*" he said automatically. "1947. Douglas Sirk."

"How come you have the sound down?"

He shrugged. "I know what they're saying," he said.

I squinted at the screen.

"That wouldn't be poor old George Sanders, again, would it?"

He nodded, and swallowed, hard.

"Are you all right, James?"

"What am I doing here?"

"What do you mean?"

"How did I get here?"

"We brought you here last night. None of us was in good enough shape to get you all the way to Mt. Lebanon."

We watched for a moment while George Sanders lit himself a long white cigarette. I looked over at the imperturbable stack of paper on my desk, at the six new sheets lying scattered beside it, covered in useless black words.

"Did I do anything last night?" he said.

"What do you mean?"

"Anything bad."

"Well, James," I said. "You stole Marilyn Monroe's nuptial jacket out of Dr. Gaskell's closet. How about that?"

There was a knock at the door, three deliberate taps, like someone testing the wood for evidence of dry rot. I looked at James. George Sanders raised a flashing monocle to his eye.

"Someone's at the door," I said.

It was a policeman, bearing an apologetic smile and the morning's rolled-up *Post-Gazette*. He was a young guy, not much older than James Leer. Like James he was tall and pale, with a sharp, mobile Adam's apple. His cheeks were a mass of tiny nicks and missed whiskers, and he was wearing some kind of sugary, varsity-halfback aftershave. His hat was a quarter size too large for his head. He had the young cop's way of standing with his chest poked out, speaking too quickly, as though rattling off, to a mock civilian, sample dialogue memorized from the training manual, at the threshold of a simulated house. His name tag said PUPCIK. I didn't ask him in.

"I'm sorry to bother you, Professor Tripp," he said. "I'm investigating a break-in at the Gaskells' house last night, and I have a couple of questions."

"Surely," I said, filling up the doorway with my frame. "What can I do for you?"

"There was a break-in at the Gaskells' house last night."

"Uh huh."

"They're friends of yours."

"Good friends," I said.

"Anyway, I understand there was some kind of party-type event at their house last night? And that you were one of the last to leave?"

"I guess I was."

"Okay, good." Officer Pupcik looked pleased with himself. Things were starting to add up. "And did you see anything? Anyone hanging around, or something, that maybe you didn't really know them?"

"I don't believe so." I looked up at the sky and bit my lip. I was thinking it over. I wanted him to know that. "No, uh-uh."

Officer Pupcik's eyebrows gathered in disappointment over his nose.

"Oh," he said.

"What'd they get?"

"What's that? Oh. They got into Dr. Gaskell's collection."

"Oh no."

"Yeah. Damn," he said, deviating somewhat from his script, "he has some pretty cool stuff." I agreed with this assessment. "Anyway, looks like they picked the lock on his vault." He shrugged. "Oh, and the dog's missing."

"That's weird."

"I know it. We figure he must have let him out. The perpetrator, I mean. He's blind and we figure he just wandered off and maybe got run over."

"The perpetrator."

"No, the dog."

"Just kidding," I said.

He nodded, then cocked his head and gave me a sharp, policemanlike look, as though realizing that he had been on the wrong page with me all along. I fell under the heading of Dealing with Assholes.

"Well," I said. "I hope you find him. Them. Good luck."

"Well, thanks. Okay." Officer Pupcik simulated a smile. "That's all, then. I won't trouble you anymore."

"If I think of anything—"

"Yes, that's right. If you think of anything, give us a call. Here." He reached into the pocket of his shirt and handed me a business card. He started to turn away, then stopped and looked back at me. "Oh," he said, "about this kid, this, uh, Leer. James Leer."

"He's a student of mine."

"That's what I understand. Do you know how I could get in touch with him, by any chance?"

"I think he lives with his aunt, out in Mt. Lebanon," I said. "I might have his number in my office on campus, if you need it."

He watched me for a few seconds, pulling at the lobe of his right ear as if trying to hear all over again all the things I'd just told him.

"That's all right," he said at last. "It can wait until Monday."

"Whatever you say."

He went down the steps to his car.

"That's a nice one," he said, nodding toward the Galaxie

in the drive. There was an odd look of pain on his face as he gazed over there, and he shook his big angular head. "Poor thing."

I had no idea what he was talking about. You would have thought he'd seen through the steel of my trunk to the body of Doctor Dee lying within.

"Uh huh," I said, closing the door. "Whatever."

I went back into the living room and looked at James. There was a sudden swell of accordion music in a distant part of the house, and then, in the next instant, a sharp series of hacks and expostulations as Crabtree coughed his way through the first cigarette of the morning. I had a sudden image of Irv Warshaw, standing by the telephone in the downstairs hall of the farmhouse, scrolling hopelessly through the functions of his watch, and I was seized with a powerful longing to put my arms around him, to brush his rough cheek against mine, to sit down to eat the bread of affliction with him and with Emily and all of the Warshaws. They weren't my family and it wasn't my holiday, but I was orphaned and an atheist and I would take what I could get.

"What do we do now?" said James.

The telephone sounded its mad alarm, and I limped slowly out to meet it.

"It's me," said Sara. "Oh, Grady, I'm so glad you're there. So many bad things are happening at once."

"Could you just hold on a minute, honey?" I said, before I hung up the phone. I walked back into my office, and switched off the television.

"How about we get the fuck out of here?" I said.

I loaned James Leer a flannel shirt and a pair of blue jeans, and pulled on my crusty old back-country boots. I dug my fisherman's vest out of the back of my closet. There was a stained little twist of weed in one of its nine pockets, which I gratefully consumed. Then I packed a canvas shopping bag with a thermos full of coffee, a bottle of Coke, a box of raisins, four hard-boiled eggs, a green banana, and half a pepperoni pizza, wrapped in foil, that I unearthed at the back of the refrigerator. For good measure I threw in a package of wieners, I suppose in case our journey included campfires, a jar of hot salad peppers, and a pickle spear wrapped in waxed paper left over from some long-ago bag lunch of Emily's. I filled the pockets of my vest with pens, rolling papers, a cigarette lighter, a ruled notebook, a Swiss Army knife, AAA maps of Idaho and Mexico, and several other potentially useful items that I found in the drawer by the kitchen telephone. I grabbed an old Navajo blanket and a flashlight from the closet in the hall. I had slipped into that familiar marijuana state which lies between happiness and utter panic, and my heart was pounding. I felt as if James and I were setting out together to fish for steelhead in a flashing Idaho stream, and at the same time that we were lighting out for Tampico with a ten-minute head start on the police.

"See you," I called out, as I abandoned my troubled house to its inmates.

It had been raining, it seemed, since February, but on this *erev pesach* the sun was shining. The sky was so blue that it pealed in my ears like a bell. Steam rose from the lawn and from the long black flower beds that lined the front walk. There were swollen pink buds on the camellia bushes, beaded with rain, and I thought I smelled an early hint of the mysterious bittersweet gas that fills Pittsburgh in the summertime, a smell at once industrial and aboriginal, river water and sulfur dioxide, burning tires and the coat of a fox. I put my hand on the Swiss Army knife in my pocket and looked out at the morning with a caffeine quiver of hope in my spine and at the tips of my fingers. Then we went down the walk to the driveway, and I saw a kind of crater in the hood of my car, a lopsided asterisk of wrinkles and pleats. *Poor thing.*

"How did that happen?" said James, running a fingertip along the jagged lip of the wound. A long flake of paint peeled away and curled around his finger like a scrap of green ribbon. "Oops."

"Shit," I said. "I don't believe it." It had completely slipped my mind. I closed my eyes. A shadow danced in a rainy smear of light, then leapt into the air and flew toward my windshield. There was the muffled rumor of a kettledrum.

"And he landed on his butt," said James.

"That's right," I said. "How can you tell?"

James Leer looked at me, then back at the hood of the Galaxie. He shrugged.

"You can see the outline of a butt," he said, and then threw his canvas knapsack into the car.

As I backed us out of the driveway, I narrowly missed destroying Happy Blackmore's Galaxie once and for all. I'd noticed the white delivery van when we came out of the house, creeping along Denniston as its driver read addresses off the housefronts, but I hadn't bothered to look for it again before I went barreling down the driveway, doing at least twenty;

you had to go fast when the car was in reverse, or she had a tendency to stall out. At the last possible instant I saw the flash of white in my rearview mirror, a pair of airbrushed punching prizefighters, ƧᗡOOƆ ƆᴎITЯOqƧ Ƨ'ꓘINAVAЯꓘ. I hit the brakes. The driver of the van floored it and pulled wildly away.

"Jesus," I said. "*I'm* off to a good start."

"Why don't you put the top down?" James suggested. "Maybe that'll make it easier to see."

I blushed, and reached up to unlatch the roof.

"I keep forgetting I can do this," I said.

On the way out of town we stopped at the Giant Eagle on Murray, and James, having turned up his nose at my stock of provisions, picked up sixty-four ounces of orange juice, a package of powdered industrial doughnuts, and a copy of *Entertainment Weekly*. It featured an article on the Fonda family of actors and there was a large photograph of handsome Henry on the cover, in a scene taken from what James at once identified as *Drums Along the Mohawk*.

"God," he pronounced, solemnly, holding out the magazine for me to see.

"He was all right," I said.

I picked up a dozen red roses in the flower department, and wrapped the stems carefully in wet paper towels from the bathroom so that they wouldn't die on the way. There was a condom machine bolted to the wall of the men's room, and I dropped fifty cents on something called a Luv-O-Pus that promised to entangle my partner in undulating tentacles of pleasure. We got stuck in a long checkout line and to pass the time I was going to show James Leer the Luv-O-Pus, but at the last minute I decided against it; I had a feeling that such an article might frighten him. While we waited to pay he downed the entire bottle of orange juice. He worked his pointy little Adam's apple up and down.

"I'm so thirsty," he said, wiping his mouth with the back of a hand. "I don't know what's the matter with me."

I laughed. "Shit, James, you're hungover."

He considered this a moment, then nodded.

"It feels kind of sad," he said.

As we drove out Bigelow I kept my eyes off the ruined hood of Happy's car and tried to put the damage, and all that it seemed to say about the way I was conducting my life, out of my mind. The top was down and I listened to the hiss of the wheels against the street, the flow of wind over the car, the sound of Stan Getz blowing faintly from the speakers and trailing out into the air behind us like a pearly strand of bubbles from a pipe. It was no use. The outline of a butt rode forever out before me, like an identifying badge.

"I thought we were going to talk to the Chancellor," said James, unhopefully, as we headed farther and farther away from Point Breeze.

"We were," I said. I looked at the flowers on the seat beside me. A gallant gesture, I thought, was the first expedient of a guilty conscience. Why did I think that Emily would be anything but sorry to see my haggard face and my odorless grocery-store roses? In any event at James's reminder the flock of guilty feelings that wheels perpetually in the chest of every pothead alighted now on Sara's roof. Had I actually *hung up* on her? Was I really leaving town with her dead dog in my trunk? "Yeah, uh, you know, maybe this isn't such a hot idea, James. Maybe we ought to turn around."

James didn't say anything. He was jammed up against his door, wrapped in his stained overcoat, knees up, elbows in, two quarts of orange juice joggling around inside him, holding on to a still-intact powdered doughnut as if it were the only ballast keeping him pinned to his seat in my car and to the spinning globe beneath us. He was miserable. Every time we went over a bump, his head wavered back and forth like the needle of a sensitive gauge. I kept heading down Bigelow, but more and more slowly as we got closer to the parkway, thinking now of Sara, now of Emily and her parents, until I reached a point of utter volitional equipoise or collapse, and we came to a red light.

"Look at them," said James. "They look like replicants."

A handsome young family was crossing the street in front of us, a slender pair of blond parents in khaki and plaid surrounded by an orderly tangle of cute blond replicant children. Two of the children swung sparkling bags of goldfish. The sun lit the flyaway ends of their hair. Everyone was holding hands. They looked like an advertisement for a brand of mild laxative or the Seventh-Day Adventists. The mother carried a golden-haired baby in her arms and the father was actually smoking a briar pipe. As they passed before the car they all looked at the crater in the hood and then gazed up at James and me in uncomprehending pity.

"The light's green," said James.

I had my eye on that baby. Its face was pressed against the woman's left breast, and it was waving its hands around in the air in a declamatory manner. Its fingers curled and uncurled and struck odd poses like the significant fingers of a stone bodhisattva. For an instant I could feel the weight of it, like an ache, in the hollow of my arm.

"We can go now, Professor."

The person in the car behind us began to honk. As the family stepped up onto the far sidewalk, just before they glided off away from us, I glimpsed the baby's face, over the

mother's shoulder. It wore an oddly crooked grin—almost as
if a muscle in its cheek were paralyzed—and a little black eye
patch over its left eye. I liked that. I wondered if I had it in me
to produce a baby with a piratical air.

"Professor?"

I did a one-eighty in the intersection and headed back toward Point Breeze.

As we pulled up in front of the Gaskells' house, I looked over
at James. The wind had blown back all his sticky black hair so
that his bangs stood straight up from his head, which gave him
a cartoon air of having just received a piece of shocking news.
I saw his eyelids flutter. The doughnut slipped from his fingers. His surprised head tilted backward and lodged in the
space between the headrest and the window. I figured he was
faking unconsciousness to get out of having to face Chancellor Gaskell, but I didn't hold that against him. After all, I'd
promised—though I doubted if he really believed me—that I
would take care of everything.

"Okay, then," I told James, climbing out of the car. "You
wait here."

There was no answer when I knocked on the front door, so
I gave the handle a try. It was unlocked.

"Sara?" I stepped inside. "Walter?"

In the kitchen there was coffee on the stove, and on the
table Sara's huge iron purse, a package of Merits, and a paperback copy of one of Q.'s novels, squashed open over a pink
Bic lighter. She was home, all right. I walked back out to the
front hall, and started up the stairs.

"Sara? It's Gra-dy! Hello?"

Expecting at any minute to be jumped in a dark corner by an enraged Walter Gaskell swinging one of Joltin' Joe's old Hillerich & Bradsbys, I stuck my head into Sara's office, the guest room, and the other upstairs rooms, and then went at last to the door of the master bedroom, where I had passed an hour just a little too recently and stupidly, I felt, to be visiting again so soon. The door was ajar, and, flinching a little, I gave it a light tap with the toe of my shoe. It swung open with a guilty creak.

"Sara?"

The bed lay buried in its trackless snowdrift of goose-down and linen. A clock ticked on the nightstand. Two pairs of slippers, one plaid, one lavender, sat side by side on the rug. The cork-lined door hung wide open and Walter's magic closet was bare; doubtless his collection had been evacuated to a safe place. Without looking down at the spot where Doctor Dee had met his fate I held my breath and stepped, as if stepping over the corpse of an Alaskan malamute, into the room. A pair of large casement windows overlooked the driveway, and I could see James Leer in the Galaxie, head lolling to one side, eyes closed, mouth open. He looked as if he really were asleep. I crossed the room to a pair of windows in the opposite wall and peered out into the backyard, beyond the ruined railbed where last night James had stood scratching at his temple with the muzzle of his gun, to Sara's little garden and, beyond that, to the big fancy greenhouse imported three years ago from France. After a moment I could make out a shadow stooping and then rising behind the steamy panes of glass.

As I went out of the bedroom I held my breath and took a look down at the rug under my feet, by the door. There was a small burnt circle as if someone had dropped a cigarette, alongside some dark brownish flecks like gravy spots on a shirtfront. Part of the circle, and no doubt some of the gravy spots, were missing where a sample had been cut from the Berber carpeting, exposing an isosceles triangle of pale green pad underneath. I poked at the blackened spot with the tip of my shoe for a moment, then went down to see Sara, in her garden, to let her know what the Pittsburgh police lab technician was going to report.

Sara's garden was rather small, some thirty feet by twenty, enclosed on all four sides by a low fence of white pickets backed with chicken wire. There were eight or nine beds, full of rich black humus, bordered by irregular red bricks set in rows half buried in the ground. Among the beds ran paths of the same brick, set into an underlayer of fine gravel, in a herringbone pattern. An uncle of Sara's, one of her father's brothers, had salvaged the bricks from the demolition of Forbes Field. The beds had been cleared out and plowed under last fall. The vines on the spindly trellises were thin and skeletal, the spigots had been wrapped with plastic and taped against frost, and the roses that ran along either side of the central alley had been cut back severely. There were a few prunish apples dangling from the apple tree, and I thought I saw the collapsed black remains of a pumpkin in one corner. Although I knew Sara had already done some spring planting, the garden looked empty and dead to me.

I walked along the brick path to the little glass building, swallowing, clearing my throat, my heart ringing hard against my breastbone. I felt certain that when I left Sara's greenhouse, having told her what I had brought myself here to say, I would never be coming back. The greenhouse was a miniature palace of glass, speckled with dew, fifteen or twenty feet tall. It was built on the plan of a Greek cross and had a high central atrium, with a peaked, hipped roof like a glass steeple. The framework was metal and wood, painted the dark green of an outfield wall. The windows were fogged but I could make out a dozen shades of green within.

I tapped on the door and it rattled under my hand.

"Sara? It's Grady."

I heard her say something that after a moment I reconstructed as a terse invitation to enter.

A jet of cool air carried me through the door, as though the greenhouse were breathing me in. The floor was gravel and my footsteps crunched and echoed off the high glass ceiling. It was so warm inside that I immediately began to sweat, and so fragrant as to be almost malodorous. I smelled potting soil and freesias, basil and rainwater, rotten wood, rubber hoses, moss, and a faint chlorine tang like an indoor pool. A thousand plants stretched out into all four arms of the greenhouse, spread across low benches, in orderly rows, sporting all manner of fronds, tendrils, and bracts, from cacti and miniature roses in pots to boxes full of tiny seedlings to a big round gardenia bush in a Mexican urn. The back part of the greenhouse was hung with fluorescent lights that cast their wide spectra over planters filled with zinnia, alyssum, phlox, and over a box of sweet pea vines that Sara had trained to climb through the empty mullions of a salvaged French door. In the central atrium, in a terra-cotta pot the size of a Volkswagen Beetle, stood a six-foot date palm, and beside it a worn purple davenport crowned with a bunch of carved grapes.

"I can't believe you hung up on me, you dick."

Sara came in from the cactus room, looking not entirely sorry to see me. She had on her gardening boots, big, steel-toed, motor-head butt kickers, black as stovepipes, scuffed and muddied and beat to shit, and a cracked old leather coat of some indeterminate color between olive and buff. It was creased and split and mud-spattered, had belt loops but no belt, and its fur-trimmed collar looked as though it had been lovingly chewed by a dog. It had belonged to her father. There was a fat paperback peeking out of the jacket's hip pocket—in case of emergency, I supposed. Underneath the coat she wore a mechanic's blue jumpsuit. Her hair was tied up in a black and green plaid scarf and as she crossed the atrium toward me she was tugging at the fingers of a pair of canvas gloves.

"Uh oh," I said, "the gloves are off."

"I hate you," she said, putting her arms around me.

"I hate you, too," I said.

We stood for a moment, holding on to each other, listening to the humming of the exhaust fans and the ticking of the heaters and the restless suspiration of the plants.

"Walter?" I said at last.

"He's there." She nodded in the general direction of campus. "But he's a basket case," she said. "We were robbed last night, Grady. They took his jacket. Marilyn's jacket. And Dee's missing."

"I heard."

She stepped away from me. "How did you hear?"

"Oh." I dropped my hands to my sides and they hung there, feeling empty and boneless. "A policeman came to talk to me this morning."

"Did you confess?"

I made myself laugh. "Actually," I said. "That's why I came to see you."

"To confess?" She gave me a sharp poke in the belly and then sat down on the purple davenport. I sat down heavily beside her. "Bad Grady." Lightly she slapped each of my cheeks with the gloves. Bad. Grady. "Your fingerprints were everywhere."

"They were?" I felt my throat tighten. "That was fast."

"I'm kidding. Hello? Kidding?"

"Ha," I said.

"Aren't I kidding, Grady?"

"Sure you are."

"What are you doing?" she asked me, looking me over. "You look like you're going camping."

"I'm going out to Kinship."

"Kinship? To see Emily?" She patted at the breast pocket of her jumpsuit, looking for cigarettes, then lowered her hand to her lap. She did not permit herself to smoke in the greenhouse. "Why? Did she call you?"

"Her father did."

"Her father."

"He invited me to their Seder. It's the first night of Passover tonight."

"Is it. I see."

"Sara."

"That's fine. No, that's really *nice*. You should be there."

"Baby—"

"No, I'm serious. They're your family. They're like a family to you. You've told me that many times."

"It's not that," I said. "I mean, I haven't, uh, decided anything yet. I'm not going up there to, you know, reconcile with Emily."

"Aren't you?"

"No."

"Are you going up there *not* to reconcile with her?"

"Well—yeah, yes, sort of. I don't know."

"I *want* you to know, Grady."

"I know."

"Now. I would like for you to decide." She patted again at the empty breast pocket. "I'm sorry, I don't mean to pressure you, but I need to know. If you're going to stay with Emily, and her family, and I think you ought to, that's a very commendable decision, then I want you to tell me that. If you're planning to go up there to Kinship and tell Emily about you and me and this baby, then I want to know that, too. If you're planning to leave Emily for me, although I certainly couldn't advise you to do that, think of the complications all this is going to cause me on my end, then I also would want to know that."

"Yes," I said.

"Yes, what?" said Sara.

I licked my lips. "I want to be with you," I said. I was not in the least certain whether I meant what I said, nor just what the implications of this statement might be, but since I intended to follow it with a tale of dog slaughter, grand theft, and an accounting of the contents of my trunk I figured it was the safest way to start. "Sara—"

"Oh, Grady," said Sara. She kissed me. We fell backward on the purple davenport, and she pressed herself against me.

"I started this garden right around the same time I fell in love with you," she said, in an incantatory, almost childish tone of voice, lying crooked against me. "It was in April. There was nothing out here. Just bare ground and dead grass. I was the same way really. Then one day I came out here to find a flower or something to put in a note to you."

She paused, and I realized she was waiting for me to take my cue. She gave my shoulder an impatient shake.

"The crocuses," I said.

"I walked out into the yard and there were crocuses everywhere. I still don't know where they came from, or who planted them. I asked you to drive me out to that equipment rental place on the South Side. It was our second date."

"It was on Opening Day."

"You liked it that I let you listen to the ball game. I got that rototiller thing and I plowed under the whole field. Then I had them come in with all that horseshit. The ground steamed for a week. Then I put up the fence. I built the beds. I planted spinach and broccoli and wax beans."

"I remember," I said.

"You're going to tell Emily about us," she said, in the same dreamy voice. She reached for my right hand and laid it atop the modest dome of her belly. "About this."

I lay on my side, looking up at the tangled iron lace of the roof over our heads. I saw that Sara, alone in a frail canoe, was drifting nearer and nearer to the roaring misty cataract of motherhood, and that she now believed I was right behind her, in the stern, madly paddling. I searched my feelings, an activity never far removed from looking for a dead rat in a spidery crawl space under the house. I was appalled to see, after five years' exposure to the unstable isotopes of my love, how many of her hopes Sara Gaskell still entrusted to me; how much of her faith there remained for me to shatter. How could I tell her the terrible things I had to tell her? Your dog is dead. You have to get an abortion.

"I'll tell Emily," I said. After a moment I took my hand from her belly, kissed her cheek, and then hauled myself to my feet. "I'd better get going. I left James Leer sitting out in the car."

"James Leer? What's he doing out in the car? Is he all right?"

"He's fine," I said. "He's sleeping off a mighty hangover, is all. I told him I'd only be a few minutes. I didn't know—"

"Are you taking him with you? Out to Kinship?"

"That's right," I said. "He's not too interested in Word-Fest, I guess, and I felt like I could use the company."

"Especially for the ride back, eh?" said Sara.

"Especially that," I said.

I kissed Sara good-bye. Then I let the greenhouse breathe me out.

When I got back to the car James slowly opened one eye and looked at me, as though afraid to expose any more of himself than this moist and bloodshot half inch to the perils of waking life.

"Well?" he mumbled as I climbed in. "Did you tell her?"

"Tell her what?" I said.

James nodded and closed the eye again. I settled back against the seat and reached out to adjust the sideview mirror, which stuck for an instant, then snapped off completely. I tossed it into the backseat, along with the roses. Then I gunned the Galaxie's addled engine, put her in reverse, and we hurtled, backward and blind, up the driveway, at forty miles per hour.

I intended to let James sleep the whole way to Kinship, if he needed it, but about ten minutes out of Pittsburgh I inadvertently dropped us into a deep pothole, and with the ensuing jolt he gasped, sat up, and looked around him.

"I'm sorry," he said, his eyes wide. He sounded very sincere, the way people do before they have fully awakened.

WONDER BOYS

"That's all right," I said. "Hey, you have that doughnut in your lap."

He looked down at the doughnut and nodded.

"Where are we? How long was I asleep?"

"Not very long. We're still making our way through the 'burbs."

This response seemed unaccountably to worry him. He looked out over his door, then mine, at the tame woods and high fences and pseudo-English chimney pots poking out over the trees, then craned around in his seat and looked behind us. I wondered if he were not still asleep and dreaming. But all at once he seemed very much awake, tapping his foot to the music on the radio, fingertipping out a little $1\frac{1}{4}$ time on the dash. He adjusted the angle of the remaining side mirror, fiddled with the door handle, rolled up his window, then rolled it down again. He picked up the doughnut, which had fallen into his lap, and brought it to his lips, then without taking a bite replaced it in the neat white ring it had left on the fabric of his overcoat. As far as I'd ever seen, James Leer was not a fidgety person, so I figured he was trying to keep his mind off feeling sick.

"You all right?" I said.

"Sure. Fine." He looked startled, as though I'd caught him thinking impure thoughts. "Why do you ask?"

"You seem a little jumpy," I said.

"Nah," he said, shaking his head, looking innocent of jumpiness at this or any other moment of his life heretofore. He picked up the doughnut, stared at it a moment, set it back down. "I'm feeling really great. I'm feeling, I don't know. Normal."

"Glad to hear it," I said. I wondered if perhaps it were all dawning on him at last; if he were beginning to realize that, having engaged, the night before, in activities as diverse as being dragged bodily and giggling from a crowded auditorium, committing grand larceny, and getting a hand job in a public place, he was now on his way to spend Passover, of all things, with the family of his dissolute professor's estranged wife, in a dented Ford Galaxie within whose trunk lay the body of a dog he had killed.

"Do you want not to do this, James?" I said, sounding more hopeful than I'd intended. "Do you want us to go back?"

"Do you?"

"Do I? No! Why would I want to go back?"

"I don't know," he said, looking a little startled.

"Buddy, this was my idea, remember? No, hey, I'm looking forward to this. I mean it. Passover. Really. Do the Ten Plagues. Eat a lot of parsley. Seriously, I'm glad I have to go out there."

"Why do you have to?"

"You know what I mean."

"Uh huh," he said uncertainly. "No, sir, I don't want to go back, either." Once again he checked his mirror, angling it one way, then another, as though worried someone might be following us.

"See any police cars?" I said.

He looked at me for a second or two and then decided I was kidding.

"Not yet," he said weakly.

"Listen," I said. "It's all right. I kind of lost my nerve a little back there, with the Chancellor, but, uh, we'll straighten everything out when we get back to town tonight. I swear. Okay? Anyway, they're an interesting family, the Warshaws. I think you're going to like them a lot."

"Okay," he said, as if I'd just given him an order. He did look like he was going to be sick.

"It's all that orange juice you drank," I told him. "Want me to pull over?"

"No."

"We're in Sewickley Heights. We could find you a nice golf course to puke on."

"*No.*" He chopped at the dashboard with both hands. The glove compartment popped open and the bag of marijuana tumbled out. He grabbed at it and started to stuff it back inside, but then he must have felt foolish, or unsophisticated, because the next instant he gave up trying to replace it, and just held the Ziploc bag, rolled up, between two fingers, like a fat translucent joint. He was blushing, or at least the skin at his ears and the nape of his neck turned red. "Please," he said. "I'm fine. Just keep driving."

"Hey, buddy, if you—"

"I'm sorry, Professor Tripp," he said. "I just hate this fucking place." I was surprised to hear him swear. Such language never appeared in his work; in fact it was almost artificially absent, even in the rawest and most twisted of his tales, as if, in the miniature Hollywood of his soul, he felt constrained to pass all his productions before a kind of inner Hays Office. "Se*wick*ley. What a bunch of, I don't know, rich—rich bastards." He looked down at his lap. "I feel sorry for them."

"You mean you wouldn't like to be a rich bastard?" I said.

"No," said James, unrolling the Baggie along his right thigh; the left thigh was still occupied by the uneaten dough-nut. "Rich people are never happy."

"Aren't they?"

"No," said James, gravely. "I mean, people with *no* money

haven't got much of a shot at happiness in life, either, of course. But rich people, I think, have, like, *none*."

"Unless they *buy* it," I said, but I marveled, once again, at James's *youngness*, appalled and envious, in the manner of a dead-armed old pitcher watching a balky phenom throw wild, terrible smoke, mistake pitches and foolish pitches and pitches that went all over the place. "That's a pretty original theory you have, I must say. 'Rich people are never happy.' I think *Citizen Kane* would've been a lot more interesting, you know, if they could have worked that theme in somehow."

"Okay," he said. "I get your point."

"Hey, don't look now, but I think one of your rich Sewickley Heights bastards likes you."

"What?" He stuffed the bag of dope under his thigh. A woman in a green Miata had pulled alongside my car. She was a good-looking blonde, no older than James, in a pair of black skier's sunglasses. She had her own top down and the wind was doing wild things to the ends of her sporty yellow hair. As she scooted past us she gave James a big smile, raised a hand, and nodded. James looked away.

"Friend of yours?" I said, watching as the girl, passing us, noticed the outline of Vernon Hardapple's butt in my hood.

"I don't know her," James said. "I swear."

"I believe you," I said.

We drove on for a time without speaking. After a little while James fished the Baggie out from under his thigh and snapped it open. He lowered his face down into the mouth of the bag, and inhaled.

"Smells like good stuff," he said, in a tone of expertise.

"And how would you know that?" I said. "I thought you didn't *do* pot. Didn't like to lose control of your emotions."

He blushed again, I supposed because he was aware that last

night, if he'd lost any further control of his emotions, he would have been careering down the middle of Centre Avenue emitting blue nuclear fire from his nostrils and trying to kick over parked cars.

"It's 'cause of my father," he said, after a moment. "He smokes it. He gets it from his doctor."

I said, "From his doctor? Is he sick?"

He nodded. "He has—my father has cancer. Of the colon."

"Jesus, James," I said. "Shit, buddy, that's too bad."

"Yeah, well. So I guess the chemotherapy makes him feel really sick. Too sick to do anything. Too sick to even go out for a walk. His business started failing. The trout pens, you know. Started getting all scummy and stuff." He shook his head, looking sad and faintly disgusted, as if recollecting the iridescent shimmer of decay on the surface of his father's fishponds. "So anyway, his doctor prescribed, you know." He gave the bag a little shake. "Want me to roll you a reefer? I do it for my dad."

"You have to *roll* them? Really? I thought that U.S. government dope was all machined and perfect. Like real cigarettes. That's what I've heard."

"Not my dad's," said James, furrowing his brow. "No. It always comes loose, in a Baggie like this."

I shrugged. We drove past the remnants of a collapsed barn, on whose roof there still faded an advertisement for Red Man, and then, immediately afterward, the sign that said we were seventy-five miles from the exit you took for Kinship, PA. I felt my heart squeeze, and something tightened up within me, as though an innermost cinch had been yanked.

"Well, sure, then," I said. "Go ahead and roll me one. If you want." I reached into my vest and fished out the little pack of Zig-Zags. "Here you go. Try not to let it all blow away, though."

He lowered the glove compartment lid again, spread a rolling paper flat across it, pinched off a small bud from the bag, dropped it into the pleat. He zipped shut the Baggie and set it under his thigh. An eddy of wind curled around the sheet of rolling paper and sent it sailing across the surface of the glove compartment lid.

"Careful," I said, "Look out, man. That stuff has to last me a long time." As I reached out to catch the skittering paper bateau I let go of the steering wheel and we bumped up onto the shoulder of the road, then off. "Jesus."

"Sorry," he said, retrieving the scattered elements of the joint. He looked at me, then started to roll up the bud, intact, as if it were a little gift he was wrapping up to give to me.

"No, James, you have to break it *up,* a little, or the thing isn't going to draw." I looked at him. "I thought you said you knew how to do it."

"I do," said James, sounding so injured that I decided just to leave him alone. I shrugged and stared ahead at the meandering black river of Pennsylvania highway I'd navigated with Emily so many times before, and which was in many ways the principal thoroughfare of her life. Driving past the red, black, and ocher towns, with their muddy baseball fields, their onion domes, their pancake houses and rusting rail yards, she marked the transit of summers and holidays, school years, birthday weekends, anniversaries, flights from the upsets and dissolutions of her romantic life in Pittsburgh. Like most women I'd known, Emily had suffered in the course of her relationships through a remarkable run of what men are pleased to call bad luck. I was not the first betrayer to come chasing after her up Route 79, with questionable intentions.

"Here," said James, handing me a lumpy but serviceable joint. "How's that?"

"Perfect," I said, and he smiled. "Thanks." I handed him my lighter, and both of us noticed that my fingers were trembling. "Could you fire it up for me, buddy?"

"All right," he said, uncertainly. "How—how are you feeling, Professor? You seem a little *jumpy* yourself." He stuck the joint between his lips and drew on it, then passed it across to me.

"I'm fine," I said. I took a long slow toke and watched the wind carry it all away when I exhaled. "I guess I might be a little nervous about going up to see my wife."

"She's really mad at you?"

"She ought to be."

He nodded.

"She's pretty," he said. "I saw her pictures in your office. Is she, what—Chinese?"

"Korean. She's adopted. Her folks adopted three Korean kids."

"Did they have any of their own?"

"One," I said. "A son. Sam. He died pretty young. Actually today's the anniversary of his death. Or yesterday. I forget how it works, with the moon, and all. They light a little candle and it burns for twenty-four hours."

He thought that over for a while, and I smoked the lumpy cigarette he'd rolled me. He'd neglected to comb out the seeds, and every so often one popcorned and spat ash across my vest. We flew past Zelienople and Ellwood City and Slippery Rock. The number of possible exits from the shrinking stretch of highway between Emily and me grew smaller, one by one, and I began seriously to regret having undertaken this journey. However badly I might want to immerse myself in her loud, sloppy, jumbled up, all-surviving family, there was no good reason not to believe that the greatest kindness I could do to Emily right now would be just to leave her alone. I had hurt her badly already and it was going to be worse when she learned that Sara was pregnant. Because she and I, for a couple of years, had tried to have a baby of our own. She was getting older and I was getting older and at the center of our marriage there was a small and all-consuming hole. When our initial efforts failed, we tried doctors and thermometers and an obsessive study of the monthly behavior of Emily's eggs, visited a special clinic, began looking into adoption. And then one day, almost magically, without ever discussing it, we just gave up. I sighed. I could feel James's eyes upon me.

"Do you think she's going to be glad to see you?" he said. "Your wife, I mean."

"No," I said. "I do not."

He nodded.

"Passover," he said, after a moment. "That's the one where you don't get to eat any bread."

"That's the one."

"What about doughnuts?"

"They're out, too, I'd imagine."

He handed me a sinker from the package and took up the one that had been languishing in his lap all this time. The blast of weed must have awakened his appetite. We took big bites and chewed on them awhile in companionable silence. Then he turned to me, his upper lip dusted with a sugary mustachio.

"Doesn't sound like much of a holiday," he said.

THREE miles off the interstate, at the point where the old state highway met the Youngstown Road, there was a diner called the Seneca, with a chrome-and-neon warbonnet for a sign. That was how I always found the shattered strip of country blacktop that led to the Warshaws' farm: just past the Seneca Diner, you took the first left, rolled over a steel bridge that crossed an insignificant fork of the Wolf River, and flashed past the general store, filling pump, and post office that were all that remained of the town of Kinship, PA. The town's schoolhouse was little more than a picturesque woodpile, and in 1977 its volunteer fire station, abandoned for a decade, had burned to the floor joists. For the last few years there'd been a sort of antique store on the ground floor of the old Odd Fellows' Hall, but now that was gone, too. Things had pretty much been deteriorating around Kinship for over a hundred years, since the original Kinship Community was abandoned and its somber-hatted population of utopians were scattered into the great expanse of general American dreaminess. Irving Warshaw's beloved springhouse was one of the few Community structures still standing, and Irene Warshaw had been trying for years to have it declared a national landmark, although not, we believed, because she cared particularly about the history of the Kinship Community. No, Irene had an idea that it would have to be a federal offense, at the very least, for an elderly man to hole up days on end—smoking El Productos, listening to Webern and Karlheinz Stockhausen, inventing magnetic paint and liquid saws and Teflon hockey rinks for desert climes—inside a building that was on the National Register of Historic Places.

Along with the old springhouse, only the barn and the boathouse on the pond were standing in the late fifties when Irving Warshaw bought the land. He'd had to build the main house from scratch, on weekends and holidays and summer vacations during the Kennedy and Johnson years. On the foundation of an earlier structure, with materials salvaged from abandoned farmsteads all over Mercer County, he'd raised up a modest two-story saltbox of weathered gray shingles, with a fieldstone chimney, an eclectic assortment of old leaded windows in the living and dining rooms, and a pair of dormers in the attic story that were set too close together and lent the house a cross-eyed expression. The floors were crooked, none of the doors hung true, and on windy days the draft of the fireplace had been known abruptly to reverse itself, filling the entire house with roiling clouds of black smoke; but Irv had done the job almost entirely himself, with some help from his late brother, Harry, and from a local named Everett Tripp, an alcoholic wires-and-pipes man who'd tried to feel Emily up when she was eight years old, and who may well have been a distant cousin of the narrator. When his sons were old enough to give him a hand, Irv set about restoring the wreck of the barn, a great gray ark staved in and keeled over in the tall grass a hundred yards from the house, which an expert from Penn State had dated to before the Civil War.

"I've never visited a real farm," said James, as we turned right, just beyond the Odd Fellows' Hall, into an alley of elm trees, huge and still leafless, that ran from Kinship Road up to the house, planted at reasonable intervals in the last century by careful utopian hands. These trees, according to some freak of

the breezes, had for many years escaped the Dutch elm disease, but now there were many gaps in the double colonnade.
Last summer I'd helped Irv bring down two blighted trees,
and it looked as though a few more had failed to bud this
spring. In a few years the whole grand structure would be
gone.

"Don't hold your breath," I said. "This is a farm like I'm an
English teacher."

"Look," said James, in a contradictory tone, pointing to
the pair of milk cows who were, along with an irritable yellow gelding, the sole current occupants of the restored barn.
"Cows."

"Don't they have those around Carvel?" I said, touched by
the childish ardor with which he returned the charitable gaze
of the cows. "I thought it was a pretty small town."

"Not all small towns have cows."

"True," I said. "The yellowish one's a horse."

James said, "Yeah? I've heard of those."

"They're good eating," I said.

I parked the car behind Emily's Bug, in the intermittent
shade of a horse chestnut tree, and we climbed out. The tree
was some eighty years old and in leaf now; in another few
weeks it would be crawling with spidery white blossoms. In
the front garden of the McClelland Hotel there'd been just
such a high, spreading, oval-shaped horse chestnut. As I
stepped out of the car my cheeks were tingling, my ears were
ringing with wind, and my hair felt permanently blown backward, like the streaming chrome hair of a hood ornament. My
ankle had stiffened in the course of the drive and I found that
I could barely stand on it.

"Check that out," I said, pointing to the lawn that lay
beyond the handsome old tree, where there stood a ragged

stonehenge of whitewashed rocks. Beneath each of these rocks, I explained to James, lay the skeleton of a Warsaw family pet, buried, in the Egyptian manner, along with its rhinestone collars and plastic T-bones or catnip-filled mice. Most of the names painted onto the rocks had long since washed away, but you could still make out the inscriptions on the final resting places of the bones of Shlumper and Farfel and Earmuffs the cat. Off to one side stood a large, jagged molar stone, all by itself. This one marked the grave of a schnauzer bought to console Emily after the drowning of her older brother, the summer that she turned nine. She'd insisted on naming the puppy after him, and when it died, Sam's name went onto the whitewashed stone, where it remained, faded but still legible. The bones of Sam the boy lay under a bronze tablet in Beth Shalom cemetery, in the North Hills, by the corner of Tristan Avenue and Isolde Street.

"I had fish when I was a kid," said James. "We used to just flush them."

"Oh shit," I said, "Emily's flowers." I leaned over into the back of the car and discovered that in the course of our journey the wind had reached in and plucked bare every last rose. We must have left a trail of petals along the highway from Pittsburgh to Kinship. It was just a six-dollar arrangement padded with baby's breath and bear grass but nonetheless at the loss of it I felt disconcerted and somehow disarmed.

"Oops," said James, looking at me with an expression halfway between pity and disapproval, the way you look at a drunken man who stands up to find that he has been sitting for an hour on his hat.

"This way," I said carelessly. I tossed the ruined bouquet onto Sam's grave. "And don't forget your knapsack."

I limped around to the laundry-room door and showed

James into the house. Nobody ever went in by the front door. We passed through the warm sugary smell of the clothes dryer and came into the steam-filled kitchen, and I caught a look of disappointment on James's face. I supposed he'd been expecting a country kitchen, pine and burnished copper, lace in the window, but Irene had remodeled at the peak or nadir of the 1970s, and her kitchen was a veritable fiesta of goldenrod and avocado and burnt orange accents, her cabinets clad in walnut Formica, adorned with elaborate gilt handles. The air smelled of scorched butter and caramelized onion and a gunpowder tang that I recognized as the smoke from Emily's Canadian cigarettes. Emily herself was nowhere to be seen. Irene and Marie, Philly's wife, stood at the stove, with their backs to us, launching raw matzoh balls into an iron pot. As we came into the kitchen they both turned around.

"Surprise," I said, thinking I would take it very hard if Irene Warshaw was sorry to see my face.

"Hello, hello!" said Irene, holding out her arms to me, wagging her head disbelievingly from side to side. Irene wasn't tall but she had a good fifty pounds on me, and when she shook one of her body parts all the rest of them tended to join in. In the country—and since Irv's retirement, five years earlier, she was nearly always in the country—she modeled her pursuits and her manner of dress as nearly as possible on those of Monet at Giverny, and she had on a broad straw hat and a knee-length blue chambray smock with billowing sleeves. She was a natural blonde, with delicate hands and feet, and in her youthful photographs one saw a girl with mocking eyes and a tragic smile, the course of whose life would conspire in time to transpose that pair of adjectives.

I kissed her soft cheek. I closed my eyes and she pressed my forehead firmly against her lips. She had a bitter, nutritious smell compounded of cooking oil, castile soap, and the five hundred milligrams of B complex vitamins she swallowed every day.

"Hello, sweetie," she said. "I'm so glad to see you."

"I'm glad to hear that," I said.

"I knew you'd come."

"How'd you know that?"

She shrugged. "I knew."

"Irene, this is James Leer, he's a student of mine. A very talented writer."

"How *wonderful*," said Irene, extending her arm past me to take hold of James's pale hand. In the early forties, at Carnegie Tech, Irene had majored in English literature and, in particular considering her long years of exposure to me, esteemed writers far too highly. Her literary taste was more exclusive and refined than Sara's, and she read with greater deliberateness, rereading and underlining choice phrases and keeping track of the characters with lists and genealogies on the flyleaf. There was a stern photograph of a besweatered, smoke-wreathed Lawrence Durrell, her absolute favorite, hanging on the wall above her secretary desk, and in her wallet she carried around a scrap of crumpled program, rescued from a trash can, on which, during the course of an awards ceremony at the Poetry Forum, a bored John Updike had sketched a carious incisor tooth that was killing him that night. I'd been trading for many years now on the goodwill that my occupation earned for me in Irene's regard. "How *are* you, James? A *writer*? And you've come to make the Seder with us?"

"I—I guess so," said James, drawing himself down deep into his filthy black coat. There was a ring of powdered sugar imprinted on one flap. "I mean, yes, if it's all right with you. I've never, uh, is it—made one? before."

"Of course! Of course!" She crinkled up her face, and smiled her most grandmotherly smile, but I saw that her blue eyes, examining James, were cold as only a grandmother's can be. James Leer had the kind of pallid and formless good looks that to a woman of Irene's age might bespeak illness, onanism, defective upbringing, or mental infirmity. I supposed it was not impossible that having grown up during a decade which preferred the colors avocado, burnt orange, and goldenrod might well have injured his brain.

"And this is Marie. My daughter-in-law."

"What's up, James?" said Marie. Born—I always got a kick out of this—during an emergency refueling stop on Wake Island, freckled, a bit wide in the hips, Marie had, unlike me, converted on marrying into the Warshaw family, and except for her childlessness she had transformed herself into a peerless Jewish daughter-in-law. Marie was in fact the best Jew in the family, far more observant than her husband or his parents. She pinned a doily to her hair on Friday nights to light the candles, and baked three-cornered cookies when it was annually appropriate, and knew all the words, in Hebrew, to the national anthem of Israel. Like many army brats she had an open and imperturbable character, which served her well in her husband's family, no two of whose members shared traits of character, or DNA, or otherwise bore any more resemblance to each other than the seventeen states and countries in which Marie had grown up.

"You look tired," she said, patting my cheek.

"I've been working hard," I said. I wondered how much she knew about Emily and me.

"How's the book?"

"Great, great. Just about done." I'd been telling her the

same thing since the days of her engagement to Philly. "Everything all ready here? Smells good."

"More or less," said Irene. "I've had so much to do. Marie's been *such* a big help. Emily, too." She looked at me. "I'm glad she decided to show up a day early."

"Uh huh," I said. I thought she might be fucking with me—as a pothead, I spent a lot of time thinking that people might be fucking with me—but there was not a hint of sarcasm in her face or tone. That didn't necessarily mean, however, that she wasn't fucking with me. Before her own retirement Irene had for thirty years run a private agency that supplied the entire Ohio Valley with Korean babies, and she was master of a certain kind of administrative deadpan I'd never learned to read.

"I shouldn't complain about having too much to do, though," she said, with a dramatic sigh. With one automatic hand she reached into a pocket of her smock, brought out a chick wrapped in flashing yellow foil, peeled it, and neatly severed its chocolate head. "It's better than being bored out of my skull."

"Aw, Irene," I said.

"I never should have let him talk me into leaving the house on Inverness," she said, chewing.

"I know," I said. During all her years there Irene had felt little affection for the house on Inverness Avenue, a cramped brick two-story, much smaller than all its neighbors, and she had been glad at last to see it sold. Since the move out to Kinship, though, the place had assumed in her mind the fabulous proportions of some lost Jerusalem or Tara. "It's been hard for you."

"It's been very hard," Marie told James.

"And I'm repeating myself, aren't I?" Irene winked at

James and sadly shook her head. Having devoted her life to the invention and licensing and construction of a thousand families all over western Pennsylvania and Ohio—the macro-management of families, so to speak—it was her melancholy fate to have ended up living far from her remaining children, in a ghost town, with a husband who spent most of his time locked up in a shed, building Wheatstone bridges and Kremlins for barn swallows.

"So where is everybody else?" I said, looking around. Beside the toaster, on a china saucer, sat the little memorial candle Irv had mentioned, in its jelly glass, its tiny fire pale and motionless. Its label, with blue mock-Hebrew characters, had been pasted on at a crooked angle, and it was priced with a fluorescent orange grocery-store sticker at 79¢.

"Deborah's lying out on the dock," said Irene, following my gaze. "She's been *no* help at all, of course. And I guess Philly—is he still down in the basement?"

"Of course. Playing with Grossman," said Marie. "Mr. Grossman got out again last night."

"Mr. Grossman?" said James. "Who's that?"

"I'm sure you'll find out," said Irene, rolling her eyes. She looked at me. "And you *know* where Irv is."

"In the springhouse."

"Where else?"

"Maybe I'll just take James out to meet him, then."

"That's a good idea," said Irene. She brushed a damp strand of hair from her eyes with the back of one arm, then made a helpless gesture that encompassed all the saucepans, crockery bowls, and empty halves of eggshells scattered across every available surface of the kitchen. "I'm afraid we're still *hours* away."

"Oh, now," said Marie. "It's not that bad."

"Oh, say," said Irene. She looked at James. "How old are you?"

"Huh?" said James, startled. He'd been looking over at the modest, all-but-invisible light the Warshaws had lit to commemorate the anniversary of Sam Warshaw's death. "I'm twenty. Almost twenty-one."

"Well, then you're the youngest." Irene tried to keep her voice sounding bright and bureaucratic, but it got a little hollow here, and you could see she was wondering how it had come to pass that in her family a twenty-year-old stranger in an ill-smelling trench coat could pass for the child of the house. Out of kindness neither she nor I looked at Marie, on whom all hopes for a grandchild, I realized, had now come ponderously to settle. "You'll have to say the Four Questions at the Seder."

"Great," said James, shrinking deep into his overcoat. "I'd love to."

"Philly will be happy about that," said Marie, sounding a little hollow herself.

"All right, then." I put my hand on James's shoulder and started for the door. When I got to the laundry room I turned. "Oh," I said, in a tone I hoped sounded airy and nonchalant and free of any tocsin of marital distress. "And, uh, where is Emily?"

"Oh, she's out on the dock, too," said Marie. "With Deb. They're talking."

"Talking," I said. Since Deborah Warshaw had spent most of the previous winter divorcing her third husband I was sure they must have a lot to talk about. "All right. Good."

"Grady," said Irene. She set down the spoon she was holding and came over to take both of my hands in hers. She looked up at me hopefully and not without a certain impatience. "I'm glad you're here." Then she nodded her head in the direction of the springhouse. "And you *know* how happy *he's* going to be."

"And Emily?" I said.

"Of course, and Emily. What are you saying? Don't be stupid."

I smiled. I supposed she was exhibiting what people nowadays refer to, with crushing disapproval, as denial. It's always been hard for me to tell the difference between denial and what used to be known as hope.

"I didn't think I *was* being stupid," I said, a little dazed by the force of Irene's optimism. All at once it seemed not impossible that my heart, that mad helmsman lashed to the wheel in the pilothouse of my rib cage, had steered me out to Kinship only to be reconciled to my wife. "I'm not sure she's going to be all that thrilled."

Irene rolled her eyes and leaned forward to give me a soft slap on the cheek.

"I hope you don't listen too closely to the things this man tells you," she said to James. She reached into her pocket, withdrew another chocolate chick, unwrapped it, and cruelly bit off its head, once again returning the remainder uneaten to her pocket. She must have had a whole pile of mangled little bodies in there.

James and I went back through the laundry room and started out the door into the yard.

"What's the matter, James?" I said. "You look a little disturbed."

He turned to me, eyes wide with panic, hands jammed into the pockets of his coat.

"Four questions about *what*?" he said.

THIS spring, as usual, the Warshaws' pond had overflowed its banks and turned the back garden into an everglades. Irene's empire of rosebushes had flooded, her stone birdbath lay washed over onto its side, and, buried to his divine nipples in mud, the statuette of Gautama Buddha that she'd set to watch over her flowers looked imperturbably out at us from behind an azalea. I limped with James across the makeshift boardwalk Irv had laid to carry you from the back door of the house, over the drowned garden, to the crooked gray shack the old utopians built to keep their meat and melons cool in the summertime. The walkway, like all of Irv's constructions, was at once intricate and ramshackle, a mismatched assemblage of two-by-fours, scrap lumber, and firewood nailed haphazardly together according to a grandiose scheme that provided for pilings, lashed guardrails, even a small bench, halfway along; the structure got more elaborate every year. I supposed that a dike of sandbags strategically placed along the pond would have been more effective, but that was not the way Irv's mind operated. As we thumped along the boardwalk I could hear coming from the springhouse the shining corners and echoing space of his beloved serial music. In his youth, before switching to metallurgical engineering, Irv had studied composition, at Carnegie Tech, with an émigré pupil of Schoenberg's, and written a few unlistenable pieces with titles like *Molecules I-XXIV, Concerto for Klein Bottle,* and *Reductio ad Infinitum. That* was the way Irv's mind operated.

Halfway to the springhouse, I stopped and looked out over the pond, blue and mottled as the hood of a Buick, roughly the shape of a sock. At the heel of the sock stood a small gray boathouse, with a miniature jetty, and on this jetty lay Deborah Warshaw and Emily, in chaise longues. Emily's chair was turned away from us, but Deborah waved and raised her hands to her mouth.

"Grady!" she called, through the trumpet bell of her cupped hands.

Emily turned around in her chair and looked at me. After a moment she raised her hand and weakly waved. She was wearing a pair of black wraparound sunglasses, and it was not quite possible at this distance to read her expression. I figured that Munch's *The Scream* was probably a safe bet.

"That's my wife," I said.

"Which one?"

"The one having a cardiac arrest. In the blue bathing suit."

"She's waving," James observed. "That's good, right?"

"I guess so," I said. "I'll bet she's pret-ty fucking surprised."

"What's the other one wearing?"

I looked. There were two pale ovals arranged across Deborah's chest, in the manner of the cups of a bikini bathing suit, ornamented at their centers with tan rosettes.

"She's wearing her breasts," I said. Beside her chair on the deck sat a squat, faceted bottle filled with a dark liquid, and a stack of what looked like magazines. These would be comic books, however. Deborah's reading skills in English were not advanced, and she rarely read anything else. I didn't really think it was a warm enough day for topless sunbathing, but it would certainly be typical of Deborah to decide that the best possible way of preparing for a family Seder was to drink Manischewitz and lie around half naked reading *Betty and Veronica*. Deborah was seven years older than Emily, but she had, paradoxically, known their parents for a briefer period of time. She was almost fourteen when she arrived from Korea, and unlike Emily and Phil she'd never quite learned to suit herself to life in the United States, in a household as patched together and ungainly as any of Irving Warshaw's inventions. She'd missed having a bat mitzvah, and I knew from Passovers past that she considered the Seder to be a kind of unnecessary and infinitely more tedious reduplication of the Thanksgiving meal. She was kind of an antimatter Emily, plain where Emily was pretty, violent where she was placid, given to rages and transports but incapable, where Emily was a master, of arrière-pensée and social calculation. It was, I always imagined, as if the Warshaws had adopted a feral child, a girl raised by wolves.

"Yo, Grady!" She drew a slow circle in the air with one hand. She wanted us to come over and say hello. Emily just sat there, motionless, holding a cigarette, the wind lifting the smooth black hem of her hair. I didn't feel ready, I realized, to face Emily yet. So I gave them a cheerful, old-slow-witted-Grady wave hello, made a great show of shaking my head, then turned and led James out to the springhouse. I knocked on the door.

"Who is it?" said Irv. When he was in the springhouse, and you knocked on his door, he never just said, "Come in."

"It's Grady," I said.

There was the scrape of a chair against a wooden floor, and then a low *oy* as Irv tried to get out of his chair.

"Stay where you are," I said, pushing open the door, stepping from the bright sunshine into the gloom and inextinguishable chill of the springhouse. The spring itself had dried up during the 1920s, but in spite of all the changes Irv had made to it over the years, the interior of the springhouse retained a cool, peppery tingle of artesian water and an air of perpetual twilight, as if it were a kind of cavern and the angular music Irv preferred merely the sound of water dripping from high stalactites into a bottomless black pool.

"Come in, come in," said Irv, putting down his book, gesturing, from his overstuffed easy chair, with great helicopter whirlings of his arms. As we came into the springhouse he braced his bad knee with his hands and lurched free from his chair. I went over to him and we shook hands, and I introduced him to James. We hadn't seen each other since January. In that time, I was surprised to see, his hair had turned entirely gray. He seemed to have taken the sequential breakups of his daughters' marriages very hard. His eyes were red, and the skin beneath them was bruised with sleeplessness. Although he'd dressed, as he always did for family occasions, in suit pants, black brogues, and a tie, his shirt was rumpled and dark at the armpits, and he'd shaved himself as badly as Officer Pupcik, leaving patches of silver stubble and numerous cuts.

"You look great," I said.

"What's the matter with your foot?" He reached to turn down the stereo. "You're limping."

I looked at James. "I had an accident," I said. When this did not seem to satisfy Irv, I added, "A dog bit me."

"A dog bit you?"

I shrugged. "Believe it or not."

"Let me see." He pointed to my ankle. "Come by the light."

"It's nothing, Irv. It's fine. What were you reading?"

"Nothing. Come, let me see."

He took hold of my elbow and tried to steer me away from his chair, toward a neighboring floor lamp with a cracked glass shade. I pulled away from him and went over to see what he'd been looking at when we came in, because I always liked to tease him for favoring such light reading as *Gas Permeable Structures in Polymer Design* and *Modal Analysis of Pre-tonal Italian Sacred Compositions of the 17th Century*. When he really wanted to unwind he might pull down something by Frege or one of his cracked old George Gamows, and chew on the end of a stinky cigar. He'd left the book facedown, flaps outspread on the arm of his chair; a hardback in plain blue library binding, with the title stamped in white on the spine: *The Bottomlands*. I felt myself blush, and I looked up to see that Irv's face had also turned bright red.

"You had to check it out of the library?" I said.

"I can't find my copy. Come." Irv pulled me over to the floor lamp. Under his regime the springhouse was invisibly but strictly divided into three parts. There was the reading room—the two wing-backed armchairs and pair of lamps, an electric space heater, and a wall lined with bookshelves filled with his metallurgical and music theory texts. In the central portion of the springhouse he had his laboratory—a stationary tub and a pair of workbenches, one cluttered, one spotless, upon which he carried out his mechanical and chemical activities, from toaster repair to the development of a substance that could stick to Teflon coating. On the far side of the room there was an army cot piled with blankets and a refrigerator replete with cans of Iron City Light, one of which—no more or less—he took, medicinally, every afternoon at five. It was an enviable setup; Irv had rediscovered, as surprisingly few men do, that the secret to perfect male happiness is a well-equipped clubhouse. We'd once tried to reckon the amount of hours he had spent out here since his retirement, and had arrived at a conservative estimate of twenty thousand. Irene, I think, would have doubled that figure.

"Here." Irv pushed my book aside and patted the arm of his chair, generating a thick cloud of dust. "Put your foot up. James, have a seat."

I took hold of his shoulder, to steady myself, and lifted my foot onto the chair. I hiked up the cuff of my jeans and carefully slid the sock down to the collar of my shoe. I hadn't bothered to rebandage the wound and the sight of it made me wince. The four holes in my ankle were dark and puckered. The flesh all around the bite was pillowy and red, tinged here and there with daubs of yellow. I looked away. For some reason I felt ashamed.

"That looks nasty," said James.

"It's infected," said Irv, leaning down to examine the wound more closely. He gave off an aroma of hair oil and leather wallet and sweat, mingled with the orange-peel-and-Listerine fragrance of his aftershave, Lucky Tiger, which he wore on special occasions. I stood over him, with my eyes closed, inhaling his familiar smell. I wondered if this was the last time I was ever going to smell it.

"When did the dog bite you?"

"Last night," I said, although it seemed like it had to be much longer ago than that. "He had his shots and all," I added; I figured this was a reasonable assumption. "So, what made you want to read that old thing, anyway?"

"I saw it in the library yesterday afternoon." He shrugged. "I was thinking of you." He clapped me on the knee, firmly, and I felt a sympathetic twinge in my ankle at the impact of his hand. "Stay put," he said. "I'm just going to clean that up for you."

He unbent and went to over his laboratory, and I stayed where I was, looking at a National Geographic map of Mars that Irv had fastened with push pins to the wall above his chair. I had to fight off an urge to burst into tears of thankfulness for his solicitude.

"So, James," said Irv. He was banging around in his drawers and cabinets, pulling out bottles, reading the labels, tossing them back. "I take it you admired Frank Capra."

I was amazed; I was sure I'd never said anything to him about James Leer and his cinemania. I looked over at James, who was standing beside the armchair, holding the copy of *The Bottomlands* in his right hand, with his left hand dangling at an odd angle behind the open book.

"He's, uh, he's one of my favorites," said James. "I mean, he was. He died last fall."

"I know he did." Irv returned with some cotton wool, a bottle of LabChem brand isopropyl alcohol, a bundle of gauze, a roll of adhesive tape, and a crinkled, squeezed-out tube of antibiotic ointment. He lowered himself to the ground a little at a time, and then knelt on his mechanical knee.

"Ooh," he said, as he winched himself down. "Wee wow."

He uncapped the rubbing alcohol and started to work with the cotton wool, dabbing delicately at my ankle. I flinched.

"Stings?"

"A little."

"You do that with a knife?" he said to James, over his shoulder.

James looked trapped. "With a needle," he said.

"What are you guys talking about?"

"His hand," said Irv. "He's got 'Frank Capra' sort of carved into it. Show him."

James hesitated, and slowly withdrew his left hand from behind the book. I saw them now, faint pink marks that might have been letters scratched into the back of his hand. I'd never noticed them before.

"Does it say 'Frank Capra' on your hand, James Leer?" I said.

He nodded. "I did it the day he died. September third."

"Jesus Christ." I shook my head. I looked down at Irv. "He's crazy about the movies," I said.

Irv squirted a dab of ointment onto the tip of his index finger.

"One would have to be," he said. Delicately he worked the ointment into the puncture marks. Thinking it over I decided that those eventual scars on my ankle would not have been acquired in any more reasonable manner than those on James's hand.

"So," I said to Irv, after a minute. "How were you liking it?"

"What's that?"

"The book. *The Bottomlands*."

"I've read it before."

"And this time?"

"It's a young man's book," he said, not unkindly. "It got me remembering how it felt to be young."

"Maybe *I* should read it again."

"You? I'd say you're in no danger of aging prematurely." This didn't sound like a compliment. "So whose dog was it that bit you?"

"Oh, the Chancellor's," I said, looking back at the map of Mars. "There was a party at her place last night."

"And aren't they going to miss you at your Wordsfest?" said Irv, drawing back to squint at my wounds. "All your students?"

"I'll be there tomorrow," I said. "Anyway, I brought one of my students with me."

"Clever of you," said Irv. "I remember the Chancellor. Nice lady."

"Uh huh," I said, keeping my eyes fixed on the towering cracked crater of Nix Olympica.

There was a knock at the door.

"Who's that?" said Irv.

"Hey, Dad. Hey, Grady." It was Philly, or rather his head and upper torso, stuck into the door of the springhouse, fingers wrapped around the doorjamb as if to prevent himself from accidentally falling into the room. Although in the past I had seen a few exchanges of genuine affection between them, the Warshaw men were awkward and ill at ease with each other. Irv had his springhouse, and Philly's domain, when he came home, was the basement, and in general they kept out of each other's way.

"That's James," I said.

Philly nodded. "Hey," he said. "Jesus, Grady, what happened to your leg?"

"I cut myself shaving."

He watched for a moment while Irv unwound a strip of gauze and tore it off with his teeth. "See Deb's tits?"

"Yep," I said. "We saw 'em."

He grinned. "So, listen, uh, Mom sent me out here to see if this dude wanted to come and see Grossman."

"Do you want to, dude?" I asked James.

"I don't know," said James, watching Philly warily. Philly Warshaw was a good-looking young man, skin the color of tea with milk, straight-jawed and slender, dressed in a spotless white T-shirt and jeans. His airman's hair was thick and spiky, and the veins stood out on his forearms. "Who is he?"

"He's a snake, man," said Philly. "He's a mongo fucking boa constrictor."

"Go ahead," Irv said. "I can take care of Grady."

James shrugged and looked at me. I nodded. He set down the book and followed Philly out the door. We heard their footsteps resound along the boardwalk as they headed toward the house.

"I certainly hope he can write," said Irv.

"He can," I said. "He's a good kid. Ouch. Maybe a little messed up."

"He's come to the right place, then," said Irv. "Hold still."

"Now, Irv."

"I don't know what's the matter with you." He wrapped one hand around my ankle, holding the bandage fast, and with the other hand brought the roll of adhesive tape to his mouth. The pressure of his fingers was firm enough to be painful. "You and Emily. If this were happening to Deborah," he said, his words a little garbled, "all right, I could understand. I'd be a little disappointed if it *didn't* happen."

"Irv, I don't know, it's just—"

"She spoke to her mother." Angrily he bit off a strip of tape and applied it to the bandage. "She doesn't seem to want to speak to me."

"It's hard for Emily," I said. "You know that."

"I know. She holds it all in." He applied a final strip of tape to the bandage, then patted at it with such gentleness that my eyes filled with tears. He looked up and managed a thin smile. "I guess she inherited that from me." Then he lowered his head and looked down at the bandages and medicines scattered around him on the ground.

"Irv," I said. I held out my hand to him and hoisted him to his feet.

"Families are supposed to get *bigger*," he said. "This one just keeps shrinking."

Then we went outside, into the last slanted shafts of the April afternoon. There was no one lying out by the pond anymore, and we leaned on each other for a moment, crippled in our various extremities, looking out at the empty chaise longues on the dock, at the sun hanging low over the bare yellow hills of Utopia.

"I'm not going anywhere," I said, just to see how true I could make it sound.

Irv smiled bitterly and clapped me on the shoulder as though I'd got off a clever line.

"Give me a break, Grady," he said.

THERE was one bathroom in the house, upstairs, at the end of the hall, in a wide, lopsided dormer all its own. It was a nice bathroom with grooved wainscoting, brass fixtures, and a big quadruped tub, but given the wild mood swings of Irving's bowels and a remarkable tendency among the women of the family to lie brooding in their bathwater, it was an overburdened facility and generally occupied when you needed it most. When I came back into the house I went upstairs to take a leak and found the heavy, paneled door shut tight. I knocked softly three times, tapping out the syllables of my name.

"Yes?"

I took a step backward.

"Em?" I said. "Is that you?"

"No," said Emily.

I gave the doorknob a twist. It was unlocked; all I needed to do was give the door a gentle push. Instead I eased the knob back, without a sound, and took my hand away. I stood looking at the closed door.

"I, uh, I need to pee, kid." I swallowed, aware of the moment that inhered in the question I was about to ask—the deep, damaged membranes of trust and intimacy I was about to lay bare. "Can I—is it all right if I come in?"

There was a splash and the faint porcelain echo of a splash.

"I'm taking a bath."

"Okay," I said to the door, resting my forehead against it. I could hear the scrape of a match and then the low angry sigh of Emily's exhalation. I counted off thirty seconds. Then I went back downstairs and out into the yard.

I walked out to the driveway and started down toward Kinship Road, looking up at the mesh of branches overhead for signs of a blighted elm tree against which it would be kosher for me to piss. The air smelled cool and slippery like wet bark, and although my wife's refusal to let me share her nakedness, however reasonable, had hurt me—even though it made my heart ache to think that I might never get to see my Emily naked again—I was feeling very glad to be out of the house, alone, carrying the happy clenched fist of my bladder inside me. Then I came around a bend in the drive and saw my sister-in-law. She was moping along about fifty feet ahead of me, wrapped in a gauzy purple dress the hem of which dragged in the gravel like a train. She was cutting at the air around her with a lit cigarette and singing softly to herself in a falsetto voice: it sounded like the slow, moaning part of "Whole Lotta Love." I knew that I ought to leave her to her unimaginable Deborah reveries but I was upset and confused about Emily, and there had been times in the past when my sister-in-law's counsel, while never useful, had provided a certain amount of welcome bemusement, like the advice of an oracular hen. She caught the sound of my tread in the gravel, and turned.

"How weird," I said by way of greeting.

"Hey, Doc!" she said.

"That's quite a dress." There were tiny silver mirrors sewn into the fabric, and the print appeared to be patterned after the psychedelic neon paisley effect you get when you shut your eyes tight and press hard with your knucklebones against them. It was the kind of dress you tend to see hanging in the closet of a woman who owns only one dress.

"Do you like it? It's from India or someplace," said Deborah, smacking me on the cheek, hard, with her compressed lips, in her version of a kiss, and giving my hand a painful squeeze. "What's weird?"

"I couldn't get Em to let me come into the bathroom and pee. She was in there taking a bath."

"She's fucking pissed at you, Doc," she said. "She heard you've been boinking this other woman." Doc was Deborah's nickname for me. She'd started out, years ago, by calling me Gravy, and hence Gravy Boat, and then the latter had metamorphosed, in a way I supposed my physique made inevitable, into Das Boot. At some point she had dropped the Boot, and then after a while Das had slid slowly into Doc, where, finding me always well supplied in any emergency with a certain pharmacological substance, it finally lodged. Deborah had come to English late, as I've said, and there was no way of telling what would happen to a phrase like "gravy boat" once it got into her brain. "Bastard." She drove a fist delicately into my stomach. "Fucking slimebag."

"Did she?" I said, not taking her abuse of me at all seriously. One of the things I'd always admired about Deborah
was the unself-conscious scabrousness of her dealings with
men in general and myself in particular. She'd arrived on
these shores with little in her luggage besides the seven great
Anglo-Saxon imprecations, and to this day she clung to them
with touching devotion, as to certain other proofs—a shriv-
eled lei of orchids, an ancient, uneaten Hershey bar the orphanage had provided for the trip—of her passage to
America. "And just where did she hear that?"

"You think I told her?"

"I don't really care," I said. "How are you, kid?"

I reached to brush a strand of hair from her right eye, and
she looked away. She had thick and lovely hair, which she
used to conceal her face, a plain face made plainer still by her
low regard for it. She hated her nose, believing it to be at once
bulbous and too small. She called it—originally, I thought, if
pitiably—her pud. Her eyes though expressive were badly
crossed, and her teeth wandered across her smile like the ker-
nels at the tip of an ear of corn.

"You don't know anything about monkeys, do you?"

"Not as much as I ought to."

"Do they make good pets? I was just thinking of getting
myself a monkey. A squirrel monkey, you know, one of those
little jobbers they have, to carry around on my shoulder. Do
you know anything about squirrel monkeys?"

"Only that they kill their masters."

Deborah showed me all her crooked little teeth.

"I still like you, Doc," she said, in her insincere way. Like
many people who have lost all but the ghost of their original
foreign accents, nothing she said ever sounded quite true. "I

just want you to know that. Everybody else thinks you're a motherfucker. But not me. I mean, I do, but I still like you anyway."

"That's great," I said. "You're the worst judge of character I know, Deb."

"Yeah, no kidding," she said, and she looked momentarily depressed. Her most recent husband, for example, a half-Korean dentist named Alvin Blumentopf to whom she had been married for all of a year, had been beaten up by loan sharks for nonpayment of racetrack debts and then convicted, two days later, of income-tax evasion, and sent to the federal prison at Marion. That Deborah had fallen in love with him almost guaranteed such a fate. "Thanks for reminding me, you know?"

She dropped her cigarette onto the road; just let go of it, half-smoked, as if it tired her. Deborah came off much tougher than Emily and I remembered that I always forgot—misled by her profane good nature and loopy style—how easy it was to injure her feelings. I stepped on the cigarette for her and ground it out.

"What a gentleman," she said. "So, okay, she wouldn't let you into the bathroom."

"She wouldn't speak to me."

"She didn't say *anything*?"

"No, but I only waited twenty minutes."

"And then you came out here to piss?"

"Yeah," I said. I started toward a nearby tree, which appeared, on close inspection, to be acceptably dead. "Mind?"

"Do I get to see your wiener?"

"You bet." I stepped behind the tree and unzipped. "Have you got a pen?"

"No, why?"

"I want to draw a little face on it for you."

"Do worms have faces?"

"Now you're depressing me," I said.

"Doc," said Deborah. "How many times have you been married?"

"Three."

"Three. Same as me."

"The same."

"And I'll bet you cheated on them, too."

"Oh, kind of."

"And *I'm* the worst judge of character you ever met?"

"Ha," I said. I finished my work, hitched up my trousers, and stepped back out into the drive. "So, aside from thinking about monkeys, what were *you* doing out here, Deb? Fleeing Egypt?"

"Oh, I don't know, I was checking around in the barnyard. Sort of looking around underneath the cow turds."

"For 'shrooms?" She nodded. "Did you find any?" Another nod. "Did you eat them?" She looked at me levelly, her eyes all pupil in the late afternoon shadow, her face expressionless. "Jesus, Deb, that's crazy."

Now she punched me on the arm and grinned broadly.

"Scared you, didn't I?" She reached into one of the side pockets of her dress and pulled out a dirty handful of skinny gray mushrooms. "I'm just kind of holding on to them for now. In case things get really dull." She shoved them back into the pocket and from the other took out her cigarettes. When she could get them she smoked a nasty filterless Korean brand called Chan Mei Chong that cost her double the price of a domestic pack and smelled like burning warthog rind.

"When I first saw Emily"—she lit the cigarette, watching the flame with her wild, crossed eyes—"yesterday, I could tell she had some kind of news to tell me. You know how all the parts of her face sort of all smoosh together around her nose?"

"Uh huh."

"I thought she was going to say that she was pregnant."

"Funny," I said, voice a little thick.

"What's funny?"

"Nothing."

"Tell me."

I have to say here that I didn't quite trust Deborah, and had no reason to believe that she trusted me. Whenever we were alone together like this I felt an awkwardness between us— we punched each other a lot, and called each other names, and rocked from foot to foot watching the smoke leave our mouths—that was partly sexual and partly social but was mostly due to our each knowing all the other's most intimate secrets, and knowing we knew them, without ever having shared a single one. She was, in other words, my sister-in-law.

"The woman in question," I said, after a moment, slowly letting out a deep breath. "The one you didn't tell Emily about."

She wrinkled her lip and blew a long gray strand of smoke toward Pittsburgh. "The Chancellor."

"She's pregnant."

"Holy shit. Does Emily know that?"

"Not yet," I said. "I just found out myself. That's kind of why I came up here."

"Huh? Are you planning to announce it at the dinner table?"

"There's an idea."

She shook her head, looked at me for an instant, then away. She picked a flake of tobacco from her lower lip.

"She's married, isn't she, your friend?"

I nodded. "To my chairman. My boss, more or less."

"So is she going to *have* it?"

"I don't think so, no. I hope not."

"Don't tell Emily, then."

"I have to."

"No, you don't. Not tonight, anyway. Fuck, what difference could it make, Doc? *Wait* a while. I mean, see what happens, you know? Why should you tell her if there isn't even going to *be* a baby? It'll hurt her feelings so *bad*."

I was impressed. Although I knew she and Emily were fairly close, it was rare to see Deborah actively displaying such concern for her sister. Part of the way she'd learned to deal with being dumped into middle of the Warshaw family was never completely to surrender the pretense that they were all a bunch of relative strangers, well-meaning but ultimately beneath her, a boatful of rude fishermen who had rescued the only survivor of the wreck of an imperial yacht. She put a hand on my arm, softly, and I wondered if perhaps she didn't have a point. Why should I hurt Emily's feelings any more than I already had? Then I reminded myself that I was always willing to listen to arguments in favor of avoiding an unpleasant chore, and I shook my head.

"I really have to. I promised I would."

"Promised who?"

"Oh," I said, "myself."

Then what's one more broken, more or less? said her look. "Are you going to stay the night?"

"I don't know. Probably not, the way things have been going."

"Then let me tell her for you. After you leave."

"No!" I regretted now that I had said anything at all to Deborah, who, along with all her genuine affection for

Michael Chabon

Emily, had also acquired, like any good elder sister, a healthy urge to see her younger sibling's jaw drop in horror. "God, you have to swear to me you won't say anything to *anyone*, Deb. Please! I just haven't figured out what I'm going to do yet, is all."

"*That's* what you're waiting for?" she said, looking pointedly unhopeful.

"Hey, fuck you," I said. "I'll figure it out. Now, come on. Do you swear?"

"Sure," she said, and her soft Korean accent fluttered in the corners of her voice. "No problem."

"Okay." I nodded, once, firmly, as if I believed her.

"Jesus, Doc," she said. "How do you manage to fuck things up so good?"

I said that I didn't know. Then I turned and faced the house.

"I'd better go rescue James from Philly," I said. "Coming?"

She looked as if she was about to say something else, but in the end she just nodded and followed after me. We walked back up the driveway toward the house, gravel crunching under our feet.

"Who is that kid, anyway?" she said. "That James?"

"He's a student of mine."

"He's cute."

"Please leave him alone."

"He told me he liked my dress."

"Did he?" I said, giving the dress a look of mock skepticism. "He's *very* polite."

"He's—? Hey, fuck you," she said, sharply, her tone no longer bantering, and I saw that I had hurt her feelings again.

She stopped in the middle of the side yard and looked down at herself. "It is ugly, isn't it?"

"No, Deb, it's—"

"Shit, I can't believe I *bought* this thing." Her voice had grown shrill. "*Look* at this!"

"I think it's beautiful," I told her. "You look gorgeous, Deb."

She went past me to the back door and opened the screen but didn't go immediately inside, and coming up behind her I saw that she was trying to catch her faint reflection in the long rippled pane of the door.

"I'm going to change," she announced, frowning. Her voice was shaking. "I look like some kind of fucking hippie tent or something. I look like there should be someone standing underneath me selling bongs."

I put a consolatory hand on her shoulder, but she knocked it away and yanked open the back door. She ran into the house, through the kitchen, and went pounding up the stairs. I was dragged by her black crackling slipstream into the kitchen, where Marie stood, all dressed for dinner, stirring the matzoh ball soup in its caldron. She looked at me, an eyebrow raised, holding an interrogative ladle in one hand.

"I'm just getting started," I told her.

I went down into the basement to rescue James Leer and found him at the Ping-Pong table, facing Philly Warshaw with a paddle in his hand. They were playing Beer Pong, a hazing ritual to which, in his wild days, Philly had subjected all suitors and young male visitors to the house, myself included. It was the consensus in the Warshaw family that Philly's wild days had endured for an unreasonably long period of time, but in the end he'd settled down, and it was only when he came out to Kinship, now, and there was no driving to be done that he drank too much; I suppose it gave him something to look forward to in family visits. I sat down on the cellar steps to watch the action.

"Take it easy, there, James," I said.

"He's all right," said Philly, taking an exaggerated swipe at the ball, painting just enough english onto it to send it skittering into the glass of beer that was stationed, on the center line, at James Leer's end of the table. "He's doing fine." He grinned. "Pound it, James."

Obediently James reached for the full pilsner glass, fished out the ball, raised the glass to his lips, and drained it in a single eternal swallow that seemed to cause him some difficulty. When the beer was gone, he hoisted the glass in my direction, an empty smile frozen on his face, as a child who is trying to seem grown up smiles around an endless salty mouthful of raw oyster.

"Hi, Professor Tripp," he said.

"How many is that?" I asked him.

"That's two."

"Three," said Philly, coming around to refill James's glass with a can of Pabst he took from the mini-refrigerator that he kept in the corner of *his* old clubhouse. Daintily James wiped the beer from the Ping-Pong ball with the tail of my old flannel shirt. His hair had come unfastened from its brilliantine moorings and stood at crazy angles from his head. He was all smirks and grins and his eyes were full of light, as they had been the night before when we burst, heads reeling, into the blazing lobby of Thaw Hall, laughing and out of breath. He was having a great time. I could see that alcohol was going to be a dangerous thing for him.

"So, what happened to your car?" Philly wanted to know. "Who's butt is that?"

"Guy jumped on it," I said. I was a little irritated with him for having lured poor James into a game of Beer Pong, but I couldn't really hold it against him. Phillip Warshaw was a born agent of chaos and a master of backspin in all its many forms. He'd come over from Korea in 1965 with a reputation for being the most willful and uncontrollable toddler in the Soodow Orphanage and had immediately started running headlong and half-intentionally through plate-glass windows and lashing neighborhood children to trees. His career as a teenage vandal was legendary at Allderdice High School; in one four-month period he and a number 12 Magic Marker had covered every flat surface in Squirrel Hill, Greenfield, and parts of South Oakland with an arcane symbology that investigators eventually identified as his birth name, written in the alphabet of his lost mother. He had found a paradise of bad behavior during his tours in Panama and P.I., and it had taken him years to adjust to married life on the base down at Aberdeen.

"A guy? What guy?"

"A guy named, uh"—I looked over at James—"Vernon Hardapple."

Philly slapped another nasty spin on the ball and just missed plunging it into James's glass again.

"*Hard*apple?"

"He was a matador," said James, without even looking at me. He readied his next serve. "Love–nine." With a flourish he put the ball in play.

"A matador. Named Vernon Hardapple."

"He was married to a Mexican," I said. "He learned it down there."

"But she left him." James slapped one back at Philly, and the ball sailed across the basement and landed in a box of old issues of *Commentary*. "Love–ten. And I guess he got a little careless in the ring."

I couldn't keep myself from smiling, but James's face remained perfectly straight, and his eyes were focused on the Ping-Pong ball.

"He got gored?" said Philly.

"Just knocked over," I said. "Broke his hip. End of his career."

"So now he fights cars in the Hi-Hat parking lot," said James. "Your serve."

"The old Hi-Hat," said Philly, spinning his first serve across the net, off the table, and then skittering around the rim of James's glass. It just missed falling in. Philly Warshaw was death at Beer Pong. "Eleven–zip. Still going there?"

"Now and then." All of a sudden I felt a little uneasy. There was something about the incident with Vernon at the Hi-Hat last night that troubled me. Why had he said the car belonged to him, quoting the letters of its license plate, eulogizing as emerald green what I'd always thought of as an unsightly shade of fly butt? I supposed, on reflection, that the car could very well have been his; Happy Blackmore had claimed to have won it in a poker game, but I'd always found this a little hard to believe, given the cosmic extent of the losing streak that Happy'd been on. I'd waited a week for him to bring the certificate of title around before learning through a colleague of his at the *Post-Gazette* that he was down in the Catoctin Mountains playing out the last foot of thread on his bobbin. "That dude with the big arms still standing there at the door? Cleon? Clement?"

"He's still there."

"That guy has twenty-two-inch biceps," he said. "I measured them one time."

"Clement let you measure his biceps?"

Philly shrugged. "I won a bet with him," he said. He glanced quickly over toward me, then blew another shot past James. "So, Grady, I hear—twelve–zip—I hear you brought us a very special kind of parsley for our Passover dipping tonight."

"Uh huh," I said, looking at James, who blushed. I imagined that he'd felt flattered by Philly's attentions; no doubt before I showed up he'd been boasting to Philly about what a big dope stud he was. "I've got a little bud in the car."

"So?"

"So?" I said, folding my arms across my chest.

Philly grinned, and then cried out in mock alarm as James succeeded in spattering a lucky shot into his beer. He raised the glass and waggled his eyebrows at me over the rim.

"Oh. Sure, okay," I said, affecting, in classic pothead fashion, a breezy unconcern with the prospect of getting stoned. "If you want." I was dying for a nice big fatty. I got up and started for the basement door. Philly sent his paddle clattering across the table.

"Are we *stop*ping?" said James, distressed.

"Gotta take a leak," said Philly, starting for the stairs. "I'll meet you'ns outside."

"Come with me, James," I said, throwing open the creaking cellar doors and starting up the stairs through the cobwebs. Before I could climb out, James gave a tug on the cuff of my trousers.

"Grady," he said. "Grady, look." I ducked back into the basement. He grinned at me and pulled me by my sleeve over to a large, foul-smelling wooden complex of crate lumber and chicken wire that sprawled across the far corner of the basement. He pointed.

"Snake," he said.

Inside the huge pen there was a chunk of dead elm, from which hung a long perfect strand of muscle, draped in decorous pleats, like a streamer. This was Grossman, the nine-foot boa constrictor who, to their considerable regret, had been rooming with the Warshaws for the last twelve years. Philly Warshaw had won Grossman in a Liberty Avenue pool hall during his senior year at Allderdice, then abandoned him to his parents' care the following fall when he enlisted. Even then, Grossman was not a young snake, and his imminent death had been foretold by veterinarians, and happily anticipated by Irene Warshaw, for as long as Philly had been promising one day to take him back. Still Grossman lived on, in his heated cage, escaping regularly, by means of various herpetical stratagems, to prey on Irene's ragged tribe of chickens and to leave incredibly foul smelling sculptures of snake dung in artistic locations all over the house.

I clapped James on the shoulder. "That's a snake, all right," I said.

James knelt down and poked a finger through a hexagon of chicken wire. He made kissing sounds.

"I think he really likes me," said James.

"He does," I agreed. I tried to remember if I had ever actually seen Grossman move. "I can tell."

James followed me up out of the basement and we went around the house to my car, brushing the spider silk from our eyebrows and lips. Evening was coming on. A paisley scarf of purple clouds and sunlight trailed across Ohio to the west. The air was dewy and the grass squeaked under our shoes. There was a smell of horseshit and onions fried in chicken fat. One of the cows out in the barnyard made a mournful comment on the burdensomeness of life. When we had nearly reached the Galaxie, to my surprise James gave a pirate cry and bolted across the last ten feet. He sprang into the air, then, with his arms pressed down against the top of the door, launched himself, as if to vault into the front seat of the open car. He had enough height, I thought, and his trajectory looked good. But at the very last instant he stopped himself and made an emergency two-point landing in the grass. He turned around, his face very serious.

"I'm having a good time, Professor Tripp," he said.

"I'm glad," I said, reaching past him for the glove compartment. I pulled out the Baggie and the papers and went to work on a joint, rolling it up on a flat stretch of my poor, mutilated hood.

"They're nice," James went on. "That Phil is cool."

I smiled. "I know it."

"Kind of not too bright."

"No," I said. "But cool."

"That's how I'd want my brother to be," he said, sounding wistful.

"Play your cards right and he could be," I said. "I think they pretty much have an open-door policy around here."

"Grady? You don't have, like, any other real family, do you?"

"No, I really don't. A couple of aunts I never see back in my hometown." I drew the ends taut and pinched them. "And the Wonders, I guess. Goddamn them."

"The Wonders?"

"The brothers in my book. They're sort of like *my* brothers." I sniffed. "I guess that's the best I can do."

"Hey, you know what? I'm the same way!" He raised the back of one hand to his brow and gave his head a tragical toss. "We're orphans!" he cried.

I laughed. I said, "You're drunk."

"You're lucky," he said, looking up at the house.

"Think so?" I drew the sweet stripe of adhesive gum across the tip of my tongue.

His eyes met mine, and to my surprise I discovered in them a hint of pity.

"Grady, you know how that guy was talking last night about, you know, having a double? Who goes around wrecking his life for him? So that he'll have plenty to write about?" He was looking at the impression of a pair of buttocks stamped into the hood of my car. "Did you think that was all bullshit?"

"No," I said, "I'm afraid I didn't."

"I didn't either," he said.

"Gra-dy! Jay-ames!" It was Irene, calling us from the porch. "It's time!"

"We'll be right there!" said James. "I guess Philly's not coming out."

"I guess not," I said. "It's kind of hard to be all wild and slip out into the yard for a doobie when you're an old married man like he is."

"A husband."

"A husband," I said, lighting the joint and taking that first long piney sip of smoke. I passed it to James. "Here."

James hesitated for a moment, holding the lit end of the joint under his nose, sniffing at it speculatively.

"Should I?"

"Go for it."

"All right." He lifted the joint in the air and nodded to me, as if raising a glass of wine for a toast. "To the Wonder brothers." He took a very long and ambitious drag, then coughed it all out. "I don't know about this stuff," he said.

"Why's that?"

"It kind of makes me feel like everything already happened five minutes ago."

"Everything did."

He took another, smaller puff, and let it rattle around inside of him for a minute. He looked up at the house Irv Warshaw had built, at the rope of honeysuckle coming unbraided along its front porch, at the shapes of people moving back and forth across its bright windows.

"I guess I'm pretty happy," he said, so flatly and as if to himself that I didn't even bother to reply.

As a Jew, Emily was never more than sporadically observant, and in the course of our marriage my view, as a gentile observer, of the annual transit of Jewish holidays across their queer lunar calendar, with all their byzantine statutes and elusive significance, had come to resemble my view, as a baseball fan, of the great test matches of the cricket schedule. But I'd always had a soft spot for Passover. I liked the fakery and slyness that went into preparing the food, the way the ubiquitous "bread of affliction" was magically transformed in the Passover repertoire into something manifold and rich— matzoh cakes, matzoh stuffing, matzoh pudding and noodles—like some humble, abundant mammal cherished by Indians for its flesh, hide, bones, organs, and fat. I liked the way the Jewish religion seemed, on the whole, to have devoted so much energy and art to finding loopholes in its crazy laws; I liked what this seemed to me to imply about its attitude toward God, that dictatorial and arbitrary old fuck with his curses and his fiats and his yen for the smell of burnt shoulder meat. In addition to all of this, I'd noticed over the years that I got a strong feeling of satisfaction from sitting down to eat a mad meal of parsley, bones, hard-boiled eggs, crackers, and salt water with a bunch of Jews, three of them Korean. It reassured me that, if nothing else in life, at least I'd fulfilled my earliest ambition simply to wander far afield, in spirit if not in space, from the place of my birth.

In our town, when I was growing up, there were only seven Jews. There were the five Glucksbringers: the ancient Mr. Louis P., who by the time I was a boy had long since retired to the Stamps and Coins department of the store on Pickman Street he'd founded fifty years before; his son, Maurice; Maurice's wife, whose name I have forgotten; and their children, David and Leona. There was Mr. Kaplan, who bought Weaver's Drugs when I was in junior high, and a pretty redheaded woman, married to one of the professors at Coxley, who attended the Episcopal church, and celebrated Christmas, but was known to be a Kaufmann from Pittsburgh. Then my father killed David Glucksbringer, leaving six. It often occurred to me to wonder if I had married into the Warshaw family in part as a way to atone for that terrible subtraction. The Warshaws, too, had lost a son; and the first year I joined them at the Seder table (Irv, Irene, Deborah, Emily, Phil, and Uncle Harry, Irv's brother, who died the next year of prostate cancer) I took the seventh chair.

This year there were eight of us, requiring two leaves in the dinner table, so that through an architectural miscalculation of Irv's, which Irene never let him forget, the dining room was too small to hold us all. Irene had to push back the easy chairs, coffee tables, and floor lamps, and squeeze us all into the living room, which took up the entire front half of the house, from the cracked and blackened fieldstone fireplace to the steep, cockeyed set of stairs that led up to the bedrooms. They'd brought all their belongings with them when they moved from the house on Inverness, and now they spent half their time rearranging the furniture and irritably tripping over footstools. They'd gone in for Danish modern in a big way during its heyday and everything was glass and black leather and abstract expanses of teak and mahogany, while the interior of the house itself was all fir flooring and knotty pine walls, yellow and splintery. Irene was always threatening to sell their old things and buy more appropriate furnishings, but they'd been here for five years now and not a hassock had been shown the door. I always figured that keeping the house jammed with reminders of their old life in Pittsburgh was both a sentimental act on Irene's part and a gesture of protest.

When James and I came in from the yard, Irv was already installed at the head of the table, nearest the fireplace, propped up on a sofa cushion. Philly, in a starched shirt with a button-down collar, his spiky hair slicked back with water, was sitting on Irv's left. They were going through a shoe box filled with yarmulkes, reading the inscriptions and trying to recollect the various afternoons and ceremonies therein commemorated. I could hear the irritable whispering of Marie and Irene in the kitchen, each advising the other not to panic, but the two Warshaw daughters were nowhere to be seen.

They were off together someplace, upstairs or outside, conferring, conspiring, helping each other dress. I felt a nasty little thrill of foreboding.

"Andrew . . . Ab . . . Andrew Abraham," Irv said, holding a blotchy purplish beanie at arm's length and frowning at the faded legend imprinted in the lining. "July . . . something, 1964. That's your cousin Andy."

"No kidding."

"Brother, I remember that one. It was up in Buffalo. Did they have gnats, God, it was awful."

Philly grinned and waggled his eyebrows at us as we joined them at the table. "Gnats, huh?" He reached into the box and pulled out a crisp gold yarmulke. "Did they get up your nose? I hate that. Hey, dudes, how are you?"

"Hi," James and I said, not quite simultaneously, and then the three of us all burst out laughing. Irv looked up, startled, trying to see what the joke was. He reached for a couple of yarmulkes and handed them to me and James.

"Up your nose," he said, as he handed James a black yarmulke and me a royal blue one, studying our faces with his engineer's eye. "In your mouth, in your ears, it was *awful*. Here you are, James. Grady."

"Thanks," said James. His face as he examined the little black skullcap was at once dubious and respectful, as if Irv had handed him a miraculous tortilla on which the face of a saint was said to have appeared.

"Phillip and Marie Warshaw," Philly read from the inside of the gold yarmulke. "May 11, 1988." He cocked his head to one side and rolled his eyes to the ceiling. "I *think* I was at that one. Wasn't that the one where the groom's father and the bride's uncle got into a huge argument about Arnold

Shoneberger and were yelling so loud at each other that all the babies in the room started to cry?"

Resisting, somehow, the urge to correct Philly's mispronunciation, Irv buried his chin in his hand and said nothing. He had worked all his life to deserve the reputation of a measured and reasoning person, and I knew it pained him to recall that devotion to his old hero had exposed him, unalterably, as the kind of man who would pick a fight with the in-laws at a wedding.

"Bat Mitzvah of—Osnat—Gleberman," I said, with some difficulty, reading from the inside of my own little hat as I donned it. "February 17, 1979."

"Osnat Gleberman?" said Philly. "Who the hell's that?"

"I have no idea," said Irv, with a shrug. "She must have been a friend of yours."

"Hey, check it out," James said, showing us the lining of his black yarmulke. "Mine says, 'Dawidov Funeral Home.' "

"Oy, here," said Irv, proffering the shoe box. "You can pick another one."

"No, thanks," said James, and he clamped the black beanie onto the back of his head.

"I never had any friends named *Osnat*," said Philly indignantly, rhyming it, as had I, with the name of the little insect that ruined Andy Abraham's Buffalo bar mitzvah.

"I believe it's pronounced 'oh-SNOT,' " said Irv, raising a pedantic finger, and the three of us burst out laughing again. "Shush!" He sat up a little in his chair, and pointed his upraised finger at the ceiling. "Here she comes." There was a faint involuntary timbre of warning in his voice, the way you announce the arrival of a notorious brawler or an ill-tempered child or a woman in a very bad mood.

We shushed, following with our ears a soft, deliberate creaking of the ceiling as it traveled over our heads and then down the rickety stairs, one by one, finally emerging into the living room in the form of Emily Warshaw. And as forms went, as Julius Marx might have added, this one wasn't half bad. She was a slight, slender woman, my wife, though broad across the hips, with hair that was always cool to the touch and a face, Crabtree used to say, like Fallingwater, all sharp outcroppings and dramatic angles. Her lips were rouged and her eyelids inked and she was dressed in black jeans, a black turtleneck, and a black cardigan sweater. When she saw me she didn't stop dead, or flee, or suffer a brain hemorrhage, or anything of the sort. She had a single moment of crushing shyness, no more, during which she glanced at James and gave him a practiced friendly smile. Then she walked right over to the empty chair beside me and, to my astonishment, sat down.

"How are you?" she said, just loud enough for me to hear. Emily had a voice that while soft, and at times even inaudible, was throaty and masculine, like the voice of a man in a crowded room talking on the telephone to a lover. On those rare occasions when she grew emotional it would rise and crack like a teenaged boy's. She met my gaze for a moment, her expression tender and surprisingly pleased, and then looked away, almost flirtatiously, as if we were strangers seated together by a designing hostess. I guessed that, so far, anyway, Deborah had managed to keep my secret. It was going to be up to me to ruin the evening.

"I'm glad to see you," I said, my voice emerging from my throat cracked by a pubescent little wrinkle of its own. Seeing Emily again I felt an intense desire to kiss her, or at least to give her fingers a squeeze, but she was sitting demurely on her hands, eyes lowered; closed off, untouchable, thinking her unimaginable Emily thoughts. I could smell the talcum powder on the nape of her neck and the clove shampoo she used on her gun black hair. I felt a bright black wobble of sex pulse across the six charged inches that separated her left thigh from my right. "This is James Leer. From workshop?"

She brushed an errant strand of hair from her eyes—she had the long, narrow eyes, like a pair of recumbent check marks, that in Korea they call buttonholes—and nodded to James. Emily was never one for handshakes.

"The movie man," she said. "I've heard about you."

"I've heard about you, too," said James.

I thought for a moment that she might ask him about Buster Keaton, one of her idols, but she didn't. She sat back in her chair, shoulders hunched, and looked like she was wishing for a cigarette. Nobody spoke for a few seconds; the advent of Emily at a party or dinner table was generally followed, in the face of the deep and devouring power of her silence, by such a period of conversational adjustment.

"Is Deb coming down?" Irv said at last.

"In a minute," said Emily, her tiny mouth twisting into a faint smirk of mock disgust. "Or maybe not."

"What's the matter?"

She shook her head. For a moment I thought she might not say anything more.

"She's all freaked out about something or other," she said, and shrugged.

As she spoke there was another creak of the ceiling, and then a loud syncopated clatter on the stairs, as if a croquet ball and a grapefruit were racing each other down to the bottom.

"Look at this," said Philly, impressed, as Deborah came into the room.

"*That's* what you're wearing to the Seder?" said Irv.

Deborah ignored him, took the chair next to her brother, and then waited, chin raised, with an air of long-suffering patience, while we all came to terms with the discovery that she had shed the unfortunate purple dress, along with her tights and shoes, and come down to the table barefoot, wearing only her bathrobe. It was a nice bathrobe, though—we all agreed about that—heavy and brightly colored and patterned with chevrons, as if it had been made from an old-fashioned trader's blanket.

"It's Alvin's," she informed us, with an exaggerated wince as she pronounced the name of her most recent ex-husband. "I figured if he can't be with us, right? At least his bathrobe could."

"That's sweet," said Philly.

"Hi, everyone," said Marie, emerging at last from the kitchen, cheeks puffed out, her thin yellow hair afly. She was carrying a silver plate on which sat a small stack of matzohs, and another, larger plate on which they were piled high. As she rounded the table you could see her taking in both that Emily and I were sitting next to each other in apparent amity, and that her other sister-in-law had made an interesting choice of festival apparel, but she said nothing, and only smiled a little wearily at Irv. She set the big plate of matzohs on the table between Emily and Deborah, and the smaller silver one in front of Irv. As she did so she laid a hand on his cheek and planted a sympathetic peck on his high forehead. Then she sat down beside Philly. Only the seat opposite Irv remained empty now.

"What's the holdup?" Irv called into the kitchen. "Come on, Irene. James is getting restless, here."

"Not really," said James.

"I'm coming, I'm coming." Irene swept into the living room, looking even more flustered than Marie, her face red, her forehead shining. She was wrapped, as on all special family occasions, in one of a number of flowing garments she had made for herself, according to her own design, drawing her inspiration, as far as I could determine, from the caftan, the muumuu, and possibly from certain episodes of *Star Trek*. "I was just having a little problem getting the Seder plate arranged. The one we bought in Mexico last winter." She carried the broad, painted earthenware plate to the table and started to set it down in front of Irv, beside the matzohs, then stopped and stood frowning at it, shaking her head. It was a pretty thing, decorated with green vines and yellow flowers and dark blue undulations, and loaded up with the usual ritual foodstuffs. "I've got the *moror,* and the parsley, the *charoses,* the bone, the egg . . . Damn it, I can never remember what this sixth little circle is for."

"What sixth circle?" said Irv, his tone implying that the problem for which she had been holding up the Seder was not only minor but would probably turn out, in the light of his impatient logic, to be nonexistent. "The horseradish, the parsley, the *charoses,* the shank bone, the egg. That's five."

"See for yourself," she said, setting the plate before him.

Irv counted off on his fingers the items that had been set into five of the plate's six round indentations, mumbling over again to himself the list of items he'd just enunciated.

"Bone, egg, and, uh . . . Oh!" He snapped his fingers. "Matzoh! It's for the matzoh," he declared.

"The matzoh." Irene slapped him on the side of his head. "The *matzoh* won't fit in there, Irv. That's ridiculous. What am I supposed to do, crumble it up? And look at *that.* Read that word there." She pointed to the Hebrew word painted in blue characters on the bottom of the empty compartment. "That doesn't say matzoh!"

Emily sat forward, leaning across me, and craned her neck to read the inscription. Her left breast brushed against my arm. She was so close to me that I could hear the creaking of her jeans.

"It says, 'Cazart,' " she offered.

"Chaz-art," Irene tried. "Chazrat."

"Chazrat?" Irv was incredulous. "What chazrat? Look, it says 'matzoh.' That's supposed to be a *mem*." He rolled his eyes and looked disgusted. "Mexicans," he said.

"It *doesn't* say matzoh."

"Maybe it's for the salt water," Philly suggested.

"Maybe it's an ashtray," said Deborah.

"Maybe it's not really a Seder plate," I said, trying to re-member if we didn't engage in this same dispute every year. "Maybe it's supposed to be for some other, similar holiday."

"I think it's *chazeret*," said Marie quietly.

"Chazeret?" we said.

Marie nodded.

"Some kind of vegetable, maybe?" She said this as if she were dredging up some fragmentary and poorly learned bit of Jewish knowledge upon which any of us would be able to improve, but I could see that she knew precisely what she was talking about, and had done all along. Marie was scrupulous about not outshining the various born and lifelong Jews among us. "Some kind of *bitter* vegetable, I think?"

"That's what the *moror* is, dear," said Irene with placid condescension. "Bitter herbs."

"I know, but I think the *chazeret* is supposed to be some-thing bitter, too. Maybe something like watercress?"

"Put some watercress, Irene," said Irv, at once, deferring,

as was generally wise in such matters, to his daughter-in-law's erudition.

"*Water*cress? Why would I have watercress?"

"For the *chazeret*." He looked annoyed, as if she were being obtuse. "There's plenty of it growing around the pond."

"I'm not going out to the pond, Irving, at *night,* in *that* mud, to harvest any *watercress*. You can forget about that."

"Or maybe endive?" suggested Marie.

"How about some radicchio?" said James, deciding to brave the waters of Warshavian ritual dispute.

"Radicchio!" cried Irene.

"I know," said Emily, with a little smile. "Why don't you put some kimchee?"

Everyone laughed at that, and an evil red rank-smelling dollop of kimchee was fetched from its sealed lead containment unit in the refrigerator. It seemed to me that things had gotten off to a very good start. Then I remembered that it didn't matter what kind of a start things got off to, that I was not going to be a part of this family much longer, and that the news I had come to impart to Emily would annihilate in an instant all the promising starts and family happiness in the world.

"Shall we begin?" said Irv. "James? Will you hand me the Haggadahs?"

He pointed to the sideboard behind us and James reached around for the stack of little booklets, which Irv then passed around. They were the same ones he always used, cheap little giveaway jobs, heavy on the English, that were emblazoned throughout with the name of a defunct brand of coffee. He pulled his eyeglasses from their plastic sleeve in the pocket of his shirt, cleared his throat, and then we set about once again to commemorate the start of a long trip across a small desert by an ill-behaved rabble of former slaves. Irv started by reading the short opening prayer that invoked in fairly conventional and politically somewhat outmoded terms the Almighty; the family, friendship, and the sense of thanksgiving; and the spirits of liberty, justice, and democracy. James turned to me, looking panicked, and I showed him the trick with Jewish books, flipping his Haggadah to what he'd thought to be its conclusion and opening it to page 1. Then I bowed my head, and listened, and looked over the top of my eyeglasses around the table. Everyone else was reading along with Irv, except for Deborah, who was not even looking at the Haggadah in her hands. I caught her eye and she stared back at me for a moment, levelly and without expression, then looked at Emily. Then she dropped her eyes to her book.

"Now we pour the first cup of wine," Irv said, when he'd concluded the opening prayer. "There are four," he told James.

"Look out!" said Philly. "James already had his four *beers*."

"He doesn't have to drink all four glasses," said Irene, looking concerned. "You don't have to drink them all, James."

I turned to James.

"Maybe you should take it easy," I said.

"Mr. Role Model," said Deborah. She looked at James. "You wanna make sure you follow this guy's example, that's for sure."

"Deb," said Emily in a tone of gentle warning, and as we raised our cups, and Irv read the blessing over the wine, I felt so grateful for this intervention by my wife on my behalf that tears almost came to my eyes. Could she really have decided to forgive me? And was I really going to throw away such unearned forgiveness, such grace? The heavy wine was hot and salty in my throat. James, I saw, drank down his whole glass.

"All right," said Irv. He pushed back his chair and got up from the table. "Now I wash my hands."

"I'd like to wash my hands, too," said Marie.

This appeared to irritate Deborah.

"Isn't it usually just Daddy who washes his hands?" she said, with mock innocence.

"Anyone can wash their hands," said Irv.

"Yes, we *all* could," said Marie, as if trying to get up a game of charades.

"Why *shouldn't* she wash her hands?" Irene said, waving a dismissive hand toward Deborah.

"Maybe you should wash *yours*," Philly said. He winked. "I'm not sure you got all the cow pie off them."

"Fuck you," said Deborah. "I hate it when you wink at me."

"May I wash mine?" said James.

"Certainly you may," said Irene, watching with a broad smile as James got up and followed Irv and Marie into the kitchen. We heard the stream of water ringing against the stainless steel sink. The smile died. "You're such a pleasant person to be around, Deborah."

"Yeah," said Philly. "What's your problem?"

Deborah glanced at me, and I felt a cheesy smile congeal on my lips.

"Okay, then, fine," she said, leaping from her chair, and for a moment I thought the meal was going to be ended before it had even begun. "I'm going to wash my fucking hands, too."

Emily looked at me and rolled her eyes, as if her sister were only being her usual impossible self. I nodded, and this moment of private derision, of silent laughter between us, made my heart seize. When the hand washers had returned from their ablutions we proceeded with the dipping of the parsley into the salt water, reading in turn from our booklets about the recollection, thereby, of Jewish hope, Jewish tears, and ancient Near Eastern fashions in hors d'oeuvres. Then Irv reached for the middle matzoh of the three stacked on the silver plate, broke it in two, and wrapped it in a napkin.

"Now," he said, turning so quickly to James, who'd been watching this procedure with dazed fascination, that the young man jumped.

"What?" he said.

"This is called the *afikomen*," said Irv, tapping the little bundle. His bushy white eyebrows knotted over his nose. "Don't you try to steal it, now."

"No, I wouldn't," said James, eyes wide.

"You're *supposed* to, buddy," I told him. "Take it easy. You hide it, and then Irv here has to ransom it back."

"There might be a little money in it for you, if you're interested." Irv set the little bundle beside his plate, slid it a couple of inches toward James, and humorously cleared his throat. "Now," he said, and took up his Haggadah again, and we all turned the page, and I saw a look of unreasoning panic enter the young man's eyes. He'd been marking it all along with a fearful thumb, and now it was here. He blanched and looked at me to save him. I clapped him on the shoulder and said, "Go to it."

"I can't read this part in Hebrew."

"That's okay. We know."

"Take your time," said Irene. "Take a deep breath."

He inhaled, and exhaled, and then, as he started in on that

old rigged four-part quiz we'd all heard Philly reel off, in weary Hebrew, so many times before—asking Irv why, on this night that commemorated a strange assortment of emergencies and miracles, he ate crackers, horseradish, and parsley and sat slumped against a crocheted orange throw pillow— the Warshaws left off their arguments, and their wry asides, and their shifting around in their chairs. Instead they just sat, motionless, listening, while James picked his way carefully through the passage, in his clear, high corrupted-altar-boy voice, as though his Haggadah were an instruction manual and there was some complicated machine there in the living room that we were all trying to assemble.

"That was very nice, James," said Irene, when he finished.

His cheeks colored, and he smiled at her as though he were in love.

"Mr. Warshaw?" he said. His voice came out sounding strangled with emotion.

"Irv."

"Irv? Could I— No."

"What James? What is it?"

"Could I have a pillow so I can, uh, recline, too?"

"Get him a pillow," Irv said.

Deborah got up and went to one of the two pushed-aside sofas, which were all but buried in throw pillows. In the cushions and bolsters that littered the house one could read, as in the strata of metamorphic rock, the handicraft fads of the Warshaw daughters—the eras of needlepoint, rug hooking, tie-dye, crochet. She brought back a cushion embroidered with a green-skinned Peter Frampton with taxi yellow curls and tucked it in behind James's back.

"Here you go, handsome," she said, patting his cheek and bringing up a deep flush of color.

Dutifully Irv set about answering the Four Questions. He looked around the table, at which sat three native Koreans, a converted Baptist, a badly lapsed Methodist, and a Catholic of questionable but tormented stripe, lifted his Haggadah, and began, unironically, "Once we were slaves in Egypt . . ." James Leer sat with his eyes fixed on Irv's gesticulating right hand, his head not quite motionless on his neck, listening to the remainder of Irv's response with the universal bogus solemnity of drunken young men trying to pay attention to something that is making no impression at all. After this we read in turn about the Four Sons, those poor ill-assorted siblings, one self-righteous, one dull-witted, one an asshole, one infantile—try to guess which one fell to me—who year after year got criticized and compared with one another in a way that I supposed had provided a useful example to Jewish parents for centuries. Next came the long retelling of the sad, operatic, but as far as I could see typical history of the Jews in Egypt, from the miraculous feats of Joseph to the slaying of Hebrew babies. Generally it was somewhere around this point that I began to engage in a little Passover reclining of my own. I sat back, closed my eyes, and felt myself drifting, abandoned and alone, in a little wicker basket on a broad muddy river, in the shadow of the murmuring bulrushes. Egypt was the expanse of lapis lazuli passing overhead, the grunt of a crocodile, the wind-chime laughter of a princess and her handmaids playing on the shore. I felt a sharp pain in my left side and my eyes snapped open. James had jabbed me in the ribs.

"My turn to read?" I said.

"If you don't mind," said Irv, dryly, looking annoyed. I looked around the table at my wife and her family. Stoned again, their faces said. Then Irv's crocodile stomach growled, long and irritably, and everyone laughed. "Maybe we had better speed this up."

So Irv hurried us through the Ten Plagues and the eating of the various recondite matzoh sandwiches. A second glass of wine was poured and blessed, and again, except for the ten drops that he spilled for the sake of those unlucky Egyptians, James knocked the whole thing back in one swallow, then gasped like a happy sailor.

"Have an egg," said Irving, "have an egg."

At last it was time to eat. As the rest of us set to work on the hard-boiled eggs, Irene, Marie, and Emily started to serve the first courses. First there were dense, cold slippery globules of gefilte fish, never one of my favorites. James conducted wary experiments on his own gray lump with a fork and the end of one finger and ignored all of Irv's exhortations to dig in.

"It's *pike*," he explained, as if this were guaranteed to whet James's appetite.

"Pike?"

"Bottom feeders," Philly assured him. "God knows what they eat."

Stealthily James interred the remainder of his fish in a grave of pink horseradish and then pushed his plate aside. He looked grateful to see the fragrant yellow bowl of matzoh ball soup when it arrived.

"So what are these a symbol of?" said James, poking at a matzoh ball with his spoon.

"What's that?" said Irv.

"These things, and those gefilder fish things," he said. "And the eggs, too. How come we're supposed to eat so many little white balls?"

" 'Cause that's what Moses had," said Philly.

"It's possible it's some sort of fertility symbol," agreed Irv.

Deborah said, "Well, it's obviously not working for this family." She looked at me, then away. "At least not for some people."

"Deb, please," said Emily, misinterpreting her sister's remark as a reference to our years of failed attempts to conceive, which in the Warshaw family were generally attributed, I knew, to the effect on my sperm count of my years of pot smoking. If only they knew, I thought; but they would soon enough. "Let's not—"

"Let's not *what*?"

"None of this stuff is a symbol of anything, okay?" said Philly, waving an arm over the table, indicating the heaped platters and serving bowls that Irene and Marie were bringing in. "All of this stuff is just, you know, you can just eat it. It's dinner."

Dinner was a roast leg of lamb, crisp and speckled with rosemary, served with new potatoes that had been roasted in the pan of crackling fat. These, along with the matzoh ball soup and a gigantic green salad trimmed with yellow pepper and red onion, had been, we were told, Irene's responsibility. Marie had provided a casserole of sweet potatoes stewed with onions and prunes, another of zucchini in a sauce of tomato and dill, and two cairns, at either end of the table, of the tasty little hollow puffs of matzoh-meal artifice, at once crusty and moist, called *bagelach*. Unfortunately, however, Philly's claim that the menu had no symbolic content was not strictly true, because it also included Emily's contribution, a kugel or pudding made, in this case, from potatoes. She'd been working on the thing, Irene informed us in a cautionary tone, all morning. As we brought the first forkfuls to our mouths the air around Emily suddenly gathered and took on a strange heaviness.

"Mmm," I said. "Great."

"Delicious," said Irene.

Everyone agreed, chewing very carefully.

At last Emily took a bite. She managed a brave smile. Then she hung her head and covered her face with her hands. One of the things Emily most disliked about herself was her haplessness in the kitchen. She was an impatient cook, hasty and careless and easily distracted. Most of her efforts arrived at the table with uncooked middles, missing ingredients, and an apology from the mortified chef. In this I think she saw a kind of parable of her life, having started out aspiring to write heart-stopping novels and short stories, and ended up generating ad copy for the biggest kielbasa in the world. It seemed to her that she must have left something out, or taken something too soon off the burner.

"It tastes like something," said Deborah, poker-faced. "Something we used to eat in school. Oh, I know." She nodded. "Paste."

I hate you, said Emily to her sister. Fuck you and go to hell.

"Sorry," she said. She looked down at her plate.

"Sweetie pie," I said, reaching out for the first time to touch her. I cupped her chin in my hand, and stroked her cool hair, and admired for the one thousandth time the surprising planes of her downturned face. Emily was a thoughtful, intense, and complicated woman with an ear for dialogue, a nice sense of the absurd, and a loyal heart, but I may well have had no better reason for falling in love with her than her face. And I don't care what you will say about me, either. People get married for worse reasons than that. But like all beautiful faces Emily's made you believe that its possessor was a better person than she was. It allowed her to pass for stoical when she was petrified, and for mysterious and aloof when she was so filled with self-doubt that she bought presents for other people when it was her birthday, framed most of her conversation in terms of apology and regret, and for all her talent could no longer manage to string twenty-five paragraphs of prose together to make a short story. "I think it tastes fine. I do."

She took hold of my hand and gave my fingers a grateful squeeze.

"Thanks," she said.

Deborah looked faintly disgusted.

"The two of you," she said, giving her head a fatigued shake. "Shit, man."

There was more at work here than Deborah's natural gift for verbal abuse, of course, though only I knew it. I'd hurt her feelings with my earlier remarks about the dress, and doubtless that explained part of her anger, but I had also, I could see, by my confession about Sara, filled her with an as yet directionless, all-encompassing sense of outrage. It was this and her sisterly loyalty, albeit twisted back on itself like a Möbius strip, that had led her to say that Emily's kugel tasted like library paste.

"So," said Irene, in a brave but reckless effort to change the subject, "Grady. How is your book going? Emily said you were going to see your editor this weekend."

"That's right," I said.

"Did he show?" said Emily, looking up, her voice all cheery, a tight smile on her face. "How is Terry?"

"Spiraling rapidly out of control," I said. "Same as ever."

"What did he say about the book?"

"He said he wants to see it."

"So are you going to let him? Did you get it done?"

I hesitated for a moment, and looked around the table. Everyone was waiting to hear my reply. I didn't blame them for that. For as long as they could remember, I'd been making vague and confident assurances that any day I would finish the thing. If and when I ever did, they would probably feel an almost physical sense of relief. I was like a massively incompetent handyman who'd been up on their roof now for years, trying to take down a gnarled old lightning-struck tree trunk that had fallen against the house, haunting every gathering, all discussions of family business, any attempt they made to sit down together and plan for the future, with the remote but ceaseless whining of my saw.

"I'm just about done," I said with a smile that morally if not in fact was a first cousin to the gap-toothed, dishonest, and faintly stupid grin of untrustworthy and drunken old Everett Tripp. "I should have it finished in the next couple of weeks."

There followed a brief silence which might have greeted a man with terminal cancer announcing that he'd just bought himself a ticket to the World Series next fall. Deborah let go a bitter laugh.

"Oh, *right*," she said.

Emily's fork rang out against her plate.

"I really wish you would stop it now, Deborah," she said.

"Stop what, Em?"

Emily started to speak, then remembered James, glanced at him, and said nothing. She picked up her fork and twirled it in the fingers of her left hand, over and over, as though looking for scratches. It would not have been at all like her to pick a fight at the dinner table and I was relieved (although secretly disappointed) to see her back down. I didn't like to think what kind of surprising mass revelations a direct challenge might bring from Deborah. But whenever tempers flared you could always count, I thought, on Emily's astonishing faculty for repression. In our eight years together we'd had exactly one fight: something to do with kirschwasser and a cheese fondue. Above all things Emily hated to draw attention to herself or cause a scene of any kind; that was how she had survived her childhood as the only Jewish girl in Squirrel Hill with an epicanthic fold.

"I wish you would just lay off Grady," she finally said, in her soft dark Casanova voice. She tried to make a little joke out of it. "Just for tonight."

Deborah sat for a moment, thinking that one over. "You're a fool, Em," she said.

"*Deborah,*" said Irv. "That's enough."

"*I'm* a fool? Look at you."

"What's that?"

"I said, 'Look at you,' " said Emily. She clutched the fork more tightly now, the joints of her fingers going white, and it occurred to me that Deborah might be getting more than she had bargained for. On that miraculous evening of the cheese fondue, I suddenly remembered, Emily had come at me with a wicked little fork. "Sitting there in your *bath*robe. You didn't even comb your *hair.*"

"Deborah, Emily, both of you," said Irene, setting her own fork down. "Stop fighting. This instant." The corners of her mouth turned up in a wry smile and she looked at James. "You're going to give our guest the right impression of our family."

Obediently and with an air of relief, Emily relaxed her grip on the fork. The tension went out of her shoulders. I was bitterly, crazily disappointed to see Emily fold.

"Sorry," she said. She smiled at James. "Sorry, James."

James nodded, looking more baffled than forgiving, and

took a long avid swallow of the California zinfandel we were drinking with dinner, as if his throat were parched. For another instant Deborah sat stroking at her unkempt black thatch of hair. Then she stood up, abruptly, tugging the flaps of her bathrobe tightly around her.

"You're always *so fucking sorry,*" she said to Emily, her cheeks twitching with pity and contempt. Her chair, one of eight blond, curvaceous tangles of Scandinavian birchwood, stood balanced on its hind legs for an instant, then tipped over and hit the floor with a loud *bönk.* As Deborah spun around, in an unsuccessful effort to catch it, the tie of her robe lashed out and knocked over her wineglass. "I've had enough Passover," she told us, superfluously. Then she opened her mouth again, and I shut my eyes, and braced myself for what she would say next.

When I heard the kitchen door slam, I opened my eyes and saw that Deborah wasn't standing there anymore. Marie had also disappeared, but after a moment she reemerged from the kitchen, carrying a damp cloth, which she used to blot the spreading purple stain on the tablecloth. At her sharp request Philly leaned over and righted the upset chair. Irv, employing his usual strategy for dealing with what he called Deborah's conniption fits, had returned to his food, working with determination on a large thick slab of kugel. James was busy reading the bottle of zinfandel, a concerned expression on his face, as though he'd just found out it was wine he'd been drinking all evening and were searching for the place on the label where they told you how to get it to stop. I looked at Emily; she was looking at her mother, who was looking, I was surprised to find, at me. I considered for one wild instant the possibility that Deborah had spilled the beans not to Emily at all, but to her mother. But then I saw what Irene was thinking. The same optimism that made it possible for her to believe that Emily and I might stay together led her never to abandon the hope that Deborah's strange behavior was brought about largely by outside forces. She was thinking that I had gotten Deborah stoned.

"Deborah," I said, smiling, giving my head a disingenuous shake. There was a rustling sound at my ear and a bright splash of blue appeared on my plate. My yarmulke had fallen into my salad.

Emily stood up.

"I'll be right back," she said, sounding determined. She went into the kitchen and out the back door, and a moment later we could hear their voices rising and falling in the flooded yard. That left six of us to sit in our chairs and stare at the pieces of broken matzoh that littered the table like pages torn out of prayer books. Marie, Irene, and Irv made several valiant attempts to start and sustain a discussion about a documentary they'd seen on PBS the night before about some Jews who were hoping to rebuild the Temple in Jerusalem, but it was all that anyone could manage to eat the food on our plates without choking and fight off the maddening desire to eavesdrop. I, of course, failed even to manage that. I couldn't hear what the sisters were saying, but the truth was I didn't really need to. I could fill in the dialogue myself.

"How about that farm in Sweden where they're already breeding all those special red heifers?" Marie said.

"I have a hard time believing your basic Ken and Janet Abramowitz from Teaneck are really going to cough up five thousand dollars to have their own personal red heifer sacrificed in Jerusalem," said Irene.

"I guess I'd better get back our deposit," Irv said.

Just then Emily came running back into the house, with an

unaccustomed thunderousness, across the kitchen floor and then out into the living room. She made directly for the hall closet, grabbed the long leather coat in which she'd fled Pittsburgh yesterday morning, and then, stopping only briefly to shoot me a tear-streaked and heartbroken look, ran back outside. We sat there, Grady and all the people who were staring at him, for another twenty seconds or so, and then, treading softly, Deborah reappeared, contentedly chewing on a mouthful of gum.

"Where's your sister?" said Irv.

"She's going for a drive," Deborah said, with a little shrug.

"Is she all right?"

"Fine."

From outside there was the irritable two-stroke cough of Emily's old Bug, and then a scrabbling of gravel as she pulled away. I hoped she would be all right, driving around in a state of shock, with those six-volt headlights, on those dark lanes. It was not unusual for her to take off in her car when she was upset, however. She found solace in traveling the roads around Kinship; down to Barkeyville, out to Nectarine, across the Ohio state line at Sharon.

Deborah took a long, slow look around the table at the wreckage of dinner and the early high spirits in which the meal had begun.

"This party sucks," she said. She walked around behind me, and as she went past I caught a bitter whiff of dirt from the pocket of her bathrobe and realized that she was not chewing on any piece of gum.

She laid a hand on James's shoulder.

"Come on, sport," she said. "Let's go hide that matzoh."

THE table had been cleared, the remnant of our tribe assembled. We hurried through the ragged end of the service. Deborah had disappeared upstairs—to wait for the mushrooms to kick in, I supposed—and Emily did not return. Irv skipped through the grace, mumbling along in tired Hebrew, stopping frequently to rub his eyes. Then it came time to open the door to Elijah the Prophet, and at Irv's request, James got himself out of his chair and stumbled into the kitchen to admit that longed-for phantom, for whom a glass of wine stood ready and waiting in the middle of the table. Many years earlier, I knew, family tradition had made it the job of Sam Warshaw to open the magical door.

"No," said Irv, his voice a little hoarse. "The front."

James looked back at Irv, then nodded slowly and went over to the front door. He had to throw his shoulder against it to get it unlocked, and it produced a suitably eerie creaking of the hinges when he pulled it open. A cool breeze blew into the room and stirred the flames of the candles, and I looked at Irv, who was watching the air around him as if he could see it moving. If Elijah ever did show up to drink his glass of wine, I knew, it would mean that the Messiah himself was on the way, and the night would be as day, and the hills would skip like rams, and fathers would be reunited with their drowned sons.

James sat back down in his chair, heavily, and gave us all a queasy smile.

"Thank you, son," said Irv.

"Hey, Irv?" I said, deciding, after all this time, to ask the

Fifth Question, the one that never got asked. "How come old Yahweh let the Jews wander around in the desert like that for forty years, anyway? How come he didn't, just, like, show them the right way to go? They could have gotten there in a month."

"They weren't ready to enter the Holy Land," said Marie. "It took forty years to get the slavery out of them."

"That could be," said Irv, looking over at James, his eyes deep and shadowy. "Or maybe they just got lost."

On this word, "lost," James suddenly tipped back in his chair, hand wrapped around yet another glass of Manische-witz, and closed his eyes. The glass slipped from his hand and chimed against the edge of the table.

"Damn," said Philly, impressed. "He passed out."

"James," said Irene, hurrying around the table to him. "Wake up." She spoke sharply, in the cool and brusque manner of a mother who fears the worst. His eyes fluttered open, and he smiled at her. "Come on, sweetie, come upstairs and lie down."

She helped James out of his chair and guided him up the creaking stairs. Just before she passed from view she turned and looked back at me, her jaw set. What kind of teacher was I? I looked away. Marie got up from the table and ran into the kitchen for another damp cloth.

Ten minutes later Irene reappeared, wearing a short black satin jacket, trimmed with a white fur collar. It was a tight fit.

"Look what James gave me," she said. "He had it in that little bag of his." She ran a hand along its collar. "Ermine."

"Is he all right?" said Philly.

She shook her head.

"I just got off the telephone with his mother." She looked at me with a puzzled expression, as though she couldn't understand why I'd told her such outrageous lies about that poor young man lying upstairs in Sam Warshaw's old bed. "They weren't home, but the housekeeper gave me a number to call. It was a country club, St. Something, they were having a party. They'll be here in two hours."

"In two hours?" I said, trying to connect the words "mother" and "country club" with what I knew about James Leer. "All the way from Carvel?"

"What Carvel?" said Irene.

"He's from a little town called Carvel. Near Scranton."

"That was a Pittsburgh number I called," said Irene. "412."

"Just a minute," said Irv. He got up from the table and brought down an old *Rand McNally Road Atlas* from the shelf under the stairs. He licked his fingertips and smoothed down his flyaway hair, looking relieved to have found a way back into the reasonable land of reference books. We searched the index three times, but there was, naturally, no listing for any-place called Carvel.

I was sitting behind the wheel of Happy Blackmore's Galaxie 500, looking up at the sky. I'd rolled myself a big fat gherkin of a joint, a cocktail weenie, a spaniel dick, and I intended to smoke it down to the skin of my lips. I was looking for the seventh star in the constellation of the Pleiades, thinking about Sara and trying not to think of Hannah. It was so quiet in the farmyard that I could hear the bones of the house creaking, and the snoring of the cattle in the barn. Every so often there was the sound of a car passing, out on the Youngstown Road, all tires and slipstream, like a sigh. The downstairs windows of the house were dark, but upstairs the lights were still on in all the rooms except James Leer's. Emily was still not back, but she had called from a pay phone to tell her mother that we should not wait up for her. I'd passed a couple of hours in front of the television with Philly, watching Edward G. Robinson pad around Pharaonic Memphis in sandals; then let myself be drawn into a sullen game of Scrabble with Irv and Irene. Finally everyone had turned in, tired of waiting for James's parents to show; they were already almost two hours late.

I couldn't help wondering how Hannah would feel when she learned that James had saddened us and won our sympathies with a false autobiography; she knew him much better than I did, which I supposed meant that now she didn't know him at all. I was still having a hard time abandoning my conception of James Leer as the working-class northeastern Pennsylvania boy damaged by grief for his dead mother. But I supposed that was only the situation of the hero of his *Love Parade*. How much of what he'd told me about himself would turn out to be the story of his novel's protagonist?

I looked up at that dark window and thought of how it was said that acute insomniacs often experienced a kind of queasy blurring of the lines between dreams and wakefulness, their waking lives taking on some of the surprising tedium of a nightmare. Maybe the midnight disease was like that, too. After a while you lost the ability to distinguish between your fictional and actual worlds; you confused yourself with your characters, and the random happenings of your life with the machinations of a plot. If that was so, I thought that James Leer probably had the worst case I'd ever seen; but then I remembered another lonely fantasist, sitting slumped in his bentwood chair with his pistol in his fingers, slowly, slowly rocking back and forth. Maybe Albert Vetch had also come to think of himself as the protagonist of one of his own stories. His solitary archaeologists and small-town bibliomanes frequently chose to shoot themselves rather than be devoured by the slavering jaws of whatever betentacled terror their unreasonable thirsts set loose upon the world, devoured by those grins as unluminous and empty as cold black space itself.

The joint had gone out, and I relit it amid the coils of the dashboard lighter. I saw now that with their creatures from beyond the Void—eye sockets vacant, maws desolate and huge—August Van Zorn's stories were all, at bottom, about the horror of emptiness: the emptiness of a matronly pair of pumps abandoned in the back of an armoire, of a blank sheet of foolscap, of a killed bottle of bourbon on a windowsill at five-thirty A.M. Perhaps Albert Vetch, like his hero Eric Waldensee confronted by the deserted rooms and corridors of "The House on Polfax Street," put a pistol to his temple because in the end there were too many whistling black holes in his room in the McClelland Hotel. This was the writer's true doppelgänger, I thought; not some invisible imp of the perverse who watched you from the shadows, periodically appearing, dressed in your clothes and carrying your house keys, to set fire to your life; but rather the typical protagonist of your work—Roderick Usher, Eric Waldensee, Francis Macomber, Dick Diver—whose narratives at first reflected but in time came to determine your life's very course.

I thought about my own luckless heroes, that motley troupe of embarrassed and discredited romantics: Danny Fixx, at the end of *The Bottomlands,* paddling his canoe into the darkness of a New Mexico cavern to hide the body of Big Dog Slaney; Winthrop Pease, in *The Arsonist's Girl,* who suffered a heart attack while digging a hole, in his backyard, for the charred remains of the tuxedo he wore to light his last great fire; and Jack Haworth in *The Land Downstairs,* ruling over and expanding the borders of his basement model-train empire, with its trim, orderly towns named for his children and his wives—while in the town aboveground, in the house over his head, his life and his family fell apart. I'd never noticed it before, but there was a persistent invocation in my work of the subterranean (that other classic theme of the horror writer), a motif of burial and concealment underground. In fact, I'd planned yet another such episode for *Wonder Boys,* one in which Lowell Wonder, after allowing Valerie Sweet to seduce him, would break into the fallout shelter of his old high school and live there for three weeks, emerging— starving, pale, and half blind—to learn that his father, old Culloden, was dead. My heroes, it seemed, were always trying either to escape from their terrible errors of judgment by crawling into caves and vaults and basements or else to cover them up—dispose of them—by laying them in the ground. In the ground, I thought. I took a deep breath and looked slowly around me, and flicked away the burnt end of the joint. Then I got out of the car, went around to the back, and opened up the trunk.

The lightbulb in the lid had burned out years before, but in the lunar-holiday radiance of the full moon it was easy to make out the contents. For a moment I stood there, looking down at the corpse and the tuba case nestled companionably against each other in my trunk. It just wasn't right, I thought, to keep Doctor Dee lying there like that. One of his ears hung twisted at a painful-looking angle to his skull, and the meat on his bones was beginning to spoil. On the back porch of the house, at angles to each other—I could feature them perfectly—stood a pair of shovels, army surplus, crusted over with a rusty oatmeal of dirt. Irv and I had used them a couple of summers ago to dig a posthole, in the front yard, for a birdhouse on a tall birch pole. It was a beautiful piece of handiwork, that birdhouse, in the form of a Russian palace with pied and twisted domes, but unfortunately the all-weather liquid nail compound Irv had formulated to hold it together had dissolved over the winter and left it scattered in particolored pieces on the snow. I looked over at the white-washed rocks scattered like knucklebones on the grass under the horse chestnut tree. Then I looked back at Doctor Dee. His blank mad eyes seemed to have fixed upon me once again. I shuddered.

"Have you out of there in a minute," I said, closing the trunk.

I went around the house to the back, found the shovels right where I'd remembered them, and carried one back into the front yard, sloshing through the flooded grass. The moon-lit headstones threw jagged shadows across the ground. I bit into the earth with the blade of the shovel and started to scoop out the dirt in a vacant spot between the graves of Earmuffs and Whiskers—a long-haired guinea pig, I seemed to re-member. When the shovel hit the dirt, because I was stoned and frightened I thought I heard angry voices coming from inside my own ears or from every corner of the farm. Each black ingot of dirt rang out against the shovel, and I was sure that any minute now somebody would come out and ask me what the hell I thought that I was doing, and I would have to tell them that I was laying another dead dog into their lawn.

After ten minutes, however, my career as a character in one of my own books was over. I couldn't dig anymore. I leaned against the horse chestnut tree and tried to catch my breath, looking down into a hole deep enough, I calculated, to hold a largish Pomeranian. So much for my fucking doppelgänger, I thought. I sighed, and my sigh was answered out on the county road, and I turned in time to see a long pale wand of light reach out and shatter against the colonnade of elms. A car was coming fast toward the house, snapping branches, bottoming out in the many potholes with a series of irritable scrapes and drumbeats. I looked back to the house. The light had come on in Sam Warshaw's old bedroom, now, and there was a shadow at the glass. James Leer watched his parents' car come up the drive.

It was a late-model Mercedes sedan, its engine percolating as though it ran on soda water. In the moonlight it looked soft and gray and stately as a felt fedora. It pulled up behind my car and sat for a minute, engine idling, headlights blaring, as if its passengers were experiencing a moment of doubt, geographic or moral. Then the driver backed it sharply to the left and executed a neat three-point turn, aiming the car out toward the road before cutting the engine; in case they needed to make a quick getaway, I supposed. A long black shoe emerged from the driver's side, pointy-toed and glinting in the light of the Passover moon. It was attached, via a dark stocking and several pale inches of calf, to a man wearing evening dress and a white tuxedo scarf that at first I took for a prayer shawl. The man was not quite as tall as James, but his frame was lanky and his shoulders looked as though they were knotted together in the same shy stoop. He held up a pale, somber palm to me, then offered his hand to the woman in the passenger seat. She was tall, too, and wide, a big woman wrapped up in the luminous white pelt of something dead, wobbling in the driveway on high, high heels. They started toward me, smiling as if they were dropping in on old friends, the man's hand applied like a cha-cha partner's to the small of the woman's back. In their somber finery and luminous white stoles they looked something like an advertisement for a French brand of mustard, and something like the couple on top of a wedding cake, and something like a pair of elegant ghosts, killed in a collision of limousines on their way to a fancy-dress ball.

"I'm Fred Leer," said the man, when he got to the steps where I was waiting. I'd left the shovel stabbed into the grass of the pet cemetery, next to the unfinished grave, and hopped up onto the front steps of the house, as if that was where visitors were always greeted. I stood there, Grady the Jolly Innkeeper, smiling, my hands clasped behind my back. "This is my wife, Amanda."

"Grady Tripp." I held out my hand to him, and he gave it a long, hard squeeze. He had a salesman's handshake, practiced and automatic. "James's teacher. How are you?"

"*Very* embarrassed," said Mrs. Leer. They followed me across the porch, over to the front door, and waited patiently while I fumbled with my keys. It'd been years since I'd had to work the locks of this house. "We want to apologize for James."

"No need," I said. "He didn't do anything wrong."

I fell into the living room, switched on the light, and saw that they were both at least fifteen years older than the silver-haired tycoon and frosted ex-cheerleader I'd seen fox-trotting toward me across the moonlit lawn of my imagination. They were dressed for the ballroom of an ocean liner, all right, but their cheeks were ruined, and the whites of their eyes were yellow, and their hair in both cases was iron gray, although he wore his cut crisp as a sailor's and hers was done in a neat little Junior League page boy. I figured Fred for sixty-five and

Amanda for a couple of years younger. James must have been a late addition to the household.

"My, this is a charming house," said Amanda Leer. She took a careful step forward into the room. The heels of her shoes were much too tall for her, considering her height and her age. They were expensive-looking black calfskin things, with black leather bows on the toes. She was wearing a modest but not at all matronly black dress, with sheer black sleeves and three flounces. Her nails were manicured and her lips rouged and she smelled of Chanel No. 5. "Oh, this is an *adorable* house."

"Grady, this is a nice place you've got out here," said Fred Leer.

I looked around the living room. All of the furniture had been shoved back into its usual disorder, with none of the chairs oriented toward one another and barely enough room for a person of my size to navigate from the stairs to the fireplace. Instead of being hung with the duck-hunting prints, pastoral landscapes, or yellowed catalog plates of antique farm equipment which seemed called for, the knotty pine walls of the cottage were a jumble of Helen Frankenthaler and Marc Chagall, aerial views of Pittsburgh and Jerusalem, bar mitzvah and graduation portraits of the Warshaw children, a Diane Arbus poster, a framed photograph of Irv posed with some beefy grinning Mellon in the belfry of the Campanile, and a couple of fairly terrible imitation Mirós that Deborah had painted in college. There was a barbed-wire tangle of Israeli sculpture taking up too much room on the lowboy. The Scrabble board was still lying out on the coffee table, abandoned in midgame, offering like a Ouija board such enigmatic counsel as UVULA and SQUIRT, and there was ice melting in a couple of tumblers by the TV.

"It's my in-laws'," I said. "I'm just here visiting."

"And your mother-in-law sounded *so* kind and concerned when I spoke to her," said Amanda Leer.

"Well, they wanted to meet you," I said. "But they got tired. It was kind of a big day around here."

"Oh, really, listen," said Fred Leer, "we were *late*." He dragged his wristwatch out of the sleeve of his snappy dinner jacket and I recognized it at once. It was the gold Hamilton, with an elongated Art Moderne face, that James would some-times wear to class and sit loudly winding when opinion in the workshop went against him. "Oh, my word, two *hours* late!"

"We just couldn't get away as quickly as we would've *liked*," Amanda said. "It's Fred's birthday today, you see, and we were throwing a party at the golf club. We've been plan-ning it all year. It was a lovely party."

"What golf club is that? Where do you folks live?" But I already knew where they lived. They were a couple of rich bastards.

"St. Andrew's," said Fred. "We live in Sewickley Heights."

So the mystic lightning that tormented the dark skies of James Leer's fiction, all that sorrowful, cabbages-and-hell Slavic Catholicism, that too was also pure sham.

"Now," said Amanda Leer, losing her Presbyterian smile. "Where is he?"

"Upstairs," I said. "Asleep. I don't think he knows you're here. I'll go get him."

"Oh, no," she said. "*I'll* go get him."

"Well, maybe you'd better let me." There was a startling implication of violence in her tone. She sounded as though she intended to yank James out of bed by his ear and drag him by this handle down the stairs and out to the car. I wondered now if it had been such a good idea to call his parents in the first place. He wasn't a child. People his age were allowed to get drunk and pass out. I might even have argued that they ought to be required to do so. "There are an awful lot of doors up there. Ha ha. You might wake up the wrong person."

"Oh, of course, you're right, Grady," she said. The smile was back. "We'll just wait for him down here."

"Hate to cause you so much trouble," said Fred. He shook his head. "I'd *like* to know what is the matter with our James, I'll tell you that."

"I know what's the matter with him," said Amanda, darkly, without elaborating. "Oh, boy."

"He sure likes movies," I said.

"Don't get me started," said Amanda.

"Don't," said James's father. "Please." He tried to make it sound humorous, but there was a hint of genteel pleading in his voice.

"Be right back," I said. "And happy birthday."

"Thank you, Grady," said Fred.

I found James not in bed but on the upstairs landing, in his long black coat, looking at me like I was the jailer come to lead him to the gallows tree.

"I don't want to go with them," he said.

"Look, James." I kept my voice low. There was a bar of light shining at the bottom of every door. I didn't want to draw an audience. I steered James into the bathroom and locked us in. "Now, James," I said, "Listen, buddy, I think you really ought to get on home."

"I'm *fine*," he said. "I'm having a good time."

"You were having *too* good a time, I'd say. I'm clearly not a good person for you to hang around with right now. James?"

He wouldn't look at me. I put a hand on his shoulder.

"James," I said. I could feel myself breaking a critical promise I'd made to him at some point in the last twenty-four hours, and I wished that I could remember what it was. "Things, listen, things—things are really weird with me these days. I—I'm floundering. Just a little bit. I—see, I have enough *blame* to take already, okay, without having to take the blame if something bad happened to *you*. Come on. I'm serious. Go home."

"That isn't my home," he said coldly.

"Oh no?" I said. "Where's your home, then? Carvel?" I withdrew my hand from his shoulder. "Or would that be Sylvania?"

He looked down at his feet, in their scuffed-up black brogues. We could hear the low murmuring of the two old people downstairs.

"Why did you tell me all of that, James?" I said.

"I don't know," he said. "I'm sorry. Really. Please don't make me go with them."

"James, they're your parents."

"They're not," he said, looking up, his eyes wide. "They're my *grand*parents. My parents are *dead*."

"Your grandparents?" I closed the lid of the toilet and sat down. My ankle was throbbing from the exertion of digging a grave for Doctor Dee, and the plunge into the stale waters of the backyard had spoiled Irv's dressing. "I don't believe you."

"I swear. My father had his own airplane. We used to fly up to Quebec in it. He was from there. Really. We had a house in the Laurentians. They were flying up there without me one day. And they crashed. I swear! It was in the newspaper!"

I looked at him. His eyes were filled with tears and his pale face was printed with the faint blue map of his bloodstream. His tone was utterly sincere.

"It was in the newspaper," I said, rubbing at my own eyes, trying to work a little keenness of judgment back into them.

"He was a senior vice president at Dravo. Seriously, he was a friend of Caliguiri and everything. My mother was, like, a big socialite, okay? Her maiden name was Guggenheim."

"I remember that," I said. It had been in the newspaper. "Five or six years ago."

He nodded. "Their plane went down right outside of Scranton," he said.

I couldn't resist. "Near Carvel?" I said.

He shrugged and looked embarrassed. "I guess so," he said. "Please don't make me go with them, okay?" He could see that I was wavering. "Go down and tell them you just couldn't wake me. Please? They'll *leave*. They don't really *care*."

"James, they care a lot," I said, although in truth they'd seemed far more concerned with my opinion of them, I thought, than with the welfare of their son. Or grandson, as the case might be.

"They treat me like a freak," he said. "She makes me sleep in the basement of my own house! It's *my* house, Professor Tripp. My parents left it to *me*."

"But why would they *say* they were your parents if they aren't, James? That doesn't make any sense."

"Did they say that?" he said, looking surprised.

I screwed up my eyes and bit my lip, and tried to reconstruct the conversation in the living room.

"I think they did," I said. "I'm not really sure, to tell you the truth."

"That would be a new one. God, they're so *twisted*. I don't know why I even gave Mrs. Warshaw their phone number. I must have been drunk." He shivered, although it was quite warm, even stuffy, in the bathroom. "They're so *cold*."

I sat up straight and studied his pale, blurred, handsome young face, trying to believe him.

"James," I said. "Come on. That man is obviously your father. You look just like him."

He blinked and looked away. After a moment he took a deep breath, swallowed, and jammed his hands into the pockets of his hard-luck overcoat. Then he looked at me, his gaze steady, and when he spoke again, his voice sounded husky and uncomfortable.

"There's a reason for that," he said.

I thought about that for a second or two.

"Get out of here," I said at last.

"That's why *she* hates me. That's why she makes me sleep in the basement." He lowered his voice to a whisper. "In the *crawl* space!"

"In the crawl space," I said, and just like that I knew he was lying again. "With the rats, and the casks of Amontillado."

"I swear," he said, but he'd gone too far, and he knew it. His eyes darted away from my face, and this time they remained averted. Those two people waiting downstairs could only be his natural parents; if she hadn't said so to me, Amanda had certainly identified herself to Irene as James's mother. I stood up and shook my head.

"That's enough, now, James," I said. "I don't want to hear any more."

I took hold of his elbow and guided him out of the bathroom. He went quietly. In the living room I turned him over to the custody of the Leers.

"Look at you," said Amanda, as we came down the stairs. "Shame on you."

James said, "Let's just go."

"What did you *do*?" She looked him up and down, horrified. "I threw that coat in the *garbage,* James."

He shrugged. "I dug it back out," he said.

She turned to me, looking, for the first time, truly grave. "He doesn't wear that thing to *class,* does he, Professor Tripp?"

"Never," I said. "No, I've never seen it before tonight."

"Come on, Jimmy," said Fred, wrapping his fingers around the thin upper stalk of James's arm. "Let's leave these good people alone. Good night, then, Grady."

"Good night. Nice to have met you both," I said. "Take care of him," I added, and immediately regretted it.

"Don't you worry about *that,*" said Amanda Leer. "We'll take care of him, all right."

"Let *go* of me," said James. He tried to pull free, but the old man's grip on him was humiliating and firm. As he was dragged out the front door into the night, James turned back to look at me, his mouth twisted and sarcastic, his eyes reproachful.

"The Wonder brothers," he said.

Then his parents hustled him across the front yard and, like a couple of kidnappers in a low-budget thriller, stuffed him without ceremony into the back of their beautiful car.

AFTER James was gone, I went to stand in the doorway of Sam's old room. The moon was shining in through the window and I could see the unmade bed, empty, admirably bare and cool. I felt myself drawn toward it. I went in and switched on the light. A few years after his death the bedroom that was Sam's in the house on Inverness Avenue had been converted into a kind of sewing room or study for Irene, but this room in the country remained his, and the decor and furnishings were those of a long-ago boy. Threadbare cowpokes on horseback tossed their curling lariats across the bedspread. The books on the shelf above the three-quarter-size desk bore titles such as *The Real Book of the Canadian Mounties, Touchdown!, The Story of the Naval Academy,* and *Lem Walker, Space Surgeon.* The headboard and dresser and the aforementioned desk formed a matched set, vaguely nautical in design, trimmed with rope and mock-iron grommets. Everything was faded and frayed, speckled with mildew and the industry of termites. Irene and Irv never articulated any conscious desire to make it a shrine or museum to their dead—their irremediably biological—son, but the fact remained that they hadn't changed a thing here, and some of his old belongings from Pittsburgh—a box turtle shell, a statue of Kali, a Reisenstein Junior High banner—had even found their way, like finger bones to the reliquary, out to Sam's bedroom at Kinship.

I sat down on the little bed and fell back. As I tried to swing my legs up onto the mattress my good ankle got caught on a cord of some sort. I sat up again, and found myself entangled in the straps of James's knapsack. When I saw that he had left it behind I felt a sharp pang of guilt. I should never, I thought, have allowed him to be stolen by those phantoms in their ghostly gray car.

"I'm sorry, James," I said. I reached into the knapsack and took out the manuscript of *The Love Parade*. I peeled off the cover page, sat back against the headboard of Sam's bed. The house slumbered around me. I was encased, sealed off, in the light coming from the bedside lamp. I started to read.

It was a period piece, I found, set during the mid-forties. It opened in some anthracite black town in the barren Pennsylvania hinterlands of James Leer's innermost soul. The protagonist, John Eager, eighteen years old, lived in a tumbledown house along the banks of a fouled river with his father, a forklift operator at the Seitz mannequin factory, and his paternal grandfather, a fearsome old bastard named Hamilton Eager who was first encountered on page 3, in the act of poisoning the boy's Chinese pug. John Eager's mother, a sickly woman who cooked in the mannequin factory lunchroom, had died the previous spring, of pneumonia, her last words to her son "You're a good-looking boy."

He was so good-looking that he was invisible, the passage went on.

He had the face of one of the Seitz company hat-forms. Nose like a shark fin. Lips red as a stop sign. Black eyes long-lashed and glassy like the eyes in the head of a deer on a wall. Nothing about his face lingered in the memory of people who saw it. Only a vague impression of handsomeness. In photographs it always looked like his head moved at the instant the picture was snapped.

The book's first hundred and fifty pages consisted of John Eager's autobiographical reverie as he rode a Greyhound bus to Wilkes-Barre to buy the gun with which, on page 163, he shot Hamilton Eager between the eyes, in payment for the poisoning of his beloved dog Warner Oland. It was a disturbing and poetic reverie that lingered overlong but at times convincingly on episodes of sexual abuse, rape, incest, deer hunting, arson, the usual James Leer brand of mock-tortured Catholicism, suicide attempts, and the young hero's moments of ecstasy in the first row of the town's grand movie house, the Marquis. The reader was not surprised to see John Eager evolve into a lonely young man who told fabulous lies to everyone and nursed a deep devout hatred of himself.

After murdering his grandfather, John Eager put in a surprise appearance at the Homecoming Dance, where he shot and killed a classmate, a bully named Nelson McCool who had been terrorizing the hero all his life, in such various and ever-crueler ways that the reader was relieved to see him finally get his reward. In the wake of these crimes, with blood pooled in the cuffs of his trousers, John Eager knelt to confess his sins, in the church of St. John Nepomuk. Then he fled, climbing onto another Greyhound that took him, in considerably fewer pages than the previous bus journey, to Los Angeles, where he tried unsuccessfully to walk onto the Fox lot, got mugged on the porch of Our Lady Queen of the Angels, and, in a scene at once tender and grim, came to the very brink of turning a trick with a washed-up hero of the silent screen before finally surrendering his unhappy soul to the Pacific Ocean at Venice Beach. In the penultimate scene, on his way out to Venice on the Red Line car, he met a rather pathetic young bottle blonde named Norma Jean Mortensen,

in whom he recognized a kindred spirit—a formless aggregate
of longing, lies, and self-contempt, hollow at the core—
whose cheap, tight sweater, laddered stockings, and naked
ambition to become the biggest star in the world helped him,
in some way I didn't quite understand, make up his mind to
drown himself.

I read without stopping and finished the book, which came
in at two hundred and fifty pages on the dot, in just under two
hours. I didn't know quite how to feel about it. The narrative
had drive and sureness of tone, and like most good first novels
it possessed an imperturbable, mistaken confidence that all the
shocking incidents and extremes of human behavior it dished
up would strike new chords of outrage and amazement in the
reader. It was a brazen, ridiculous, thrilling performance, with
a ballast of genuine sadness that kept the whole thing from
keeling over in the gale-force winds of melodrama. Whether
because he had outgrown them, forgotten them, or finally
tired of hearing me and his peers complain about them, James
had largely abandoned his silly experiments with syntax and
punctuation, and the prose throughout, although quirky and
clotted with similes, did a good job of persuading, at least for
the duration of each sentence and paragraph, that the events
therein described really had come to pass.

And yet when I closed the book I could not help feeling
that in some way much of it was irremediably false. The impressive use of period details, never misplaced or anachronis-
tic, nonetheless felt dutiful and deliberate—there were dozens
of references to hat fashions and big bands and great chrome
automobiles—and had clearly been derived secondhand from
old movies. Apart from certain disturbing recollections of
childhood and early adolescence, and the strange episode

with the powdered and ascoted old star, *most* of *The Love Parade* seemed to have been crafted out of echoes and fragments and secondhand threads. The people spoke, amused themselves, and reacted to one another like people in movies. The things that happened were kinds of things that happened in movies. Other than along certain emotional tangents there was little in the book that felt as if it had actually been lived. It was a fiction produced by someone who knew only fictions, *The Tempest* as written by isolate Miranda, raised on the romances in her father's library.

I set the manuscript on the nightstand beside me. Maybe, I thought, I was not the fairest possible judge of what James Leer had done. In my heart, I knew, I was jealous of the kid: of his talent, although I had talent of my own; of his youth and energy, although there was no point in regretting the loss of those; but mostly of his simply having *finished* his book. For all its flaws, he could be proud of it. The dynamic of ostracism and imagination and the malfunctioning of a broken family were well presented, and the scene on the streetcar with the inchoate Marilyn, if not entirely convincing, was imagined with a fan's ardor, and came as a genuine and pleasant surprise. And there was one scene, early on, which had haunted me all through the reading of the rest of the book and which, I found, troubled me still. I reached for the manuscript and opened it to page 52, to the scene in which the narrator recounted, in brutal terms, the August day in 1928 on which old Ham Eager raped his son's new wife.

So the old man caught her like a pigeon by the neck. He forced her face into the dusty yellow mattress of his bed. All the breath went out of her. He had been down by the road picking blackberries and the ink was on his fingers.

John Eager, the narrator went on, in the same dispassionate tone, was born nine months afterward. The passage as I read it had raised the hairs on my neck, and now I found I was no longer quite sure that James Leer had lied to me, even though I knew that the best liars keep on lying successfully long after they've been discovered. I didn't really believe that Fred Leer was James's father as well as his grandfather, but still I couldn't suppress the sudden swell of guilt in my chest for having allowed those two elegant spooks to cart him off. Setting the manuscript aside again, I stood up, and paced around the room, and thought about James Leer.

Why *The Love Parade*? James seemed to have chosen it, as usual, more for its status *as a title* than for any evident connection to the plot or characters of his story. There was a kind of sympathetic magic in the way James titled his fictions, as if by producing works called *Stagecoach* and *Greed* he hoped to make of himself not simply a writer but an entire studio; to raise, on the patch of vacant scrub that was his life, a teeming city of costumers, soundmen, hoplites, buccaneers, and Kickapoo Indians, where he could be producer and director, screenwriter and gaffer and makeup artist, the walk-on destined for stardom and the leading lady at the peak of her career. I had known plenty of movie lovers in my life, from imaginary drag queens who idolized the great female faces to nostalgia addicts who climbed into a movie as into a time machine or a bottle of whiskey and set the dial for "never come back"; and to one degree or another the obsession, like all obsessions, implied a certain windy emptiness within. For James, I thought, the attraction must be to the fluid identities of the actors and actresses: the press-office biographies, the stage names, the roles and characters constantly adopted and shed. And—it was clear from his novel—he'd been powerfully affected by the image of community, of small-town life, that was fostered in so much classic Hollywood product.

He was intelligent enough to know, however, that this image was an illusion—his ambivalence about that illusion was reflected in *The Love Parade*—and damaged enough to be fascinated by the dark reverse of the Hollywood medallion, by the starlet in the corner of a party scene in *The Bad and the Beautiful* who later took ninety-two Nembutals and fell from her veranda, by the sorrow of a blacklisted screenwriter, by the sad pathology of a screen lover's sex life, by the fate of Sal Mineo, Jayne Mansfield, Thelma Todd. For all of this the perfect figure, I thought, may have been the inscribing of the two words "Frank Capra" into his hand. Capra was always thought of as a great sentimentalist, but the world of his films was filled with shadows—only one man's life, remember, separated Bedford Falls from the garish nightmare of Potters-ville—in which there often lurked the specter of ruin and suicide and shame. In his sorrow over his hero's death James had taken the whole idea of small-town America implied and romanticized by the name Frank Capra, and carved it with a needle into his flesh.

I sat down on the bed, hugged myself, stood up again. I picked up *Lem Walker, Space Surgeon* and read that throughout the graduation ceremonies at the Academy of Medicine on Altair IV, the skies were troubled with positron storms. I opened the drawers in Sam's old desk and found them bare except for a Pez candy and a 1964 penny. I tried to shake the feeling that of all the people I had broken faith with in my life, James Leer was the one least able to withstand the betrayal.

"All right," I said aloud, looking with regret at James's knapsack, wishing with my wizened, selfish, black little raisin of a soul that I could just lie there in Sam Warshaw's bed, smoking dope and reading about a nasty little outbreak of Cetusian fever among the Hive People of Betelgeuse V. But my black little heart was trapped in the backseat of a gray Mercedes, making the long, silent trip back to Pittsburgh. "I guess that's what I'll do."

I picked up the manuscript and the knapsack and went downstairs. At the bottom of the staircase I lost my balance and did something bad to my other ankle. I hopped into the kitchen and picked up the phone. I dialed my house. Hannah answered. I told her where I was.

"We miss you," she said loudly. In the background I could hear Wilson Pickett, Hannibal's elephants, gunplay, hysterical women, and something that might have been the rattle of dice.

"Crabtree's there," I said. It was hard to keep my voice down.

"He's having a party."

"Jesus," I said. "That's a terrifying thought." I slid James's manuscript back into the knapsack, and fastened the clasp. "Try to make sure he doesn't leave, all right?"

"Uh huh. Listen, Grady!" She was shouting now. "Listen, I have to tell you something. There was a policeman here, Grady. Earlier tonight. Something like Popnik."

"Pupcik. I know him." Irene had left the black satin jacket draped over the back of one of the kitchen chairs. I picked it up and held it to my face. The fur collar gave off a faint bitter whiff of vitamin B. "What'd he want?"

"I don't know. He said he wanted to talk to you. Grady, are you coming home?"

The back door rattled and slammed, and a moment later Emily came into the kitchen, reeking of tobacco, makeup smeared into a Pierrot mask, moving stiff-jointed and half sideways like a spooked cat. As she brushed past me our eyes met, and looking into those two blurred dark circles, I felt like one of August Van Zorn's heroes, in the instant before his hapless narrative broke off with a final terrible dash. There was nothing in them. It was an empty gaze, a hole in the fabric of the world.

"Get out," she said.

I hefted James's knapsack and slung the stolen jacket over my shoulder. I lifted the receiver to my lips.

"I was just leaving," I said.

As I made my way along the avenue of elm trees I felt the wheels of the Galaxie bump abruptly up and over something big. There was a sickening instant of slippage when I hit the brakes. I clambered out of the car and went around to the back, where, in the bloody glow of the taillights, I found a kind of distended loop of cable stretched across the roadbed, frayed badly at one end. I had run over Grossman. At first I panicked and got back into the car, intending just to drive away and never come back and keep on driving until I hit Wood Buffalo or Uranium City. I put the car in gear, but ten yards farther along the road I stopped again and went back to gather up the surprisingly heavy remainder of Grossman. Nobody in that house, I thought, would ever miss this ruinous and unreliable member of the family. So I carried him over to the car, opened the trunk, and pitched him in there with the tuba and Doctor Dee.

OF the drive back to Pittsburgh I remember only the struggle to roll three joints one-handed and the intermittent companionship of a radio station, playing a tribute to Lennie Tristano, that turned out to be WABI, the low-watt voice of old Coxley College, drifting in on some ghostly undertow in the ether. Around two o'clock I pulled off the deserted parkway and headed up toward Squirrel Hill. I was going home, but I didn't intend to stay there longer than it would take me to retrieve Crabtree—assuming he was still operative. I had decided to try something reckless, senseless, and stupid, and in any such attempt there could be no more useful companion than Terry Crabtree.

My house was ablaze in the middle of our slumbering street, lit up like a landing strip. As I came up the front walk I heard the racy laughter of a saxophone, and the glass in the windows hummed a walking bass line. My house was crawling with writers. There were writers in the living room, with their shoes kicked off, watching one another dance. There were writers in the kitchen, making conversation that whipsawed wildly between comely falsehood and foul-smelling truths, flicking their cigarette ash into the mouths of beer cans. There were a half dozen more of them stretched out on the floor of the television room, arranged in a worshipful manner around a small grocery bag filled with ragweed marijuana, watching Ghidrah take apart Tokyo. On the sofa behind them a pair of my students, young writers of the Angry School who pierced their lips and favored iron-buckled storm-trooper footwear, had welded themselves into a kind of impromptu David Smith. On the stairs leading up to my bedroom sat three New York agents, better dressed and less drunk than the writers, exchanging among themselves delicate constructions of confidentiality and disinformation. And there were so many Pittsburgh poets in my hallway that if, at that instant, a meteorite had come smashing through my roof, there would never have been another stanza written about rusting fathers and impotent steelworks and the Bessemer converter of love.

There was only one writer in my office. She was sitting alone on the Honor Bilt, with the door closed, her knees pulled up under her sweater so that the pointy tips of her boots peeked out from under the hem. Her head was bowed, and she was concentrating on a thick manuscript stacked on the sofa beside her, twisting a long yellow strand of hair around one finger and then untwisting it again.

"Hey," I said, coming into the room, closing the door behind me. I looked over at my desk. It was only then I realized that I'd left the house that morning with *Wonder Boys* lying out in the open where anyone—where Crabtree—could get at it.

"Oh!" said Hannah, slapping back onto the stack the page she'd been about to set to one side, covering it with both hands, as though it were something she herself had written and didn't want me to see. "Grady! Oh, God, I'm so embarrassed. I hope you don't mind. It was just sort of lying out." She wrinkled up her nose at the thought of her own misbehavior. "I suck."

"You suck not," I said. "I don't mind at all."

She reassembled the scattered slices of the Grady's Wheel of Cheese, upended it, carefully tapped it against the sofa cushion, and set the thing down on an arm of the sofa. Then she got up and came over to get her arms around me.

"I'm so glad to see you," she said. "We tried to find you *every*where. We were worried."

"I'm fine," I said. "I just had to deal with a little outbreak of Cetusian fever."

"How's that?"

"Nothing." I nodded toward the manuscript balanced on the edge of the sofa. "Did, uh, did *Crabtree* happen to see any of that, do you know?"

"No, I don't know," said Hannah. "I mean, I wouldn't think so. We were gone all day, over at WordFest. We didn't get back until late." She grinned. "And he was pretty busy after that."

"I'll bet he was," I said, reluctantly disentangling myself from her. "So, listen, where is the old Crab, anyway?"

"Who knows? I've been in here for a couple of hours. I don't even know if he's here or—oh, no, don't go!" She redoubled her hold on me. "Stay, where are you going?"

"I really need to talk to him," I said, though all of a sudden the prospect of getting back into my car, and driving all the way out to Sewickley Heights on my unreasonable errand, struck me as less than appealing. I could just stay here with Hannah, and forget all about Deborah and Emily, and Sara and the pale smiling tadpole in her belly, and above all that poor lost liar Jimmy Leer. She was holding me and I closed my eyes and in my mind I followed her downstairs to her apartment, and lay beside her on her sateen comforter, under the Stieglitz portrait of Georgia O'Keeffe, and plunged my hand down into the mouth of her cowgirl boots, and ran my fingers along the damp slender arches of her feet. "I really need—"

"The Horse" came on, out in the living room, and Hannah grabbed hold of my hand.

"Come on," she said. "You need to dance."

"I can't. My ankles."

"Your *an*kles? Come on."

"I can't." She got me to the door and pulled it open, letting in a bright blast of horn charts. She rocked her skinny cowgirl hips a couple of times around. "Look, Hannah, James got himself—he got himself into a little bit of trouble tonight. I need Crabtree to help me go get him out."

"What kind of trouble? Let me come."

"No, I can't say, it's nothing. Look, he and I'll go get James, okay, it won't take long, we'll bring him back, and then I'll dance with you. All right? I promise?"

"He shot the Chancellor's dog, didn't he?"

"He did?" I said, pushing the door closed again. "Shot what?"

"Somebody shot their dog last night. The blind one. That's what the police think, anyway. The dog's missing, and they found some spots of blood on the carpet. And then I heard Dr. Gaskell dug a bullet out of the floor."

"Jesus," I said. "That's terrible."

"Crabtree thought that it sounded like something James would do."

"He doesn't even know James," I said.

"Who does?" said Hannah.

You don't, I thought. I gave her hand a squeeze.

"I'll be right back," I told her.

"Can't I come with you?"

"I don't think you should."

"I know savate."

"Hannah."

"Oh, all *right,*" she said. Back home in Provo, Hannah had nine older brothers, and she was accustomed to the abandonment of boys. "Can I at least keep reading *Wonder Boys* until you come back?"

It hadn't really sunk in until now that someone had actually been reading my book. It was a painful and exhilarating thought.

"I guess so," I said. "Sure."

Hannah poked a finger between my belly and my belt buckle and tugged until I nearly fell against her.

"Can I take it down into my room and be alone with it?"

"I don't know," I said, taking a step backward. I was always, I thought, taking a step away from Hannah Green. "How are you liking it?"

"I think I'm loving it."

"Really?" I said. Hannah's praise, though lightly given, struck me with unexpected force, and I felt my throat constrict. I saw how lonely a pursuit the writing of *Wonder Boys* had become, how sequestered and directionless and blind. I'd shown some early chapters to Emily, and her only memorable comment at the time had been "It seems awfully male." I'd laughed this off, but ever since then I'd been the book's only reader, the prophet, founder, and sole inhabitant of my own failed little Pennsylvanian utopia. "All right, then. Sure you can."

She brought her face very close to mine. Her lips were chapped and she'd daubed them with balm that smelled of vanilla.

"I kind of think I'm loving you," she said. "Too."

Oh, what the hell, I thought. Maybe I'd better just stay.

"Tripp's here?" said Crabtree from somewhere out in the hall. His voice sounded plaintive and so relieved that I felt a pang of guilt at the sound of it. "Where is he? Tripp?"

I started, and pulled away from her.

"Don't let him see that thing, okay?" I said. "Hide it till we leave." I gave her a peck on the cheek and stepped out into the hall. "I'll see you soon."

"Be careful," she said, brushing at a strand of hair that had gotten caught in the lip balm at the corner of her mouth.

"I will," I said.

As long as she was falling in love with me, I might as well start making her promises I didn't intend to keep.

I found Crabtree out in the hallway, all by himself, watching the people in the living room attempt to re-create the Horse. He had one hand in his pocket and the other wrapped around a bottle of sparkling water. It seemed that in my absence he was willing to surrender the pretense that he was still Crabtree the Tricksy Spirit, the artist as mischief maker, and to stand slouched against the wall, alone in the middle of his own party, looking sober, lonely, and bored. He was wearing another of his double-breasted metallic suits, of a soft, almost imperceptible blue like the light given off by a black-and-white television. His eyes behind his round glasses were lusterless, his cheeks puffy and splotched. As he watched the dancers he reminded me of James Leer, lingering last night in the Gaskells' backyard, a friendless and envious boy in the dark, gazing up at a radiant window.

When he saw me his face resumed its usual calm smirk,

however, and he nodded, once, and looked back into the living room.

"There he is," he said, as if all unaffected by my abrupt reappearance, as if he hadn't been wandering the house seconds before like a revenant, crying out my name. "Where'd you get to?"

"I went up to Kinship."

"I heard."

"How are you?"

"I'm dying." He rolled his eyes. "This WordFest gig is without question the most tedious exercise you have *ever* put me through, Tripp."

"Sorry," I said.

"Look at those people." He shook his head.

"They're writers," I said. "Poets are not bad dancers as a rule. But we're a little light on poets this year."

"Those are fiction people."

"Most of them." I shrugged my shoulders a few times quick. "We like to do that Snoopy kind of thing with our shoulders."

"And *everyone's* straight at this thing. Don't you have *any* queers in Pittsburgh?"

"Sure we do," I said. "I'll call them."

"And then you fucking *drive off* this morning with the rest of my little medicines in your car."

"I did? They are?"

"Uh *huh*. At least I hope so. I think they're in your trunk. You must have knocked them loose last night when you were ransacking my bags."

"I'm sorry," I said. "Really. Listen, buddy, come outside with me."

He folded his arms and affected a prim expression. "I don't want to get off now."

"We're not going to get off," I said.

He glanced over at me, then away. "You're al*ready* stoned."

"I know it."

"You look like hell, Tripp."

"I know, I know, Crabtree, come *on*. I need you, man. I need you to come with me."

"Come with you where?"

"Buddy." Without intending to I found myself imitating Hannah's manner with me. I hooked my finger over his belt buckle and gave it a sharp tug, and pulled him toward me and the front door. Crabtree dug in his heels and stayed where he was. "Won't you just come with me if I ask you to?" I said. "Do I have to tell you where?"

"No, you don't." He unhooked my hand from his belt, turned it palm up, looked at it, and then tossed it back at me, as if refusing a corsage. He was bored enough to have forgotten that he was only pretending to be petulant. "You didn't tell me where you were going this morning."

"I know, I know, all right, I'm an asshole." I didn't blame him for being angry with me. I'd gotten him invited to WordFest, promising him our first chance to be together in months—years—then vanished, leaving him to attend dull seminars and oversimplistic lectures and to throw himself his own party with a bunch of woolen and funkless straight people. "I'm really, really sorry."

"So how *was* everything up there, anyway?"

"Nice. Awful."

"Emily still leaving you?"

"I would think so." I shook my head. "To tell you the truth, it was a disaster. James—"

"*My* James?" Crabtree brightened, and touched his fingertips possessively to his breastbone. "Did he go with you? Is he here *now*?"

"No, and that's why I need you, buddy." I lowered my voice and brought my lips very close to his ear. "He kind of got himself—"

"Arrested?" he cried.

"Hush. No, kidnapped."

"*Kid*napped? Who by?"

I paused a moment for effect. "His parents," I said.

Crabtree's father was a Pentecostalist preacher somewhere out in Hogscrotum County, MO, and his mother was the editor-in-chief of a magazine for knitting-machine enthusiasts. "She can make you anything," went a favorite line of his. "She made me a queer." He had been lost to the clutch of Satan since early adolescence and hadn't seen them in years.

"His *parents*?" It must have sounded to his ears like the direst of fates.

"He has 'Frank Capra' carved into the back of his hand."

"Let me get my coat," said Crabtree.

Launching himself like a swimmer from the wall, he dashed into the kitchen, retrieved his trench coat from the back of a chair, filched a half-empty bottle of Jim Beam from the kitchen table, and knocked back a swallow. Then he lit a cigarette and tied the belt of his overcoat around him. He slipped the Jim Beam into the left pocket of his coat, and on his way past the refrigerator stopped to fill the other pocket with a couple of little bottles of Mickey's malt liquor. When he came back into the hall he was grinning and wide awake.

"Let's buy a gun!" he said happily.

We went out to my car, and I was about to get in when Crabtree said, "Hey!"

He was standing at the back of the car, tapping on the lid of the trunk with the fingers of one hand.

"What?" I said, though I knew at once. "Oh." I walked slowly around to the back. "I thought you said you didn't want any."

"I was lying."

"I had a feeling."

"Open the trunk."

"How about we wait—"

"Open it."

"I'm serious, Crabs, I—"

"Now."

I opened the trunk.

"Holy Jesus," said Crabtree. "You offed the husky dog."

"No, wait a minute, Crab—"

"Phew!" The smell by now was indescribable, a compound of burnt aging automobile stinks and the natural odors of death and blood—sweet as garbage, acrid as gasoline, the smell of a thousand rubber tires rolled in batshit and then set on fire. "What *is* that?" Drawing the rest of his body away from the car, he extended his neck and poked his head out over the trunk, maneuvering it back and forth, over and back, as though it were a camera on a very long pole. Gingerly he withdrew his head and turned his wondering lens on me. "Is that a *snake*?" he said.

"Part of one," I said. I put my hands on the lid of the trunk and started to slam it. "Come on. I'll explain on the way out."

"Not so fast." He grabbed hold of my wrist. "I want my medicines." After a brief struggle he wrested the trunk lid away from me and raised it once more. "I don't care if you have a dead cassowary in there." Carefully he reached into a far corner of the trunk and, wrinkling up his nose, started to feel his way around.

"Ick," he said.

WE pulled into Sewickley Heights around three A.M. and rolled with the top down through its sinuous dark streets. The sidewalks were overarched with immense sycamores and lined with high hedges that hid the grand houses behind them. Crabtree was holding a Greater Pittsburgh street map and, pressed between his lips, an overdue notice from the college library, which had been mailed two weeks before to a James Selwyn Leer at 262 Baxter Drive. The Leers were un-listed, as we'd discovered in a Shell station telephone booth, but the ever-resourceful Crabtree had dug around in James's knapsack and found the notice, stuck between two pages of the Errol Flynn biography. He had the knapsack balanced on his lap.

"The address on the manuscript?" said Crabtree, angling the street map, the better to catch the dim glow of the glove compartment light. "5225 Harrington?"

"His aunt's house. In Mt. Lebanon."

"I'm looking at the index, here. There's no such street."

"How surprising."

Driving out to the suburbs I'd filled Crabtree in on most of what had happened to James Leer and me since I'd taken his shiny little pistol away from him the night before; the things I had learned and unlearned about him. I skipped the part about Marilyn Monroe's jacket, though. I told myself I had the thing all nice and folded up into a neat little bundle on the backseat, so I ought just to leave it like that until tomorrow, when I would drive James over to the Gaskells' and finally set everything straight; but the truth was that I was embarrassed. I didn't want to have to try to explain to Crabtree what James and I were doing up there in the Gaskells' bedroom in the first place. So I said that it was just a crazy accident that James had shot Doctor Dee. As I talked about James and his book, Crabtree seemed to grow convinced not only that the young man must be a good writer—he gave *The Love Parade* a quick editorial flip-through on the way out, reading by the light from the glove box—but that he, Terry Crabtree, Agent of Chaos, was the switch failure on the tracks toward which James Leer's train was inexorably hurtling. I offered him a little account of my sad dealings with Emily and the Warshaws, too, but he didn't seem all that interested, frankly, in my problems, or at least that was what he wanted me to think. He was still angry with me for having abandoned him that morning. As for *Wonder Boys,* he made no mention of it, and I was afraid to ask. If he'd looked at it and had nothing to say to me, then that told me plenty right there.

"Baxter's next," he said, looking up from the map.

I took it, guessing left. The numbers started at 230 and went up. I cut the lights, and as we drew closer to 262 I cut the engine, too. Silently we coasted until we pulled up abreast of the Leers' driveway. There were pillars on either side, topped with stone pineapples. A fence of nasty-looking iron javelins ran off for a hundred feet in either direction and disappeared into the shadows. We got out of the car and gently let the doors fall shut. Then we took a couple of tentative steps into the Leers' driveway, a rolled-out winding ten-mile

river of finest country-club gravel, round as polished hema-
tites and opals, that described a number of lazy meanders
across the hundred feet of lawn which separated us from the
wide front porch. The porch had to be wide, in order to wrap
itself all the way around the Leers' house, an eccentric pile of
fieldstone and shingles, bristling with awnings and trusses and
pointy dormers that stuck out in every direction, all jumbled
together under a collection of gambreled eaves. The front
door and indeed a fair portion of the facade were illuminated
by floodlights hidden in the hedge.

"Jesus," I said, keeping my voice low. "There must be fifty
or sixty windows on that thing, Crabtree. How are we going
to find *his*?"

"They keep him chained up in the basement, remember?
We just have to find the cellar door."

"If he was telling the truth," I reminded him. "About anything."

"If he wasn't telling the truth about anything," said Crabtree, "then what the fuck are we doing here?"

"Good point," I said.

We started up the drive to the house, and as we drew closer
I saw a long, thin ribbon of light stretched across the trees off
to the left. Somewhere upstairs, on the far side of the house, a
lamp was burning in a window.

"They're still awake," I said, pointing. "His parents."

"They're probably up filing their teeth," said Crabtree,
whose genuine sympathy and mounting desire for James Leer
were characteristically tempered with ridicule. "Come on."

I followed him around the near end of the house and we
went into the backyard. He seemed to think that he knew
where he was going. The gravel crunched loudly under my
feet and I tried to get that toe-heel, toe-heel Indian stealth

walk going, but it was too painful, and in the end I just tried to be quick about it.

There was no cellar door, or evidence of anything like a cellar, but there was a ground floor, an exposed cement foundation at the back of the house with two windows let into it, on either side of a glass-paned door. The windows were neatly curtained with dotted swiss, brightly lit from within. On the other side of the door a woman was singing, in a soft low rueful voice.

> *Why should I care*
> *Though he gave me the air?*
> *Why should I cry, heave a sigh, and wonder why?*
> *And wonder why?*

"Doris Day," said Crabtree.

I smiled at him; he nodded.

"James Leer," we said.

I drummed lightly on the glass, and after a few seconds' delay James Leer opened the door. He was wearing a pair of red pajamas, too short in the leg and cuff, sagging in the seat, shot through with holes, ink-stained. His hair was mussed and his eyes were bright and somehow he didn't seem very surprised to see us. At first, actually, he didn't appear even to recognize us. He scratched at the back of his neck with the sharpened end of a pencil and blinked his eyes.

"Hey," he said, tossing his head as if shaking off the remnants of a dream. "What are you guys doing here?"

"We're springing you, Leer," said Crabtree. "Get some pants on."

"I can't believe you made fun of my bathrobe," I said.

We pushed past him, into a room that I'd been picturing to

myself as a punitive cell: naked lightbulbs, an iron cot in one corner draped with a tattered coverlet, Sheetrock walls un-adorned except for a thin splotchy coat of white paint. Instead we found ourselves standing in a large old cellar, more or less finished and as wide as the house itself, inhaling a comforting, subterranean smell of river mud, secondhand books, and moldering blankets. The low ceiling was held up by massive oak beams, and the floor had been painted, in the era when this was a fashionable effect for servants' quarters, to look as though it were covered by a red Persian rug. This false carpet had been worn down to gray floorboard for the most part, but in the corners and along the edges of the room there were still bright patches of geometry and blood. The room was lit by a dozen antique electric candelabras, some of them as tall as James, a grove of gilded and iron black trees connected to a pair of wall outlets by an elf knot of extension cords. The walls, not Sheetrock but some kind of heavy gray masonry, were lined with books, piled high into twisting stairways, sag-ging arches, spindly Gaudí steeples, and above the spires of this paper city hung the still photographs, posters, and other movie ephemera James and his obsession had managed to amass. To the right of the door, under a black velvet canopy that sagged, baroque, enormous, and rotten with wormholes, stood James's bed, like a foundered galleon. Beside the giant bed there was a nightstand, with a top of pink marble en-closed in a tiny gilt balustrade, on which he had a box of Kleenex, an empty juice glass, and a masturbatory jar of Vase-line. The bed was still made, and James had neatly folded the old clothes I'd lent him and stacked them neatly at its foot. There was no sign of the black overcoat.

"I like what you've done with it," said Crabtree, sidestep-ping one of the iron trees, looking around the room. Some of the bulbs in the candelabras' branches were the kind that pretend to be flickering flames. "When's Captain Nemo moving in?"

James blushed, though whether at the question or at the sudden proximity of Crabtree I couldn't say. He seemed to be a little frightened of Crabtree, which was not necessarily unwise of him.

"It's just a bunch of my gran's old stuff," he said, taking a step away from Crabtree. "She was going to throw it out."

"Your gran?" I said. "That's who I met tonight?"

James didn't say anything.

"Hey, I heard all about all of it, the parents, the grandparents, and I believe you, okay?" said Crabtree with patent but, as ever, somehow credible insincerity. "That's why we're here." He glanced over toward James's desk, beside the television, an elaborate rolltop number with gilt handles and a matching oak swivel chair. On the desktop there was an old manual Underwood with a piece of paper rolled into the carriage, a paragraph arrested in midphrase, and beside the typewriter a neat pile of paper, the uppermost sheet half covered in single-spaced text. "What were you writing?"

James looked taken aback by the question. He hurried over to the desk, gathered up the typescript, and stuffed it into one of the drawers.

"Just another story," he said. He slammed the drawer closed. "It sucks."

"Bring it," said Crabtree, beckoning to James with one hand. "I want to read it."

"What? You mean now?" He looked over at an electric office clock that hung from the wall beside his bed. He'd replaced the standard face with a black-and-white photograph of a plump, wild-eyed movie actor with a pair of mad mustaches whose face was familiar to me—he was a character actor from the thirties. "But it's so *late*."

"It's not late, man, it's *early*," said Crabtree, making an argument and fixing James with a look I myself had succumbed to many times at three-thirty in the morning when Crabtree felt persuaded that there were hours more of fun to be had. "I thought Grady said you didn't want to be here anyway."

"I didn't," said James, succumbing. "I don't."

"So all right, then."

James grinned. "All right," he said. "Let me get dressed."

"Wait," I said. They both turned to look at me. "I don't know about this."

"What's the matter?" said Crabtree.

"I have to tell you, James," I said. "I'm feeling like you've been fucking with me again."

"Why?" He looked alarmed. "What did I do now?"

"You made it sound like they were going to bring you home and throw you into a weasel pit," I said. "You live in a fucking castle, here, buddy."

James looked down at his hands.

"James," said Crabtree, "did you tell Grady that your parents—"

"They're my grandparents." He looked up at me defiantly. "They are."

"Sure they are." Crabtree smiled thinly. "Did you tell him that your *grandparents* were going to bring you home, James, and throw you into a weasel pit?"

"No, I don't think so."

"Well, then." Crabtree punched me on the arm, as if to say, There now, you see? "Go get dressed."

"All right." He went over to the bed and scooped up the

pile of clothes I'd lent him that morning. "Can I—could I wear these again, Professor Tripp?" he said.

I looked at him and then shrugged.

"Ah, what the fuck," I said.

He flinched, and I saw that somehow I'd hurt his feelings. He nodded, slowly, and stood there for a minute, fiddling with the collar of my flannel shirt. Then he turned and walked away, dragging his feet a little. He disappeared through one of a pair of doors at the back of the room. After a second we could hear the whirring of a bathroom fan.

"So modest," said Crabtree with admiration or mock admiration.

"Huh."

"Oh, come on, Tripp. Why're you so mad at him?"

"I don't know," I said. "I'm not really mad at him, I guess. It's just all that crap about his parents not being his parents, you know? I mean, what is that?" I shook my head. "I guess I just want to know once and for all what the truth is about the little bastard."

"The truth," said Crabtree. He went over to a nearby pile of books and hefted the three uppermost titles. They were hardcovers, in plain, dark bindings. "That's always been real important to you, I know."

I held up my right hand to him and showed him my fist.

"Imagine a finger," I suggested.

"I think you ought to go easy on the kid."

"Yeah? Why's that?"

"Because yesterday you left him sitting all by himself in the dark."

I lowered my fist and said, "Oh."

I didn't know what else to say to that. I took a closer look at James's movie memorabilia and saw that it was no mere act of dark teenaged whimsy that had led him to cut the dead director's name into the back of his hand. The kid was a Capra fanatic. All along the wall behind the desk, above piles of videocassettes labeled MR. DEEDS, LOST HORIZON, et cetera, above stacks of screenplays bound in black vinyl with some of the same titles printed in block letters on their fore edges, were lobby posters from fifteen or sixteen of Capra's films, some of them familiar to me, some of them bearing outlandish titles such as *Dirigible* or *American Madness,* and dozens of still photographs and lobby cards—most of them drawn, it seemed to me, from *It's a Wonderful Life* and *Meet John Doe.* This wall comprised the capital of James's moviemania, so to speak, from which the empire had then spread upward, across the heavy beams of the ceiling, and down onto the other walls of his room, settling in large prosperous colonies that were dedicated to some of Capra's great stars: Jimmy Stewart, Gary Cooper, Barbara Stanwyck, in framed photos, posters, and lobby cards representing much of their other work, great and obscure, from *Annie Oakley* to *Ziegfeld Girl.* In the farthest corners of the room the empire of James's obsession seemed to disintegrate into a kind of vague borderland of Hollywoodiana, where it had established a few remote outposts—Henry Fonda, Grace Kelly, James Mason.

Then, picking my way carefully among the candelabras and piles of books and videocassettes, I stepped around to the great black shipwreck of his bed and found on the wall behind it a group of about forty glossy photographs of movie actors whose common theme, or link to Frank Capra, eluded me. There was Charles Boyer, and a delicate woman I thought might have been Margaret Sullavan, and, once again, the grinning, plump-cheeked, mustachioed face of the man in James Leer's clock. As with this fellow, many of the actors in the photographs had familiar faces that I couldn't quite place; several meant nothing to me at all. At the center of the group, however, there were a number of well-known photographs of Marilyn Monroe—naked and aswim in red velvet, reading *Ulysses,* holding down her skirt against a blast of subterranean air—and looking at these, I realized what I was seeing. This was a rival empire, I thought, setting out to conquer the walls of James's room: the upstart Kingdom of Hollywood Suicide. I supposed the satin jacket would have fit right in.

"Did Herman Bing off himself?" I said, pointing to the man with the flying mustaches. "Would you know Herman Bing if you saw his picture?"

"Check this out," said Crabtree, ignoring my question. He waved a couple of heavy handfuls of books. "These are *library* books."

"So?"

"So, they were due"—he looked up at me, waggling his eyebrows—"two years ago. This one's three years overdue." He reached for another book and checked the scrap of paper pasted onto its fly. He whistled. "This one's *five.*" He picked up another. "This one was never even checked *out.*"

"He stole it?"

Crabtree was scrabbling through all the books now, knocking over towers, upsetting arches.

"They're *all* library books," he said, crab-walking in a crouch along the foot of the wall. "Every single one of them."

"Hey," said James, emerging dressed in my too-large dungarees, rolling up the vast sleeves of my flannel shirt.

"Looks like you're going to have some *monster* fines, here, Mr. Leer," said Crabtree.

"Oh," said James. "Ha. I—uh, see, I never—"

"It's cool," said Crabtree. Abruptly he snapped shut one of the stolen books and handed it to me. "Here." He stood up and took James by the arm. "Let's blow."

"Uh, there's only one problem," said James, unhooking himself from Crabtree. "The old lady's been coming down here, like, every half hour, I swear, to check on me." He glanced over at the face of Herman Bing. "She'll probably be down in like five minutes."

" 'The old lady,' " said Crabtree, winking at me. "Why's she keep checking on you? What's she think you're going to do?"

"I don't know," said James, coloring. "Run away, I guess."

I looked at James, remembering the sight of him in the Gaskells' backyard, the trembling flash of silver in his hand. Then I looked down at the spine of the book Crabtree had handed me and saw, to my amazement, that it was a rebound copy of *The Abominations of Plunkettsburg*, by August Van Zorn, property of the Sewickley Public Library. According to the circulation label it had been checked out three times, most recently in September of 1974. I closed my eyes and tried to clear my head of this proof of the uselessness of Albert Vetch's art, of all art and energy and human life in general. There was a sudden rumble of nausea in my belly and the familiar spray of white noise across the inside of my skull. I waved my hand in front of my face, as though shooing away a cloud of bees. I saw that I could write ten thousand more pages of shimmering prose and still be nothing but a blind minotaur stumbling along broken ground, an unsuccessful, overweight ex–wonder boy with a pot habit and a dead dog in the trunk of my car.

"We need a decoy," said Crabtree, "is what we need. To lie in your bed and look like you."

"Yeah, like a couple of big hams," said James. "They do that in *Against All Flags*."

"No," I said, opening my eyes. "Not a couple of hams." They looked at me. "Have you got some kind of a tarp, down here, or something? An extra blanket? Something heavy?"

James thought about it for an instant, then jerked his head toward the doors at the back of his room. "Through there. The one on the left. In the closet, there're some blankets. What are you going to do?"

"I'm going to empty my trunk," I said.

I walked back to the door next to the bathroom and came into a dark room that smelled less musty and riverine than James's. I flipped on the lights and saw that it was a kind of informal recreation room, with unvarnished fir walls and Berber carpeting on the floor. There was a wet bar at one end, and a large old Philco television, and in the very center stood a billiards table. The bar top was bare and the television unplugged and there was not a cue stick in sight. The closet James had mentioned was just beside the door, and in it, on a lower shelf, I found a pile of tattered coverlets and blankets. None of them looked quite large enough for the purpose I had in mind, but there was a striped Hudson Bay, just like the one old Albert Vetch used to spread across his lap against the chill winds blowing in from the Void. I threw this one over my shoulder and went back into James's room. James and Crabtree were sitting on the bed. Crabtree's hand had vanished inside James's shirt—my shirt—and he was moving it around in there with an air of calm and scientific rapture. James was looking down, watching through the window of his open collar as Crabtree felt him up. As I came into the room he looked at me and smiled, a sleepy, vulnerable expression on his face, like someone caught without his glasses on.

"I'm ready," I said softly.

"Uh huh," said Crabtree. "So are we."

I raised the lid of the trunk very slowly, to keep it from squeaking. Doctor Dee, Grossman, and the orphaned tuba lay there, in the moonlight, sleeping their various sleeps. I tossed the blanket around Doctor Dee, tucked its corners under his pelvis and withers, and then hoisted his stiff body into my arms. He seemed to have grown lighter since last night, as though the matter of his body were leaking away in the form of an ill-smelling gas.

"You're next," I promised Grossman. I didn't know what I was going to do about the tuba.

"All right if we stay here?" whispered Crabtree, through his open window, as I came around the car. I heard the rattle of the little vial of mollies in his hand.

"I'd prefer it," I said.

I looked in at James, sitting in the backseat beside Crabtree. He had the glassy eyes and gelid smile of someone bearing up under a mild irritation of the bowels. I could see that he was trying very hard not to be afraid.

"You all right with this, James?" I said, with a toss of my head that encompassed the body of Doctor Dee in my arms, the immense and shadowy backseat of my car, the Leer estate, moonlight, disaster.

He nodded. "If you hear a weird sound like an elevator," he said, "run."

"What will that be?"

"It'll be an elevator."

"I'll be right back," I said.

I carried Doctor Dee along the gravel drive, around the back of the house, to James's room. To free one hand I rested the dog's body against the door, turned the knob, and stepped inside. Holding Doctor Dee in the crook of one straining arm I yanked back the covers on James's bed and dropped his dead body onto the mattress. The springs of the mattress rang like a bell. I pulled the covers up over his head and left a black tuft of fur protruding from the top. This is such a stupid thing to do, I thought; but it looked so convincing that I couldn't keep from smiling.

When I went back into the billiards room to put away the Hudson Bay blanket, I noticed another array of photographs on the wall over the Philco. These were not movie stills, however. They were old family pictures, none more recent than a shot of a five-year-old but unmistakable James Leer, dressed in a red-and-black cowboy getup, gravely brandishing a pair of chrome six-shooters. There was one of an unknown handsome man holding baby James in his arms, with the Duquesne Incline train cars rising and falling on the wintry hillside behind them, and another of James wearing a tiny red bow tie and sitting on the lap of a much younger Amanda Leer. The rest of the pictures were standard studio portraits from prewar Europe and America, brilliantined men, lard-cheeked babies in frilly gowns, sepia-toned women with marcelled curls. I probably wouldn't have remarked them at all if one were not the exact duplicate of a photograph that was hanging from a wall in my own house, in the long downstairs hallway where Emily had carefully framed and nailed up a history for herself.

It was a photograph of nine serious men, young to middle-aged, dressed in dark suits and posed in stiff chairs behind a glossy velvet banner. The man in the center of the group, small and dapper and looking faintly angry, I knew for Isidore Warshaw, Emily's grandfather, who'd owned a candy store on the Hill not far from the present location of Carl Franklin's Hi-Hat. ZION CLUB OF PITTSBURGH, read the appliquéd letters on the banner, in an arc over a large Star of David. There was a second motto sewn on underneath the star, in shiny Hebrew characters. I was so surprised to find this photograph on the wall of someone else's house that it took me a minute to realize I wasn't looking at the *same* photograph. Then I noticed the tall, thin fellow sitting off to one side of the picture, legs crossed at the knee, staring away to his right while all of the other men faced the camera. He'd always been there; I'd noticed him, without ever quite seeing him, a thousand times before. He was thin, dark-haired, and handsome, but his features had an unformed, blurred appearance, as if he'd moved his head at the instant the shutter opened and closed.

I heard a sound, a low, sorrowful half-human moan like the call of a lighthouse in a fog. For a weird instant I thought that I was hearing the sound of my own voice, but then I could feel it resounding deep in the house, rattling all the hidden joists and rafters and the glass in the picture frames on the wall. The elevator. Amanda Leer was on her way down, perhaps to make certain that her son hadn't followed George Sanders and Herman Bing into the Great Dissolve.

I switched off the light and hobbled back out to James's room. As I was about to switch off the light in there, as well, and take my leave of the haunted house of Leer, my gaze fell on the old manual Underwood parked on the desk, its black bulk ornamented, like an old-fashioned hearse, with a ribbon of acanthus leaves. I went over to the desk and yanked open the drawer into which James had stuffed the piece he'd been working on when we arrived. It consisted of ten or eleven tries at a first paragraph, each of them a sentence longer than the previous one, all of them heavily marked up and re-arranged with arrows. The uppermost sheet went something like

ANGEL

She went wearing dark glasses to eat the Passover meal with his family, her pale famous hair tied up in a scarf pat-terned with cherries. They quarrelled in the cab on the way to his parents' apartment and made up in the elevator. Her mar-riage had failed and his was failing. She wasn't at all sure the time had come for her to meet his family and neither she knew was he. They had dared one another into taking this leap like children balanced on the railing of a bridge. The good things in her life had often proved illusory and she didn't know if there was really deep water flowing down there below them or only a painted blue screen.

He told her that on this night in Egypt three thousand years ago the Angel of Death had passed over the homes of the Jews. On this night ten years ago his brother had killed him-self and he warned her a candle would be burning on the table in the kitchen. She had never considered the idea of death as an angel and it appealed to her. It would be a workmanlike angel with a leather apron, shirtsleeves rolled, forearms rip-pling with tendon and muscle. Six years later just before she killed herself she would remember

By now the moaning of the elevator had sharpened to a regular rusted squeak, like the sound of an ancient iron water pump, and it was growing louder every second. The house shuddered and sighed and ticked like a heart. I didn't have much time. I replaced the manuscript, closed the desk drawer, and headed for the door. As I went past the bed I happened to look over at the empty glass I'd noticed before on James's nightstand, and saw now that it had an orange price sticker on its side that said 79¢. He'd stolen Sam's memorial from the Warshaws' kitchen. I went over to the nightstand and picked up the empty glass. Sometime during its twenty-four-hour career, I saw, a moth had flown down into the *yahrzeit* candle and been drowned in the pool of wax. I reached in and pried away the body of the errant moth and laid it in my palm. It was a small, unremarkable, dust-colored moth with tattered wings.

"Poor little fucker," I said.

The elevator landed like the blow of a hammer on the ground floor of the house. There was a rattle of cagework and the squeal of hinges. I dropped the dead moth into the pocket of my shirt, turned out the light, and then ran out into the deep, silent, Episcopalian darkness, solemn and sweet-smelling as night on a golf course.

When I was safely in the car again I gunned the engine and rolled us away from the gates with their sober pair of pineapples.

"James," I said, when we were halfway down the block and gaining speed. I checked the rearview mirror, half-expecting to see a wraithlike nightgown dancing in anger at the foot of the Leers' driveway. There was nothing but moonlight, dark hedgerows, and a distant black vanishing point. "Are you *Jewish?*"

"Sort of," he said. He was sitting in the backseat, reunited with his knapsack, looking wide awake. "I mean, yes, I am, but my grandparents—they kind of, I don't know. Got rid of it, I guess."

"I always thought—all that Catholicism in your stories—"

"Nah. I just like how twisted that Catholic stuff can get."

"And then tonight I had you figured for Episcopal for sure. At least Presbyterian."

"We go to the Presbyterian church, actually," said James. "*They* do. At Christmas. Shoot, I remember one time we went to this restaurant, in Mt. Lebanon, and I ordered a cream soda? And they *yelled* at me. They said it was *too Jewish*. Cream soda, that's about as Jewish as I ever got."

"Dangerously close," said Crabtree, solemnly. "Next thing you know you would have been strapping that little box onto your forehead."

I said, "So what did you think of Passover, then? Of the Seder? Of the Warshaws?"

"It was interesting," said James. "They were nice."

"Did it make you feel Jewish?" I said, thinking that perhaps this was the reason he'd stolen the burnt-out candle from the Warshaws' kitchen. "Being with them?"

"Not really." He sat back and tipped his head backward, looking up at the cold stars through the bare canopy of tree limbs overhead. "It made me feel like I wasn't anything." He said something more after that, but with his head tilted back his voice emerged pinched from his larynx, and the wind passing over the car carried his words away.

"I didn't catch that last part," I told him.

"I said, 'Like I'm nothing,'" he said.

WHEN we got back to my house the front door was wide open and all the lights were on. The stereo was playing softly in the living room.

"Hello?" I called. I went into the living room. It was deserted. There were crushed tortilla chips on the rug, cassettes and album jackets scattered everywhere; a giant Texas-shaped ashtray, which someone had left balanced on the arm of a wing-backed chair, had since tipped over onto the seat cushion, spilling butts and ashes all over the pale striped fabric. I went through the dining room, into the kitchen, and then checked out the laundry room, looking for survivors, collecting empty beer cans and turning off the lights as I went.

"There's nobody here," I said, circling back out into the hallway, where I'd left Crabtree and James; they too had vanished. I started down the hall after them, to see if I could interest anyone in blowing a joint with me and then searching the late-night dial for a good infomercial or a Hercules movie, but I didn't get far before I heard the tongue of Crabtree's door latch click discreetly against the jamb.

"Crabtree," I called, in a panicked whisper.

There was a pause, and then his head emerged into the hall.

"Ye-es?" he said. He looked a little exasperated. I'd caught him just as he was tucking his napkin into the collar of his shirt, licking his lupine chops. "What, Tripp?"

I stuck my hands into the pockets of my jacket. I didn't know what to say. I wanted to ask him to pull an all-nighter with me, the way we'd used to do, sitting on opposite sides of a nine-pack of Old Milwaukee, inveighing against our enemies, smoking black cigars, speculating for hours on the meaning of a certain enigmatic question in the lyrics of "Any Major Dude." I wanted to tell him that I didn't think I could face another night in the emptiness of my bed. I wanted to ask him if there was anything in my life that was real and coherent and likely to remain the same way tomorrow.

"Here," I said. From one of the hip pockets of my jacket I produced the fabled Lov-O-Pus I'd bought this morning at the Giant Eagle, on the way out to Kinship. I tossed it at him, and he caught it in one hand. "Wear it in good health."

He read the tentacular promises made in wiggly green letters on the label of the Lov-O-Pus condom. He smiled.

"Thanks," he said. He started to close the door.

"Crabtree!"

He stuck his head back out into the hall.

"What am I going to do now?"

He shrugged. "Why don't you go finish your book?" he said. There was a nasty and unmistakable gleam in his eye, and I saw that he had taken a look at the manuscript of *Wonder Boys;* there was no question about it. "Aren't you just about done?"

"Just about," I said.

"There you go," he said. "Why don't you give it a good hour and wrap the whole thing up?"

Then he drew back into the bedroom and firmly shut the door.

I went into the kitchen again, pressed my ear against the door to the basement, and listened for a few minutes without hearing anything but the slow deep breathing of the old house itself. The wood felt cool against my cheek. My ankle was throbbing, and I realized that it had been hurting for the last hour without my having noticed. All at once it was killing me, and I told myself that I really ought to drive to the E.R. at Shadyside and have someone take a look at it. Instead I went over to the wreckage of bottles, tumblers, and plastic wineglasses on the kitchen table and administered a tall dose of Kentucky anesthesia. Then I carried the glass of bourbon down the front hall and into my office. The manuscript was gone from its accustomed resting place on my desk, and I panicked for an instant before remembering that Hannah had taken it down into her bedroom to read.

"Hey."

I turned. There was a man sitting on the Honor Bilt, watching the television with the sound off. It was my old student, the one who'd dropped my class after coming to the conclusion that I was only a cheap Faulkner imitator with nothing of value to impart. He sat slumped backward on the sofa with a forty-ounce bottle of beer pressed between the ripped knees of his jeans, smiling at me as if we were the oldest of friends and he'd been waiting all night for me to show up. A copy of *The Land Downstairs* lay open on his lap but he was not giving it his close attention. In fact I thought he had it upside down.

"How are you?" I said. "Is it Jim?"

"Jeff," he said.

"Welcome," I said with mock solemnity, trying to let him see that I thought he had a lot of nerve but that it was nonetheless cool for him to be there. "What are you watching?"

"The news," he said. "The news from Bulgaria."

It was a wildly colored, out-of-focus program, streaked and pitted by the ionosphere. The newsreader had on a blazer the color of a taxicab and wore a vast hairdo like a thick sable hat. According to the reference date in the corner of the picture the transmission was already a few days old, but I didn't suppose that mattered when the whole thing was in Bulgarian and turned all the way down. I sat down on the sofa and watched with Jeff for five minutes.

"Well," I said, standing up. "Good night."

"Ciao," said Jeff, without looking up.

I went down to Hannah's room. All the lights were on, and she was lying on her bed, surrounded by the scattered pages of *Wonder Boys,* asleep. She was dressed in a white nightgown, lace at the bodice. Her feet were bare. They were thick, wide, ordinary feet, with long crooked toes. I sat down on the edge of her bed and hung my head. From this vantage I could see the little moth lying in my pocket. I fished him out and stared at him for a while.

"What are you holding in your hand?" said Hannah.

I started. She was looking at me through half-closed lids, not really awake. I uncurled my fingers, revealing the moth, embalmed in a thin white coating of wax.

"Just a moth," I said.

"I fell asleep," she told me, her voice cobwebbed with sleep. "I was reading."

"That good, huh?" I said. There was no reply. "How far did you get?"

But her eyes had fluttered closed again. I looked at the clock. It was four thirty-two in the morning. I collected the parts of my manuscript, slapped them together, and set them on the nightstand beside her bed. Her bedclothes were all knotted and twisted, so I shook them out and let them fall billowing over her like parachute silks. I covered her feet, kissed her cheek, and wished her good night. Then I turned out the lights and went back upstairs to my office. Jeff had fallen asleep, too, stretched out shoeless on the Honor Bilt. I switched off the television, went over to my desk, and sat down to work.

I was still typing away and Jeff was still sleeping at nine o'clock, when the policeman came to take James Leer away.

PALE, pink Terry Crabtree was sitting, propped up by two feather pillows and a throw cushion, in the wreckage of the bedclothes, naked except for a pair of pin-striped blue boxers, his legs drawn up to his chest. His body hair ran more to blond than I remembered, and the light of a Sunday morning, coming in through the window behind him, discovered a faint golden aura around his thighs and his shins and at the backs of his hands. He held the typescript of *The Love Parade* balanced against the tops of his knees with one hand, and with the other he was stroking at his bedmate's hair. This was the sole part of James Leer visible when I came into the bedroom: the rest of him could only be inferred amid the heap of blankets and twisted sheets at Crabtree's side, from which the hair of his head emerged, in the vicinity of his pillow, exactly like the great black shock of Doctor Dee's fur. Discarded shirts and trousers struck poses on the floor around the bed. There was a kind of autumnal stain in the air that reminded me of the smell of leather work gloves, a high-school locker room at homecoming, the inside of an ancient canvas tent. I swung halfway into the room, hanging on the doorknob. Crabtree looked up at me and smiled. It was a kindly smile, lacking in all irony. I hadn't seen its like on his face in years. I was sorry to have to wipe it away.

"Is he awake?" I said, relieved not to have interrupted them in the act of exploring each other's lunar surfaces, or engaging in some other Crabtreevian activity that would have obliged James to speak to Officer Pupcik whilst dangling by his ankles from the ceiling, dressed as an owl. "He has a visitor."

Crabtree raised an eyebrow and studied my face, trying to read in it the identity of James's visitor. After a fruitless few seconds he leaned across the bed and peeled back the walls of James's cocoon, exposing the whole of his head, his downy neck, the pale smooth expanse of his back. James Leer lay curled up like a child, his face to the window, immobile. Crabtree pursed his lips, then looked up at me and shook his head. Sound asleep. The smile on his face was indulgent and almost *sweet,* and the thought crossed my mind that Crabtree might be in love. That was too disturbing a notion to entertain for very long, however, and I dismissed it from my mind. I'd always counted on and found comfort in Terry Crabtree's unique ability to regard all romantic love with genuine and pitiless scorn.

"He's pretty worn out, I imagine, poor kid," he said, pulling the covers back over James's head.

"Regardless," I said. "He's going to have to wake up."

"Why?" said Crabtree. "Who is it? Old Fred?" He grinned and made a sweeping gesture with one hand to encompass all the odors and disorders of the room. "Send him on in."

I said, "A policeman."

Crabtree opened his mouth, then closed it. For an unprecedented instant he could think of nothing to say. Then he set the typescript of *The Love Parade* on the night table beside him, lowered his lips to James's ear, and whispered, too low for me to hear what he was saying. After a moment James moaned, softly, then got his head up off the mattress. He craned it around toward me, squinting, newly hatched, his brilliantined hair sticking up at all angles from his head.

"Hey, Grady," he said.

"Good morning, James."

"A policeman."

"Afraid so."

After another moment he managed to roll himself all the way over, onto his back. He sat up on one elbow, blinking one eye and then the other, working his jaw in circles, as if experimenting with the functions of a brand-new body. The blankets slid from his shoulders, leaving him naked to the waist. The skin on his belly was mottled with sleep. On his shoulder he wore red traces of Crabtree's lips and incisors.

"What does he want?"

"Well, I guess he wants to ask you about what happened at the Chancellor's house on Friday night."

James didn't say anything. He lay there, without moving, his left temple resting companionably against the upper part of Crabtree's right arm.

"You *snore*," he told Crabtree.

"So I hear," said Crabtree, nudging James lightly with his shoulder. "Go on, Jimmy," he added. "Just tell them what I told you to tell them."

James nodded, slowly, looking down with longing at the deep declivity growing cold in the center of his pillow. Then his eyes opened wide, and he looked up at me.

"Okay," he said. He gave his head a determined nod, then swung his legs around, stood up, and went bare-assed to the foot of the bed, where he found his BVDs. He dressed himself deliberately and quickly. As he pulled on his shirt he noticed the long archipelago of hickeys on his shoulder. He ran his fingers softly across them, and looked over at Crabtree with a smile that was crooked and half grateful. He didn't seem particularly distressed or bewildered, I thought, on awakening to his first morning as a lover of men. While he worked his way up the buttons of my old flannel shirt, he kept glancing over at Crabtree, not in any mawkish way but with deliberateness and an air of wonder, as if studying Crabtree, memorizing the geometry of his knees and elbows.

"So," I said. "What did you tell him to tell them?"

"Oh, that he's very, very sorry for shooting the Chancellor's dog, and that he's willing to do anything to make it up."

James nodded, and bent to pick up his socks.

"I don't think it's going to be that easy," I said.

James stood up. "I left my shoes in the hall," he said.

"I don't really think you're going to need *shoes*," said Crabtree. "The guy's not going to arrest you."

A floorboard creaked, and there was a jingle of metal from down the hall. We all looked at one another.

"Mr. Tripp?" called Officer Pupcik. "Everything all right back there?"

"Yeah," I said, "we're coming." I put my hand on James's shoulder and steered him toward the the door. "Come on, *Jimmy*."

As he started out of the bedroom, James turned to Crabtree and nodded toward the manuscript on the bedside table.

"So," he said. "How is it?"

Crabtree raised his chin, tipping his head back until the ends of his hair brushed his shoulders, and looked at James through narrowed eyelids. It occurred to me that an editor was a kind of artistic Oppenheimer, careful to view the terrible flash of an author's ego only through a thick protective lens.

"It's not bad," he said, not quite tonelessly. "Not bad at all."

James grinned, and he ducked his head once in childish delight. Then he grabbed his shoes and brushed past me and went skipping down the hall toward the front door, where I'd left Officer Pupcik waiting for him out on the porch.

Crabtree sat up and opened his eyes wide again.

"I want to publish this," he said, picking up the manuscript and thumping it once with the heel of his hand. "I hope they'll let me. I've got to think they will. It's brilliant."

"Great," I said, feeling a little twinge. "A little more help from you and Officer Pupcik, there, and he can be the next Jean Genet. It's been a while since somebody wrote a good book in jail."

He wrinkled up his nose. "I don't think killing someone's dog's all that big a *deal,* Tripp. Isn't it basically just a kind of vandalism?"

"Didn't he tell you about the jacket, Crabtree?"

Crabtree shook his head, and his expression got a little vague; I had him worried now. And that was a disturbing notion, too.

"Look at it this way," I told him. "You won't have any trouble getting him off the book page."

Ｊ AMES and the policeman stood on the porch, side by side, looking in through the front door like a couple of paperboys come to collect. I was relieved to see that the handcuffs were still dangling from Officer Pupcik's utility belt.

"I'm real sorry, Mr. Tripp," the policeman said, "but I

Michael Chabon

have to run James here on over to the campus. Dr. Gaskell wants to talk to him."

I nodded, and shrugged my shoulders at James, palms upraised, consigning him yet again to the custody and judgment of others. For once there was no concomitant look of reproach in his eyes. He only smiled, and followed his captor down the porch steps, going lightly.

"Just a minute, James," I said, grabbing for the car keys on the deal table by the door. The two men stopped and turned back. I dangled the keys before me and jerked my head toward the side of the house. "There's something you'd better take with you, don't you think?"

"Oh, yeah," said James, blushing a little—but only a little. He was feeling all tender and well-fucked and strange, you could see, crepey and delicate as the unfurling petal of a flower. It was hard for him to be embarrassed about anything. He'd forgotten all about the jacket, I supposed, and he couldn't have cared less what dire fate lay in store for him that morning in the office of his department chair. He was just going along with things now, waiting to see what happened next. "I think I saw it on the front seat."

"What's that?" said Officer Pupcik.

"Walter's jacket," I said. "Dr. Gaskell's, uh, his property. It was all a misunderstanding. It was really all my fault. I said I would show him something upstairs, and he didn't understand that it wasn't mine, and—" I stopped. I could see Officer Pupcik's eyes starting to glaze over. No explanation is ever concise or truthful enough to suit a policeman. "Anyway, James would like to give it back."

"Oh," said Officer Pupcik, "and that's a problem, then, isn't it?" He nodded, once, looking pleased with himself for having figured it out. "You've got her in the shop." He hoisted a thumb over his shoulder in the direction of the driveway. "Couldn't stand seeing her with that nasty ding in the hood, huh?"

"What's that?" I said. "I don't— Jesus."

I had followed them down the porch steps, and now I looked, past the flower beds, over to the driveway. There was nothing in it but a bloody black oil stain on the cement.

"Oh, shit," I said.

"What's the matter?" said Officer Pupcik.

"Grady?" said James.

"It'll be all right, James," I said, temporizing, trying to think where I could have left the car last night. I'd walked all the way home from campus after the lecture, yes, and—no, that had been two nights ago. "Just try to explain everything to Dr. Gaskell as well as you can. I'll be along with the jacket as soon as I get it back."

"So, where is she?" said Officer Pupcik.

"What's that? Oh, she's at the body shop, uh huh. That's right. Damn, I wish I'd thought to get that jacket out of her before I dropped her off."

"Wull, hey, you'ns want me to drive you over there?"

"Yes, sure, uh, well, no," I said, cleverly. "That's all right. I don't think I'm quite ready to leave the house yet." I gave what I hoped would pass for a humorous pull on the flap of Mrs. Knopflmacher's bathrobe. "I have to get dressed. I'll have Crabtree—my editor, Terry Crabtree—drive me over there. Go on ahead, James. We'll catch up with you."

James nodded, appearing somewhat less certain now of the serendipitous drift of things. Officer Pupcik laid a custodial hand on his elbow and guided him over to the squad car. I followed them down to the foot of the driveway, my hands thrust with utmost cool into the geranium pockets of my big chenille robe. As they climbed in on their opposite sides the two young men looked back at me wearing nearly identical expressions of distrust.

Just before he started the car Officer Pupcik rolled down his window. He was holding a pair of aviator sunglasses in his hand but didn't seem quite ready to slip them onto his face.

"So, let me get this straight," he said. "You're saying, you have Dr. Gaskell's property, or you know where it is, is that it?"

"That's right. Safe and sound."

"And as soon as you get it from your car, which you left at a body shop, you'll be bringing it right on over to him."

"You betcha."

He nodded, slowly, made one last furtive examination of Mrs. Knopflmacher's bathrobe, and put on his sunglasses. Then he rolled up his window and drove away with James. I gave a weak little wave, and I was still there, waving at the empty street like a mad queen on a parade float, when Crabtree appeared at my shoulder a minute later.

"Where are they taking him?" he said. He'd pulled on one of my old T-shirts over his boxer shorts, and he was wearing a pair of Birkenstock sandals I had at some point years ago pilfered from his closet. The shirt, come to think of it, was one of his, too; it was a promotional pocket-T, acquired from a pharmacist lover, which claimed, in lavender script, that Ativan chased the clouds away. I wondered if he were planning now to reclaim everything I'd ever taken from him. "What's this about a jacket? What did he do?"

"I think I told you about it once," I said. "A black satin jacket. With a fur collar? Marilyn Monroe wore it when she married Joe DiMaggio."

"Oh, *yeah*," said Crabtree, wrapping his arms around himself. It was a breezy morning, with a chill hint of rain in the air. "I always wanted to get a look at that thing."

"I took James upstairs to show it to him. I guess James felt sorry for it."

"And?"

"And so while I was out in the hallway, you know, wrestling with Doctor Dee—he boosted it."

"How like him," said Crabtree. The tungsten glint of irony had returned to his voice. "So? I don't see why that's a problem."

"Don't you?"

"He can just give it back."

"Uh huh. That's awfully good thinking, Crabs."

He squinted at me, trying to determine why I sounded like I was fucking with him.

"Well, so where is it?" he said.

"Lying on the backseat of the car."

Crabtree looked over his shoulder toward the driveway.

"I see," he said, after a moment. "And where did we *leave* the car last night? I can't quite seem to remember."

"I feel reasonably certain that we left it right about where you're looking."

"Huh? Holy shit, Tripp, what, the car's been stolen?"

"Not exactly," I said. "I think it sort of got *repossessed*."

"Repossessed? How could it be? I thought you said the fucking thing was some kind of a payoff from Happy Blackmore. I thought he owed you money."

"It was," I said. "He did. Only I'm starting to think the car wasn't exactly Happy's to give me, if you know what I mean. He never did bring me any pink slip for it. I haven't been able to register it yet." I felt myself blush. "Happy kept saying he had the title in his files."

"In his *files,*" said Crabtree, looking arch. "Happy Black-more."

"I know," I said. "Sounds pretty stupid, now."

Several years before, Crabtree had advanced Hap several thousand dollars to ghost the autobiography of a catcher, a rising star who played for Pittsburgh and hit the sort of home runs that linger in the memory for years. Old Happy had spent months engaged in what he called—straight-faced—his preliminary researches before delivering an outline so poorly constructed and filled with inaccuracies that Crabtree and his bosses had immediately moved to cancel the contract. Not long afterward the power-hitting subject himself had died in a car wreck, out on Mt. Nebo Road, leaving nothing in Happy's notorious "files" but the fragments and scribblings of a ghost.

"Maybe it's around here somewhere," I said, hopelessly.

"Sure. Maybe you parked in someone else's driveway by mistake."

"I wouldn't put it past me," I said. "Ha ha."

"Ha," said Crabtree. "Neither would I."

We went into the house and pulled on shoes and pants, and then took a walk around the block to look for the Galaxie. The morning felt cold and inauspicious, and I was sorry to see that after yesterday's sunshine the usual heavy clouds had returned, low and threatening and so brilliant they hurt the eyes. As we walked I told Crabtree about my exchange with Vernon Hardapple at the Hi-Hat.

"How did he find you?"

"I don't know. Maybe Happy—oh."

We'd almost made it back to the house, now, and as we approached the foot of my driveway I spotted a twisted white scrap of paper lying in the grass. I knelt down to pick it up, shook the dew from it, and handed it over to Crabtree.

"I think I might've lost a bunch of these that night," I said. "I dropped my wallet."

" 'Grady Tripp, Novelist'?" said Crabtree, reading the soiled business card on which, over my address and telephone number, this dubious legend was engraved.

"Sara gave them to me, for my last birthday," I said, trying to keep from blushing. "I think she was trying to cheer me up."

"Sweet," said Crabtree. He slipped the card into the pocket of his T-shirt. "All right, then. Clearly Vernon came and took his car back."

"Clearly."

"So."

"So?"

"So we're just going to have to find him, and the car, and get the coat back from him." He nodded, encouraging himself. "I can talk to the guy. I can talk to anyone."

"I know you can, Terry, but—"

"We have to, Tripp." His expression was oddly grave. "I—I don't—I wouldn't want anything to—anything bad to happen to James." He glanced at me, a little sheepishly, then punched me on the arm. "What are you looking at? Fuck you."

"Nothing," I said.

"I like him."

"Yeah, I guess I like him, too," I said. We started up the walk to the house. "I'll ask Hannah if we can borrow her car."

"It seems to me that girl would let you borrow her pancreas," observed Crabtree. He looked at me, then; it was the first close examination he had given me all morning. He wasn't, I thought, especially impressed by what he saw. The wind had picked up, and I shivered, and all of a sudden it occurred to me that when Terry Crabtree gazed at me with such an air of cool and unconcerned appraisal he was no longer really seeing me, his oldest friend, in whom all the outlandish promises of life and every chance for glory intimately and anciently inhered. He was seeing only the pot-addled author of a bloated, boneless, half-imaginary two-thousand-page kraken of a novel, a hoax whose trusting and credulous pursuit had cost him tens upon tens of thousands of dollars and, seemingly, his career.

"Oh, hey," he remembered to ask me, "what's going on with the two of you, anyway?"

"Nothing," I said. "I've been trying my best to leave her alone."

"Amazing," said Crabtree.

The front door was open, and deep in the house I heard the melancholy wheezing of an accordion. Hannah was awake and making breakfast; there was a clamor of pots from the kitchen. I was suddenly afraid of having to face her, and I wondered at this; and then in the next instant I realized that what I feared was not Hannah but her opinion of *Wonder Boys*. I felt intimations of disaster there; my book was at last going forth into the world, not, as I'd always imagined, like a great black streamlined locomotive, fittings aglint, trailing tri-colored bunting, its steel wheels throwing sparks; but rather by accident, and at the wrong time, a half-ton pickup with no brakes, abruptly jarred loose from its blocks in the garage and rolling backward down a long steep hill.

"Crabtree," I said, stopping him at the threshold. "We

don't even know Vernon's real name. 'Vernon Hardapple'—
we just made that up."

"Oh, that's right." Crabtree looked bemused. I could see
he was trying to assemble the things we did know about the
roostery high-haired man with the terrible purple scar on his
face. "You know," he said, after a moment, "if you think
about it, we kind of made the whole *guy* up."

"No wonder he fucked us over, then," I said.

HANNAH Green and the inevitable Jeff were cracking eggs
into a crockery bowl and peeling strips of bacon from the
package. Heartbroken Argentine music came blowing up the
stairs from the basement, and as we walked into the kitchen
we found Jeff lecturing a skeptical Hannah on the origins of
the tango in the death grip and knife play of latent homosex-
ual love, an argument which I recognized as cribbed from old
George Borges. Maybe, I thought, this Jeff character had
something to recommend him; there was a certain thematic
aptness, after all, in trying to make a girl through the plagia-
rism of Borges.

"I mean, look at the way they dance—it's all about sod-
omy," he was saying, charmingly.

"Get out of here," said Hannah, picking large fragments of
eggshell out of the bowl.

"I'm serious."

"Jeff," said Crabtree, shaking his head sadly. "Jeff, we have
to have a talk."

"Oh, hi!" said Hannah, looking up. She gave me an awkward, oddly formal wave. She had on a long purple nightshirt

over her cracked red boots. Her index finger wore a smart eggshell hat. Her eyes were bright, her cheeks pink, and when she spoke she sounded well-rested and strong and a bit over-eager, like someone whose fever has just broken. "You fellas want some eggs?"

I shook my head and then pointed toward the basement door.

"Can I talk to you a sec, Hannah?" I said.

"Was that *you* snoring, man?" I heard Jeff say to Crabtree as we started down the basement stairs. "You sound like a fucking rock tumbler."

"What's up?" said Hannah, looking concerned.

I told her that James had been taken away by the police, and that rescuing him would be a simple thing, but that in order to rescue him we would need to borrow her car. The sudden disappearance of my own vehicle I explained with a vague but suitably ominous allusion to Happy Blackmore. No, I said, shaking my head in the same vague and ominous but supremely self-possessed manner, it would be better if she herself didn't come along. She and Jeff should just head on over to WordFest, and in an hour—easy—James, Crabtree, and I would be joining them. That was all I told her—it was all I thought I needed to tell her—but to my surprise she did not immediately agree to let us take her car. She hugged herself, stepped backward toward her bed, and sat heavily down. The manuscript of *Wonder Boys* stood in a stack on her night table, spotless, smooth-edged, all its corners true. Hannah regarded it for several seconds, then turned her face to me. She was biting her lower lip.

"Grady," she said. She took a deep breath, then slowly let it out. "Are you at all stoned, by any chance?"

I was not, and I swore to her that I was not. The claim

sounded completely false to my ears. I could see she didn't believe me, and, in the way of these things, the more I promised her, the falser I sounded.

"Okay, okay, ease up," she said. "It's not really any of my business. I wouldn't even—I mean, normally—"

I was surprised by how upset she seemed. "What, Hannah? What is it?"

"Sometimes I think you smoke too much of that stuff."

"Maybe I do," I said. "Yeah, I do. Why? I mean, what makes you say so?"

"It's not— I didn't want to—" She reached for *Wonder Boys*. Its weight bent her hand at the wrist, and when she dropped it onto her lap it resounded against her knee bones like a watermelon. She looked down at its first page, at the initial run of sentences I'd written and rewritten two hundred times. She shook her head and started to speak, then closed her mouth again.

"Just say it, Hannah. Come on."

"It starts out great, Grady. *Really* great. For the first two hundred pages or so I was *loving* it. I mean, you heard me last night."

"I heard you," I said, my heart squeezing itself into a tight fist of dread.

"But then—I don't know."

"Don't know what?"

"Well, then it starts—I mean parts of it are still wonderful, amazing, but after a while it just starts—I don't know—it gets all spread out."

"Spread out?"

"Okay, not spread out, then, but jammed too full. Like that thing with the Indian ruin? Okay, first you have the Indians come, right, they build the thing, they die out, it falls apart, hundreds of years go by, it gets buried, in the fifties some scientist finds it and digs it out, he kills himself—all that goes on and on and on, for, like forty pages, and, I don't know—" She paused, and blinked her eyes, and wondered for a moment at the novelty of administering criticism to her teacher. "It doesn't really seem to have anything to do with your *characters*. I mean, it's beautiful writing, amazingly beautiful, but . . . And all that about the town cemetery? All the headstones, and their inscriptions, and the bones and bodies underneath them? And the part about their different guns in the cabinet in the old house? And the genealogies of their horses? And—" She caught herself devolving into simple litany and broke off.

"Grady," she said, sounding more than a little horror-struck. "You have whole chapters that go for thirty and forty pages *with no characters at all!*"

"I know." I knew, but it had never quite occurred to me to put it to myself this way. There were, I was suddenly certain, a lot of things about *Wonder Boys* that had never occurred to me. On a certain crucial level—how strange!—I had no idea of what the book was really about, and not the faintest notion of how it would strike a reader. I hung my head. "Jesus."

"I'm sorry, Grady, really, I just couldn't help wondering—"

"What?"

"I wondered how it would be—what this book would be like—if you didn't—if you weren't always so stoned all the time when you write."

I pretended to become indignant. "It wouldn't read half as well," I said, sounding more dishonest to myself than ever. "I'm sure of that."

Hannah nodded, but she didn't meet my eyes, and the tips of her ears turned red. She was embarrassed for me.

"Wait till you finish it," I said. "You'll see."

Again she didn't reply, but now she managed to bring herself to look at me, and her face was the face of a woman who, having at the last moment discovered that all of her fiancé's claims and bona fides were false, all of his credentials forged, has unpacked her trunks and cashed in her ticket and now must tell him quickly that she will not sail away. There was pity there, and resentment, and a Daughter-of-Utah hardness that said, Enough's enough. However far she'd gotten in her reading last night and this morning, the thought of pressing onward to the end was obviously too onerous for her even to contemplate.

"Anyway," I said, glancing away. I cleared my throat. It was my turn to be embarrassed. "Is it all right about the car?"

"Of course," she said, with cruel charity and a backward wave of her hand. "Keys are on the dresser."

"Thanks."

"No problem. You guys take good care of James, now."

"We will." I turned away. "You betcha."

"Grady," she said.

I looked back, and she held out the manuscript to me as though returning a ring. I took it, grabbed the keys, and started back up the stairs.

So Crabtree and I undertook a final pilgrimage to the Hi-Hat, provincial capital of the empire of our friendship throughout the long period of its decline. It was the only place we could think of to go looking for the Shadow, that implacable high-haired hobgoblin we'd invented and set loose on Friday night. At his own insistence Crabtree was behind the wheel, and going too fast. He drove Hannah's rattling old Renault like a Frenchman, upshifting and downshifting as though linked in an intimate horsemanlike relationship to the engine. In his hands and eyes and in the cant of his thin shoulders there was a cool, expectant agitation I hadn't seen in years. For the moment, at least, he seemed to have managed to pole his own raft out of the fog of failure, and other such bad habits, in whose midst we'd been floating now for so long. As he drove, drumming on the dash, sucking on a Kool, I could see that he was going over all the accidents, likelihoods, and possible outcomes of this expedition, considering alternate strategies and tactics. Ordinarily it would have made me glad to see him thus alive with all the narrative possibilities of our trouble. It was like old times; he was writing his name in water. But whenever we stopped for a red light he would glance over at me, and his expression would go blank, incredulous, faintly pitying, as if I were only a bedraggled hitchhiker picked up in a rainstorm on the road between Zilchburg and Palookaville: a nobody headed nowhere, smelling vaguely of wet wool. I had the feeling that if our present venture failed I would not play a central role in his next attempt to rescue James Leer.

I rode shotgun, watching the stolid brick houses of Pittsburgh go past, feeling stunned and useless in the wake of Hannah's criticism, and hoping nevertheless to retrieve the Baggie of dope I'd left in the glove compartment of the Galaxie. We were halfway to the Hill before I became aware that I was still clutching the manuscript of *Wonder Boys* in my hands, crinkling its title page with my fingers. No wonder I looked so pathetic to Crabtree, a broken down old illusionist carrying his moth-eaten scarves, greasy tarot cards, and amazed testimonials from defunct czars and countesses in a paper suitcase on his lap. I'd never intended to bring the thing along, and I had a feeling that it was probably a mistake to have done so; but I hadn't intended not to bring it along, either, and although I felt embarrassed there was, as always, something reassuring about the watermelon weight of it on my thighs. Neither of us said a word.

The storefronts along Centre Avenue were barred and shuttered, the door handles chained, the broken sidewalks deserted except for a party of girls in starchy pink and yellow and ladies in broad hats who were coming down the steps of the A.M.E. church on the corner of the Hi-Hat's block. Crabtree guided us into the parking lot of the Hat, where on Friday night that flickering Shadow had danced its corrida with the Galaxie. It was empty of everything but a stiff breeze and a broad whirling fairy circle of paper cups, losing numbers, the want ads, a hair net, fluttering sheets of waxed paper stained with barbecue sauce. The black steel doors of the club were closed tight, a corrugated shutter covered the kitchen window, and the place had the usual forlorn appearance of a nightclub in the daytime, unplugged, unmagical, closed up like a frozen custard stand on a deserted stretch of boardwalk in the winter.

"Oh, well," I said.

"Oh, well, nothing," said Crabtree, backing out, dragging the wheel around, putting the car in first. "We're going to— Hey."

I looked. At the other end of the alley, where it gave onto the next street, sat a red sports car, parked at a crazy angle and blocking our path, as though its driver had been in too great a hurry to drive it any farther and had abandoned it just so. It was one of those angular new Japanese models that bear such a disturbing resemblance to the naked skull of a rat.

"Think that's Carl Franklin?" said Crabtree.

"How about if I go see," I said.

"There's an idea."

I nodded. I set the manuscript on the seat and got out of the car. Crabtree looked at it and for a moment I thought he was going to pick it up. He left it lying there. He reached into his pocket for his cigarettes.

"Go on," he said, pushing in the dashboard lighter. "We don't have all that much time."

I went over to the pair of black doors and one-two pounded on them. I watched a lipsticked cocktail napkin chase itself around an oblong patch of mud beside the door. Years ago there had been an evergreen hedge planted here, a survivor from swankier days at the Hi-Hat, which in the summertime bore tiny white flowers as heady as gardenias, but it had proved too attractive a target for the local Six-Inch Rifle Club, and now there was only the patch of mud. I reckoned the shade of lipstick on the napkin as Rose Sauvage. A minute passed. I looked back at the car, praying as I turned my head, He'll be reading it. He was not. He sat blowing smoke, hands on the wheel, brow furrowed, examining me for signs of an imminent failure of nerve. I pounded on the door, harder this time, and waited, then looked back at Crabtree and shrugged. He spun his hand at the wrist several times in an impatient circle, and I started back to the Le Car. At that moment I heard the report of a heavy bolt being drawn, and the squeal of hinges, and behind the windshield of Hannah's car Crabtree's eyes widened. I whirled and found myself looking at a naked chest, hairless, damp, incandescent with muscle, beautiful in color as a slab of raw liver. Clement, the doorman, was not only shirtless, but the fly of his jeans was unbuttoned, revealing two inches of red silk underpants. He was not at all happy to see me.

"Hey, Clement," I said. "Sorry to bother you."

"Uh huh." The interior of the club was dark behind him but I could hear the slow exhalation of a saxophone and then the irresistible carnal reasoning of Marvin Gaye. Clement folded his twenty-two-inch biceps across his chest. The smell of pussy was on him, around him, drifting out of the gap in his trousers, the smell of cumin and salt pork and sawdust hot off the saw. "You are, though."

"I know, and I mean it, I'm really sorry. You know me, don't you?" I laid a hand over my wildly beating heart. "Name's Tripp. I used to come here a lot."

"I know your face."

"Great, okay, well, listen, I'm, uh, my friend and I are looking for someone. Little guy. Tall hair. Black. He has a big nasty scar on his face. Kind of looks like he has an extra mouth, right here."

I touched my fingers to my cheek. Clement's eyes tightened at the corners for an instant, then relaxed.

"Yeah?" he said. He raised the fingers of his left hand to his nose and idly sniffed at them. Presently it became clear that this was all he intended to say for the moment.

"So do you know him?"

" 'Fraid not."

"Really? I bet he comes here all the time? He's just a little guy. Looks like a jockey." His name's Vernon, I almost added.

Clement took a step backward, and with an expression on

his face of profoundest mock regret, started to shut the door.

"We're closed, Gee," he said.

"Wait!" I reached out and grabbed hold of the door with both hands. I did it without thinking and my intentions were largely symbolic, but I soon found myself pulling with all the strength in my arms. I didn't want that door to close on me. "Buddy—!"

Clement smiled, flashing a gold incisor, and let go of the door. I flew backward, clinging like a windsurfer to my steely black sail before I lost my footing and sat down, hard, in the patch of mud by the door. The sound of my impact was impressive but not especially dignified. Clement took a step toward me and stood looking down, hands on his hips. He breathed carefully, like a runner pacing himself. I figured I had about two seconds to tell him something good. I offered him all the money in my wallet and whatever was in Crabtree's, too. He refused it. The golden tooth winked at me. Clement was the kind of man who smiled only when he was angry. I made him a second offer, and this time he held out his hand to me and helped me to my feet. I looked back at the patch of mud, in which I had impressed my unique personal cartouche. Then I hobbled over to the car, peeling the seat of my jeans away from my skin.

Crabtree had rolled down the window. His eyebrows were arched and he was smirking his Crabtree smirk but there was something unamused in the expression of his eyes.

"Well," I said, leaning against the door.

"Well?"

I swallowed and looked away. I wiped my muddy fingers against one thigh. I told him what I had promised Clement in exchange for the Shadow's name.

"No way," he said, but without hesitating he reached into

the breast pocket of his linen jacket and pressed a slender plastic prescription vial into my hand. "So he knows him, huh? Who is he?"

"That's what I'm about to find out."

"Peterson Walker," said Clement, slipping the vial carelessly into the back pocket of his jeans. "People call him Pea. He used to fight."

That figured; Happy Blackmore drew a fair portion of his unsavory acquaintance from the eye cutters and ring rats of the upper Ohio valley.

"A flyweight," I guessed.

He shrugged. "More like a fleaweight," he said. He works for a sporting-goods store. I forget the name. Downtown, Second, Third Avenue. Something with a K."

"Is it open on Sundays?"

"Man, what I look like? The fucking Yellow Pages?"

"Sorry," I said. I turned to leave him. "Thanks a lot."

"Ain't going to get your car back," said Clement, sounding suddenly friendly. I stopped and faced him again. "But you might go and get yourself smoked." This prospect seemed in an abstract way to interest him. "Pea's been looking for that car for months, man. Saying it used to belong to his brother and shit."

"What happened to his brother?"

"He got himself smoked." He cocked his large head to one side and scratched idly at his neck. "Couple of guys from Morgantown. Had something to do with a horse. I heard they was really trying to smoke Pea Walker."

"Oh, yeah," I said. "I heard that, too." I could see this was difficult for Clement to believe. "So this Pea guy carries a gun, huh?"

"That's right. Big fat German nine."

"I suppose that's the kind of thing you would know," I said, considering his reputation as a master of confiscation. "Is that kind of thing pretty common around here?"

"Ain't no such thing as a flyweight with a gat," observed Clement sagely, as he closed the black steel doors.

"Amazing," said Crabtree when I got back into the car and told him what I'd learned. He was grinning now. "We had the story pretty much right."

"Except for the sport, I guess, yeah."

"Nice to know we're still skilled at that."

"Nice," I said. We pulled back out onto Centre and headed downtown. Unlike Crabtree, who seemed in the last twelve hours to have found a cure for all his heartsickness, I felt clammy, mud-stained, and tired, and I was so desperate for a joint that I could smell from here the burnt spearmint flavor of the Baggie in the Galaxie's glove compartment.

"What?" said Crabtree.

"What what?"

"You sighed."

"Did I?" I said. "It's nothing. I guess I was just wishing I could have been skilled at something else."

"Like what?"

I hefted the manuscript that I held in my lap.

"Like writing novels, for example," I said. "Ha ha."

He nodded and adjusted his lips into a smile to acknowledge my little joke. We came to a stoplight and he slowed. The light turned green and he started off again and we sat there in Hannah's tiny car that smelled of stale carpet and damp earth, not talking about *Wonder Boys*.

"Is it really that bad?" I said.

"Oh, no! It really has the makings, Tripp," said Crabtree mildly. "There's a lot there to admire."

"Fuck," I said. "Oh, my God."

"Look, Tripp—"

"Please, Terry, spare me the editorial boilerplate, okay?" I bowed my head until my brow hit the dashboard. For a moment I hung there, looking down, suspended like a bridge over the meandering turbid river of *Wonder Boys*. "Just tell me what you thought. Be honest."

"Tripp—" he began, then paused, searching for gentle phrasings and diplomatic constructions.

"No," I said, sitting up, too quickly, so that the blood drained from my head and left a net of winking phosphenes in front of my eyes. I was afraid I might be about to have another one of my episodes and so I started talking, fast, to drown out the white noise of the blood in my veins. "Listen, I've changed my mind, forget it. Don't tell me what you thought. I mean, enough of this game. Enough! I admit I'm not done with the damn thing, okay? All right? Shit, that's obvious. I'm nowhere near being done. I've been working on the thing for seven years, and for all I know I've got another seven years to go. Okay? But I am going to finish it."

"Sure you are. Of course."

"And maybe it has some problems. It wanders. All right. But it's a great book. That's fundamental. I know that. That's one thing I know."

We were downtown by now; the great sinister bulk of Richardson's County Jail loomed ahead of us. It's a famous building and no doubt deservedly so, but with its keeps and turrets, its towers peaked like hangman's hats, the empty stone eye sockets of its somber face, it always looked to me like a mad castle, filled with poisoners and dwarfs, in which children were baked into cookies and pretty songbirds roasted alive on long spits. This part of town was, if anything, even more deserted than the Hill; there was no one out walking on this blustery Sunday morning, and the streets were all but empty of cars. It would have been easy to spot a fly green Galaxie.

"You still haven't been honest with me," I said.

"You said you didn't want me to."

"Because I don't."

"All right, then."

"But tell me anyway."

"It's a mess." His voice was soft and not uninflected with pity. "It's all over the place. There are way too many characters. The style changes every fifty pages or so. You've got all this pseudo–García Márquez stuff, with the phosphorescent baby, the oracular hog, and so on, and I don't think any of that stuff is working too well, and then—"

"How much of it did you read?"

"Enough."

"You have to keep with it," I told him. "You have to read on." I was making the argument I had made to myself, over the years—to the harsh and unremitting editor who lived in the deepest recesses of my gut. It sounded awfully thin, spoken aloud at last. "It's that kind of a book. Like *Ada*, you know, or *Gravity's Rainbow*. It teaches you how to read it as you go along. Or—Kravnik's."

"What's that, Gombrowicz?" said Crabtree. "I never read that."

"Kravnik's Sporting Goods. I just remembered." I'd seen it a hundred times before, without ever really noticing it, on Third Avenue, near Smithfield. "Turn here. Left. I think it'll be the first right, there, down the left-hand side of the street. Seriously, Crabs, how much of it did you read?"

"I don't know. I skipped around."

"Approximately, though. How much? Fifty pages? A hundred and fifty?"

"Enough. I read enough, Tripp."

"Fuck, Crabtree, how much of it did you read?"

"Enough to know that I didn't want to read any more."

I didn't know what to say to that.

"Look, I'm sorry, Tripp. I'm more than sorry. I shouldn't have said that." He didn't seem all that sorry. He was still spinning the wheel with aplomb, blowing giddy clouds of menthol smoke out the window. He was on the trail of Pea Walker and ready to negotiate for James's salvation. "There's nothing I can do with a book like that. Not now, I mean. It has too many problems. I hate to say it like this, Tripp, but I'm trying to be honest. For a change. I just can't expend any time on *Wonder Boys* at the moment. I'm hanging by, like, three little molecules of thread at Bartizan. You know that. I need to hand them something fresh. Something snappy and fast. Something kind of pretty and perverted all at the same time."

"Something like James," I said.

"He's my only hope," said Crabtree, as we pulled up in front of Kravnik's Sporting Goods and Outfitters. "If it isn't already too late."

"Too late," I said, feeling hollow.

Kravnik's took up the ground floor of a ten-story fireproof commercial block that, like most of the obsolete skyscrapers in this part of downtown, must once have been a bold flower of nineteenth-century capitalism. Its windows were filmed over with grime, and its stone face was tattooed with handbill glue. The sign, with its enormous red *K,* was ornamented at one side with a grotesque caricature of Bill Mazeroski, his skin bleached green by thirty years of weather. Translucent blue sunshades had been drawn over the grimy windows, so that they were all but impenetrable to the eye. It was one of an ever-dwindling number of such classic Pittsburgh establishments—half buried in dust and soot and an enigmatic mantle of central European gloom—that deal in rendering vats, piroshki presses, artificial wigs, and that regardless of the hour or day of the week always look as if they have been closed since the death of Guy Lombardo. There was a sign tacked to the front door of Kravnik's, however, that claimed otherwise, in bright red letters.

"We're in luck," I said. "It's open."

"Great," said Crabtree. "Look, Tripp, just give me a couple of months, all right? Take a couple more months. Take a year. Pare it down. Finish the thing. I'll be in a much better position to help you, you know, when you're really done."

"A couple of months." I felt no sense of relief at finally being granted the reprieve I'd dreamt of for so many weeks. The promise had a weak, bureaucratic ring to it, and anyway—pare it down? How would I know what to pare when I wasn't even sure anymore of what the whole thing was about? "Look," I said, pointing, trying to sound cheerful. " 'Free Parking in Rear.' "

He nosed the car into a narrow passage that ran between Kravnik's and the building beside it. As we pulled past the front of the store I tried to see in through the filthy aqueous windows but could glimpse only the dimmest outlines of headless mannequins, equipped for bizarre or outmoded sports—bearbaiting, the hammer throw, the hunting of stoat. We emerged into a large, irregular loading area, cluttered with Dumpsters and discarded wooden pallets, part of which served Kravnik's as a makeshift parking lot. A few other narrow passages opened into the lot at odd intervals amid the surrounding buildings, and the whole thing was split down the middle by a broad central alley, running parallel to Third Avenue, all the way from Wood Street to Smithfield. There were half a dozen parking spaces designated as belonging to Kravnik's and Crabtree pulled obediently into one of them, lining up between the stripes. Three spaces closer to the back of the store sat the Galaxie, empty, windows rolled; and beside this a ten-year-old Coupe de Ville whose license plate read KRAVNIK. The parking lot was otherwise deserted.

"Wait here," I said, opening my door. I set *Wonder Boys* down on the seat, and fished around in my pocket for the keys to the Galaxie. "Be ready to leave quickly."

"I'm ready now," said Crabtree, half humorously. "Seriously, Tripp, don't you think we ought to just talk to him? I wasn't planning on our having to, you know, actually burgle anything this morning."

"The guy isn't going to want to talk to us," I said. "He doesn't trust us. He doesn't like us."

"How do you know that? Why wouldn't he?"

"Because he thinks we're friends of Happy Blackmore."

"Good point," said Crabtree. "Hurry it up."

I stepped quickly over to the Galaxie and peered in through the rear window, shielding my eyes with the flat of my hand. The jacket had slipped down onto the floor behind the driver's seat, but I could see that it was still folded fairly neatly and apparently unharmed. I got the door unlocked, grabbed the jacket, and tucked it under my arm. Then I climbed across the front seat and reached for the glove compartment. I felt a thrill of despair in my belly. There was no way the little bagful of Humboldt County would still be there. When I popped the lid, I knew, I would find only a deranged assortment of Mexican road maps and a race card from Charles Town marked with the names of Happy Black-more's unlucky picks.

The reefer was still there. The glove compartment, I sup-posed, was as serviceable a stash for Pea Walker as it had been for me. I slid back out of the car, triumphant, and in my exultation jammed the rolled Baggie into the hip pocket of my sport jacket with a little too much zeal. My hand passed clear through the pocket, deep into the lining of the jacket itself. "Shit," I said, feeling a little stab of panic at the sound of tearing silk, and that was when it hit me that Crabtree didn't plan to publish *Wonder Boys* at all. He was just going to write me off as a loss. The air seemed suddenly to have gone out of my lungs, my heart stopped beating, the sky was empty of birds and the wind died and I had ruined the pocket of my favorite corduroy jacket. Then I breathed in; a pigeon sailed overhead, and the wind sent a ghostly tent of newspaper scraping across the empty parking lot. I looked back at the Le Car and saw Crabtree watching me go about my thieving business, tapping on the accelerator every few seconds, a look of mild concern on his face.

Without stopping to think about it, I climbed back into the Galaxie and took my accustomed place behind the wheel. I had the keys to this car: at the moment it seemed to me that I didn't have very much else. The thing to do, I considered, was to back it out of the parking lot, take off down that long alley toward Smithfield Street, cross the Monongahela, and drive away from Pittsburgh at whatever speed that ancient Michigander engine could attain. There was nowhere on earth I wanted to drive it, but that was not the same thing as having a good reason to stay. I settled in, adjusted the rear-view mirror, and slid the seat all the way back. I smelled a new but oddly familiar odor in the car, something gingery and sharp that at once made me feel less wildly numb and filled my chest with a faint welcome throb of regret. It was the smell of Lucky Tiger; Irving Warshaw and Peterson Walker wore the same brand of cologne. I smiled and slipped the keys into the ignition, but then I hesitated. Before I went anywhere, I would finally see myself rid of the things I'd been dragging around behind me all weekend like a ribbon of ringing tin cans.

"What are you doing, man?" said Crabtree as I climbed out of the car again. "I think I hear someone."

Without answering I went around to the back of the Galaxie and opened the trunk. The tuba and the remains of poor Grossman were still lying there, apparently undiscovered. Grossman had done nothing overnight to improve the smell back here, and I wondered if Walker hadn't been liberally dousing the interior of the car with Lucky Tiger in a doomed battle against the stench of rotten boa. I grabbed the battered instrument case in one hand, then took hold of Grossman with the other. He was stiff and heavy and gnarled as an ashplant.

"What the hell is that?" said Crabtree.

"What's it look like?" I said. I figured the question would keep him occupied for a while. At the far side of the parking lot stood a disorderly battalion of green Dumpsters, and I headed toward them. Just as I started across the alley with my surrealistic burden I heard the squeal of a car low on power-steering fluid taking a tight curve, and looked up to see a familiar white delivery van, barreling toward me along the narrow passage Crabtree and I had come through a few minutes before. Pea Walker was in the passenger seat, and there was a much larger man, a white guy with a shaved scalp, behind the wheel, aiming the van straight at me. The guy's tongue was curled at the corner of his mouth, as if he were concentrating very hard on attaining his goal. At a word from Walker, however, he cut the wheel and interposed the van between me and Hannah's car, trapping me among the Dumpsters. Then he hit the brakes.

Walker hopped down from the van and without a word came toward me, a sprightly little hop in his gait, cocking his head to one side as if delighted to see me again. He was dressed in a splendid aubergine tracksuit and an elaborate pair of sneakers, his shoes and suit embellished like a Mayan codex with all sorts of cryptic glyphs and pictograms. He was carrying a big bottle of something twisted up in a plain brown sack, and now he set it down on the ground beside him, regretfully, and gave it a fond little pat on the head.

"Yo, Booger, the guy in the car," he called to his friend.

Obediently the other fellow jumped down from the cab and went after Crabtree, who chose the odd defensive maneuver of sounding the Le Car's horn a few times in succession. When that proved unsurprisingly ineffective he started to roll, backing out of the parking space, then executing a quick three-point turn that put him in the alley, pointed toward Wood Street. In the process, and quite by accident, he managed to knock down Booger, the bald boy, and iron out the wrinkles in his right foot with one pass of the left rear tire.

"Jesus!" said Booger. He lay there on the ground, propped up on his elbows. He looked insulted. I turned my attention back to Pea Walker, watching for the gun Clement had mentioned, but to my surprise as he came at me Walker brandished only his fists, working them around in the air before him like a kitten reaching for a string. They were thick and misshapen as the knuckles of an apple tree. I had at least a hundred pounds on him. I smiled. Walker smiled too. His eyes were bloodshot, his head teetered on his neck, and he was missing several fairly important teeth from that smile of his. I wondered if he knew.

Right as I was considering the strategic value of just letting the guy hit me a few times with his washed-up-flyweight fists, he reached into the waistband of his purple warm-up suit and pulled out a ridiculously big piece the width of whose muzzle was exceeded only by that of his desolate smile. His firing hand wasn't all that steady, but I supposed that at this range it didn't need to be.

I made a feint to the left, and then cut toward the rolling Le Car. I was not so mobile, however, with my tuba and snake part, and he danced in front of me, cutting me off from Crabtree again.

"Hey, Pea," I said.

"What up?" he said.

We stood there for a minute, a mangy, overweight purblind minotaur and a broken-down and toothless Theseus with a shaky shooting hand, facing each other at the common center of our disparate labyrinths. The wind had picked up considerably and the air around us was filled with dust devils and rattling gusts of rubbish.

"Tripp!" said Crabtree, in warning or as a kind of desperate wish. He was drifting off down the alleyway, slowly, as if he meant to give me one last chance to join him before he abandoned me once and for all.

Walker looked over at the Renault, and while his head was turned I raised the heavy staff of Grossman's body over my head and—like Aaron, the silver-tongued shadow of Moses—hurled it at him. It struck him squarely in the face, with a loud crack, and he fell backward. The nine flew out of his hand and went clattering like an old roller skate across the parking lot. I ran down the alley, kicking through drifting strands of debris, swinging the tuba out ahead of me, the jacket tucked under my arm. I had my eyes fixed on the rickety knees of Booger, who was up again and hobbling after the Le Car—rather halfheartedly, it seemed to me. He probably had no idea whom he was chasing, or why. As for Crabtree, he could easily have outpaced Booger but he was still crawling along the alleyway at two miles per, with the passenger door hanging open, waiting for me. As soon as I drew even with the unfortunate Booger I brought the tuba around, aiming cruelly for his kneecaps. My aim was a little off, though, and I hit him in the belly instead, knocking the breath from his lungs in a single gust. He stumbled for a couple of steps before toppling over. A filthy tangle of packing tape and newspaper came rolling at him along the alley like a tumbleweed and adhered momentarily to the side of his head before blowing on past.

"You hit me with a tuba," he said, looking at me with an air of hurt surprise.

"I know," I said. "I'm sorry."

A sheet of paper came whistling up and flattened itself against my face. I peeled it away. It was a piece of twenty-pound bond and glancing at it I found that it described the most awful moment of an inglorious chapter in the medical career of Culloden Wonder, chief scoundrel and patriarch of that inglorious clan. I looked over at the Le Car, and saw that Crabtree had been driving so slowly not because he was waiting for me but because he was engaged in an ongoing battle with the open door of the car, trying, all at the same time, to close it, to flee the alley, and, if possible, to prevent the wind from carrying off every last page of my novel. The air was filled with *Wonder Boys;* I saw now that its pages made up a fair portion of the trash that was blowing through the alleyway and across the parking lot. Pages were settling like fat snowflakes on Booger, and brushing up like kittens against my legs.

"Jesus," I said. "Crabtree, stop the car!"

Crabtree stopped and climbed out, and together we started to try to save what we could, plucking sheets of paper from the air, raking them like leaves from the pavement.

"I'm so sorry, man," he said. He made a leaping grab for one high-flying page but missed by an inch, and it sailed away. "I didn't notice."

"How many pages did you lose?"

"Not too many."

"Are you sure?" I said. "Crabtree, it looks like a fucking blizzard out here."

There was a small explosion behind us. We turned and saw Walker crouching on one knee by the white van, the nine held out at the end of a wavering arm.

"Shit!" said Booger, clutching at the sudden bright blossom on the sleeve of his right arm.

"Jesus Christ," said Crabtree, grabbing hold of me, dragging me toward the car. "Come on!"

I threw the tuba into the backseat, handed Crabtree Marilyn's jacket, and climbed in beside him, and then we abandoned my novel to the parking lot of Kravnik's Sporting Goods, leaving it to stream out behind us like the foamy white wake of a boat.

BREATHLESS with success, Crabtree immediately set about reca-
pitulating the events of the last twenty minutes, fixing the least
details of our escapade in place with the narrative equivalent
of watchmaker's tweezers and embellishing the overall con-
tours of the plot with the rhetorical equivalent of a fire hose.
"Did you see that Booger's tattoo? On the back of his
hand? It was the ace of hearts, but the heart was black. I could
smell his breath, Tripp, he'd been drinking a Yoo-Hoo, I
swear to God. I thought he was going to kiss me. Christ, he
was ugly. Both of them were. How about that gun, huh? Was
that a nine millimeter? It was, wasn't it? Jesus. Those bullets
sounded like fucking hummingbirds."
There was already a short chapter in Crabtree's hypothetical autobiography entitled "People Who Have Shot at Me,"
and now as he drove us out to the college he painstakingly
revised it, commencing with an episode that had befallen
both of us some eleven years earlier, when I'd helped him try
to sneak his lover at the time, the painter Stanley Feld, into
the East Hampton home of an art-collecting lawyer who'd
reneged on a promise to let Feld visit the painting he considered his best work; like all our greatest escapades this was a
noble enterprise in theory rendered hopelessly foolish from
the first moments of execution, in this case by Feld's having
neglected to mention that the collector in question was an
art-loving Mafia lawyer, and that not only his collection but
his entire walled estate was guarded by heavily armed half-
men whose aim, fortunately, was less than perfect. From this
incident, in which a round of automatic weapons fire tore the

branch off a spruce tree several feet over our heads, Crabtree made the natural transition to the two angry shots fired at him, six months later, by Stanley Feld, one of which lodged in his left buttock.

Now he had a new section to add to this favorite hypothetical chapter, and I could see that he was delighted to do the work.

"Chaos," he said, rolling his window down, breathing it in like the smell of cut grass or the ocean. He shook his head admiringly. "What a mess."

"No kidding," I said, looking down at the pathetic remnant of *Wonder Boys* in my lap. I ought to have been pounding on the dashboard, I thought, and eulogizing sweet chaos, the opposite and the inhibitor of death, and stating, for the record, that Vernon Hardapple's breath had carried an anise whiff of Italian sausage and a rusty tang of beer. Ever since the day, nearly twenty-five years before, that I'd first fallen under the spell of Jack Kerouac and his free-form Arthurian hobo jazz, with all its dangerous softheartedness and poor punctuation, I had always, consciously and by some unthinking reflex of my heart, taken it as an article of faith that escapades like the rescue of James Leer from his Sewickley Heights dungeon, or the retrieval of the missing jacket, were intrinsically good: good for the production of literature, good for barroom conversation, good for the soul. Chaos! I ought to have been gulping it down the way Knut Hamsun, perched atop a locomotive as it hurtled across the American heartland, swallowed a thousand miles of icy air in a successful attempt to rid his body of tubercles. I ought to have been welcoming the bright angel of disorder into my life like the prickling flow of blood into a limb that had fallen asleep.

Instead, I spent the whole trip out to the college trying to assess and come to grips with the fatal blow that had been dealt to the manuscript of *Wonder Boys*. Crabtree, as it turned out, had managed to prevent exactly seven pages from blowing out of the car. They were all impressed with the watermark of his Vibram soles, or pebbled like the surface of a basketball with a relief of asphalt; part of one page had been torn away. Two thousand six hundred and four pages—seven years of my life!—abandoned in the alley behind Kravnik's Sporting Goods, with a run-down Ford and three quarters of a dead snake. I shuffled through the remains, numb, wondering, a busted shareholder in the aftermath of a crash, clutching the sheaf of ink and rag paper that only an hour before had been all my fortune. It was a completely random sample from the novel, pages bearing no relation to one another except for two which coincidentally both dealt with the birthmark on Helena Wonder's behind that was shaped like her native state of Indiana. I allowed my head to fall backward against the headrest. I closed my eyes.

"Seven pages," I said. "Six and a half."

"Naturally you have copies," said Crabtree.

I didn't say anything.

"Tripp?"

"I have earlier drafts," I said. "I have alternate versions."

"You'll be all right, then," he said.

"Sure, I will. It'll probably come out better next time."

"That's what they say," he said. "Look at Carlyle, when he lost his luggage."

"That was Macaulay."

"Or Hemingway, when Hadley lost all those stories."

"He was never able to reproduce them."

"Bad example," said Crabtree. "Here we are."

He turned into the long avenue of tulip trees that led up

Founder's Hill to the center of campus, and I directed him toward Arning Hall, where the English faculty kept office hours. We parked in the tiny faculty lot, in the space reserved for our Miltonist. Crabtree checked his watch and ran a cocksure hand through his long hair. There was still half an hour until the Farewell, the closing ceremonies of WordFest, was scheduled to begin—thirty minutes to set up his monte table and his trick manacles and his box with the hidden chamber, and tie a few balloon animals for Walter Gaskell. He reached into the backseat for the black satin skeleton key that would spring James Leer. Then he got out of the car and pulled on his own suit jacket. He shot his cuffs and worked a stiffness out of the muscles of his neck. He lit another Kool Mild.

"Wanna come?"

"Not particularly."

Crabtree ducked his head back into the car and gave me a quick once-over, more for his benefit than my own, the way an actor about to go onstage will nervously check the costume of a fellow cast member whose cue is still two scenes off. He slid my eyeglasses up the bridge of my nose with his index finger.

"You going to be all right?"

"You bet. Uh, Crabtree," I said. "Tell me if I'm wrong. It sounded to me like you aren't going to do this book at all. Am I wrong about that?"

"Yes. Look, Grady, I don't want you to think . . ." He let the sentence go. It was hard seeing Crabtree unable to choose among all the different unthinkable things he didn't want me to think. "But—perhaps—in a sense—perhaps this"—he nodded toward the little puddle of *Wonder Boys* in my lap— "is for the best."

"Kind of a sign, you're saying."

"In a sense."

"I don't think so," I said. "In my experience signs are usually a lot more subtle."

"Uh huh. All right." He stood up again and tugged on the lapels of his jacket. "Wish me luck."

"Luck."

He slammed the door.

"So you still want to be my editor?" I said, staring straight ahead, my voice deadpan and, I hoped, self-mocking.

"Of course. Give me a break." His voice cracked with impatience or mock impatience. "What do you think?"

"I think that you do," I said.

"I do."

"I believe you." I didn't believe him.

"All right," he said. He looked in through the car window at me again, his face suddenly the pale, bony country-boy countenance of twenty years earlier. "I guess it's probably better if you don't come with me."

"I guess it is," I said. It hurt me to have to say it. All male friendships are essentially quixotic: they last only so long as each man is willing to polish the shaving-bowl helmet, climb on his donkey, and ride off after the other in pursuit of illusive glory and questionable adventure. Not once, in twenty years, had I declined to second Crabtree, to share the blame for and to bear witness to his latest exploit. I wanted to go with him. But I was afraid—and not only of having to confess to Walter Gaskell my role in the killing of Doctor Dee and the ignominious means by which I'd come to know the combination of the lock on the secret closet. At least I knew what needed to be said to Walter, more or less. But if there was the question of expelling James Leer to be decided, then the Chancellor was the one to make that decision—Sara was going to be at this meeting, too. And I had no idea what I wanted to say to her, or to the quickening little packet of cells in her belly. I looked down at a page I had designated as 765b and spoke into the collar of my shirt.

"Next time," I said.

He nodded, and coughed into his fist, and set off across the parking lot toward Arning Hall, leaving me with the tuba, which seemed so intent on following me everywhere that I now began to regard it with some uneasiness. I watched Crabtree bounce up the worn granite steps of Arning Hall. He held the satin jacket by the shoulders and gently shook it out, as though shaking crumbs from a tablecloth. Then he disappeared into the building.

Thoughtfully or thoughtlessly he had left the keys in the ignition, and I switched on the radio. It was tuned to WQED. A local arts reporter I didn't particularly admire was interviewing old Q. about his life and work and personal demons. I reflected for a moment on the journalistic euphemism that allowed personal demons to writers who were only fucked up.

INTERVIEWER: So then, would you say, perhaps, that it was a kind of, and I know it's an overused phrase, but, a catharsis for you, then, revealing, or discovering, if you like, in your story "The Real Story"—to use the word "discover" in its original sense, of course, of "lifting the cover from"—the depths to which a man—a man perhaps in some ways very much like you, although naturally not, of course, you—in his hopeless and even, I daresay, oddly heroic quest for what he calls "the real story"—will sink? I'm referring now to the scene in the Laundromat where he steals the nonprescription antihistamines out of the old woman's handbag.

Q.: Yes, right. [*Embarrassed laugh*] Some of those babies pack a
real wallop.

I switched over to AM and spun the radio dial until I hit
polka music. I opened and closed my window a few times,
fiddled with the rearview mirror, adjusted my seat, opened
and closed the glove compartment. Hannah kept hers very
neat, and well stocked with the road maps that had gotten her
from Provo to Pittsburgh two years before. There was a flashlight, and a small box of tampons, and a flat tin of Wintermans
little cigars. This, I thought, looked vaguely familiar.

I snapped it open and found that it contained, of all things,
a sheaf of tight little marijuana cigarettes, expertly rolled. I
wasn't at all surprised by their precision because I had rolled
them myself, and given the box to Hannah on her birthday
last October. At the time I'd rolled her a dozen; there were
still twelve of them in the can. I ran one under my nose and
inhaled its corky, hybrid smell of marijuana and cheroot. The
stuff I'd rolled, I remembered, was pharmaceutical quality,
the most powerful Afghan Butthair ever to make its way into
the Ohio River Valley. I jabbed the dashboard cigarette
lighter, sat back, and waited. In the mirror I caught a glimpse
of the tuba that had been stalking me all weekend, and shuddered. I thought of one of the last stories August Van Zorn
wrote before he gave up his mastery of a minor literary form
in favor of suburban humor and shaggy dog stories. It was a
story called "Black Gloves." It concerned a man, a failed
poet, who had committed some unspecified but horrible
crime, and who kept finding—in a bar, on the platform beside him while he waited for a train, in one room of every
house he visited, in his study draped over a bust of Hesiod, in
the very blankets of his bed—a pair of black ladies' evening

gloves. He threw them in the ash can, tossed them into the river, set them on fire, buried them in the ground. They reappeared. One night he awakened with their empty fingers wrapped around his throat.

The cigarette lighter popped out, and I jumped. The pages of *Wonder Boys* spilled onto the floor at my feet and pooled around my ankles. I took one hit off the terrible joint and clutched the skunky green smoke in my lungs. I exhaled. In that tiny interval, between inhalation and blowing out, I became disgusted with myself. I squeezed the tip of the joint, tucked the remainder back into the Wintermans tin, snapped shut the lid, and set the tin back into the glove compartment. Then, trying to refrain from any sudden movements that might alarm the tuba, I crept out of the car, mounted my donkey, and set off on the crooked road after Terry Crabtree.

THE disposition of James Leer was debated not in the Benedictine gloom of Walter's office on the third floor of Arning Hall but in the cool, aseptic terrarium of the Administration Building—a late modernist structure built by a pupil of a pupil of Frank Lloyd Wright's son—in the bright desolation of charcoal carpeting and steel furniture that was the Office of the Chancellor. I'd caught up to Crabtree halfway between Arning and Admin, and we went in to face the Gaskells together. The door to the anteroom was a single thick pane of glass, and as we walked off the elevator we could see James Leer slumped on a low couch inside, legs thrust out and hooked at the ankles, hands folded in his lap, looking very bored. When he saw us coming with Marilyn's jacket he sat up and waved, a little uncertainly, as if he couldn't decide whether our appearance portended bad news or good. I was not too sure myself. One hit of that fabled marijuana had been enough to trouble the edges of everything with a woozy shimmer of indeterminacy. I was sorry I'd smoked it. Sooner or later I was always sorry I'd smoked it.

"Why, look who it is," said Crabtree. "Our Lady of the Flowers himself."

"I'm hosed," James said, not entirely regretfully, as we came in.

"Kicked out?" I said.

He nodded. "Yes, I think so. I'm not completely sure. They've been in there for a while." He lowered his voice. "Actually, I think they were having a fight or something."

"Jesus," said Crabtree, working a last anticipatory kink out of his neck.

We listened; there was a man's voice, an unintelligible but reasoned murmur. I didn't hear Sara.

"They aren't fighting now," I said.

"Here goes," said Crabtree. He knocked.

"They stopped fighting when Fred and Amanda showed up," said James.

Crabtree's hand froze in midknock.

"Are they in there, too?"

"Yup," said James. "I told you, I'm hosed."

"We'll see about that."

"They brought the dog with them."

"We're hosed," I told Crabtree.

"Maybe *you* are."

"I don't look stoned?" My heart began to pound. The classic aim of a pothead is always to look perfectly straight—and if possible operate complicated machinery—while immense

shrieking nebulae are coming asunder in his brain. To fail at
this—to be found out—carries a mysterious burden of anxiety
and shame. "How are my eyes?"

"You look like you've been gassed," he snapped. In my
sudden paranoia I was no longer certain he was so glad to have
me along. "Just get my back, all right? Let me do the talking."

"Oh, of course," I said.

Sara opened the door. To her credit both as an administrator and as the lover of an irregular man, she did not look
particularly surprised to see either of us.

"Come in," she said, rolling her tired eyes. Then she saw
the jacket. That surprised her. "You got it? Walter, they got
it!"

Walter Gaskell unfolded himself from his chair and hurried
toward us. For a moment I thought that he had aimed himself
at my head, and I took a step backward, but he didn't even
look at me. He went straight for the black satin prize. Crabtree stood erect, the jacket draped across one arm, presenting
it for Walter's inspection with pride and a refined air of concern, like a sommelier with a bottle of very old claret. Walter
took it from him with equal delicacy and then looked it over
carefully for signs of damage.

"It seems to be all right," he announced.

"Oh, thank heavens. Well, James Leer! You are *very*
lucky!" said Mrs. Leer, appending, with her eyes, "to be
alive." She and her husband had risen from their chairs when
we came in, and now Mr. Leer wrapped his bony arm around
her in a way that was at once reassuring and triumphant, as if
to say, There, I told you everything would work out fine. I
imagined that he was always telling her something like this, in
the vain hope that such lessons in grace had a cumulative
force and that one day she would see that, for the most part,

everything did. It struck me that the chief obstacle to marital contentment was this perpetual gulf between the well-founded, commendable pessimism of women and the sheer dumb animal optimism of men, the latter a force more than any other responsible for the lamentable state of the world. She was dressed for a funeral in a belted black dress, black stockings, and a pair of black pumps, and her pale hair sat atop her head as motionless as a nurse's hat. Fred had evidently been dragged into town from the golf links. He was fond, it appeared, of pistachio plaid. Amanda Leer shook herself free from her husband's reassuring arm and walked right up to me.

"Now listen, everyone," Crabtree began, trying to interpose himself between Mrs. Leer and me. She skirted him and got up into my face. Her dress gave off a sour tang of cedar.

"You have a lot of nerve, mister," she said.

"I'm sorry," I said.

Her sharp tone caught Walter's attention and he looked up from the jacket.

"Yes," he said, still without quite meeting my gaze, not so much afraid to look at me, I thought, as embarrassed for my sake. My cannabinolic paranoia shot up another notch. Could *all* of them tell that I wasn't straight? "You and I need to talk."

"I guess we do," I said. I wondered how much Sara had told him. The safest assumption, I decided, was, probably, all of it.

Crabtree gave Walter's arm a reassuring squeeze.

"Walter, if we could just—"

"I don't think you'll find anyone in this room who's very happy with you right now, Grady," said Sara, ominously. She looked over to a corner of her office where there was an immense nylon duffel of the sort used by skiers to carry their gear. I didn't have too many doubts about what was inside. The image of Doctor Dee lying dead and zippered in a nylon bag struck me at that moment as incredibly poignant. I suddenly recalled his penchant for arranging sticks into almost intelligible hieroglyphic patterns in the grass of the Gaskells' backyard. He had spent his entire life feverishly trying to communicate some important message that no one had understood and that had now died with him, undelivered. At the thought of this I did a surprising thing. I was surprised by it, anyway. I sat down, with a loud creak, in one of the cowhide-and-chrome office chairs, covered my face in my hands, and started to cry.

"Grady." Sara came over and stood beside my chair, near enough to touch me. She didn't touch me. "Terry?" she said, her voice half pleading, half accusatory. She thought Crabtree must have given me something from his fabled pharmacopoeia. I was a drinker when we met, of course, but it had been several years since she'd last seen me in tears, and never when there were other people around. I should add here that when I say that I sat down and started to cry I don't intend to convey an impression of copious tears aflow and lusty Pucciniesque sobbing. I was capable of only the most trite display of macho grief, choked, all but silent, a slight dampness around my eyes, like someone trying to stifle a yawn.

"Yes." At last Crabtree, having watched me steer the entire operation off the road and into the brambly shoulder, slid over and took control of the wheel. "Mrs. Leer, Mr. Leer, how do you do. My name is Terry Crabtree, I'm a senior editor at Bartizan. I've been reading James's work this weekend, and I've discovered for myself what a brilliant young talent he is. You must be very proud of him."

"Oh—well . . ." Fred Leer watched his wife's expression for a cue. She nodded. "Of course we are. But—"

"Walter, if you and James and the Leers would like to come with me—Sara, is there someplace we could talk? Walter, I have a number of things I need to discuss with you. I had a chance to read your book."

"Did you? But I—I feel I ought to—"

"I was very impressed."

"Walter," said Sara, her tone crisp and administrative. "Why don't you show Mr. Crabtree and the Leers into the Hurley Room? I'll look after Professor Tripp."

Walter hesitated a moment, looking at his wife. His craggy face was pinned up at the corners in a hard smile that might have been angry or merely tolerant. I could still feel him deliberately not looking at me. Of all the ways he could have chosen to react to my presence, I figured a disgusted hauteur was neither the least desirable nor the least deserved. He held the jacket over one arm and petted its collar with soft automatic strokes. His emptied-out gaze was fixed on the face of his wife. He was giving her one last chance, I thought. She put her hand on my shoulder. He nodded and followed Crabtree and the Leers out of the office.

"What's gotten into you, Professor Tripp?" said Sara.

At first I didn't say anything. I couldn't seem to catch my breath.

"I lost my book," I managed to say, finally identifying the source of my tears. The thought of old Doctor Dee vainly arranging his sticks in the grass had made me feel terrible pity, and not—naturally—for him. "I lost *Wonder Boys*."

"All of it?"

"Except for seven pages."

"Oh, Grady." She knelt down on the floor beside my chair

and pulled to her bosom the addled head in which vast shrieking universes were flying apart. She lay her cool palm against
my forehead as if checking for fever. Her tone was acerbic but
tender. "You're such a putz."

"I know."

She began to search my temples for gray hairs. When she
found one she gave it a ruthless yank.

"Ouch. How many?"

"Dozens. It's very sad."

"I'm old."

"Very old." She yanked another one, and held it out before
her with a philosophic air like a conventional Hamlet with his
skull. "So I told Walter everything."

"I figured. Ow. He already knew, right?"

"He said not."

I lifted my head and looked at her.

"Does he still love you?"

She considered this question. She poked her tongue in her
cheek and thought it over. She rocked back on her heels and
rolled her eyes, trying to recollect their conversation.

"It didn't come up," she said. "Do you—still love Emily?
Don't answer that. What did she say when you told her about
us?"

Had I told Emily about Sara and me? All at once I couldn't
remember. I could still feel the cool imprint of Sara's hand on
my forehead.

"No," she said, when she saw that an answer was not going
to emerge anytime soon from my spavined brain. "Don't answer that either. Just—just tell me what you're going to do."

I was suddenly aware of my lungs, of their inexplicable and
regular functioning, of the rhythm of my breath that was always there, audible, visible, palpable. Why didn't my lungs

just stop? What would happen if they did? What if the only thing that had kept my lungs working all these years was the simple fact that I never gave them a moment's thought?

"Grady?"

"I can't breathe," I said.

That good academician Sara Gaskell read something more into this statement than I had intended. She scrambled to her feet and jumped back, away from me, as if I had taken a swing at her. I was saying, she thought, that I felt smothered by her and by the spawn of Grady. Perhaps I was.

"Okay," she said, waving me to the door. "Out. Goodbye."

"No. I'm sorry." I extended a conciliatory hand to her. "I didn't mean it, I—I'm just so tired."

"Just so stoned, you mean."

"No! I only had one hit! Truthfully! Then I put it back!"

"What a breakthrough!" she said. She checked her watch. "Quarter to two! Jesus. The Farewell." When she looked up at me again her eyes were narrow and cold and not entirely devoid of hatred. I had been wasting her time, and that was the worst thing you could have done to Sara Gaskell.

"All right, Grady, you stay, *I'll* go. I have to take care of this whole James Leer thing before the Farewell. You can just sit here and breathe, all right? Do a lot of breathing. Breathe, and smoke pot, and sit here, and see if you can squeeze out a few more of those absurd little tears of yours."

"Sara—"

I stood up, took a step toward her, and made the cynical and pathetic last attempt those who knew me well would have learned by now to expect.

"Sara," I said, "what if I told you that I wanted to marry you?"

She flattened her left hand against my stomach and held it there a moment, keeping me literally at arm's length. Then, as if I were teetering on a narrow shelf of rock, high above a canyon, with my back to the blue abyss, she gave me the gentlest of shoves. Before I fell I noticed, with a pang, the pale glint of her wedding band. Then I hit the floor, hard.

She stepped over me, into the outer office, and then strode off toward the Hurley Room, her heels knocking marble, the hem of her pleated skirt flicking at the air behind her like the tooth of a lash. After a moment I heard voices echoing in the hall and the chime of the elevator. Then I heard nothing at all. And that, those who knew me well would unquestionably have concluded, was exactly the response I deserved.

I didn't want to attract attention, slipping into the auditorium of Thaw Hall, and so I climbed the stairs to the balcony and took a seat at the back. There were fewer people here to listen to Walter Gaskell deliver his customary valedictory, however, than there'd been two nights earlier for Q.'s lecture, and after a few minutes I was able to move all the way down to the loge, to the very last seat on the left. Pinned by an arabesque button to the wall beside my head hung one end of a deep velour swag, heavy with dust. I pressed myself against it, inhaling its thick smell of mildewed flag, and gazed out over the five hundred heads below, trying to pick out Sara's.

Crabtree I spotted right away, in the front row, slouched, in shirtsleeves, watching Walter with a very sleepy and complacent look on his face. If he were a cat he would have been licking the blood and feathers from his whiskers. He had dressed James for the assembly, I saw, in his own mushroom-colored sport jacket, worn over my old flannel shirt. James was sitting right there beside him, spine erect, hands folded politely in his lap, his earnest Adam's apple working its way up and down as he drank in the urbane good counsel of his queer old dean—the standard Walter Gaskell homily, in that room full of agents and editors, to go forth and work hard at one's craft, always without regard to such vulgar concerns as finding an agent or an editor.

When someone at the end of their row coughed, James turned, and happened to look up, and spotted me in my corner. I was startled: I'd felt almost safe, lurking there like John Wilkes Booth behind the dusty velour drape and the scrim of my own loneliness. James's eyes got very wide, and he was about to turn and give Crabtree a poke in the ribs, but I put a finger to my lips and drew a pleat of dusty velour sideways across my face. Although he looked doubtful, he nodded, solemnly, and turned back to the stage. At the sight of James in Crabtree's jacket I experienced a sharp pang of abandonment, out of all proportion to the unremarkable circumstance of male lovers sharing clothes. I felt suddenly bereft not only of Crabtree and his love but of my earliest bright image of myself, of my trajectory across the world. It's not fashionable, I know, in this unromantic age, for a reasonably straight man to think of finding his destiny in the love of another man, but that was how I'd always thought of Crabtree. I guess you could say that in a strange sort of way I'd always believed that Crabtree was my man, and I was his. It was only proper, I supposed, for the first thing in my life that had ever felt right to be the last one to be proven wrong.

In any case, I hadn't come here to find Crabtree. I sat forward in my seat and resumed my inspection of the people in the endless rows below me, looking for Sara Gaskell. I had managed for the moment to forget about my breathing, but the drug was still at work in my brain and now I seemed to have become overconscious of the muscles and machinery of my throat. I was thinking so intently about the swallowing reflex that it became impossible for me to swallow. I couldn't find Sara, and all that scanning of the shifting mass of heads down there below me made me feel sick.

"Looking for someone?"

It was Carrie McWhirty, the long-suffering author of *Liza and the Cat People*. She was a prematurely motherly girl, with steel-rimmed glasses through which she scowled at me, looking more than a little revolted. I wondered if there were already stories going around.

"Carrie," I said. "I didn't see you there."

"I know," she said, sounding sad as a bassoon. "Were you looking for Hannah?" She pointed. "She's over there."

I knew that I shouldn't have, but—so—I looked. Hannah was sitting several rows from the stage, off to the right-hand side of the orchestra, on the aisle. She was nodding her head, every so often, and smirking into her cupped hand, and I could see that the person on the other side of her was entertaining her more than Walter Gaskell—doubtless at the latter's expense. Her hair was pulled back in a clip, exposing her neck. A hand appeared around the back of her head and settled lightly on her left shoulder, and she suffered it. She kicked her long legs in their bright red boots. The printed program slid from her lap, and when she leaned down to retrieve it I saw beside her a cheerful pink face framed in long hair even fairer than hers. I sat back and closed my eyes.

"Who is that guy?" said Carrie. "Do you know him?"

"His name's Jeff," I said.

For a long time after that, I couldn't bring myself to open my eyes. I sat there, listening to Walter's soft voice, with its faint granite echo of New York. He seemed to be winding down, now; he related a few purportedly amusing incidents of the last few days, none of which concerned the murder of a dog, the theft of a sacred garment, or a wife who was carrying another man's child in her womb.

"And now," he said, "I have some good news. A round of congratulations is in order." He paused. He had come, at last, to the Plums. Someone at WordFest had found a publisher for her children's book, *Blood on a Bustier.* Another participant, a fellow I knew who wrote features for the *Post-Gazette,* had landed his crime novel, *The Loneliest Prawn,* at Doubleday. I may, thinking back on it, have those titles reversed. There was applause, which, I imagined, the people in question rose to their feet and acknowledged.

"It's especially exciting," Walter went on, "to announce that our own James Leer, a student here, has found a publisher for his first novel, which I believe is called *The Lovely Parade.*"

I opened my eyes in time to see Walter nodding genially to James in the front row, a look on his face of amazing warmth and benevolence. People were clapping and calling out to James but he just sat there, with his hands in his lap, staring straight ahead, at nothing, at the dust of Thaw Hall hanging in the lights of the stage. When Crabtree gave him a jab in the rib cage, James rose to his feet as if jerked by a cord. Carrie McWhirty pointed at him and whispered to the person on the other side of her, "I had a class with him." James turned to face the five hundred people behind him, and the fifty above him, standing there looking lost and alarmed as a child caught in the midst of a startled flock of pigeons. On his lanky frame Crabtree's jacket fit remarkably badly. It gaped at the collar and showed an inch of pale wrist. His shoes were the same old pair of dented black Packards, and the red plaid work shirt lent him a rubish air. He stood there like that, looking like a scarecrow hung from a nail, until the applause first slowed, then sputtered, and then died out altogether. The entire hall was silent, and James just stood, shifting from foot to foot, swallowing, looking as though he might be about to throw up. I saw that it was not the delicious moment described by cinema and fiction when the butt of jokes and resentment, when the mad boy, was applauded. The admiration of his tormentors was itself a kind of torment.

"The guy's kind of an alien probe," said Carrie. "If you know what I mean."

"Take a bow, James," called Hannah Green, loud enough for everyone in the auditorium to hear. There was laughter. James looked at her. He had gone bright red in the face. After one last innocent moment of feeling like an alien probe, he spread out his hands and hung his head and, as he must, took his first sweet bow as a wonder boy. Then he tumbled back into his seat like a blown umbrella and covered his face with both hands.

Walter Gaskell cleared his throat.

"Finally, and perhaps not least importantly," he went on, sounding impatient, "Terry Crabtree, of Bartizan, has also decided to publish my own book, *The Last American Marriage,* parts of which some of you are already familiar with."

Wild, wholehearted, obsequious applause. Crabtree smacked James on the shoulder and then gave it a fond squeeze; another successful narrative from the quick aquiferous pen of Terry Crabtree. Walter took a rapid, dignified bow of his own, thanked the secretaries and volunteers, quoted Kafka on the subject of axes and ice, wished us all a productive year, and then, with a Vincent Price cackle, un-leashed the fledgling writers like a tattered flock of bats. The lights came up. People started to file out.

"Are you coming, Professor Tripp? Mr. Q. is throwing one last party at the Gaskells'," said Carrie. "He asked me to come," she added.

"No, I don't think so," I said. I watched Jeff follow Han-nah up the aisle, his hand at the small of her back. They stopped to congratulate James, who stood pulling at the cuffs of his jacket in a ring of well-wishers.

"Okay, then," said Carrie, sounding doubtful. "I'll see you, Professor Tripp."

"You betcha," I said, and then I saw Sara, at the other end of the auditorium, by the side exit. She was looking right at me, I thought. I stood up to go after her and raised a hand, but as I was in the act of wildly waving she turned and walked, without a sign, out of Thaw Hall.

I offered Carrie McWhirty a gelid little smile, and when she had left me alone I sat down, heavily, like someone bur-dened with a fever. I put my hand to my forehead and thought I detected a febrile sheen. The clamor of parting con-versation down in the lobby swelled briefly, then died. Sam Traxler came in, carrying a vacuum cleaner and a milk crate filled with cleaning supplies, and walked the aisles and rows of the auditorium, gathering up the larger pieces of trash and stuffing them into a plastic bag. After a while he disappeared, and I was alone. I had lost everything: novel, publisher, wife, lover; the admiration of my best student; all the fruit of the past decade of my life. I had no family, no friends, no car, and probably, after this weekend, no job. I sat back in my chair, and as I did so I heard the unmistakable crinkle of a plastic bag. I reached into the torn hip pocket of my jacket and passed my hand through the hole, into the lining, where I found my little piece of Humboldt County, warm from the heat of my body.

There was a creaking of hinges below me. Sam Traxler came back into the auditorium and started for his shiny chrome vacuum cleaner. Just as he was about to switch it on, I called out to him. "Yo, Sam."

Without any apparent surprise he looked up, slowly, as if people were always calling to him from the empty balconies.

"Oh, hey, Professor Tripp," he said.

"Sam," I asked him. "Do you get high?"

"Only when I'm working."

I leaned out over the balcony, aimed the Baggie toward him, and tried to toss it, like a dart or a paper plane. It caught in a pleat of one of the velvet swags that draped the balconies of Thaw Hall. I leaned out farther, bracing my legs against the seat behind me, and gave the stiff drapery a tug. The Baggie shook loose and went fluttering earthward like a leaf. Sam came across the hall, bent over, and picked it up. Now I had nothing at all.

"Holy shit," he said. "Are you serious?"

I assured him that I was, and then I smelled blood in my nose, and the air around me filled with winking diodes and strands of luminous pearls. There was a submarine roaring in both my ears as if someone had clamped a pair of conch shells over them.

"Oh," I said, balanced there on my belly like a Steinway on a second-story window ledge. Then I felt the block and tackle, as it were, give way. To be honest, I'm not really sure what tipped me. A body the size of mine is subject to the play of the mysterious gravitons that influence oceans and mountainsides. When I fell I would have broken across all those empty seats below me like the Monongahela River in flood. And in the interest of full disclosure I feel compelled to add that for one suspended instant, just before I lost consciousness, I truly relished the prospect. Then I pitched forward, grabbed a couple dusty handfuls of velvet, and started down.

I felt a sharp jerk on my collar. The top button of my shirt sprang loose and winged me on the cheekbone. I felt myself being hauled slowly back over the balcony, then pitched onto my back. Smooth hands pressed against my forehead. Just before I closed my eyes for good I had a momentary vision of Sara's face. It seemed to be looking down at me from some indeterminate height.

"Grady?" she said, wondering. "What are you doing, you idiot?"

I opened my mouth, and tried to answer her question, but I couldn't manage it. The furrow of tenderness in her voice gave me reason to hope, and I felt a sharp pain in my chest at the sudden expansion of the last hopeful muscle in my body.

I rose like a kite, in fits, tethered to the mortal husk of Grady Tripp by a thin pearly string. Below me Pittsburgh lay spread, brick and blacktop and iron bridges, fog in its hollows, half hidden by rain. The wind snapped at the flaps of my jacket and rang in my ears like blood. There were birds in my hair. A jagged beard of ice grew from my chin. I'm not making this up. I heard Sara Gaskell calling my name, and looked down, way down into the fog and rain of my life on earth, and saw her kneeling beside my body, blowing her breath into my lungs. It was hot and sour and frantic with life and tobacco. I swallowed great mouthfuls of it. I grabbed hold of the opalescent thread and reeled myself in.

Wʜᴇɴ I woke I found myself in a dim hospital room, lying naked under a powder blue paper gown, taking my evening glucose through a neat little hole in my left arm. It was a nice semiprivate room, with cheerful Bloomsbury print wallpaper, a whisk broom of everlasting in a vase on the windowsill, and a view of an impressive old black stone church across the street. A faint banner of blue sky flew from the steeple and stretched across the top of the evening. The curtain was drawn between us but I could see the foot of my neighbor's bed and beyond it the cool blue corridor of the ward.

"Hello?" I called out to the other side of the curtain. "Excuse me? Could you tell me what hospital this is?"

There was no immediate reply and I imagined the person in the next bed lying with his jaw wired shut, comatose, aphasic, somehow unable to respond. But I knew the room was simply empty. I watched the last strands of blue fade from the evening sky outside the window with the feeling that a great loneliness was descending upon me.

"Sara?" I said.

I was aware of a vague irritation at my right wrist and I rubbed my arm against the sheets for an idle minute before I looked down and saw the plastic ID bracelet with my name and a legend of numerals that encoded all the particulars of my collapse. Above this in neat black script was printed the name of the hospital. It was a well-known and expensive hospital with a less than spotless local reputation, fifteen minutes by taxi from Thaw Hall. I looked at the clock radio on the table beside my head. It was seven twenty-four. I'd only been out for two hours.

At seven-thirty the attending physician came in. He was a resident, a young man with overlong hair, a pointed nose, and blue eyes as cold and disturbing as Doctor Dee's. He needed a shave, and he wore the sad, swollen mien of a doctor at the end of a shift, like a traveler walking off an airplane after thirty hours in the air. His name tag said GREENHUT. He looked so profoundly disappointed in me that I wondered for a moment if he was someone I knew.

"So," he said.

"I passed out." I decided not to tell him that I had also, as nearly as I could determine, died.

"You did."

"I've been doing that a lot lately," I said.

"Uh huh," he said. "You've also been smoking a lot of marijuana, I understand."

"Kind of a lot. Do you think that's why I've been having these spells?"

"Do you?"

"It's possible."

"How long have you been having them?"

"My spells?" I said, sounding a little too much like Blanche DuBois for my own comfort. "About the last month, I guess."

"See if you can stand up. Just watch your tube, there."

I tugged myself tender as a dance partner to my feet.

"How's that feel?"

"Pretty good," I said. As a matter of fact I felt steadier on my feet and clearer of head than I had in a long time, quite possibly several years. The pain in my ankle was almost gone.

"How long have you been smoking marijuana, Grady?"

"A while," I said.

"How long?"

"Spiro T. Agnew was our vice president, I believe."

"That's probably not the problem, then. Any major changes in your lifestyle over the last month?"

"One or two." Immediately I thought of *Wonder Boys*. It was almost exactly one month since I'd begun my ill-advised attempt to slap an ending onto it. Thinking it over, I saw that the spells had increased in both frequency and intensity as the effort went awry and Crabtree's arrival drew near. "I haven't been eating as much. I've been drinking a lot the past couple of days, which isn't good for me, I know."

"And your wife left you."

I sat back down on the edge of the bed. My blue paper dress crinkled loudly.

"Is that in my chart?" I said.

"I spoke with the woman who saved your life," he said, his voice flat and free from melodrama, as though everyone had such a woman, or knew, at the very least, where one could be hired.

"Uh huh." I touched my fingers to my lips, still tender and sore from the repeated pressure of Sara's lifesaving kiss.

"She's worried about you," said Dr. Greenhut. Surreptitiously he glanced at his watch. To make this gesture less apparent he wore the watch turned around, with the face strapped to the inner part of his wrist. He was a nice kid, and trying to take an interest in my case, but I could see that I was only a minor knot of turbulence in the laminar flow of exhaustion across his life. "You ought to see a doctor, Mr. Tripp. An internist."

"I'll do that," I said.

There was a pause. Dr. Greenhut looked down at the clip-board in his hands, then back at me. "I think you really ought to consider seeing a therapist, too."

"You heard about the dog," I said.

He nodded. He grabbed a leather armchair behind him, dragged it over to the foot of my bed, and cautiously lowered himself into it, as if he feared he might not be able to get back out.

"You have a drug problem, Grady, all right?" He said this without any particular gentleness or disdain. "And it seems clear that you haven't been caring for yourself. You're mal-nourished. Okay? That dog bite on your ankle? It's infected. You're lucky they brought you in when they did. Another day or two and you might have lost the foot. We had to pump you with a massive dose of antibiotics."

"Thank you," I said, in a weak little whisper.

"As for your spells, I don't know. You've been experienc-ing a good deal of anxiety, lately, I understand. That may explain them."

"They're anxiety attacks?"

"Possibly."

"That's a little disappointing."

He rubbed lightly at the corner of his mouth with a knuckle. I supposed that he was too tired to smile.

"So is my friend—Sara—is she still here?"

"No," he said, allowing a faint flicker of pity into his eyes. "She said she had a houseful of party guests."

"I have to see her," I said. "Are you going to give me a hard time if I want to check out?"

"Mmm." He reviewed my case carefully for a few seconds, without recourse to the notes on the aluminum clipboard under his arm. In the end I believe he based his decision on a certain look of desperation in my eyes.

"Tell you what," he said. "I'll let you walk, on one condition."

"What's that?"

"That it's the last stupid thing you ever do."

"I better get back in bed then," I said. He didn't reach for his mouth this time. "Just kidding."

"Look," he said, openly consulting his wristwatch now. "I can't really keep you in here if you want to leave. I'll speak to the nurse. I'm going to write you a prescription for a course of ampicillin, for that bite of yours, all right? Have it filled on your way out, and make sure you follow it all the way to the end."

"To the end," I said. "Hey, thank you."

But he was already out the door, the tails of his jacket billowing out behind him. A minute later a nurse came in and unhooked me from my dinner. I put on the mud-stained jeans and the shirt that smelled of flopsweat and the corduroy jacket with the torn pocket. It was as I started out of the room that I learned the identity of my silent neighbor in the next bed.

"Don't forget your snare drum, Mr. Tripp," said the nurse. "Or whatever that thing is."

It was, of course, that black, hulking shadow, that brass Alecto, the Tuba of August Van Zorn. It rode down in the elevator with me, and followed me across the lobby to the doors of the hospital, and watched while I stood there reckoning the walking distance to Sara's house and struggling with the unfamiliar exercise of forming a resolve. If my repaired ankle held up, I could make it in half an hour, but then

Michael Chabon

what was I going to say to her when I got there? The past
weekend had made two things clear to me: first, that as I
presently lived it, mine was not a life into which a baby ought
responsibly to be introduced, and second, that when this
pregnancy was terminated, my relationship with Sara would
not survive the procedure. She had—understandably, I
guessed—chosen to view this as a definitive moment in the
hitherto imprecise history of our love: from this point on we
would be either the conjoint parents of our child, or else a
couple of embittered ex-lovers, looking back on five wasted
years. It was awful luck that my pot-hobbled spermatozoa had
managed to rally themselves for one last mad fallopian adventure, and that five years' worth of love, good companionship,
and the exhilaration of sneaking around should come in the
end to a referendum on my fitness as a father, but there it was.

I switched the tuba to my other hand. I tried to picture
myself eight months hence, holding to my shaggy breast that
sweet freakling, that tiny chimera, part Sara, part Grady, part
some random efflorescence of the genes. I pictured a big-
headed, hollow-eyed Edward Gorey baby, in an antique
nightdress, with tight-clenched little fists and a vandalistic nature. Let's say, I said to myself, just for the sake of argument,
that bringing another beastly mutant Tripp into the world
was not by definition a bad idea. How did one generally
know if one wanted a baby or not? In all the time Emily and
I had supposedly been trying to knock her up, it had never
occurred to me to ask myself if I wanted our effort to suc-
ceed—maybe because in my heart I'd never believed that any
relationship long exposed to the malign radiations of my character was actually capable of bearing any such fruit. Did one
really *feel* the need for a child—as a craving in the nerves, a
spiritual yearning, the haunting prickle of a lost limb?

I dragged the tuba back into the lobby and over to the information booth, which was staffed this evening by an elegant old volunteer in a striped smock. Her hair was silver and her nails were French-polished and she was wearing an emerald brooch. She was reading Q.'s third novel—the one about the sex-mad coroner—with a look of distasteful absorption.

"Do you have any babies in this hospital, by any chance?" I said, when she looked up. "You know, where you can look at them behind the glass?"

"Well," she said, laying down the book, "yes, we have a nursery, but I don't know—"

"It's for a book I'm writing."

"Oh? Are you a writer?" she said, interested now but eyeing the tuba suspiciously.

"I'm trying," I said. I hoisted the tuba. "The symphony keeps me awfully busy."

"Really! My husband and I went just last Friday night, how do you like that? *Harold in Italy*. Oh, we have regular tickets, I'm sure we must have seen—"

"Actually, it's an orchestra in Ohio," I said. "The, uh, Steubenville Philharmonic."

"Oh."

"We're very small. We play a lot of weddings."

She looked me over more carefully now. I gripped the front of my shirt where the button was missing and tried to look like I had a musical soul.

"Fifth floor," she said at last.

So the tuba and I went to take a look at the babies. There were only two on display at the moment, lying there in their glass crates like a couple of large squirming turnips. A man I presumed to be the father of one of them was leaning against the observation window, an old guy like me, sawdust on his trousers, hair Brylcreemed, his shop foreman's face beefy and half asleep. He kept looking from one to the other of the babies, biting his lip, as if trying to decide which one to spend his hard-earned dollars on. Neither of them, his face seemed say, was exactly a bargain, head dented, skin purple and crazy with veins, spastic limbs struggling as if against some invisible medium or foe.

"Boy," I said, "would I like to have me one of those."

The man caught the irony in my tone but misunderstood it. He looked at me, then jerked a thumb in the direction of the baby that must not have been his. His lips made a tight little smile.

"I got news for you, buddy," he said. "You already do."

SOMEWHAT more than half an hour later, I turned into the leafy street at the heart of Point Breeze where in vanished days the heirs to great fortunes in steel and condiments had disported in the grass, knocking balls through silver wickets with gold mallets. I walked down to the Gaskells' house along the sinister iron fence. It was a cool spring evening in a river town at the foot of the mountains. A fine mist hung in the air. All the lights in the street looked haloed and soft, as if rubbed up by the thumb of a sentimental pastelist. I was still carrying the tuba, for no reason other than that, in my current circumstances, it passed for good company. That's another way of saying it was all I had. The Gaskells' house was lit from every window, and as I came up the walk I heard the suave tinkling of a vibraphone. I didn't hear any raised voices or other sounds of human merrymaking, but this didn't surprise me, because the last party of the WordFest weekend, wherever it was held, was generally a survivors' ball, low-key and hungover and poorly attended. I set the tuba down beside me and rang the doorbell.

I waited. All the leaves in the trees began to clatter and shake. Two seconds later it was pouring down rain. I knocked. I tried the heavy latch with my thumb, and it gave. I pushed through the door, feeling a sharp thrill of dread.

"Hello?" I said.

The place was deserted. I circled the ground floor from the living room, into the kitchen, and through the swinging saloon doors into the dining room. Everywhere I saw the signs of recent habitation: plastic cups kissed by women, cigarette butts in ashtrays, abandoned hats and sweatshirts, even an empty pair of shoes. An air of eerie, postdisaster calm hung over the whole scene, as in the wake of a death ray or sparkling toxic cloud.

"Anybody home?" I called out to the second floor, then started to follow the tentative course of my voice up the stairs. There was no reply. A drop of rain ran down the back of my neck and produced a vibraphone shiver along my spine. The front door was still open and the whispery laughter of the rain in the trees and puddles outside harmonized weirdly with the skeleton tap dance of the vibes. An empty house, a reckless and foolish man climbing to his doom, the ghostly music of an orchestra of imps and bonedaddies: I had become the hero of a story by August Van Zorn. Maybe, I thought, I had never been anything else. At this, there was a loud thump right behind me, as of a body hitting the floor, and I jumped, whirled around, prepared to be swallowed by the slavering maw of the Eldest Black Nothingness itself; but it was only the tuba. It had fallen over sideways onto the porch—either that, or it was attempting to locomote.

"I can't turn my back on you for a second," I told it, not quite not joking.

I backed quickly down the stairs and stood very still in the foyer, keeping an eye on the tuba and trying to think what could have happened, and where everyone had gone. I had a view down the hallway into the kitchen, and I could see through the back windows that there was a light burning out in the yard. So I went into the kitchen again and pressed my face against the glass. Inside Sara's greenhouse one of the cool violet GroLites was aglow. There was no reason not to suppose that she must sometimes leave a light burning out there, and it was hard to believe she would have chosen this moment to see how her sweet peas were coming along. Nevertheless I pulled the collar of my jacket up over my head and ran splashing across the yard. I knocked on the door a couple of times, then pulled it open and allowed myself to be inhaled into that strange glass house with its stink of fish emulsion and flowers and rot. I'd never been inside at night before. There was only the one light on, off in one of the other rooms, and I stood there, trying to adjust to the dim light and the heavy air, wild with a smell of rank vanilla and sweet decay that I presently identified as narcissus. It was overpowering; you could almost hear it humming in your ears like bees.

"Sara?" I said.

The murmuring of flowers seemed to grow louder as I went deeper into the greenhouse, but when I went into the central atrium I discovered that it was not some heady perfume working on my nerves—only the ironic and elliptical snoring of a modern master of the short-story form. On the old purple davenport, under the potted date palm, Q. lay unconscious. His shirttails had come untucked, his fly was unbuttoned, and on his feet he wore only a pair of red-toed sock-monkey socks, caked with mud. Those were his shoes, then, abandoned in the living room. Even in his dreams, apparently, Q. and his doppelgänger were still going at it, because although his brow was knotted in anguish, the rest of his face looked peaceful, even self-satisfied, as if he were enjoying some well-deserved rest. In addition to the mud on his stocking feet there was a goldfish of dried blood on the pocket of his shirt and a telephone number or message to himself scrawled across the back of his left hand. I leaned over to try to read what it said. It was too smeared to make out, but appeared to begin with a *C.* CROATOAN, I thought, might not have been inappropriate. I switched on an overhead light.

Q.'s eyes snapped open.

"No!" he said, reaching out, his fingers outspread, as if to ward me off.

"Easy, man," I said. "You'll be all right."

He sat up.

"Where am I? What is that smell?"

"That's plant breath," I said. "You're in Sara's greenhouse."

He sat up and rubbed his face and gave his jowls a shake. Then he looked around, up at the spiky leaves of the palm tree, down at his muddy socks. He shook his head.

"Nope," he said.

"No idea how you got here, eh?"

"None."

I gave his shoulder a little squeeze.

"That's all right," I said. "Try this one. All the people at that party. Any idea where they might have gone to?" I nodded in the direction of the house. "Place is empty. Looked like people must have cleared out in a hurry. Left all their cups and cigarettes and whatnot lying around." I looked at my watch. It was not quite nine o'clock. "Seems like things broke up kind of early."

"Yeah, uh, right——" he began, tentatively. "Sara." He nodded. "She cleared them all out."

"She what?" I couldn't believe Sara would do anything so indecorous in public—such behavior would not become the vision of sound and gracious chancellorhood she had so carefully elaborated for herself. My heart sank. "That's not like Sara." There was only one explanation: she had decided, once and for all, to rid her aging womb of the spawn of Grady. I was gripped by a sudden irrational certainty that she had, in fact, already done so—that she'd chased everyone out of her house and then driven off, alone and hysterical, to the office of some night doctor, in a tragic part of town. "Why did she do that?"

"I don't remember," Q. said, and then he remembered. He looked up at me, his eyes wide and pleading, as though I'd been sent out here to punish him for whatever it was he'd done. He lowered his head.

"I think I broke Walter Gaskell's nose," he said into his collar.

"You're kidding. Oh, my God."

He looked defensive. "Maybe not." He pinched the spherical tip of his nose. "I just barely clipped him with the thing." He nodded reassuringly to himself as the details started to come back to him. "It wasn't like I got him with the sweet spot."

"The sweet spot?"

"I was swinging one of his bats. A big one, thirty-six

ounces, all yellow and stained. Like a kind of an old tusk. It used to belong to Joe DiMaggio." His lined face softened a little as he remembered. "A beautiful thing."

"I know the one," I said.

"Still a lot of tension in it, somehow. When you swung it. Like there was still something powerful in there trying to get out."

"I guess there must have been," I said. "I guess it kind of got out and broke Walter's nose."

"Uh huh," he said. He cocked his head a little to the side, and his voice was sharp. "At least I didn't *steal* it, though."

"Good point," I said. "So then, what, did she take him to the hospital? Sara, I mean." Here I had come all this way looking for her, and she'd probably been in the emergency room at the hospital the whole time.

"I don't know. He was bleeding and shouting and I was probably shouting a little, too. Sara came in, at some point, and they shouted at each *other* for a while. Sorry, I don't re-member what about. Then she chased everyone out of the house. If she's not there now, I don't know where she went."

"And Walter?" I said.

Q. lifted an eyebrow, and sort of pointed with the un-shaven tip of his chin in the general direction of the door to the greenhouse. He smiled. I looked at him for a mo-ment, not understanding. Then I caught the doppelgänger glint of mischief in his eye. He wanted me to turn around. I turned around, half-expecting to see the tuba standing there behind me.

"Hello, Grady," Walter said.

He was looming in the shadows of the greenhouse, dan-gling the tar-stained old DiMaggio bat at his side. This was an item he had acquired last fall, in the grip of a frenzy of acquisition so intense that he'd forgotten all about Sara's birthday, and had subsequently tried to make a lame and insincere sort of present out of the brittle stick of ash wood itself. That proved to be a fatal insult to the health of their marriage, as far as Sara was concerned, and if she ever found herself able to leave him once and for all, this bat, nominally hers, would be one of the reasons. It was one of a small number of bats purporting to be that swung by Joe D. all during his famous streak of 1941, and therefore worthy of a certain amount of devotion, as I had tried to explain to Sara at the time. In his other hand, Walter was holding a plaid ice bag, pressed against the bridge of his nose. There was blood on his white oxford shirt.

"Hey, Walter," I said.

"I'm sorry about your nose, Walter," said Q. "I must have been pretty drunk."

Walter nodded. "I'll be all right."

"And," I said, "I, uh, I know this is going to sound pretty fatuous, right about now, Walter, but I want you to know that I'm really sorry, too. About everything. I feel really, really bad." I paused and licked my lips. The truth was that I didn't actually feel so bad. I just didn't want Walter trying to doctor me up with that bat. "I—I wish I could make it up to you."

"I really don't think you ever could, Grady," Walter said. He rolled the bat back and forth against his thigh, and his fingers worried the worn old tape on the handle. I remember he didn't look angry, or especially retributive, or happy in that way people look in the movies when the revenge of which they've been dreaming curls up the wicked corners of the lips. His eyes were ringed with fatigue, he had an ice bag over his nose, and he wore, more than anything, the harried air of a dean after a night of quarreling with the accounting firm and contemplating painful cuts in his budget for next year. "The department is going to have to place you on a disciplinary leave, of course."

"Okay," I said. "That makes sense."

"For an indefinite term, I'm afraid. You may well lose your position. I'll certainly do my best to see that you do."

I looked at Q. He was glancing back and forth from me to Walter, calmly but with a certain air of frustration I thought I recognized. He was wishing he had a pen so that he could make a few notes.

"You're a goddamn fraud, Grady. You've produced nothing at all since you've been here," Walter went on, softly. "That's seven years. Close to eight." He named two of my writing colleagues in the department. "In the past seven years they've brought out nine books between them. One of *hers* won a national award, as I'm sure you know. What have *you* done, Grady?"

These were the very words, the charges I had been dreading and anticipating for so long, but in all that time I had never managed to come up with an adequate response. I hung my head.

Q. cleared his throat. "*Besides* sleeping with your wife, you mean," he said, helpfully.

Walter lowered the ice bag and dropped it to the ground. The bat shot up from his side and began to describe tight little arcs in the air between us. He was clutching it in both hands now, waggling his fingers on its shaft, his face bloodied and swollen but his Doctor Dee eyes remarkably blue and calm.

"Are you going to use that on me?"

"I don't know," he said. "I might."

"Go for it," I told him.

So he did. And I believe that most of the violence that

occurs between men is the product, in one way or another, of flippancy and smart remarks. I told him to go for it, and he came at me and swung the historic bat. I got my arm up but he still managed to land a glancing blow on my left temple. My glasses went flying. A large rock rang out against a taut sheet of metal, and a flashbulb blew, and a luminous retinal rose bloomed and withered in the innards of my eye. It hurt, but not as much as I might have predicted. After blinking experimentally a few times I picked up my glasses, set them on my nose, drew myself erect, and, with the same over-elaborate display of dignity, like a drunk's, walked out. Unfortunately for my brave show of imperviousness and self-possession I went the wrong way, and ended up somewhere in the rearmost wing of the greenhouse, where my legs got tangled in a bale of chicken wire, and I fell over.

"Grady?" Walter called, sounding genuinely concerned.

"I'm fine." I found my feet, extricated myself from the jingling haystack of wire, and set a course for where I remembered the door to be. On my way back across the atrium I went past the purple davenport and stopped.

"Did you get all that?" I said to Q.

He nodded. I thought he looked a little pale.

"I have a question for you," I said, pointing. "What's it say there on your hand?"

He looked down at the smear of blue ink on the back of his left hand and frowned. It took him a few seconds to remember.

"It says, 'Frank Capra,'" he said. He shrugged. "Something I saw tonight. I think there might be a book in it."

I nodded, and held out my hand to him, and we shook. On my way out I brushed past Walter Gaskell and stumbled a little, and he put a hand out as if to steady me. For an instant

I could have collapsed into his arms. But I knocked his prof-fered arm away and strode across the whirling yard to the house.

I climbed the back steps and walked through the house, feeling a little less woozy with every step. When I got to the front porch the tuba was there waiting for me. I was almost glad to see it. I stood in the light spilling out through the open door behind me, rain on the lenses of my eyeglasses, rain run-ning down the sides of my nose, trying to work up the nerve to walk back to the empty house on Denniston Street. I looked into the foyer to see if by any chance someone had left behind an umbrella, or if there was something I could use to cover my head. There was nothing. I turned, and took a deep breath, and heaved the tuba up over my head, to give me a little shelter. Then I started for home. The thing was too heavy to carry in this way for very long, however, and after a while I lowered it and just went ahead and got wet. My clothes grew heavy, and my shoes squeaked, and the pockets of my jacket filled with rain. Finally I sat down on top of the tuba and waited there, like a man clinging to an empty barrel, for the flood to carry me off.

The flood, I thought. This was the true, original ending I'd always planned for *Wonder Boys*. One April day, after a heavy winter, the Miskahannock River would overflow its banks and wash away the entire troubled town of Wonderburg, PA. For that very last paragraph I had always envisioned the image of a young girl and a crookbacked old woman, poling a skiff down the long main hall of the Wonder house. There was something in this vision of the tiny boat in which all that remained of the Wonders went spinning out the front door of the house, to be lost amid the debris and flotsam of the world, that moved me to the point of tears. Automatically I patted my pockets for a pen and a sheet of paper to make some notes. There was something in the hip pocket of my jacket. It was the seven surviving pages of *Wonder Boys,* folded and porous with rain. I laid them against my thigh and carefully spread them flat.

"Well?" I said to the tuba. "What do you say we finish this thing right?"

I took hold of the sheaf of paper and folded it over. I bent down the uppermost corners, lifted the lowermost couple of flaps, and tucked and pleated those last seven pages until I had worked them into a soft and waterlogged little boat. Then I set this unlikely craft in the gutter at my feet, and watched it pitch and career away down the street toward the Monongahela River and the open sea. And thus, as it was foretold in the prophecies of witch women and in a nine-page outline I'd made on an April afternoon five years earlier, wild water came and carried off the remnant of the Wonders. I stood up, and found that my head was remarkably clear, and that all its former lightness seemed to have passed, like an electrical current, into my limbs. My hands were dizzy, my feet reeled, my heart weighed nothing at all. I wasn't happy—I'd poured too many years of my life, too many thousands of hard-won images and episodes and elegant turns of phrase, into that book not to part with it in utter sorrow. Still, I felt light. I felt as if I had been raised in the crushing precincts of the planet Jupiter, and then set free, massive and buoyant, to bound along the streets of Point Breeze, covering nine feet at a stride, with only the tuba to keep me from floating entirely off the earth.

After I'd been walking along for a while in the general direction of home, shivering, thinking the circular thoughts of a man who's been clocked with a Louisville Slugger, a car pulled up alongside me and sat burbling by the curb, lighting up the rain in a broad glittery fan outspread before it. It was a red Citroën DS23. The rain spattered against its black canvas top.

I carried the tuba over to the curb, bent down, and looked into the car. It was warm inside there, and everything was lit by the soft amber light of the dash. There was a smell of damp ash and the wet wool of Sara's topcoat, and a faint trickle of advertising from the radio. She made a face at me as I leaned in, bugging out her eyes a little, so that I would know she was angry but not entirely without humor. Her hair was slicked back with rainwater and her face was flushed and someone had kissed her on the cheek with orange lipstick.

"Need a lift?" she said, with mock smoothness. She affected not to be surprised to have come upon me thus but I could tell by the way that she held her mouth so perfectly straight, and by a certain telltale dilation of her nostrils, that she had been panicking for hours and might be panicking still.

"I've been looking all over for you," she said. "I went back to the hospital, I went by your house—Jesus, Grady, what happened to your head?"

"Nothing," I said, touching a hand to my left temple. Yes, it was swelling nicely. "Okay, Walter hit me with a baseball bat." Also, it seemed to me, now that I had something to focus my vision on, I could not quite get my left eye to come into true with my right. "I'm all right. God knows I had it coming."

"Are you sure?" She narrowed her eyes and studied me. She was trying to determine if I was stoned. "Why are you squinting like that?"

"What squinting, I'm fine, I'm not stoned," I said, and to my amazement I discovered that this was the truth. "Honest."

"Honest," she repeated doubtfully.

"I feel great." This was also the truth, except insofar as my actual body was concerned. "I'm so glad to see you, Sara. There's so much I want to tell you—I feel—I feel so *light*—" I began to tell her about the way I had died, and the last voyage of the good ship *Wonder Boys*, and the sudden magical weightlessness of my old Jovian frame.

"I have my suitcase in the trunk," said Sara, cutting me off, as usual, before I could muddy the waters of an important discussion with any of my Mercutian prattle. "Is Emily coming home?"

"I don't think so."

Her eyes narrowed again.

"No," I said. "Nuh-uh. She isn't coming home."

"Could I stay with you, then? Just for a little while. A couple of days. Just until I find someplace else to go. If," she added quickly, "that's what you want me to do."

I didn't say anything. The rain redoubled in force, and the tuba was dislocating my elbow, but I couldn't bring myself to put it down, and Sara hadn't asked me to get into the car yet. I had a feeling my answer might have a lot to do with whether she ever would. I stood there, getting rained on, remembering the promise I had made to Dr. Greenhut.

"Okay, fine," said Sara, putting the car in gear. She started to roll slowly forward.

"Wait a second," I said. "Hold on."

The taillights on the roof of the car lit up.

"Okay," I said, hurrying to catch up to her. "Of course you can stay with me. Please. I'd love it."

After that I waited for her to smile, and ask me into the car, and drive me home and lay me down on the Honor Bilt to sleep for the next three days. But Sara wasn't ready to end the negotiations.

"I've decided I'm going to keep it," she informed me, watching my face for the effect of this announcement. "In case you were wondering."

"I was."

She took her hands off the wheel for the first time and turned them outward, fingers spread, a nameless gesture more eloquent and wondering than a shrug.

"It's just started to seem like a good thing to have," she said. "If I'm not going to have anything else."

"Think so?"

"At the moment."

I stood upright, stepped away from the curb, and took a last look up, through the rain, at the empty sky over my head. Then I put down the last of my burdens and reached for the passenger door.

"I guess there's no point in hanging on to this tuba, then," I said.

ONE of the strangest bits of jetsam to wash up in the aftermath of the flood that carried me, eventually, all the way back to the town where I was born was a black satin jacket, with an ermine collar, slightly worn at the elbows and missing a button. Although she was, by law, entitled to ask Walter to sell off his whole precious collection and let her take half the proceeds out of the marriage with her, Sara offered to waive her rights to all the rest of it—the flannel jerseys, the three thousand bubble-gum cards, and above all that tar-stained bat—if he would let her keep the jacket. I would have been more than willing never to see the thing again, but to her it was a reminder, at once ironic and cherished, of the weekend that had sealed our fate. Everything else they owned she conceded to Walter, who proved willing to exchange a small if significant principality in order to hold on to the rest of his mighty empire. When the two of us were at last free and clear of our past entanglements, social and professional, Sara and I were married here, at the Town Hall, by a justice of the peace who was a distant cousin of my grandmother, and for the ceremony, almost but not quite as a joke, Sara wore the jacket. I didn't think this was a very favorable omen, but it was my fourth marriage and any talk of omens was, to a certain extent, beside the point.

For more than a year after *Wonder Boys* blew apart in that alley behind Kravnik's Sporting Goods I was unable to do any writing at all. I dumped the whole exploded clockwork of draft chapters and character sketches and uninsertable inserts into a liquor box and stuck them under the bed. My life was in turmoil, and, maybe because I couldn't see very well out of my left eye anymore, it took me a long time to get back my sense of narrative balance and my writerly perception of depth. I got to know my lawyer and a number of other Pittsburgh attorneys, quit smoking pot, and did my best to be a husband, and a father to my son. Sara landed the position of dean of students at Coxley College and arranged for me to be hired, part-time, by the department to which Albert Vetch had devoted so much of his life, and we moved back to this old hill town, with its houses the colors of dead leaves, where a neon sign burns on a cold night with an aching clearness and it is always football season. And then, one Sunday afternoon after we had been living on Whateley Street for a couple of weeks, in a rented house a block from the corner of Pickman where the old McClelland Hotel still stands, I brought the liquor box out from under the bed, took it into the backyard, and, under a tangle of wisteria, buried it in the cold black ground.

I do my writing in the morning, now, if the boy will let me, and in the afternoon when I'm not teaching, and sometimes in the evening when I get home from the Alibi Tavern. On a day when my work hasn't gone well, I like to spend a couple of hours at the Alibi's dented steel bar, and you will find me there on Tuesday nights after the advanced workshop lets out. You can look for the half-blind minotaur with the corduroy sport coat and the battered horsehide briefcase, at the far end of the bar by the jukebox, holding on to a mug of Iron City cut, for the sake of his health, with thin, sweet lemonade. If you sit long enough on the neighboring stool he will probably mention that he is working hard on a novel about baseball and the Civil War, or a memoir of Berkeley in the early seventies, or a screenplay, called *Sister of Darkness,* based on a number of interlinked stories penned by another obscure local man of letters, who wrote under the name of August Van Zorn. Usually he sits with one or two much younger men, students of his, wonder boys whose hearts are filled with the dread and mystery of the books they believe themselves destined to write. He has known a number of famous and admired authors in his time, and he likes to caution and amuse his young companions with case histories of the incurable disease that leads all good writers to suffer, inevitably, the quintessential fate of their characters. The young men listen dutifully, for the most part, and from time to time some of them even take the trouble to go over to the college library, and dig up one or another of his novels, and crouch there, among the stacks, flipping impatiently through the pages, looking for the parts that sound true.

WEREWOLVES IN THEIR YOUTH

Michael Chabon

Werewolves in Their Youth is a masterful collection of stories, featuring a cast of characters haunted by their pasts and attempting to make sense of their futures. Serious, yet shot through with wit, humour and compassion, these nine short stories demonstrate Chabon's ability to weave together comedy and tragedy with unforgettable results.

£6.99   1 85702 985 2

HABITUS

James Flint

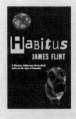

A hilarious satire on the state of humanity that entwines the troubled lives of Joel, a mathematical genius, Judd, the disaffected son of a Hollywood star, and Jennifer, a precocious schoolgirl, as they search for meaning in the millennial world.

£6.99   1 85702 832 5

SHOPPING
Gavin Kramer

Meadowlark is a lonely man with a portrait of the
Queen pinned to his apartment wall. Sent to work in the
Tokyo office, he soon becomes lost in a world of besuited
Englishmen who, slaves to the office by day, cruise the
neon-lit nightspots by night. But before long Meadowlark
undergoes an eerie change that shocks his colleagues; he
falls in love with a fourteen-year-old Japanese girl.

£6.99   1 85702 958 5

ALLAN STEIN
Matthew Stadler

When his affair with a fifteen-year-old boy turns into
reality, Matthew jumps at the chance to forsake Seattle
for the leafy boulevards of Paris. There he becomes
embroiled in a mystery concerning some missing Picasso
drawings featuring Allan Stein – nephew of Gertrude
Stein and possibly the model for Picasso's 1906 painting
of a naked boy leading a horse – Matthew is soon
overwhelmed by his attraction to the teenage son of
the household in which he is staying.

£6.99   1 84115 108 4

ME AND THE FAT MAN
Julie Myerson

Amy is a married, small-town waitress with a chaotic past who picks men up in the park, gives them sex for money and pays it straight into the Nationwide. When a stranger called Harris walks into her life and demands that she meets his friend Gary, the fat man of the title, she is confused and beguiled. But who's using whom and why?

£6.99   1 85702 833 3

THE HAPPIEST DAYS
Cressida Connolly

Each of these deceptively simple stories challenges the things you know about a person, showing that it is possible to be intimate strangers. Familiar emotions – love and loss, jealousy and loneliness – are dissected and shown anew.

'That rare and wonderful hybrid, tales which are both utterly unexpected and beautifully written . . . I'd recommend them to anyone.' *Daily Mail*

£6.99   1 85702 715 9

GIRL NOBODY
Tomek Tryzna

Marysia Kawczak moves from the flatlands of rural
Poland to the city. Her passionate friendships with the
two most glamorous girls in her new class explode her
assumptions and fill her adolescent world with colour
and confusion. But Marysia discovers her adored friends
are not, as it seemed, vying for her soul, but are playing
a cruel game against her.

£6.99   1 85702 661 6

THE MAGICIAN'S ASSISTANT
Ann Patchett

Shortlisted for the 1998 Orange Prize for Fiction

It comes as a surprise to Sabine after the death of
Parsifal, when the magician's mother and two sisters
appear from nowhere to request her help. Accepting
their plea, she uproots from her beloved Los Angeles to
the frozen wastes of Nebraska where she discovers her
own magical powers that may finally help her find love.

£6.99   1 85702 815 5

All Fourth Estate books are available from your local bookshop,
or can be ordered direct (FREE UK p&p) from:

Fourth Estate, Book Service By Post, PO Box 29,
Douglas, I-O-M, IM99 1BQ

Credit cards accepted.

Tel: 01624 836000   Fax: 01624 670923

Or visit the Fourth Estate website at:
www.4thestate.co.uk

Please state when ordering if you do **not** *wish to receive further
information about Fourth Estate titles.*